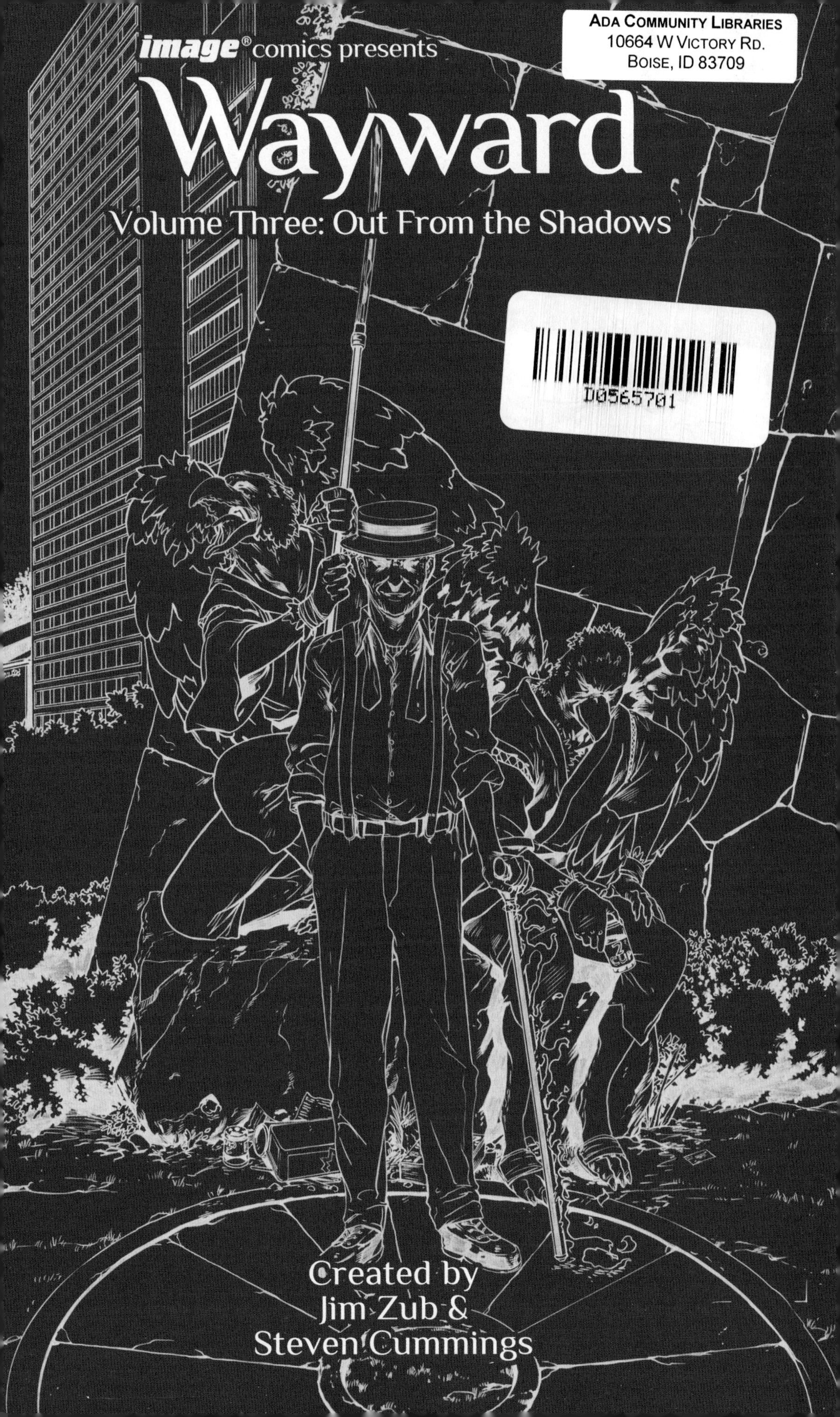
image® comics presents
Wayward
Volume Three: Out From the Shadows
Created by
Jim Zub &
Steven Cummings

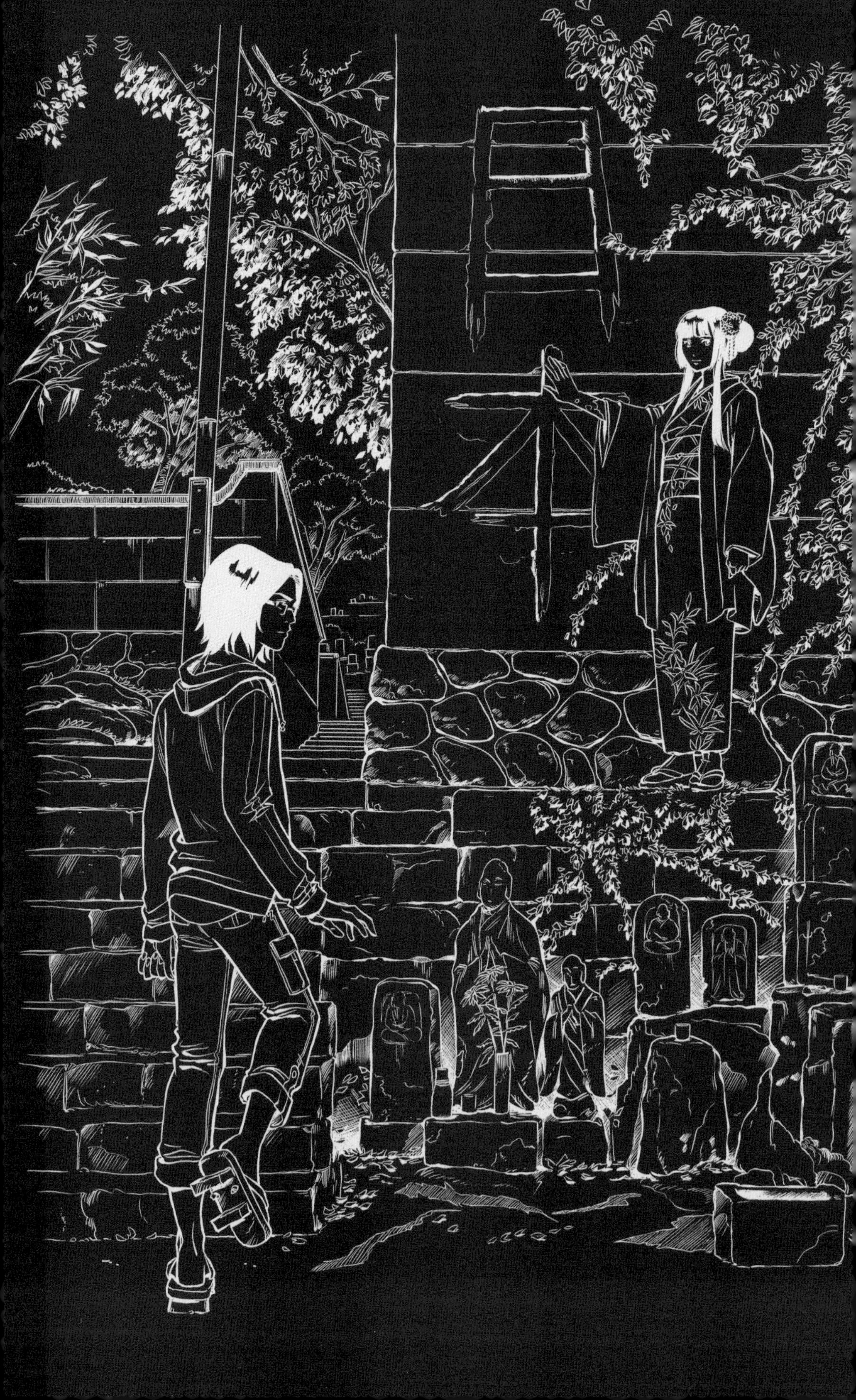

story
Jim Zub

line art
Steven Cummings

color art
Tamra Bonvillain

color assist
Brittney Peer

color flats
Ludwig Olimba

letters
Marshall Dillon

back matter
Zack Davisson

Previously

A group of teenagers living in Japan discover that they have strange supernatural powers. **Emi Ohara** can alter the form of manmade objects and change her body to match their materials. **Nikaido** absorbs and controls emotions. **Shirai** feeds on the energy of spirits to sustain and empower him. **Ayane** is not a teen at all, she's a shape shifter formed from supernatural energies channeled through generations of cats. At the center is **Rori Lane**, a half-Japanese half-Irish girl called a 'Weaver', a powerful conduit for the strings of fate that define power and destiny.

Soon after these powers emerge, the teens are hunted by **Yokai**, mythical Japanese creatures and spirits. The Yokai sense these striplings are the next generation of supernatural power in Japan but they're not willing to give up the power they've built over the centuries.

At the end of their latest battle, Rori summons a powerful spell that shatters five nodes of power being used by the Yokai, a blatant act of war with far-reaching consequences...

IMAGE COMICS, INC.
Robert Kirkman – Chief Operating Officer
Erik Larsen – Chief Financial Officer
Todd McFarlane – President
Marc Silvestri – Chief Executive Officer
Jim Valentino – Vice-President

Eric Stephenson – Publisher
Corey Murphy – Director of Sales
Jeff Boison – Director of Publishing Planning & Book Trade Sales
Jeremy Sullivan – Director of Digital Sales
Kat Salazar – Director of PR & Marketing
Emily Miller – Director of Operations
Branwyn Bigglestone – Senior Accounts Manager
Sarah Mello – Accounts Manager
Drew Gill – Art Director
Jonathan Chan – Production Manager
Meredith Wallace – Print Manager
Briah Skelly – Publicity Assistant
Sasha Head – Sales & Marketing Production Designer
Randy Okamura – Digital Production Designer
David Brothers – Branding Manager
Ally Power – Content Manager
Addison Duke – Production Artist
Vincent Kukua – Production Artist
Tricia Ramos – Production Artist
Jeff Stang – Direct Market Sales Representative
Emilio Bautista – Digital Sales Associate
Leanna Caunter – Accounting Assistant
Chloe Ramos-Peterson – Administrative Assistant
IMAGECOMICS.COM

special thanks
Danica Brine
Nishi Makoto
Christine Marie
Ann O'Regan
Mr. Blahg and Grace

Chapter Eleven

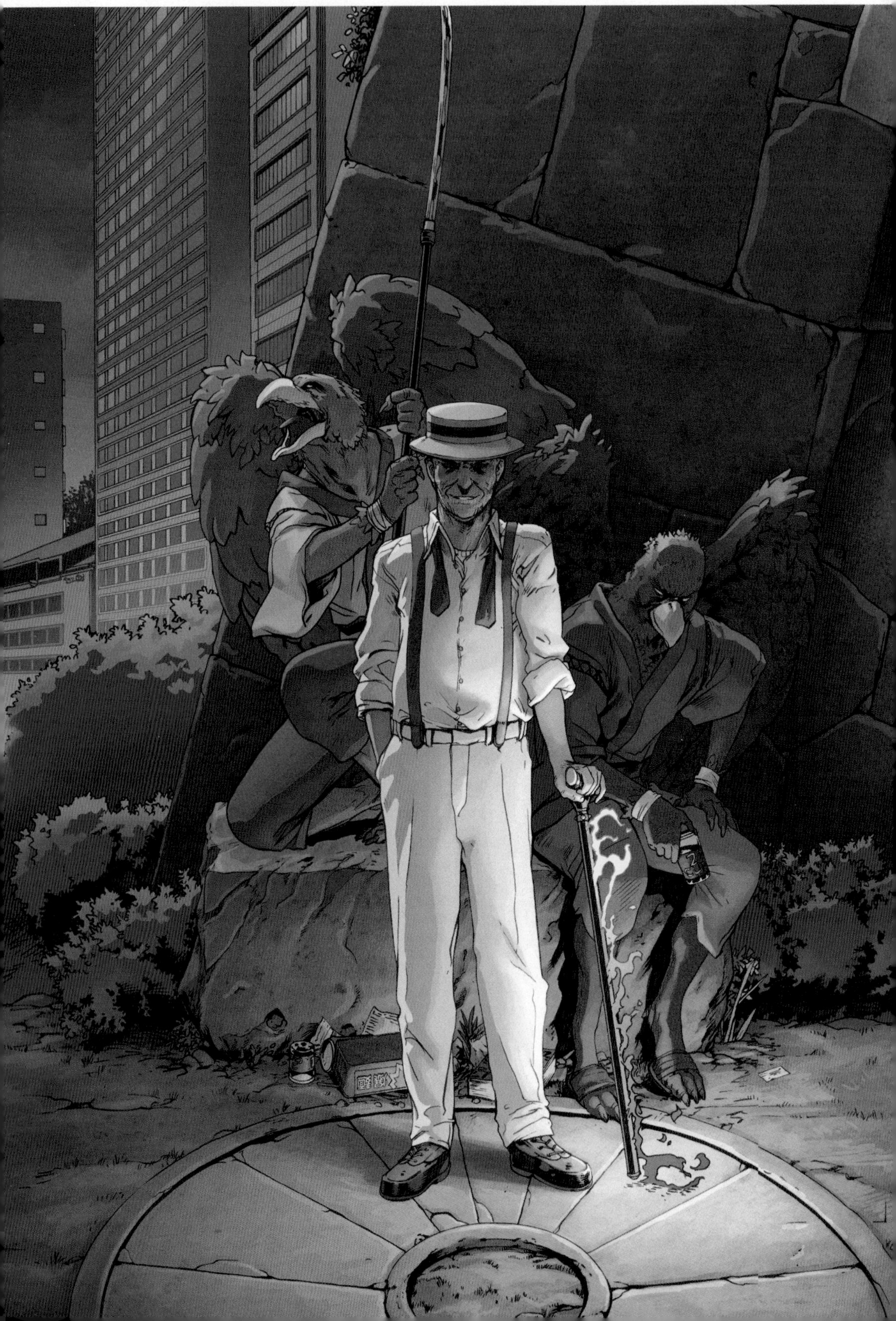

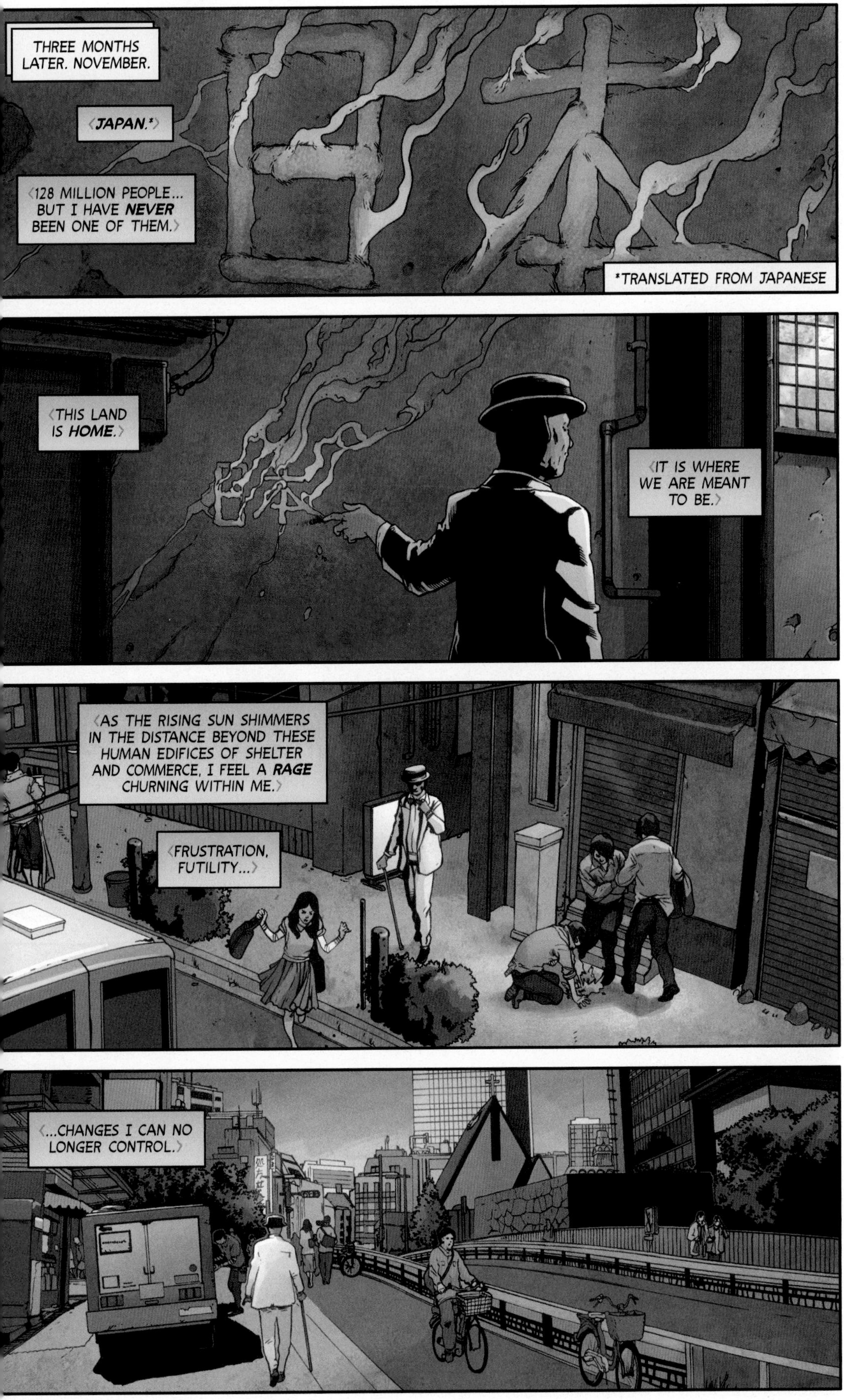
THREE MONTHS LATER. NOVEMBER.
‹JAPAN.*›
‹128 MILLION PEOPLE... BUT I HAVE ***NEVER*** BEEN ONE OF THEM.›
日本
*TRANSLATED FROM JAPANESE
‹THIS LAND IS ***HOME***.›
‹IT IS WHERE WE ARE MEANT TO BE.›
‹AS THE RISING SUN SHIMMERS IN THE DISTANCE BEYOND THESE HUMAN EDIFICES OF SHELTER AND COMMERCE, I FEEL A ***RAGE*** CHURNING WITHIN ME.›
‹FRUSTRATION, FUTILITY...›
‹...CHANGES I CAN NO LONGER CONTROL.›

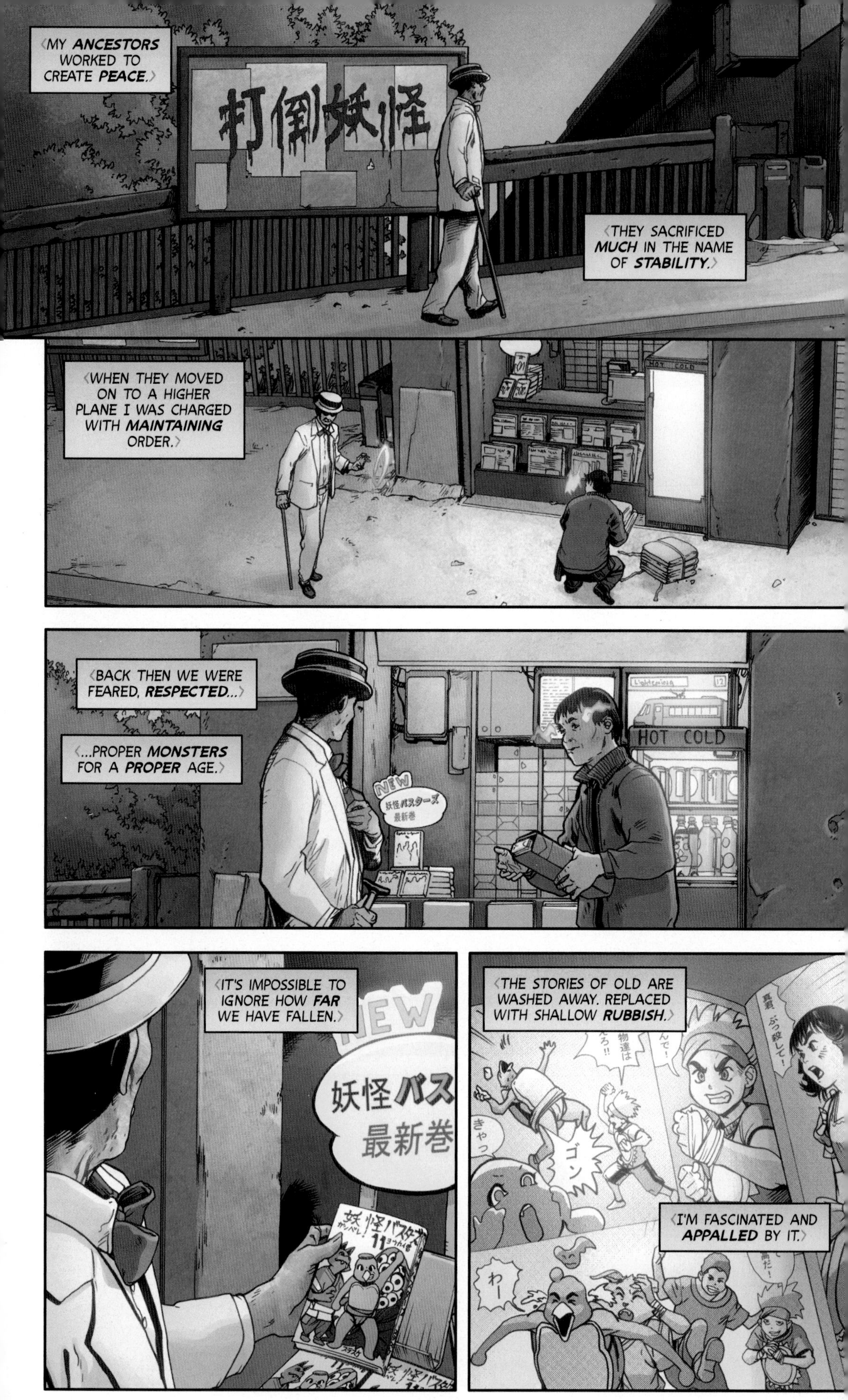

⟨MY ANCESTORS WORKED TO CREATE PEACE.⟩
打倒妖怪
⟨THEY SACRIFICED MUCH IN THE NAME OF STABILITY.⟩
⟨WHEN THEY MOVED ON TO A HIGHER PLANE I WAS CHARGED WITH MAINTAINING ORDER.⟩
⟨BACK THEN WE WERE FEARED, RESPECTED...⟩
⟨...PROPER MONSTERS FOR A PROPER AGE.⟩
NEW
妖怪バスターズ
最新巻
HOT COLD
⟨IT'S IMPOSSIBLE TO IGNORE HOW FAR WE HAVE FALLEN.⟩
NEW
妖怪バス
最新巻
⟨THE STORIES OF OLD ARE WASHED AWAY. REPLACED WITH SHALLOW RUBBISH.⟩
きゃっ
ゴン
⟨I'M FASCINATED AND APPALLED BY IT.⟩
わー

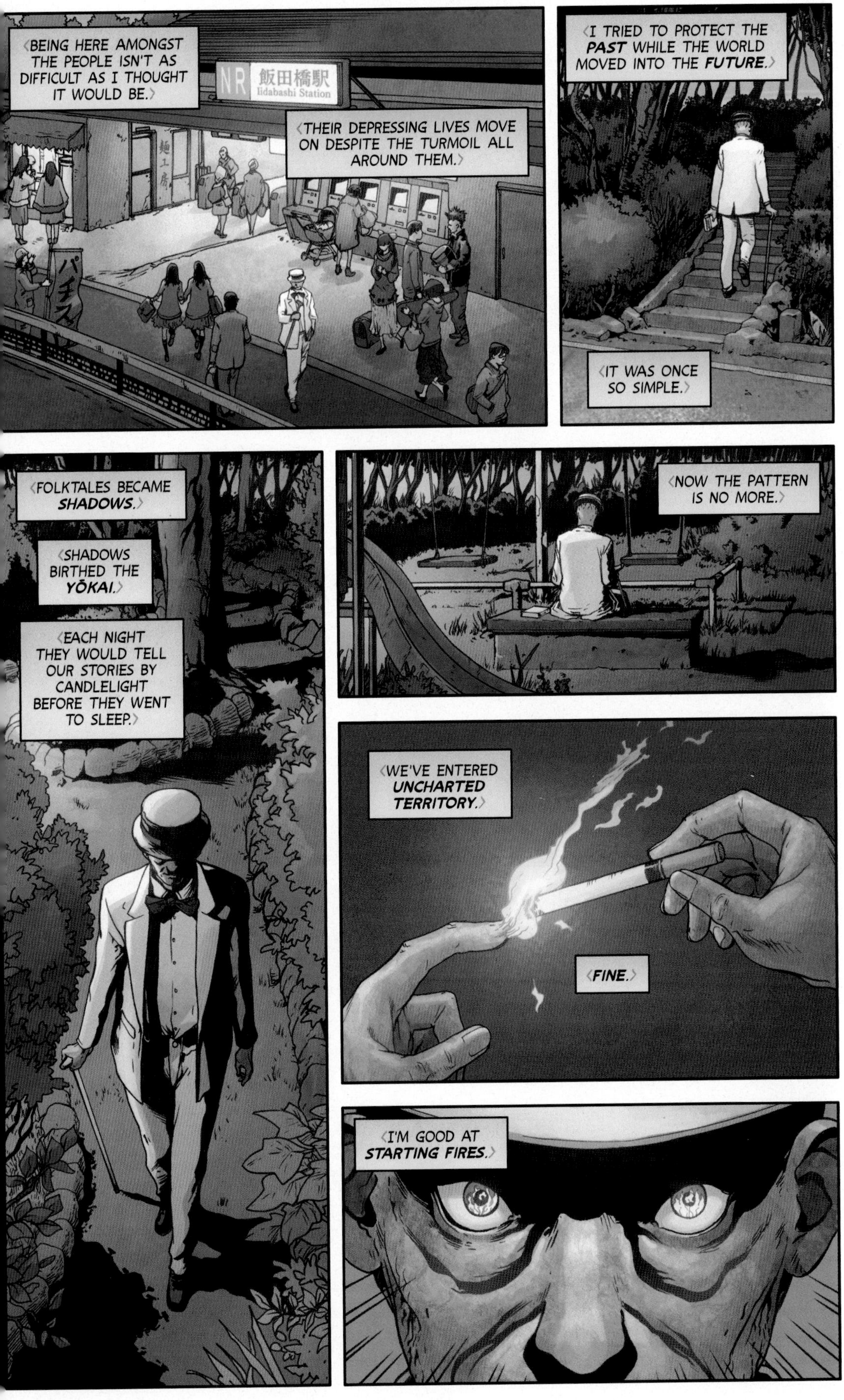

〈BEING HERE AMONGST THE PEOPLE ISN'T AS DIFFICULT AS I THOUGHT IT WOULD BE.〉
NR 飯田橋駅 Iidabashi Station
〈THEIR DEPRESSING LIVES MOVE ON DESPITE THE TURMOIL ALL AROUND THEM.〉
〈I TRIED TO PROTECT THE ***PAST*** WHILE THE WORLD MOVED INTO THE ***FUTURE***.〉
〈IT WAS ONCE SO SIMPLE.〉
〈FOLKTALES BECAME ***SHADOWS***.〉
〈SHADOWS BIRTHED THE ***YŌKAI***.〉
〈EACH NIGHT THEY WOULD TELL OUR STORIES BY CANDLELIGHT BEFORE THEY WENT TO SLEEP.〉
〈NOW THE PATTERN IS NO MORE.〉
〈WE'VE ENTERED ***UNCHARTED TERRITORY***.〉
〈***FINE***.〉
〈I'M GOOD AT ***STARTING FIRES***.〉

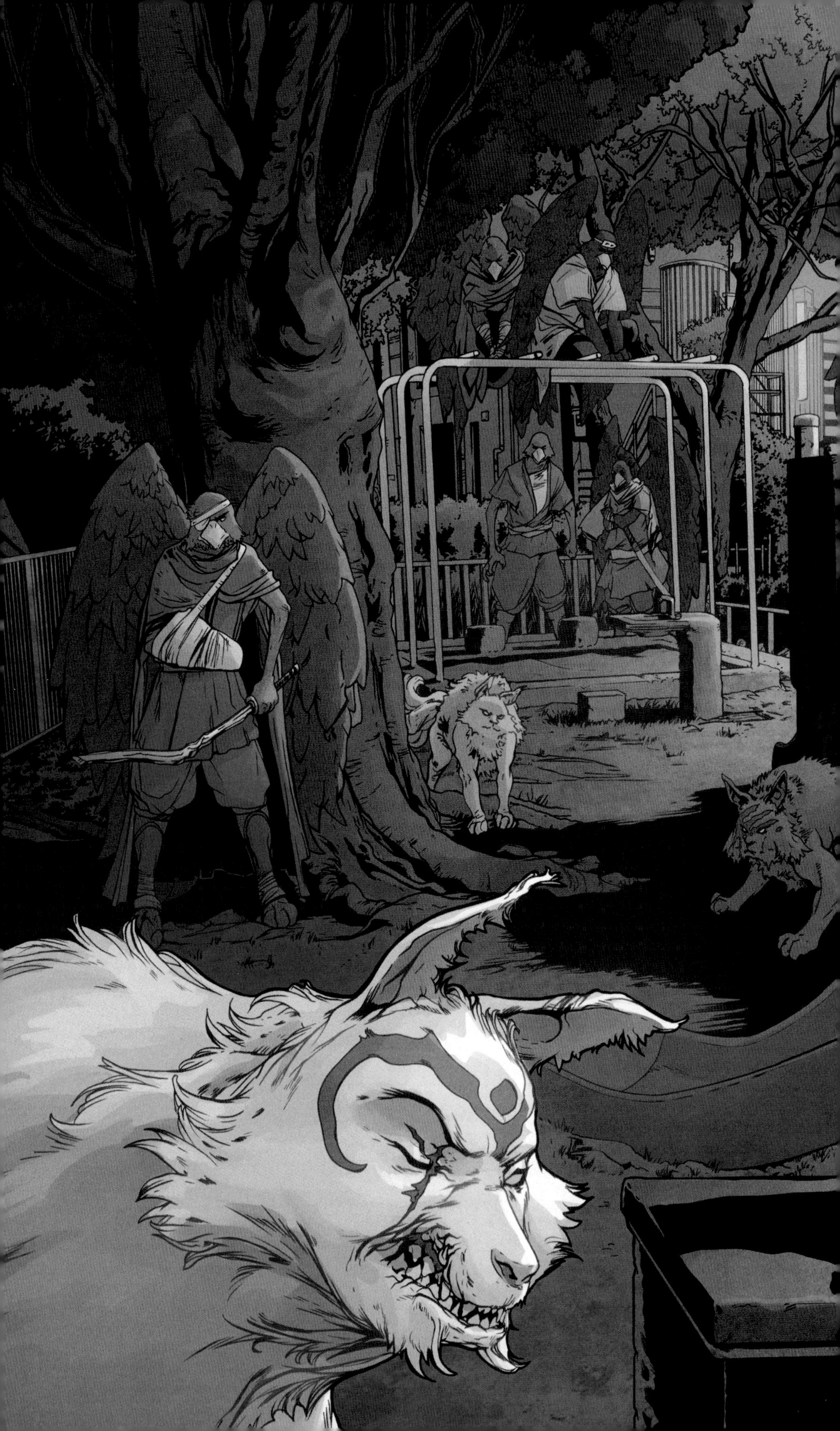

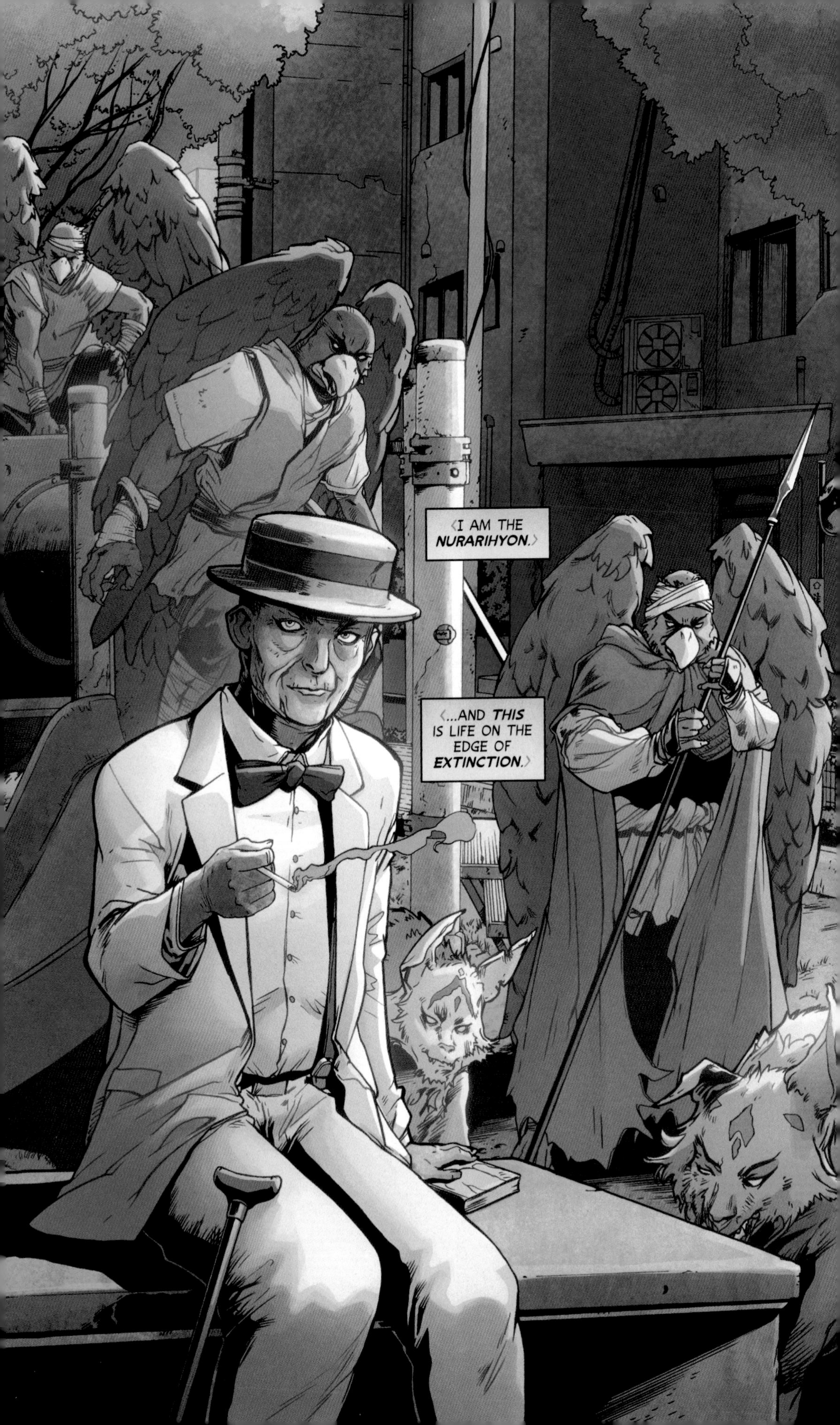
‹I AM THE NURARIHYON.›
‹...AND THIS IS LIFE ON THE EDGE OF EXTINCTION.›

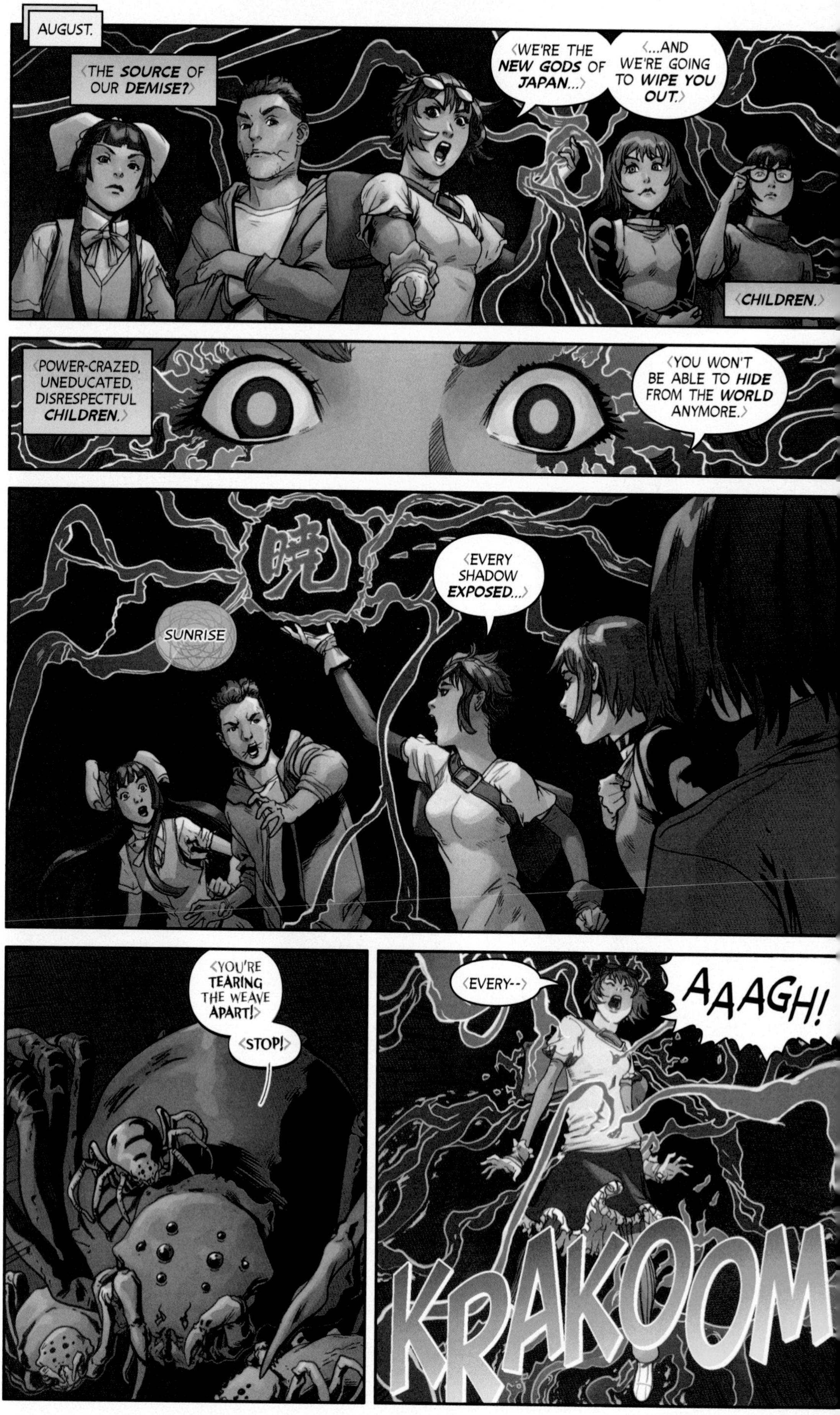
AUGUST.
⟨THE SOURCE OF OUR DEMISE?⟩
⟨WE'RE THE NEW GODS OF JAPAN...⟩
⟨...AND WE'RE GOING TO WIPE YOU OUT.⟩
⟨CHILDREN.⟩
⟨POWER-CRAZED, UNEDUCATED, DISRESPECTFUL CHILDREN.⟩
⟨YOU WON'T BE ABLE TO HIDE FROM THE WORLD ANYMORE.⟩
暁
SUNRISE
⟨EVERY SHADOW EXPOSED...⟩
⟨YOU'RE TEARING THE WEAVE APART!⟩
⟨STOP!⟩
⟨EVERY--⟩
AAAGH!
KRAKOOM

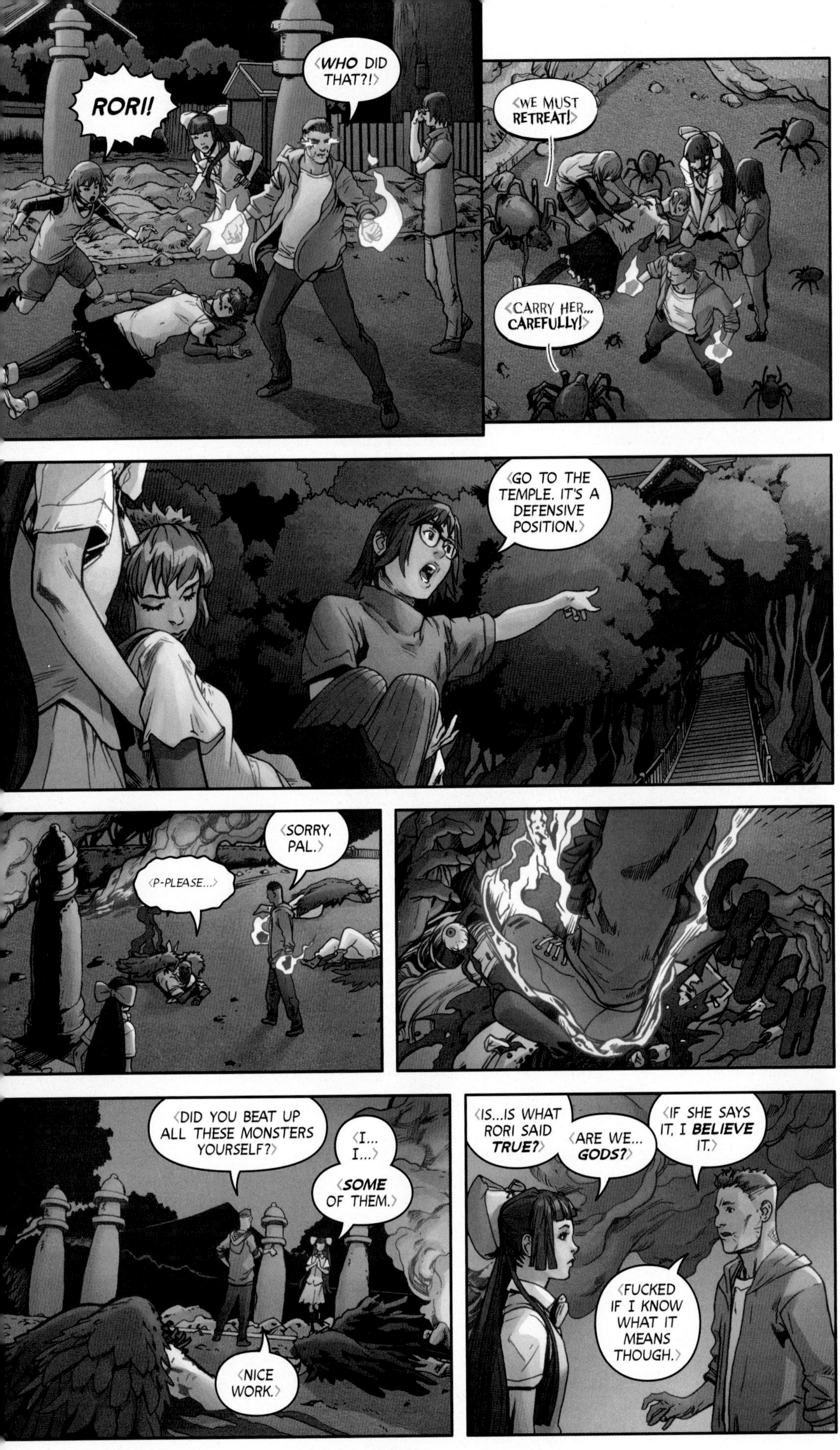
RORI!
‹WHO DID THAT?!›
‹WE MUST RETREAT!›
‹CARRY HER... CAREFULLY!›
‹GO TO THE TEMPLE. IT'S A DEFENSIVE POSITION.›
‹SORRY, PAL.›
‹P-PLEASE...›
CRUSH
‹DID YOU BEAT UP ALL THESE MONSTERS YOURSELF?›
‹I... I...›
‹SOME OF THEM.›
‹NICE WORK.›
‹IS...IS WHAT RORI SAID TRUE?›
‹ARE WE... GODS?›
‹IF SHE SAYS IT, I BELIEVE IT.›
‹FUCKED IF I KNOW WHAT IT MEANS THOUGH.›

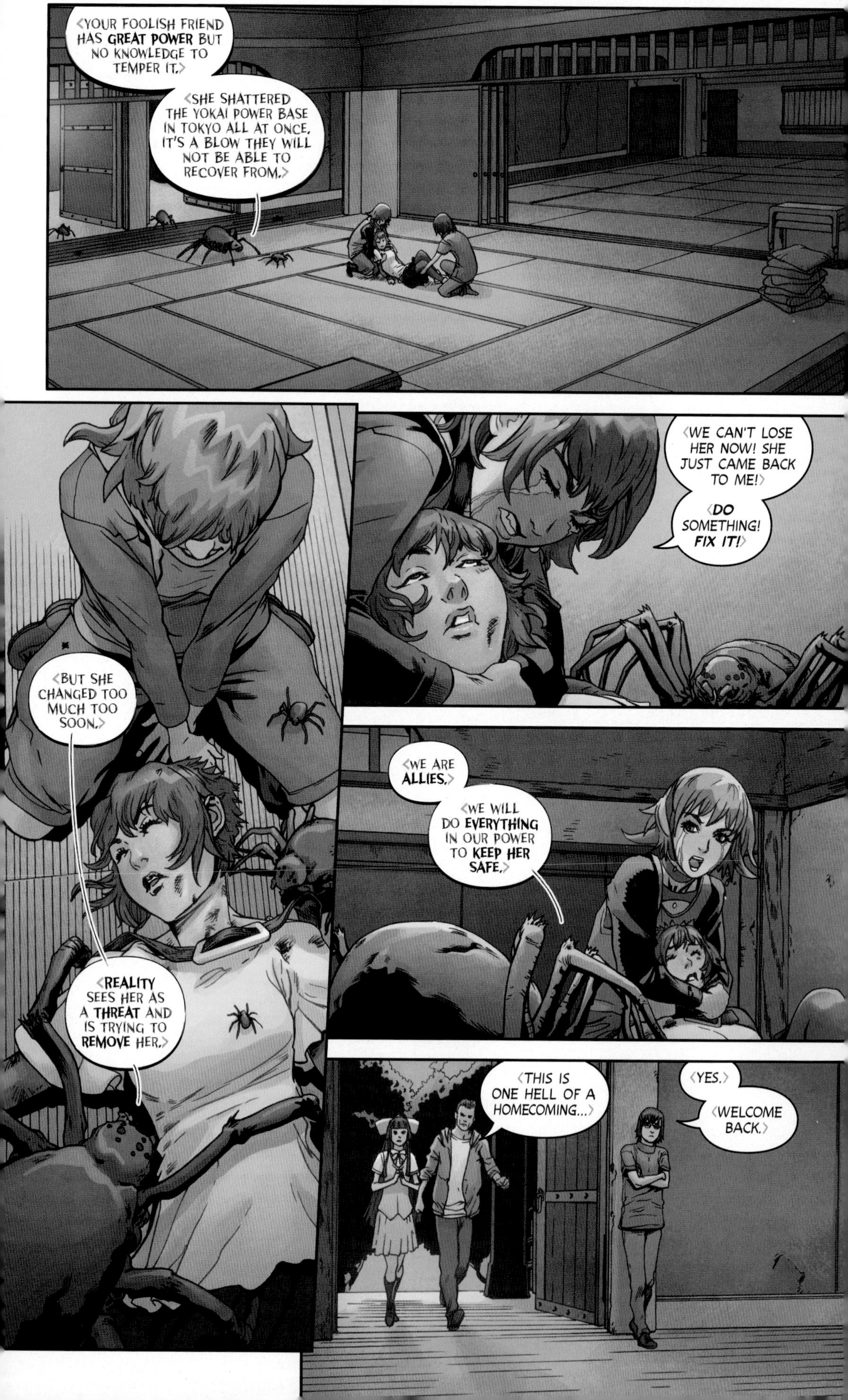

<YOUR FOOLISH FRIEND HAS GREAT POWER BUT NO KNOWLEDGE TO TEMPER IT.>
<SHE SHATTERED THE YOKAI POWER BASE IN TOKYO ALL AT ONCE, IT'S A BLOW THEY WILL NOT BE ABLE TO RECOVER FROM.>
<BUT SHE CHANGED TOO MUCH TOO SOON.>
<REALITY SEES HER AS A THREAT AND IS TRYING TO REMOVE HER.>
<WE CAN'T LOSE HER NOW! SHE JUST CAME BACK TO ME!>
<DO SOMETHING! FIX IT!>
<WE ARE ALLIES.>
<WE WILL DO EVERYTHING IN OUR POWER TO KEEP HER SAFE.>
<THIS IS ONE HELL OF A HOMECOMING...>
<YES.>
<WELCOME BACK.>

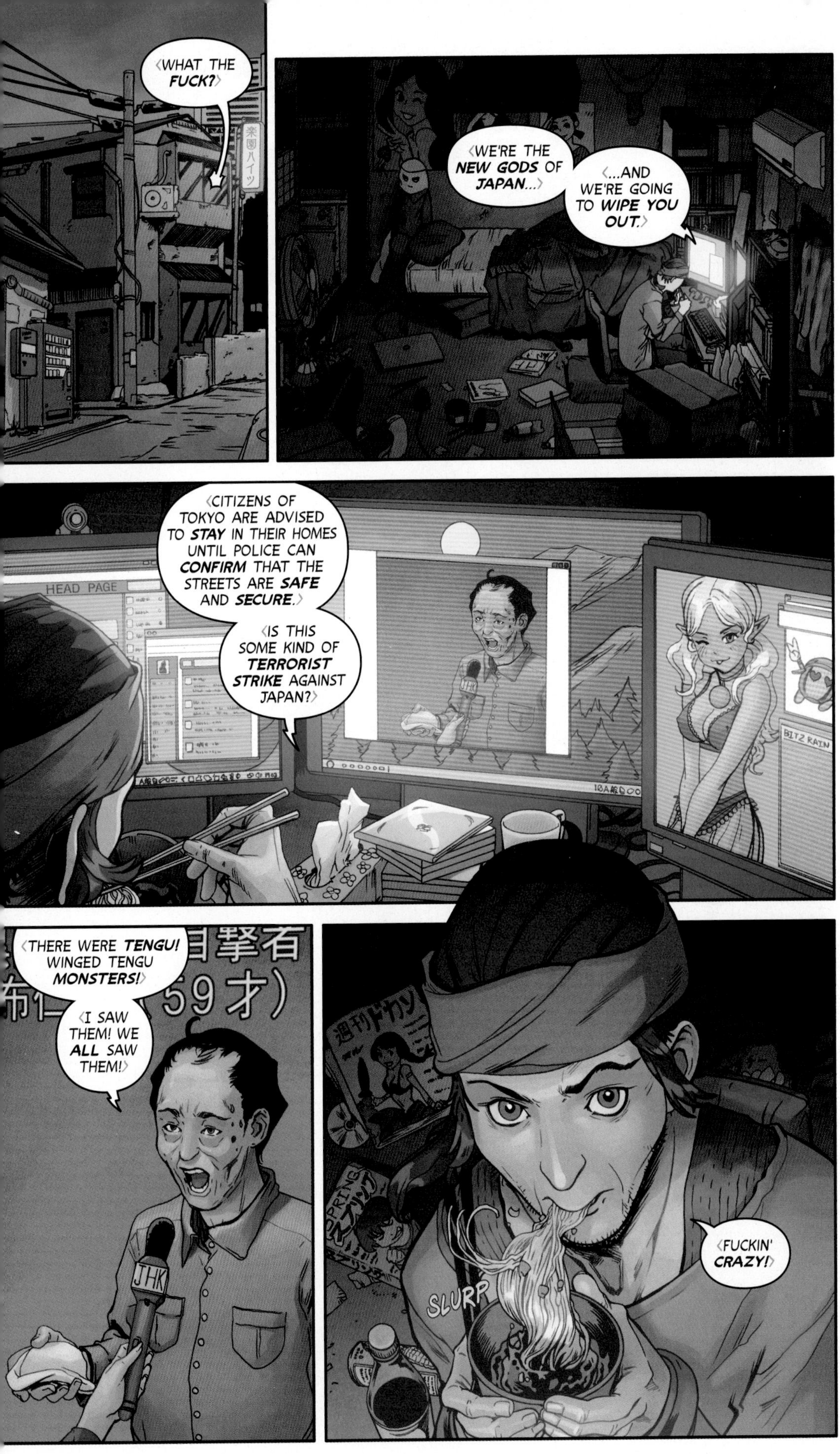

⟨WHAT THE FUCK?⟩
楽園ハイツ
⟨WE'RE THE NEW GODS OF JAPAN...⟩
⟨...AND WE'RE GOING TO WIPE YOU OUT.⟩
HEAD PAGE
⟨CITIZENS OF TOKYO ARE ADVISED TO STAY IN THEIR HOMES UNTIL POLICE CAN CONFIRM THAT THE STREETS ARE SAFE AND SECURE.⟩
⟨IS THIS SOME KIND OF TERRORIST STRIKE AGAINST JAPAN?⟩
JHK
BITZ RAIN
⟨THERE WERE TENGU! WINGED TENGU MONSTERS!⟩
⟨I SAW THEM! WE ALL SAW THEM!⟩
目撃者
59才)
JHK
週刊ドカン
SPRING
⟨FUCKIN' CRAZY!⟩
SLURP

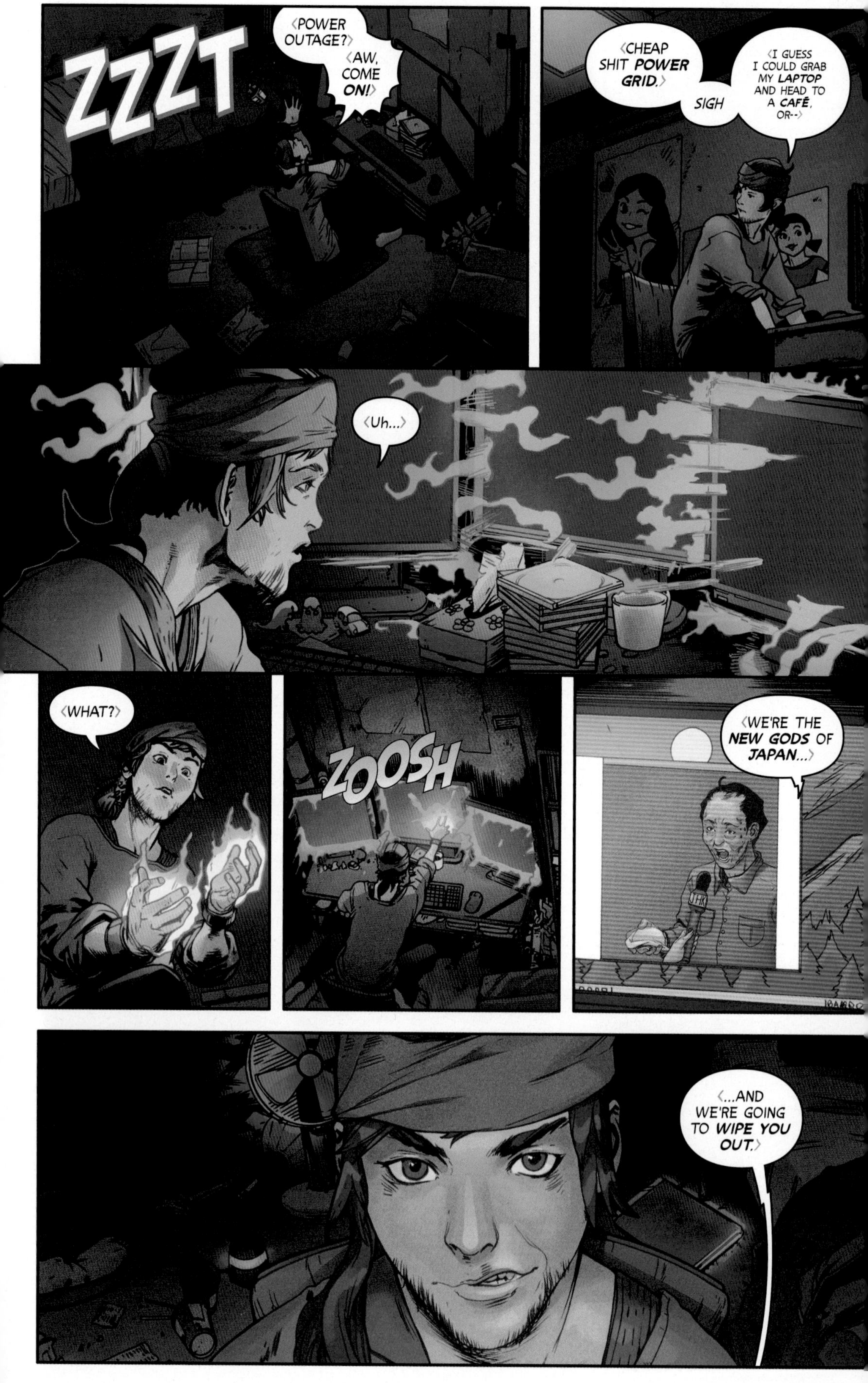
ZZZT
⟨POWER OUTAGE?⟩
⟨AW, COME ON!⟩
⟨CHEAP SHIT POWER GRID.⟩
SIGH
⟨I GUESS I COULD GRAB MY LAPTOP AND HEAD TO A CAFÉ, OR--⟩
⟨Uh...⟩
⟨WHAT?⟩
ZOOSH
⟨WE'RE THE NEW GODS OF JAPAN...⟩
⟨...AND WE'RE GOING TO WIPE YOU OUT.⟩

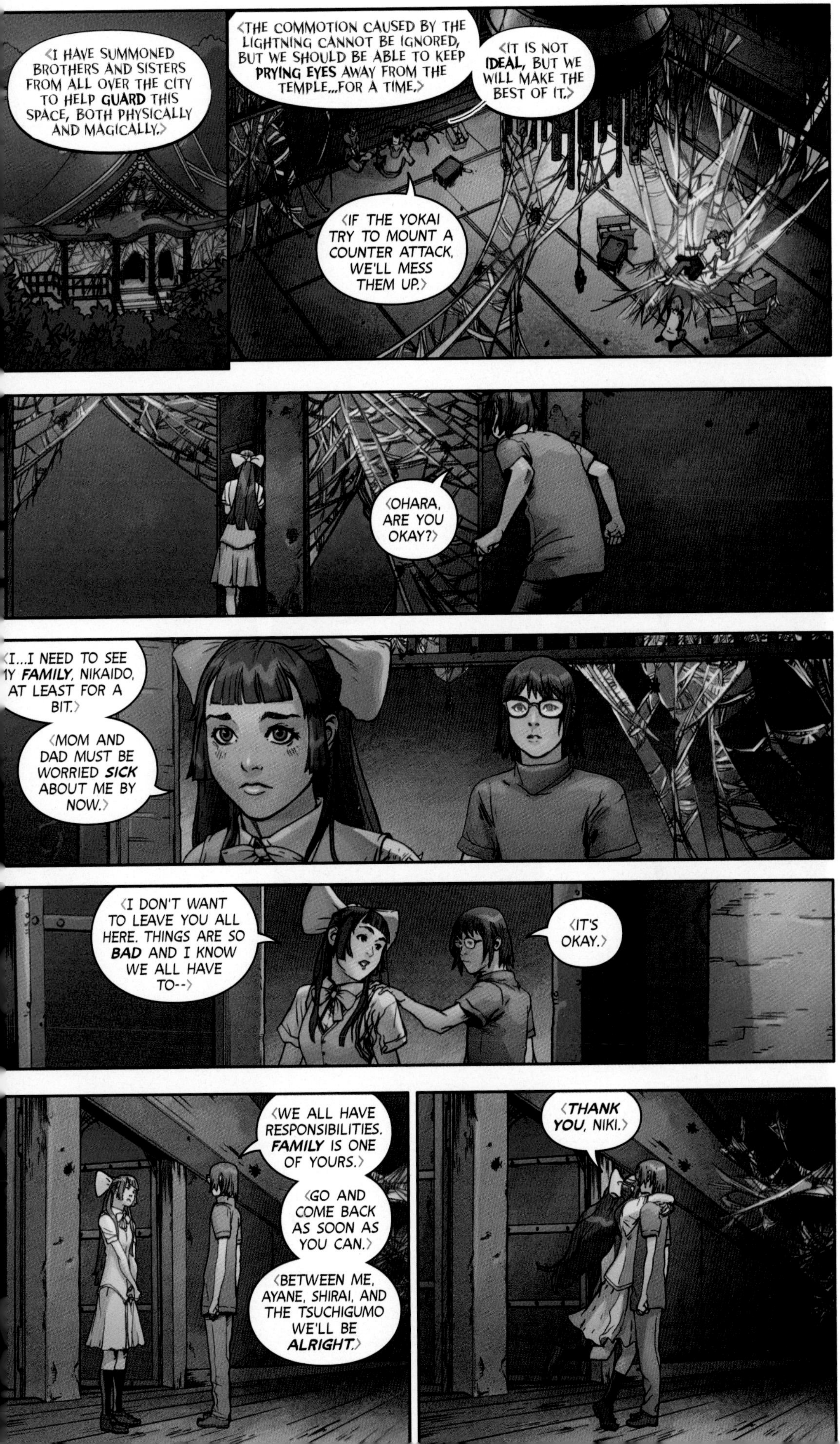

<I HAVE SUMMONED BROTHERS AND SISTERS FROM ALL OVER THE CITY TO HELP **GUARD** THIS SPACE, BOTH PHYSICALLY AND MAGICALLY.>
<THE COMMOTION CAUSED BY THE LIGHTNING CANNOT BE IGNORED, BUT WE SHOULD BE ABLE TO KEEP **PRYING EYES** AWAY FROM THE TEMPLE...FOR A TIME.>
<IT IS NOT **IDEAL**, BUT WE WILL MAKE THE BEST OF IT.>
<IF THE YOKAI TRY TO MOUNT A COUNTER ATTACK, WE'LL MESS THEM UP.>
<OHARA, ARE YOU OKAY?>
<I...I NEED TO SEE MY ***FAMILY***, NIKAIDO, AT LEAST FOR A BIT.>
<MOM AND DAD MUST BE WORRIED ***SICK*** ABOUT ME BY NOW.>
<I DON'T WANT TO LEAVE YOU ALL HERE. THINGS ARE SO ***BAD*** AND I KNOW WE ALL HAVE TO-->
<IT'S OKAY.>
<WE ALL HAVE RESPONSIBILITIES. ***FAMILY*** IS ONE OF YOURS.>
<GO AND COME BACK AS SOON AS YOU CAN.>
<BETWEEN ME, AYANE, SHIRAI, AND THE TSUCHIGUMO WE'LL BE ***ALRIGHT***.>
<***THANK YOU***, NIKI.>

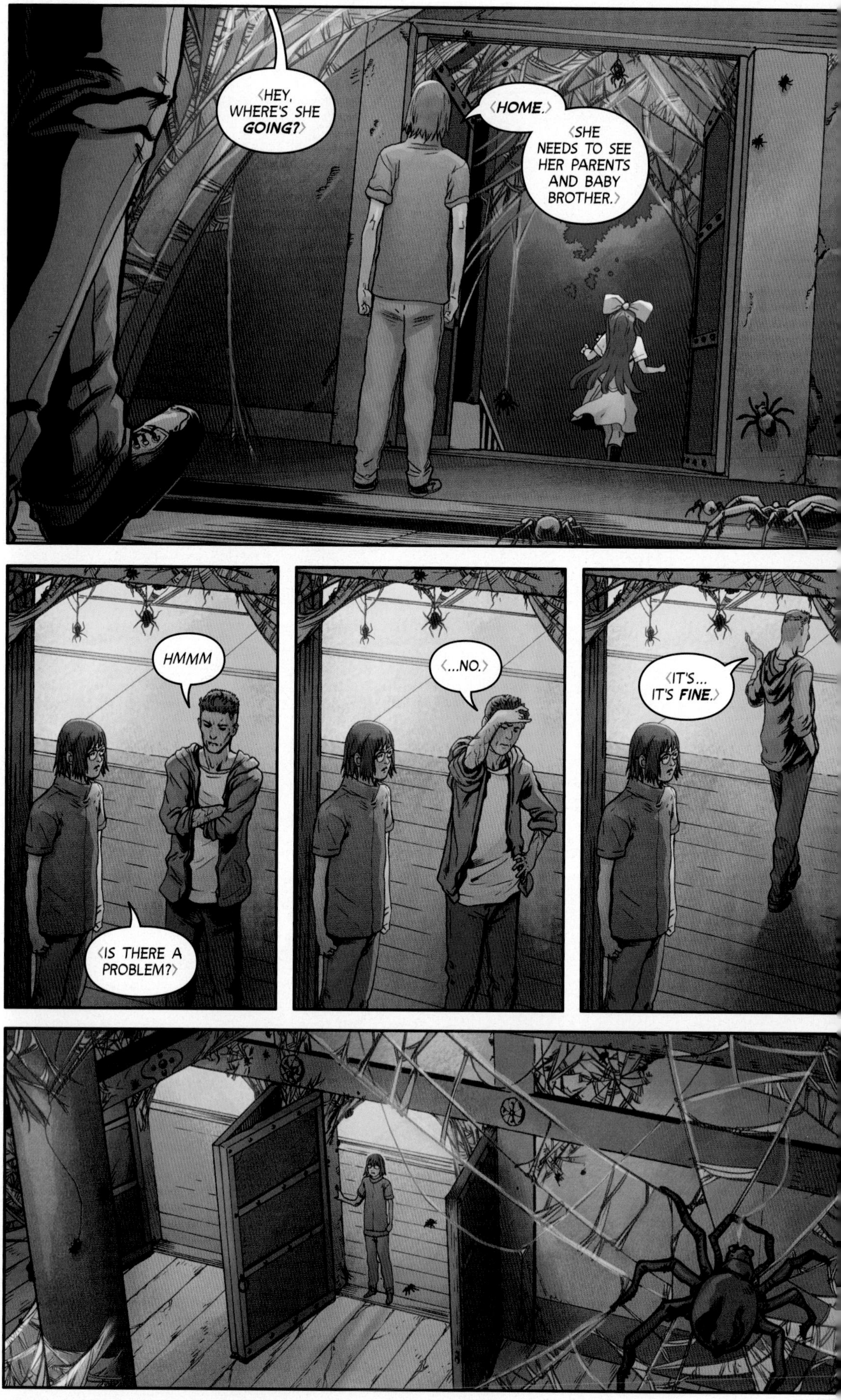

⟨HEY, WHERE'S SHE *GOING?*⟩
⟨*HOME.*⟩
⟨SHE NEEDS TO SEE HER PARENTS AND BABY BROTHER.⟩
HMMM
⟨IS THERE A PROBLEM?⟩
⟨...NO.⟩
⟨IT'S... IT'S *FINE.*⟩

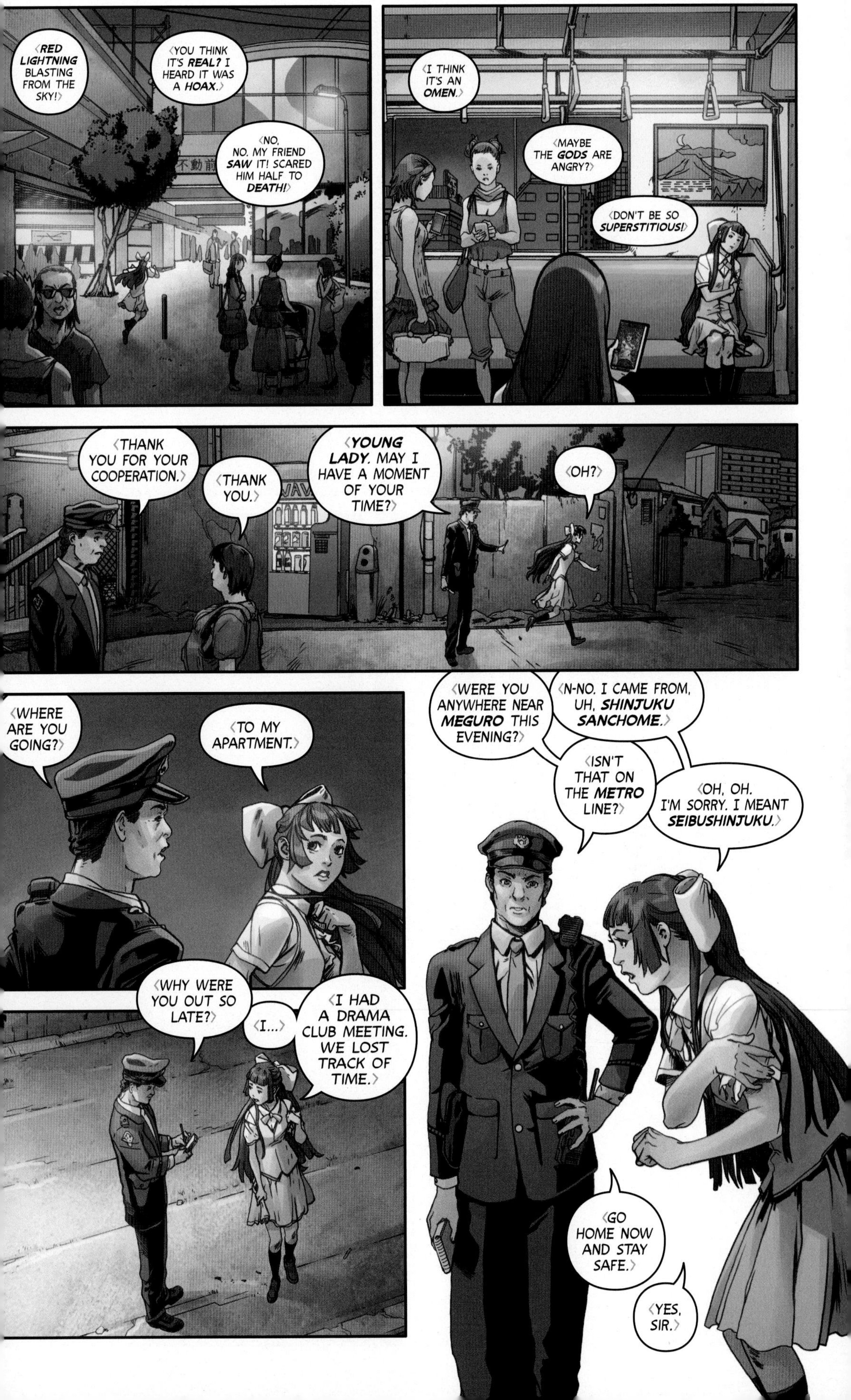

‹RED LIGHTNING BLASTING FROM THE SKY!›
‹YOU THINK IT'S REAL? I HEARD IT WAS A HOAX.›
‹NO, NO. MY FRIEND SAW IT! SCARED HIM HALF TO DEATH!›
不動前
‹I THINK IT'S AN OMEN.›
‹MAYBE THE GODS ARE ANGRY?›
‹DON'T BE SO SUPERSTITIOUS!›
‹THANK YOU FOR YOUR COOPERATION.›
‹THANK YOU.›
‹YOUNG LADY. MAY I HAVE A MOMENT OF YOUR TIME?›
‹OH?›
‹WHERE ARE YOU GOING?›
‹TO MY APARTMENT.›
‹WHY WERE YOU OUT SO LATE?›
‹I...›
‹I HAD A DRAMA CLUB MEETING. WE LOST TRACK OF TIME.›
‹WERE YOU ANYWHERE NEAR MEGURO THIS EVENING?›
‹N-NO. I CAME FROM, UH, SHINJUKU SANCHOME.›
‹ISN'T THAT ON THE METRO LINE?›
‹OH, OH. I'M SORRY. I MEANT SEIBUSHINJUKU.›
‹GO HOME NOW AND STAY SAFE.›
‹YES, SIR.›

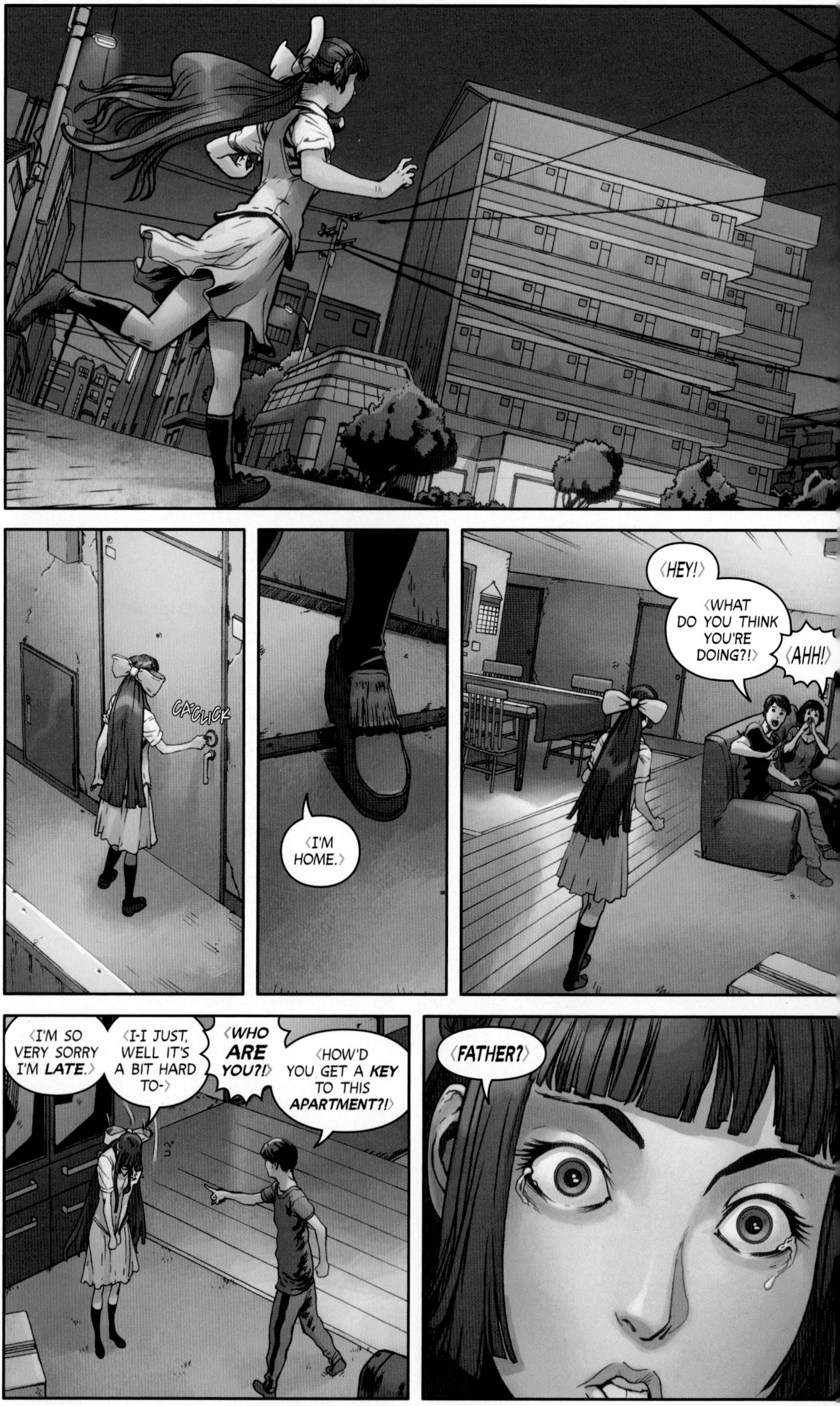
CA'CLICK
〈I'M HOME.〉
〈HEY!〉
〈WHAT DO YOU THINK YOU'RE DOING?!〉
〈AHH!〉
〈I'M SO VERY SORRY I'M LATE.〉
〈I-I JUST, WELL IT'S A BIT HARD TO-〉
〈WHO ARE YOU?!〉
〈HOW'D YOU GET A KEY TO THIS APARTMENT?!〉
〈FATHER?〉

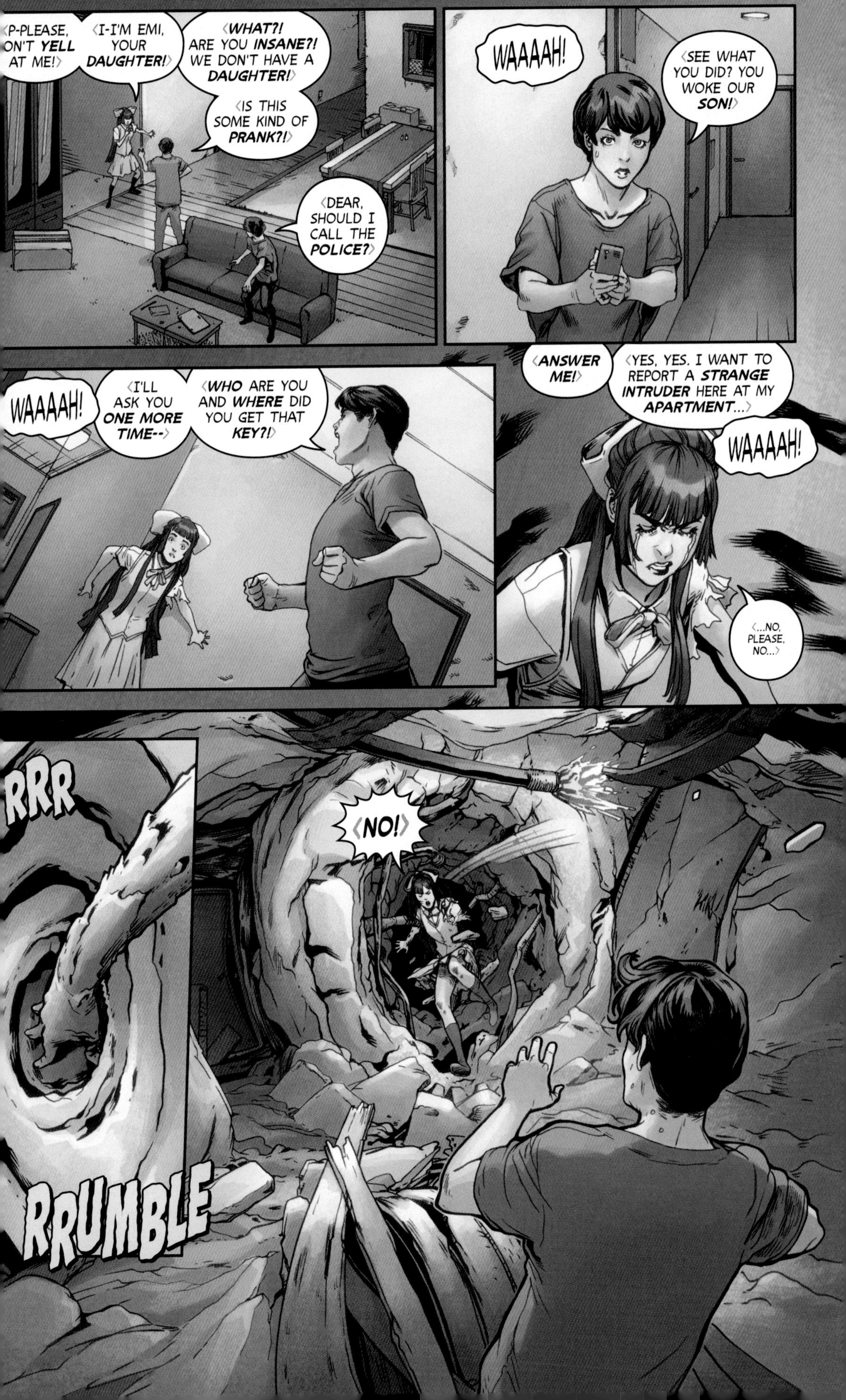
‹P-PLEASE, ON'T YELL AT ME!›
‹I-I'M EMI, YOUR DAUGHTER!›
‹WHAT?! ARE YOU INSANE?! WE DON'T HAVE A DAUGHTER!›
‹IS THIS SOME KIND OF PRANK?!›
‹DEAR, SHOULD I CALL THE POLICE?›
WAAAAH!
‹SEE WHAT YOU DID? YOU WOKE OUR SON!›
WAAAAH!
‹I'LL ASK YOU ONE MORE TIME--›
‹WHO ARE YOU AND WHERE DID YOU GET THAT KEY?!›
‹ANSWER ME!›
‹YES, YES. I WANT TO REPORT A STRANGE INTRUDER HERE AT MY APARTMENT...›
WAAAAH!
‹...NO, PLEASE, NO...›
RRR
‹NO!›
RRUMBLE

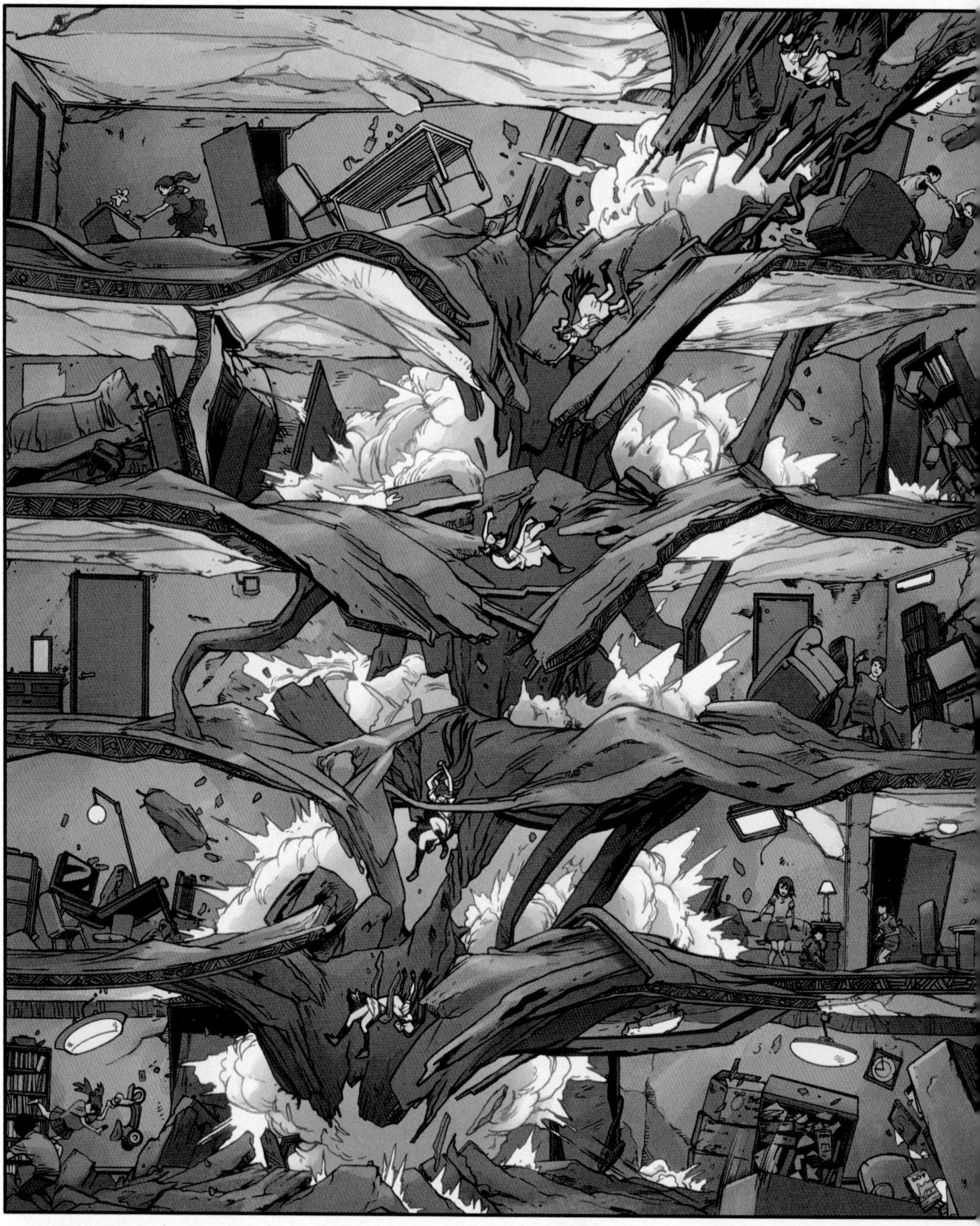

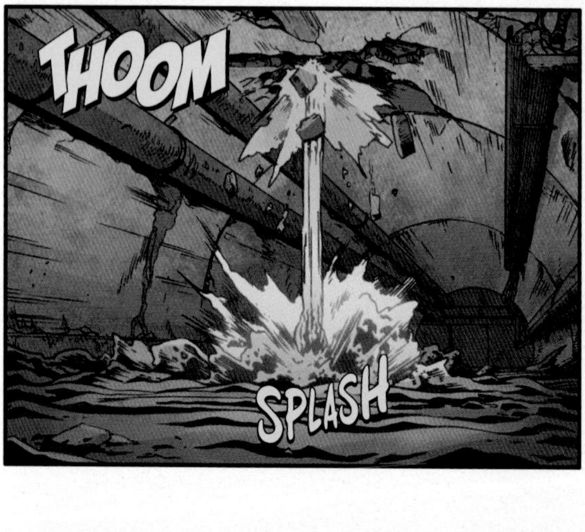
THOOM
SPLASH

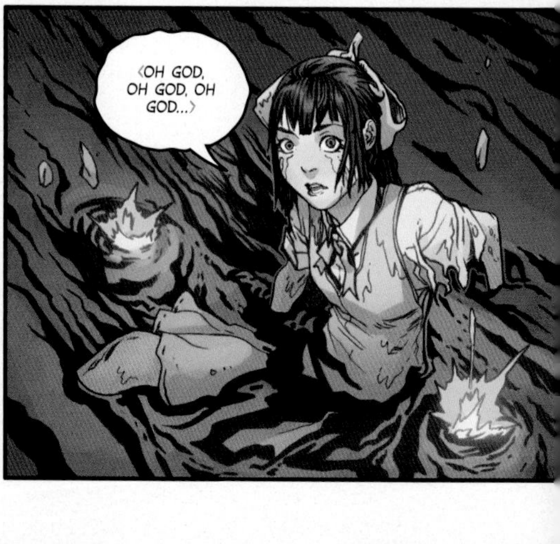
‹OH GOD, OH GOD, OH GOD...›

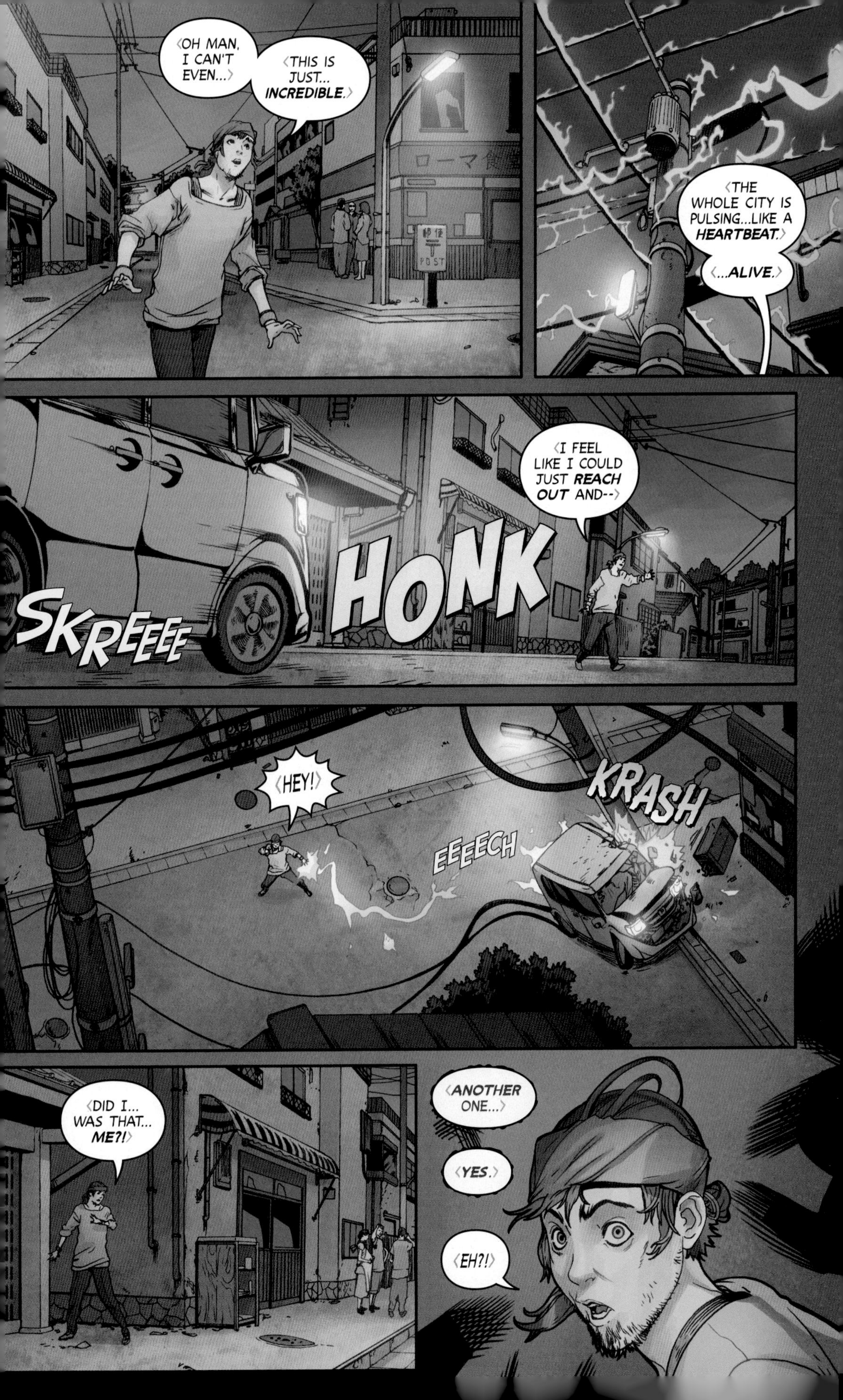
⟨OH MAN, I CAN'T EVEN...⟩
⟨THIS IS JUST... **INCREDIBLE**.⟩
⟨THE WHOLE CITY IS PULSING...LIKE A **HEARTBEAT**.⟩
⟨...**ALIVE**.⟩
ローマ食堂
POST
⟨I FEEL LIKE I COULD JUST **REACH OUT** AND--⟩
SKREEEE
HONK
⟨HEY!⟩
KRASH
EEEECH
⟨DID I... WAS THAT... **ME?!**⟩
⟨**ANOTHER** ONE...⟩
⟨**YES**.⟩
⟨EH?!⟩

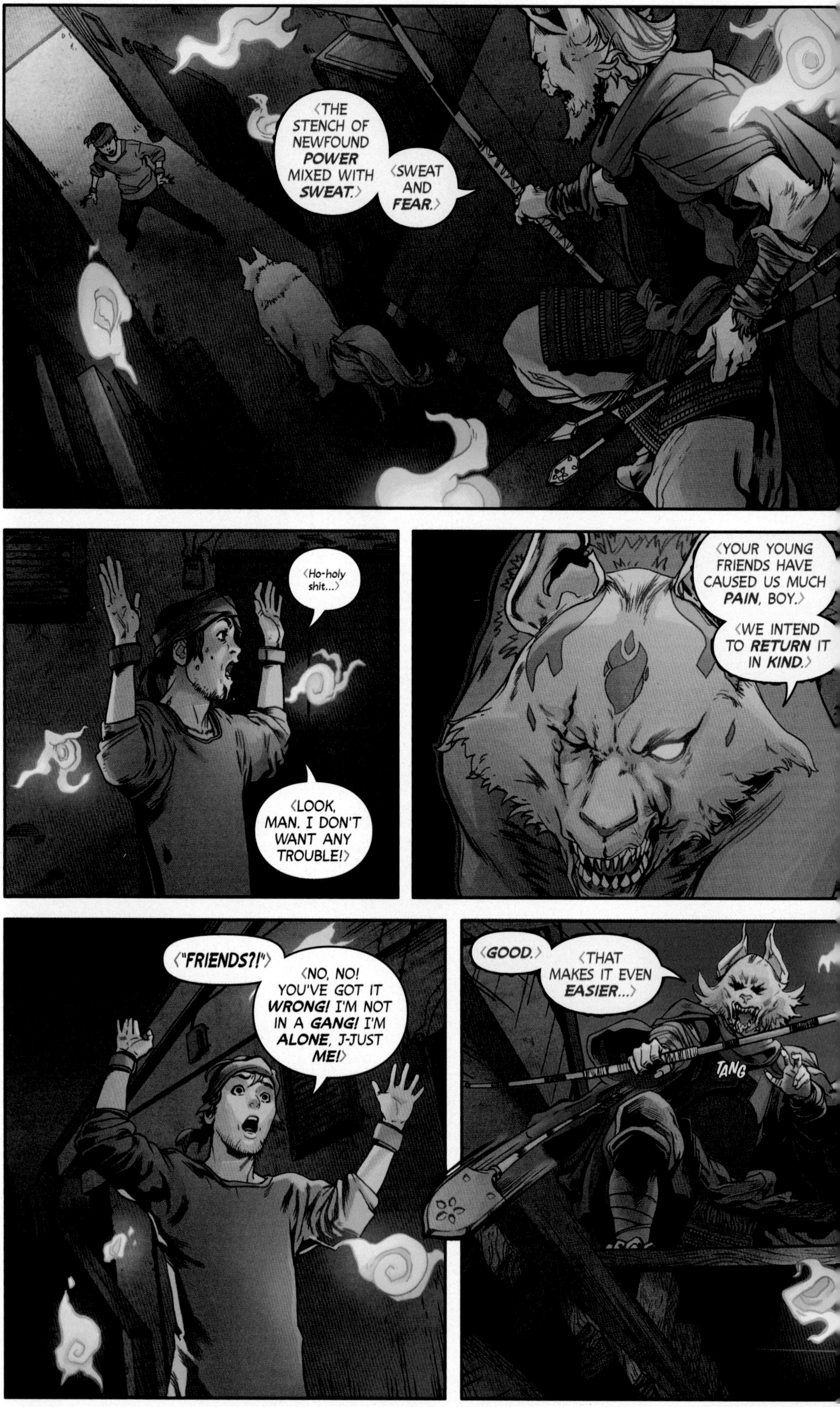
‹THE STENCH OF NEWFOUND POWER MIXED WITH SWEAT.›
‹SWEAT AND FEAR.›
‹Ho-holy shit...›
‹LOOK, MAN. I DON'T WANT ANY TROUBLE!›
‹YOUR YOUNG FRIENDS HAVE CAUSED US MUCH PAIN, BOY.›
‹WE INTEND TO RETURN IT IN KIND.›
‹"FRIENDS?!"›
‹NO, NO! YOU'VE GOT IT WRONG! I'M NOT IN A GANG! I'M ALONE, J-JUST ME!›
‹GOOD.›
‹THAT MAKES IT EVEN EASIER...›
TANG

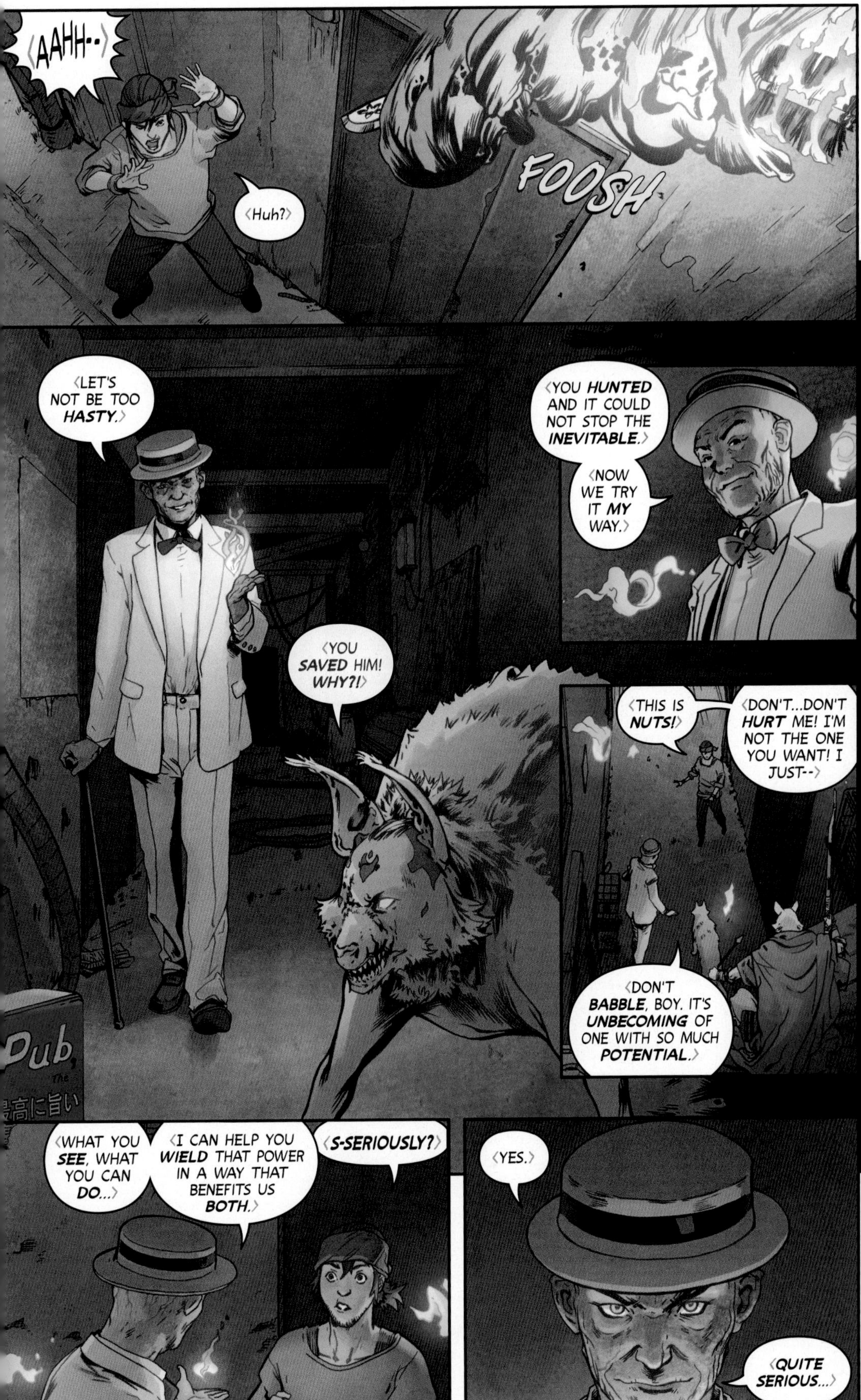
⟨AAHH--⟩
FOOSH
⟨Huh?⟩
⟨LET'S NOT BE TOO HASTY.⟩
⟨YOU HUNTED AND IT COULD NOT STOP THE INEVITABLE.⟩
⟨NOW WE TRY IT MY WAY.⟩
⟨YOU SAVED HIM! WHY?!⟩
⟨THIS IS NUTS!⟩
⟨DON'T...DON'T HURT ME! I'M NOT THE ONE YOU WANT! I JUST--⟩
⟨DON'T BABBLE, BOY. IT'S UNBECOMING OF ONE WITH SO MUCH POTENTIAL.⟩
Pub
The
最高に旨い
⟨WHAT YOU SEE, WHAT YOU CAN DO...⟩
⟨I CAN HELP YOU WIELD THAT POWER IN A WAY THAT BENEFITS US BOTH.⟩
⟨S-SERIOUSLY?⟩
⟨YES.⟩
⟨QUITE SERIOUS...⟩

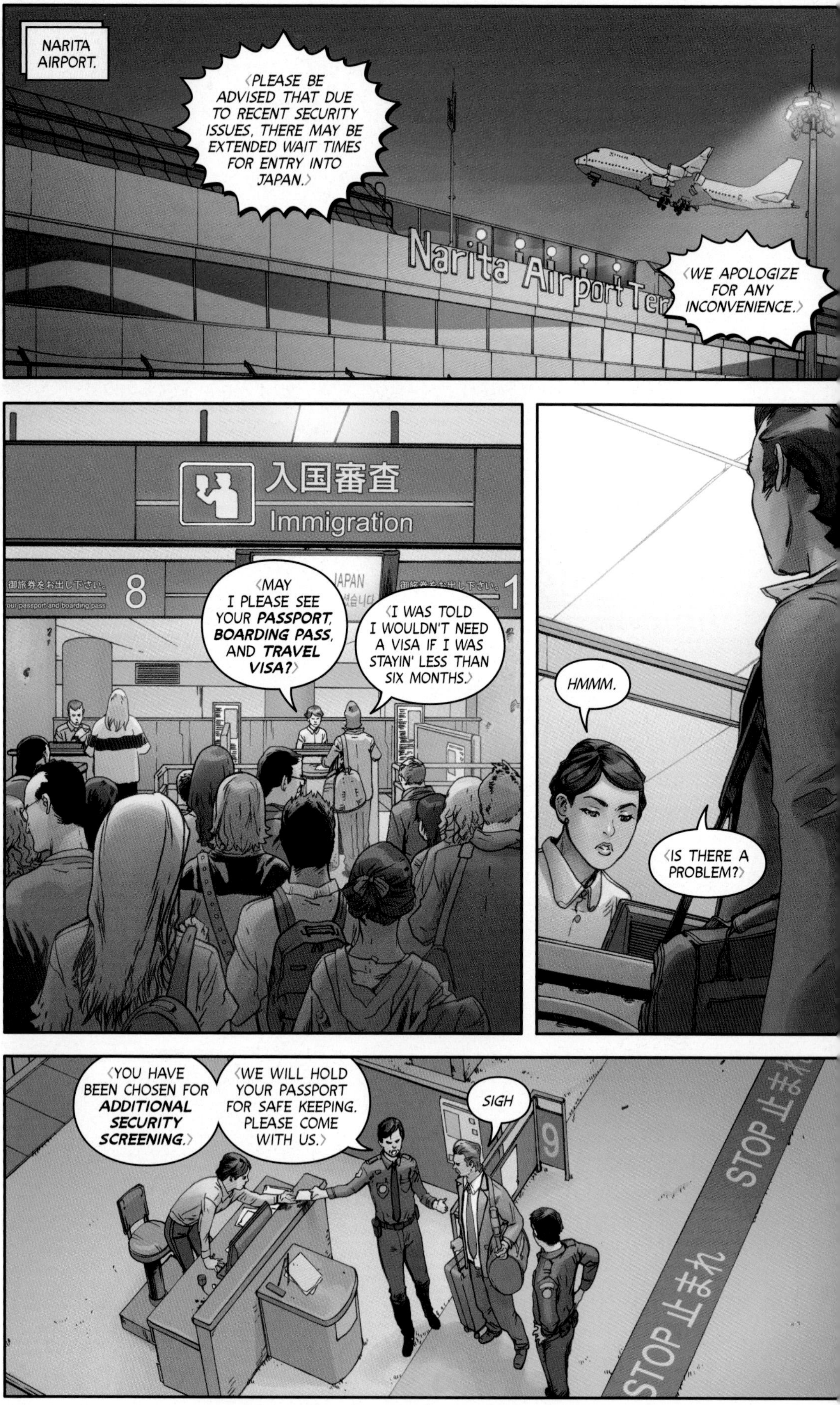

NARITA AIRPORT.
‹PLEASE BE ADVISED THAT DUE TO RECENT SECURITY ISSUES, THERE MAY BE EXTENDED WAIT TIMES FOR ENTRY INTO JAPAN.›
Narita Airport Ter
‹WE APOLOGIZE FOR ANY INCONVENIENCE.›
入国審査
Immigration
御旅券をお出し下さい。
8
1
JAPAN
‹MAY I PLEASE SEE YOUR **PASSPORT, BOARDING PASS,** AND **TRAVEL VISA?**›
‹I WAS TOLD I WOULDN'T NEED A VISA IF I WAS STAYIN' LESS THAN SIX MONTHS.›
HMMM.
‹IS THERE A PROBLEM?›
‹YOU HAVE BEEN CHOSEN FOR **ADDITIONAL SECURITY SCREENING.**›
‹WE WILL HOLD YOUR PASSPORT FOR SAFE KEEPING. PLEASE COME WITH US.›
SIGH
9
STOP 止まれ
STOP 止まれ

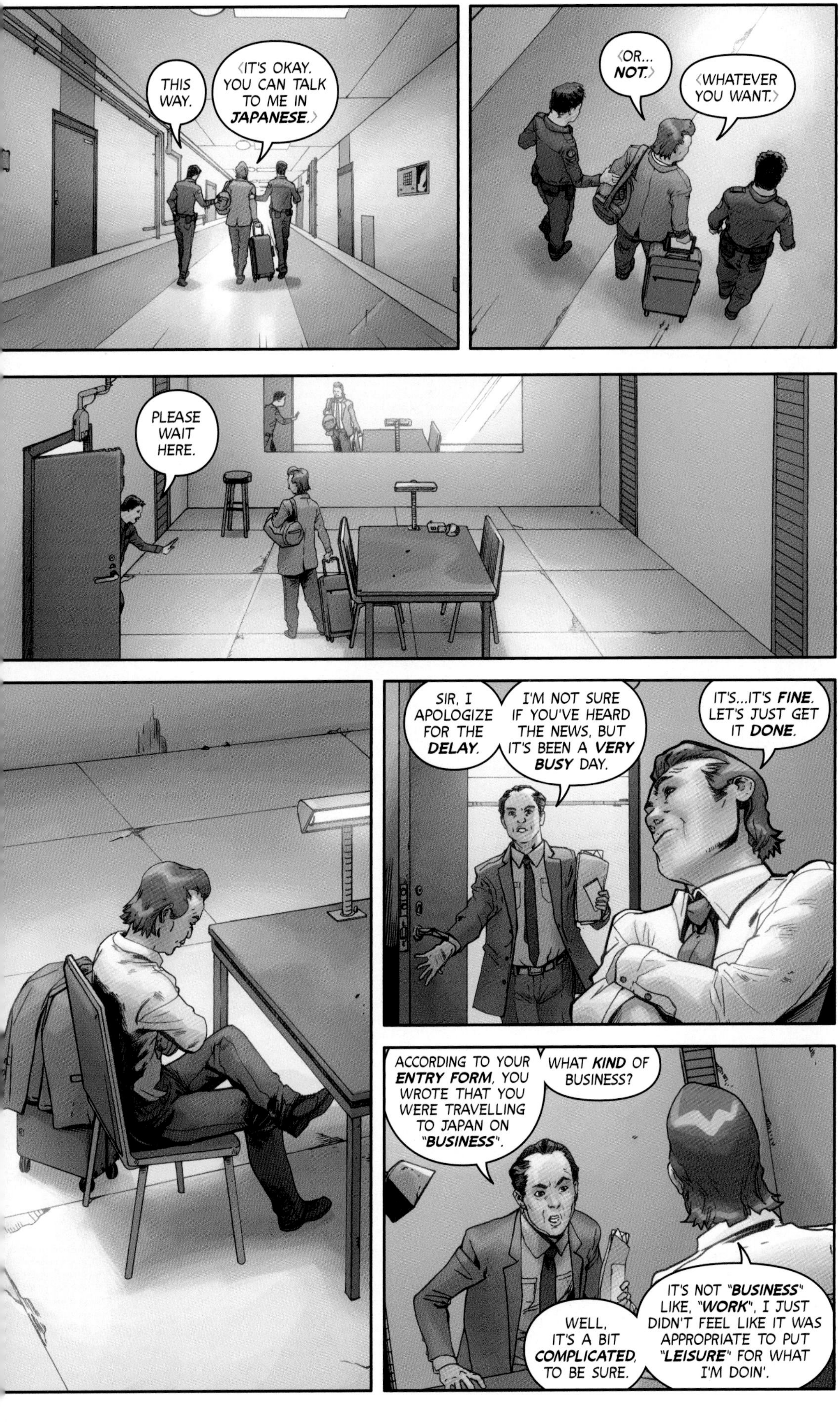

THIS WAY.
‹IT'S OKAY. YOU CAN TALK TO ME IN **JAPANESE**.›
‹OR... **NOT**.›
‹WHATEVER YOU WANT.›
PLEASE WAIT HERE.
SIR, I APOLOGIZE FOR THE **DELAY**.
I'M NOT SURE IF YOU'VE HEARD THE NEWS, BUT IT'S BEEN A **VERY BUSY** DAY.
IT'S...IT'S **FINE**. LET'S JUST GET IT **DONE**.
ACCORDING TO YOUR **ENTRY FORM**, YOU WROTE THAT YOU WERE TRAVELLING TO JAPAN ON "**BUSINESS**".
WHAT **KIND** OF BUSINESS?
WELL, IT'S A BIT **COMPLICATED**, TO BE SURE.
IT'S NOT "**BUSINESS**" LIKE, "**WORK**", I JUST DIDN'T FEEL LIKE IT WAS APPROPRIATE TO PUT "**LEISURE**" FOR WHAT I'M DOIN'.

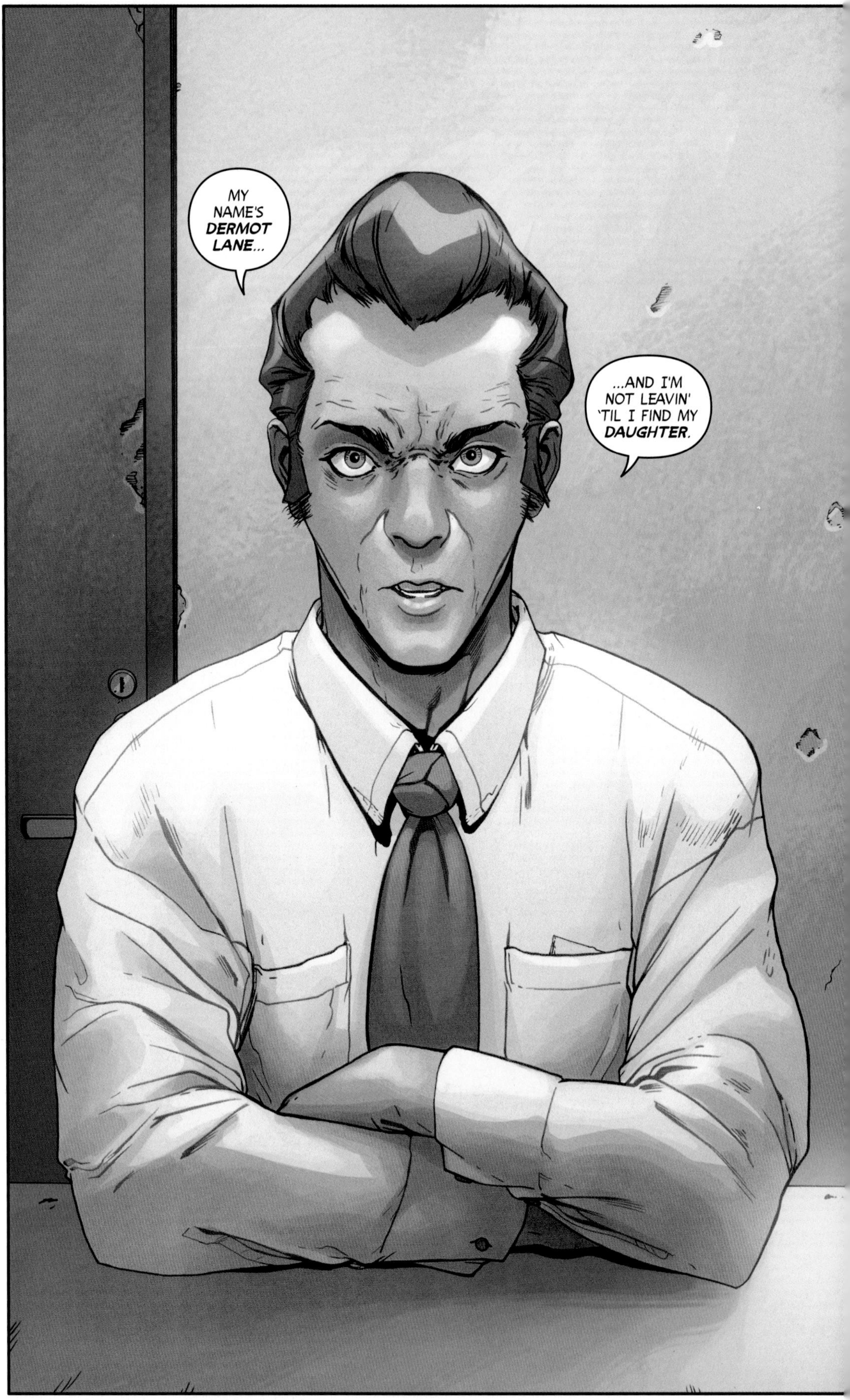
MY NAME'S *DERMOT LANE*...
...AND I'M NOT LEAVIN' 'TIL I FIND MY *DAUGHTER*.

Chapter Twelve

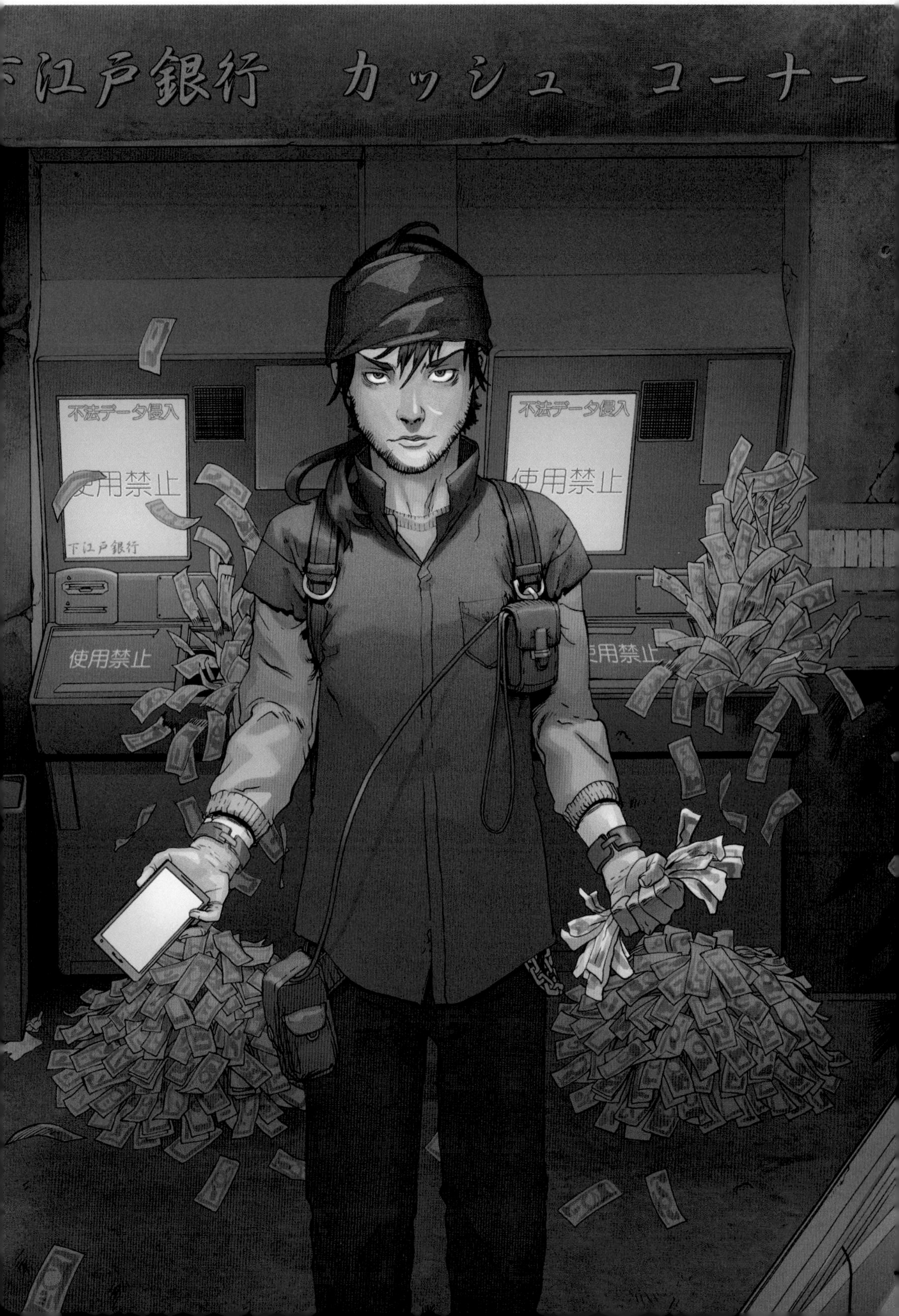

江戸銀行 カッシュ コーナー
不法データ侵入
使用禁止
下江戸銀行
使用禁止
不法データ侵入
使用禁止

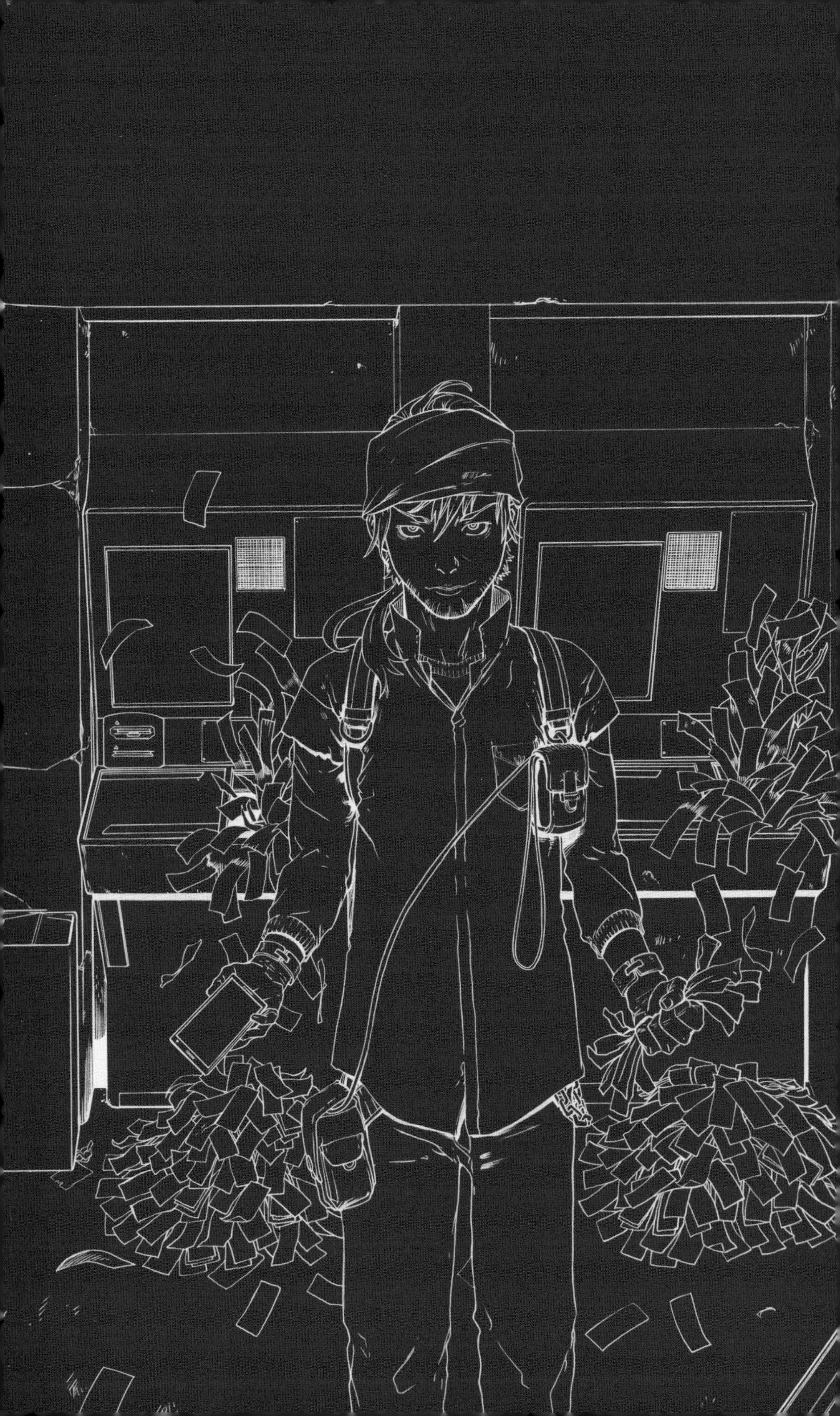

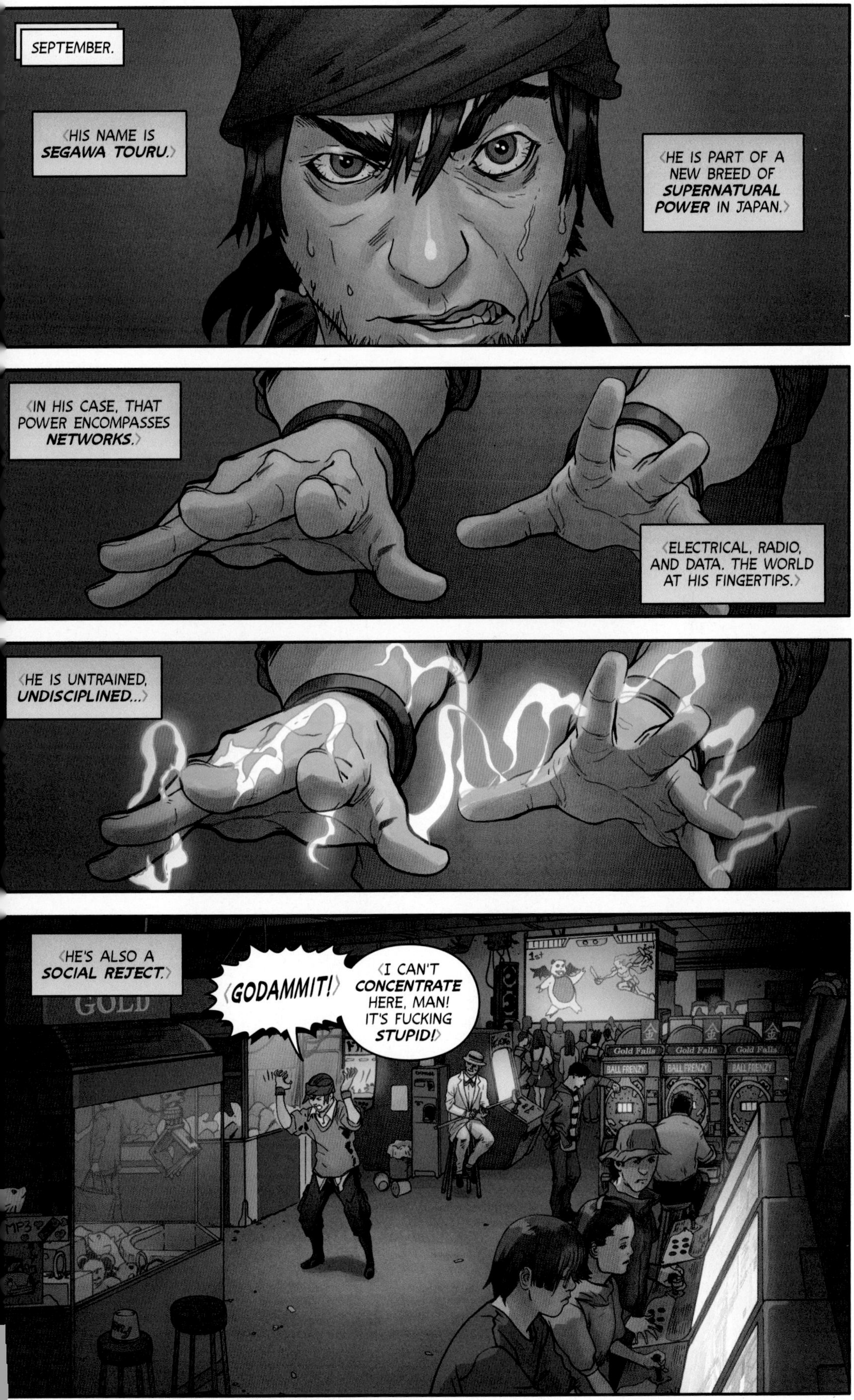
SEPTEMBER.
⟨HIS NAME IS SEGAWA TOURU.⟩
⟨HE IS PART OF A NEW BREED OF SUPERNATURAL POWER IN JAPAN.⟩
⟨IN HIS CASE, THAT POWER ENCOMPASSES NETWORKS.⟩
⟨ELECTRICAL, RADIO, AND DATA. THE WORLD AT HIS FINGERTIPS.⟩
⟨HE IS UNTRAINED, UNDISCIPLINED...⟩
⟨HE'S ALSO A SOCIAL REJECT.⟩
GOLD
⟨GODAMMIT!⟩
⟨I CAN'T CONCENTRATE HERE, MAN! IT'S FUCKING STUPID!⟩
Gold Falls
BALL FRENZY
Gold Falls
BALL FRENZY
Gold Falls
BALL FRENZY
MP3

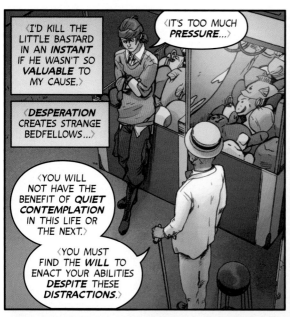

‹I'D KILL THE LITTLE BASTARD IN AN *INSTANT* IF HE WASN'T SO *VALUABLE* TO MY CAUSE.›

‹*DESPERATION* CREATES STRANGE BEDFELLOWS...›

‹IT'S TOO MUCH *PRESSURE*...›

‹YOU WILL NOT HAVE THE BENEFIT OF *QUIET CONTEMPLATION* IN THIS LIFE OR THE NEXT.›

‹YOU MUST FIND THE *WILL* TO ENACT YOUR ABILITIES *DESPITE* THESE *DISTRACTIONS*.›

‹CONSISTENCY COMES THROUGH PRACTICE.›

‹I WANT YOU TO TRY AGAIN, BUT *THIS* TIME--›

‹ONE SEC. I'M *HUNGRY*. LEMME LOOK UP SOME GOOD UNAGI *PLACES* AROUND HERE...›

"HUNGRY?!"

‹*HUNGER* FOR POWER, NOT *SUSTENANCE*!›

‹WE MUST FIND THE TRIGGER WITHIN YOU, THE--›

KRESH

‹WHAT THE *FUCK?!*›

‹YOU *BROKE M* PHONE!›

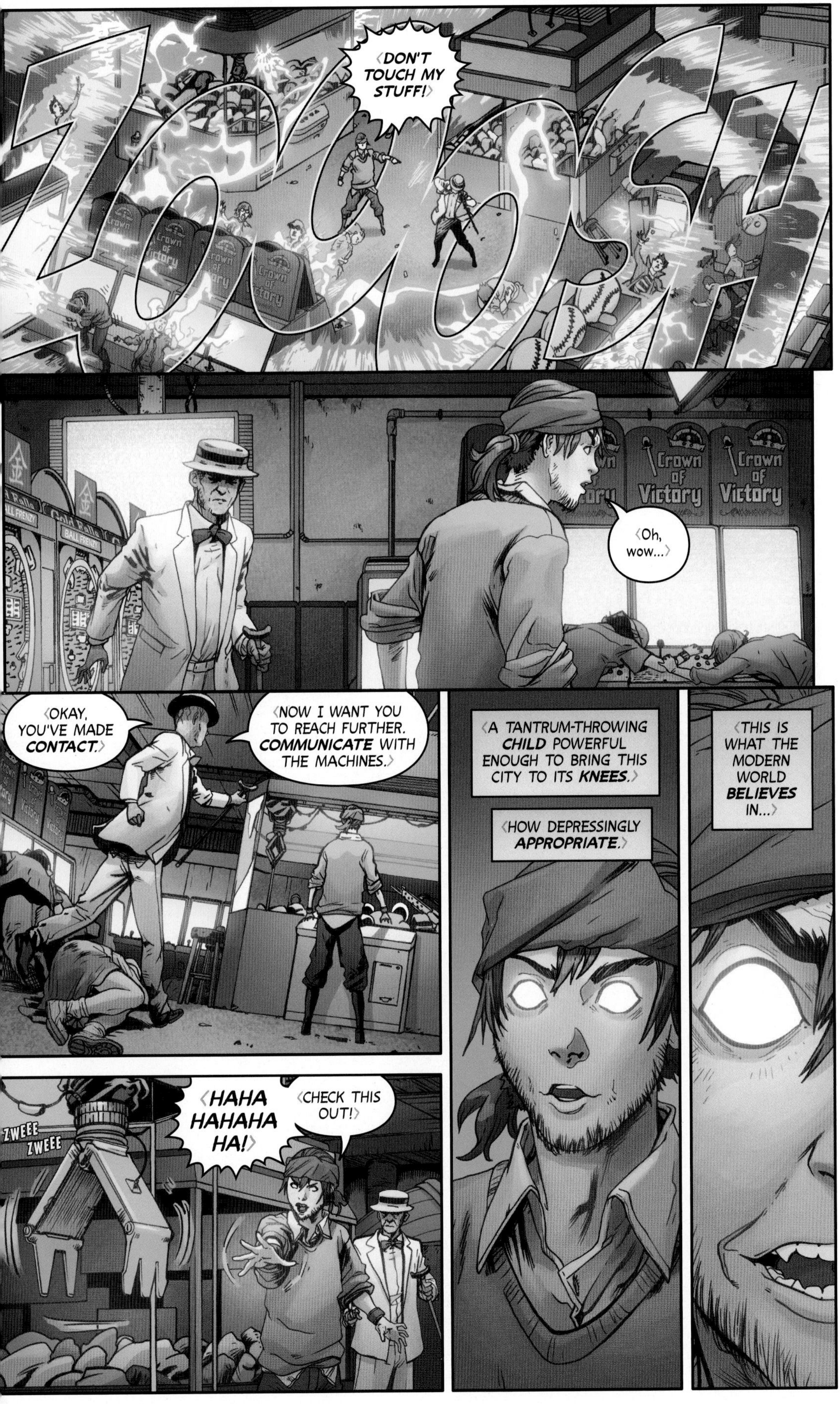

ZOOOSH
‹DON'T TOUCH MY STUFF!›
Crown of Victory
Crown of Victory
Crown of Victory
‹Oh, wow...›
Gold Balls
BALL FRENZY
Crown of Victory
Crown of Victory
‹OKAY, YOU'VE MADE CONTACT.›
‹NOW I WANT YOU TO REACH FURTHER. COMMUNICATE WITH THE MACHINES.›
‹A TANTRUM-THROWING CHILD POWERFUL ENOUGH TO BRING THIS CITY TO ITS KNEES.›
‹HOW DEPRESSINGLY APPROPRIATE.›
‹THIS IS WHAT THE MODERN WORLD BELIEVES IN...›
ZWEEE ZWEEE
‹HAHA HAHAHA HA!›
‹CHECK THIS OUT!›

〈...THESE ARE THEIR GODS OF *YOUTH* AND *MADNESS*.〉

UNHHHHH!

〈RORI'S *AWAKE!*〉

〈RORI, IT'S ME, *AYANE!*〉

DO YOU *HEAR* ME? I'M RIGHT *HERE!*

〈HER BODY IS PRESENT BUT HER MIND IS STILL *LOST* IN THE *WEAVE,* SHE CANNOT SEE OR HEAR US.〉

AHHHH!

〈WHAT... WHAT'S SHE DOING?!〉

〈YOU HAVE TO *HELP* HER!〉

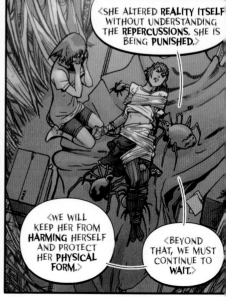

〈SHE ALTERED *REALITY* ITSELF WITHOUT UNDERSTANDING THE *REPERCUSSIONS,* SHE IS BEING *PUNISHED.*〉

〈WE WILL KEEP HER FROM *HARMING* HERSELF AND PROTECT HER *PHYSICAL* FORM.〉

〈BEYOND THAT, WE MUST CONTINUE TO *WAIT.*〉

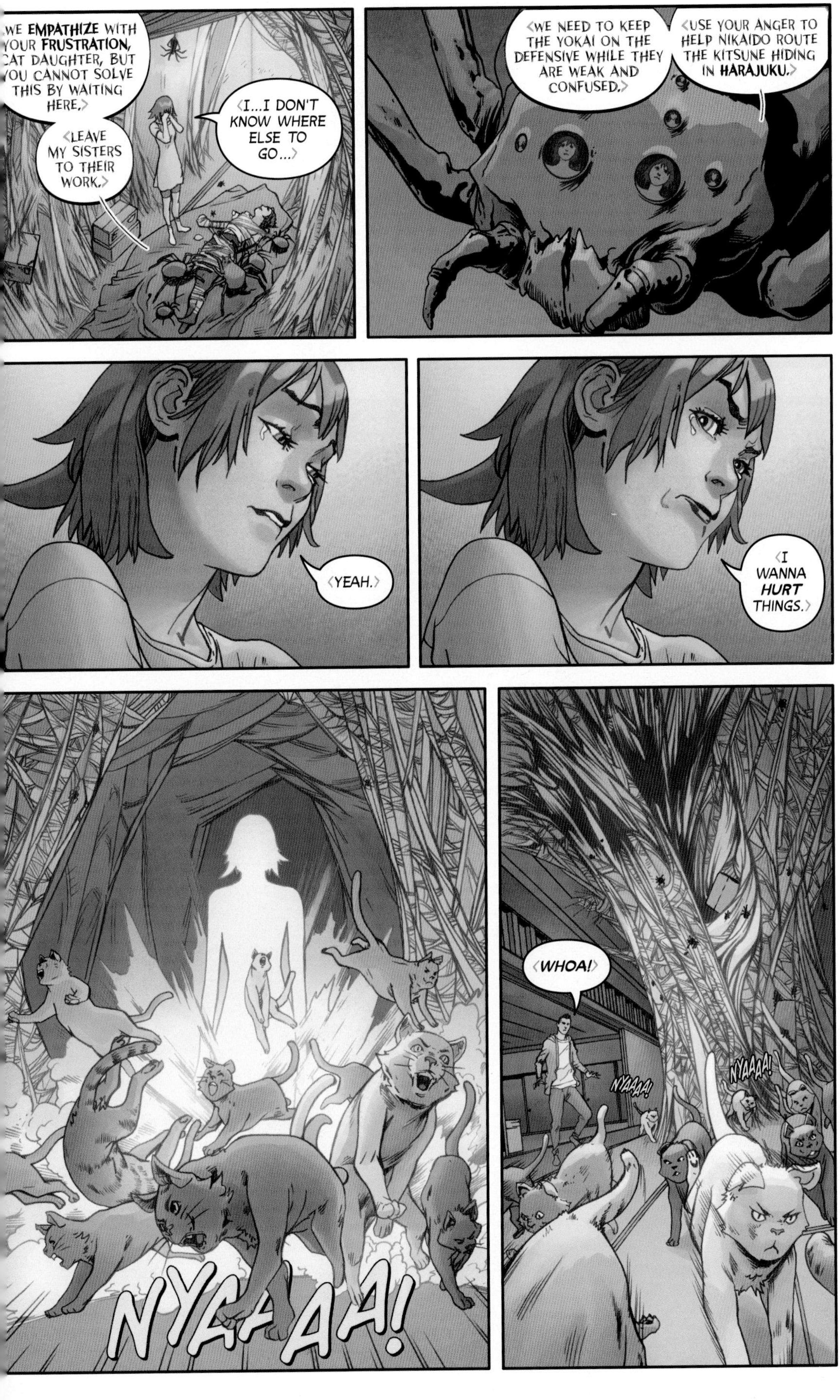

‹WE **EMPATHIZE** WITH YOUR **FRUSTRATION**, CAT DAUGHTER, BUT YOU CANNOT SOLVE THIS BY WAITING HERE.›
‹LEAVE MY SISTERS TO THEIR WORK.›
‹I...I DON'T KNOW WHERE ELSE TO GO...›
‹WE NEED TO KEEP THE YOKAI ON THE DEFENSIVE WHILE THEY ARE WEAK AND CONFUSED.›
‹USE YOUR ANGER TO HELP NIKAIDO ROUTE THE KITSUNE HIDING IN **HARAJUKU**.›
‹YEAH.›
‹I WANNA ***HURT*** THINGS.›
NYAAAA!
‹***WHOA!***›
NYAAAA!
NYAAAA!

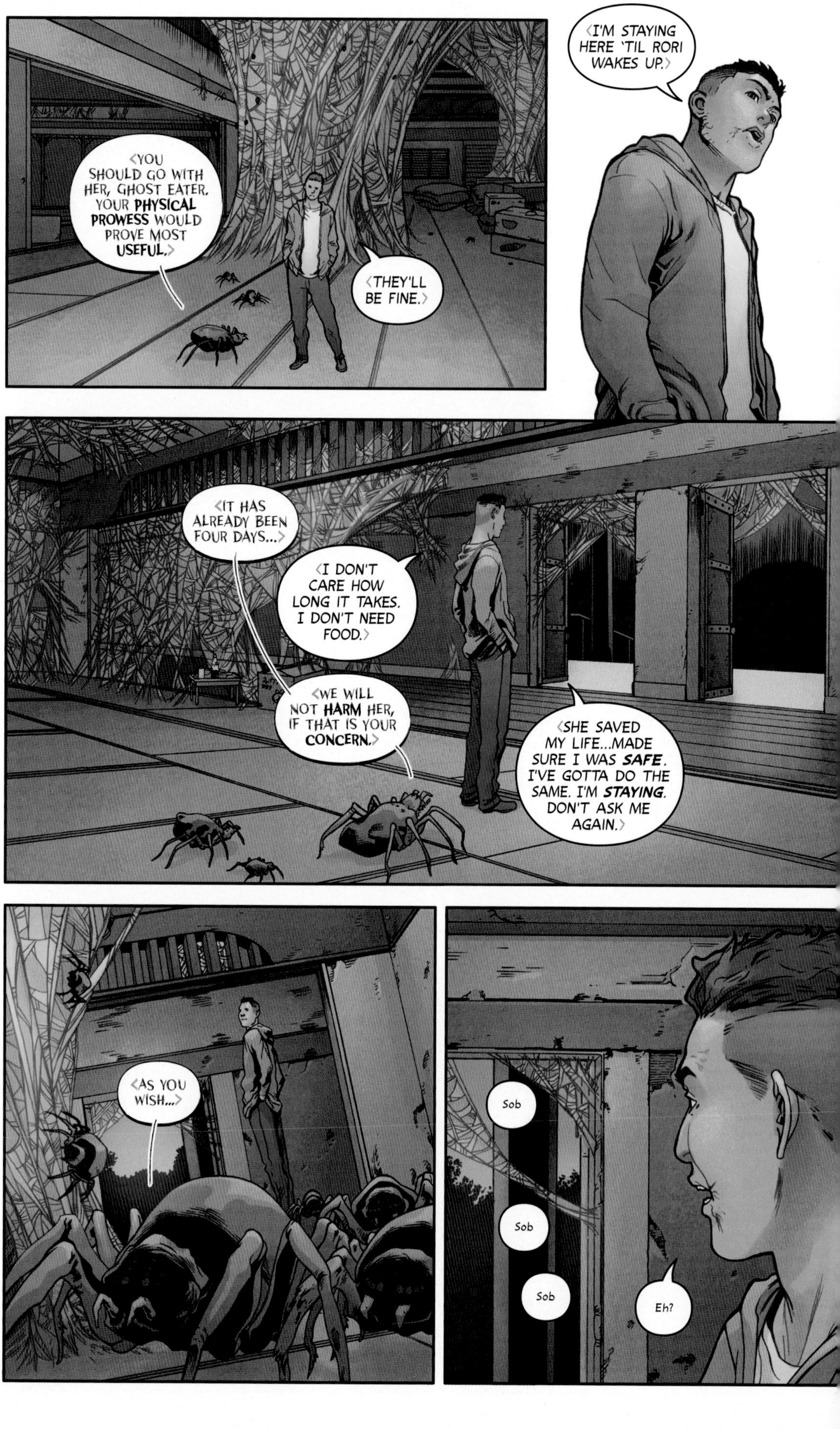

<YOU SHOULD GO WITH HER, GHOST EATER. YOUR **PHYSICAL PROWESS** WOULD PROVE MOST **USEFUL.**>
<THEY'LL BE FINE.>
<I'M STAYING HERE 'TIL RORI WAKES UP.>
<IT HAS ALREADY BEEN FOUR DAYS...>
<I DON'T CARE HOW LONG IT TAKES. I DON'T NEED FOOD.>
<WE WILL NOT **HARM** HER, IF THAT IS YOUR **CONCERN.**>
<SHE SAVED MY LIFE...MADE SURE I WAS ***SAFE***. I'VE GOTTA DO THE SAME. I'M ***STAYING***. DON'T ASK ME AGAIN.>
<AS YOU WISH...>
Sob
Sob
Sob
Eh?

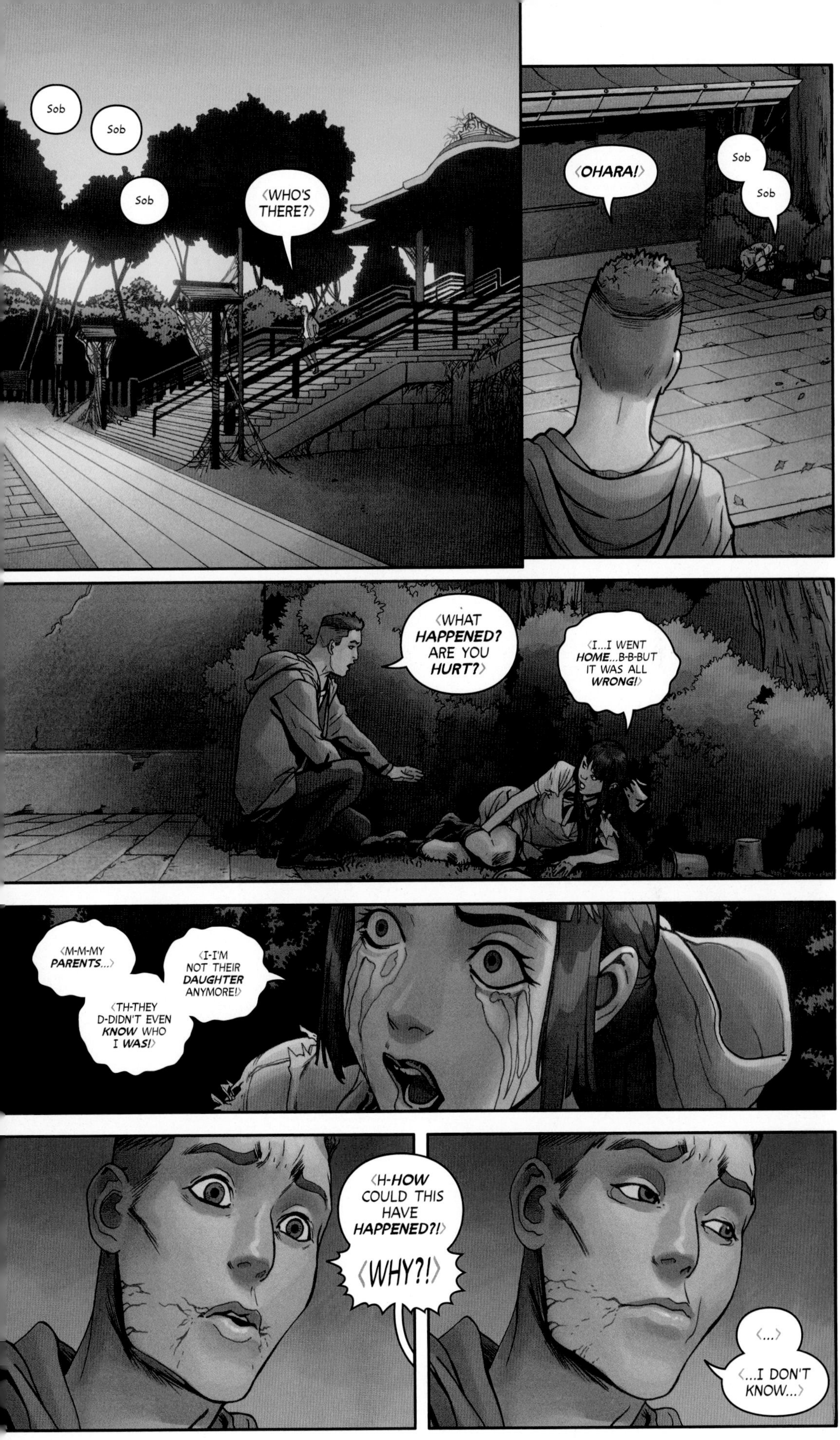
Sob
Sob
Sob
⟨WHO'S THERE?⟩
⟨OHARA!⟩
Sob
Sob
⟨WHAT HAPPENED? ARE YOU HURT?⟩
⟨I...I WENT HOME...B-B-BUT IT WAS ALL WRONG!⟩
⟨M-M-MY PARENTS...⟩
⟨TH-THEY D-DIDN'T EVEN KNOW WHO I WAS!⟩
⟨I-I'M NOT THEIR DAUGHTER ANYMORE!⟩
⟨H-HOW COULD THIS HAVE HAPPENED?!⟩
⟨WHY?!⟩
⟨...⟩
⟨...I DON'T KNOW...⟩

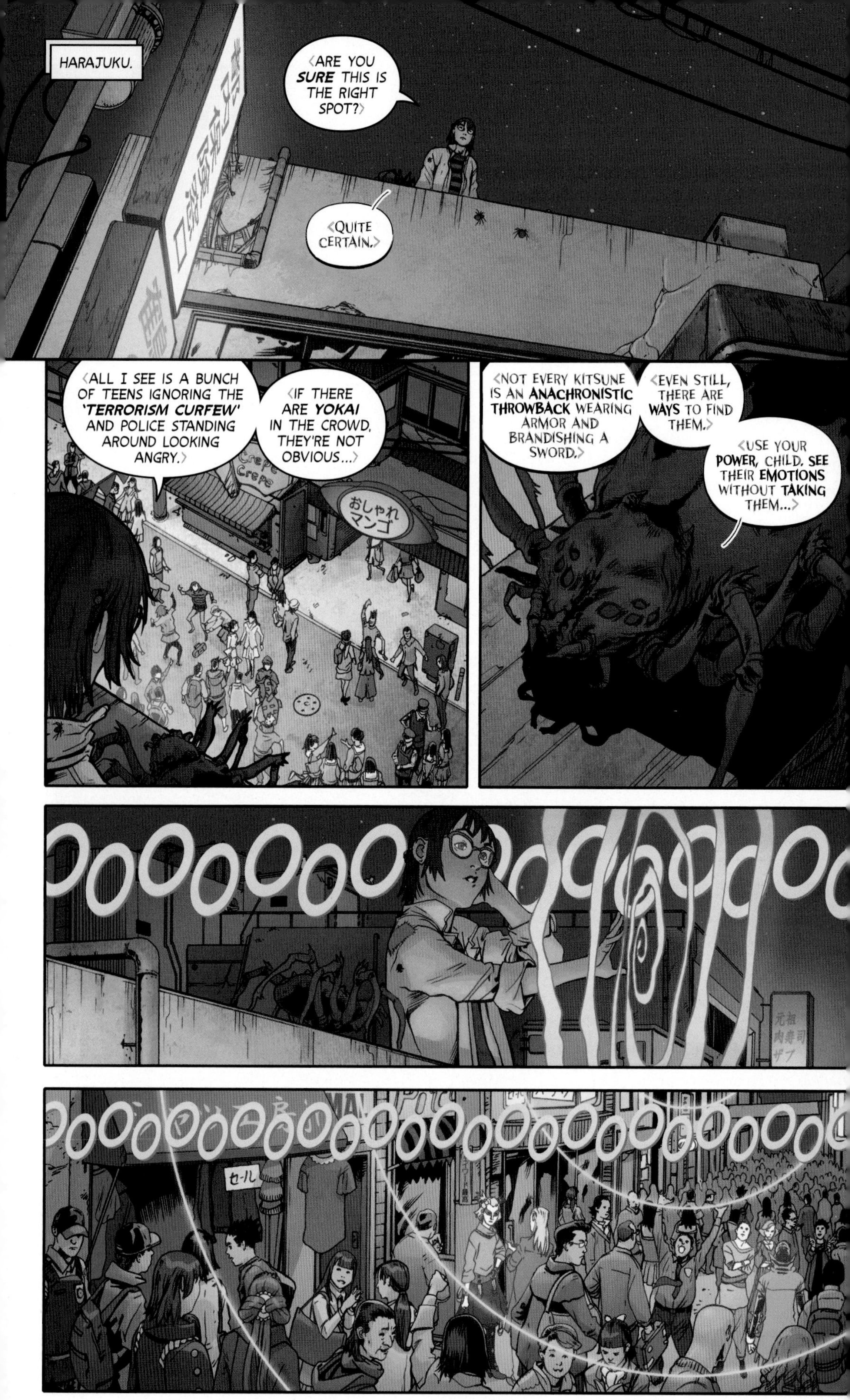

HARAJUKU.
<ARE YOU *SURE* THIS IS THE RIGHT SPOT?>
<QUITE CERTAIN.>
<ALL I SEE IS A BUNCH OF TEENS IGNORING THE ***'TERRORISM CURFEW'*** AND POLICE STANDING AROUND LOOKING ANGRY.>
<IF THERE ARE ***YOKAI*** IN THE CROWD, THEY'RE NOT OBVIOUS...>
Crepe Crepe
おしゃれ マンゴ
<NOT EVERY KITSUNE IS AN **ANACHRONISTIC THROWBACK** WEARING ARMOR AND BRANDISHING A SWORD.>
<EVEN STILL, THERE ARE **WAYS** TO FIND THEM.>
<USE YOUR **POWER**, CHILD. **SEE** THEIR **EMOTIONS** WITHOUT **TAKING** THEM...>
セール

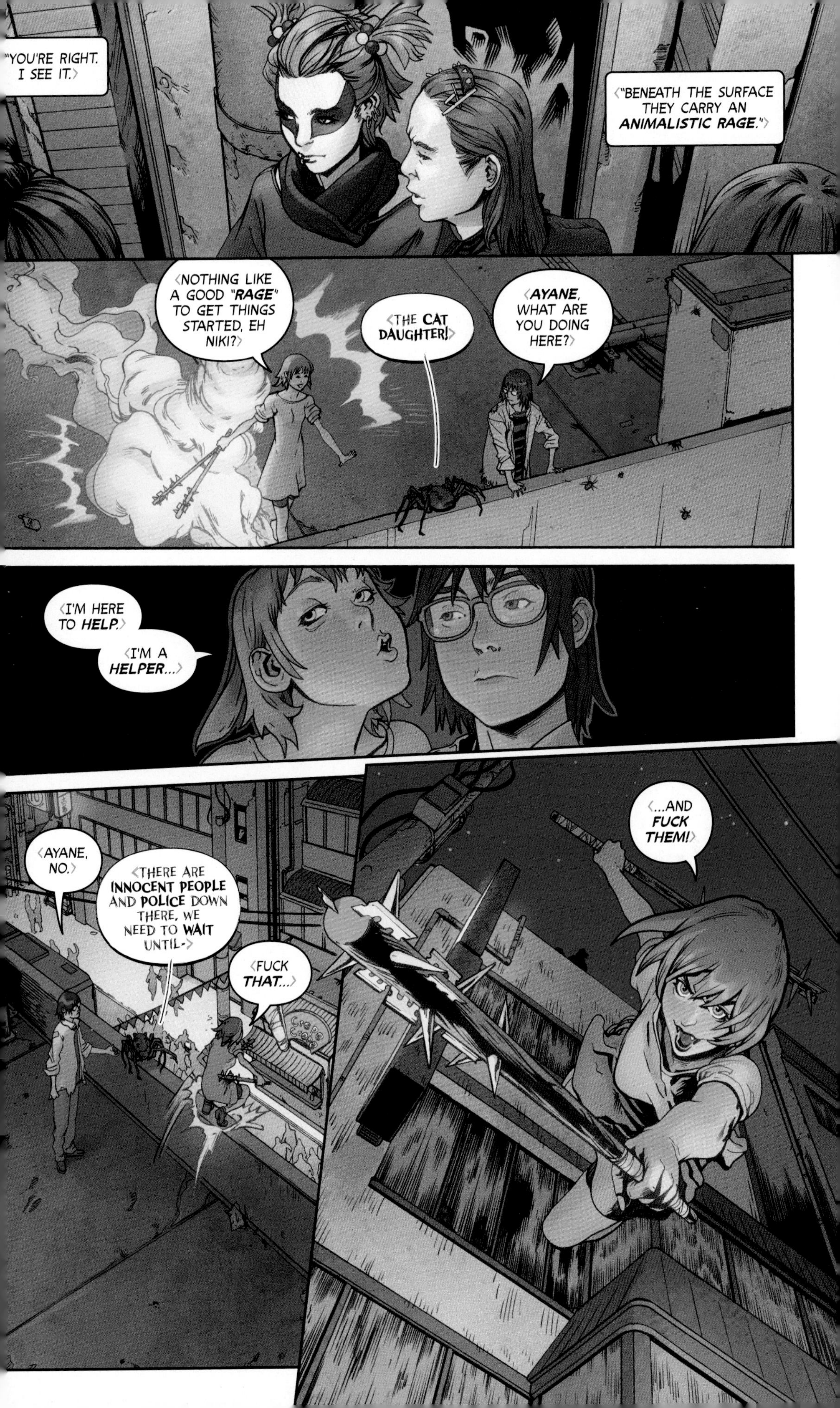
"YOU'RE RIGHT. I SEE IT.>
<"BENEATH THE SURFACE THEY CARRY AN ANIMALISTIC RAGE.">
<NOTHING LIKE A GOOD "RAGE" TO GET THINGS STARTED, EH NIKI?>
<THE CAT DAUGHTER!>
<AYANE, WHAT ARE YOU DOING HERE?>
<I'M HERE TO HELP.>
<I'M A HELPER...>
<AYANE, NO.>
<THERE ARE INNOCENT PEOPLE AND POLICE DOWN THERE, WE NEED TO WAIT UNTIL->
<FUCK THAT...>
<...AND FUCK THEM!>
Crepe Crepe

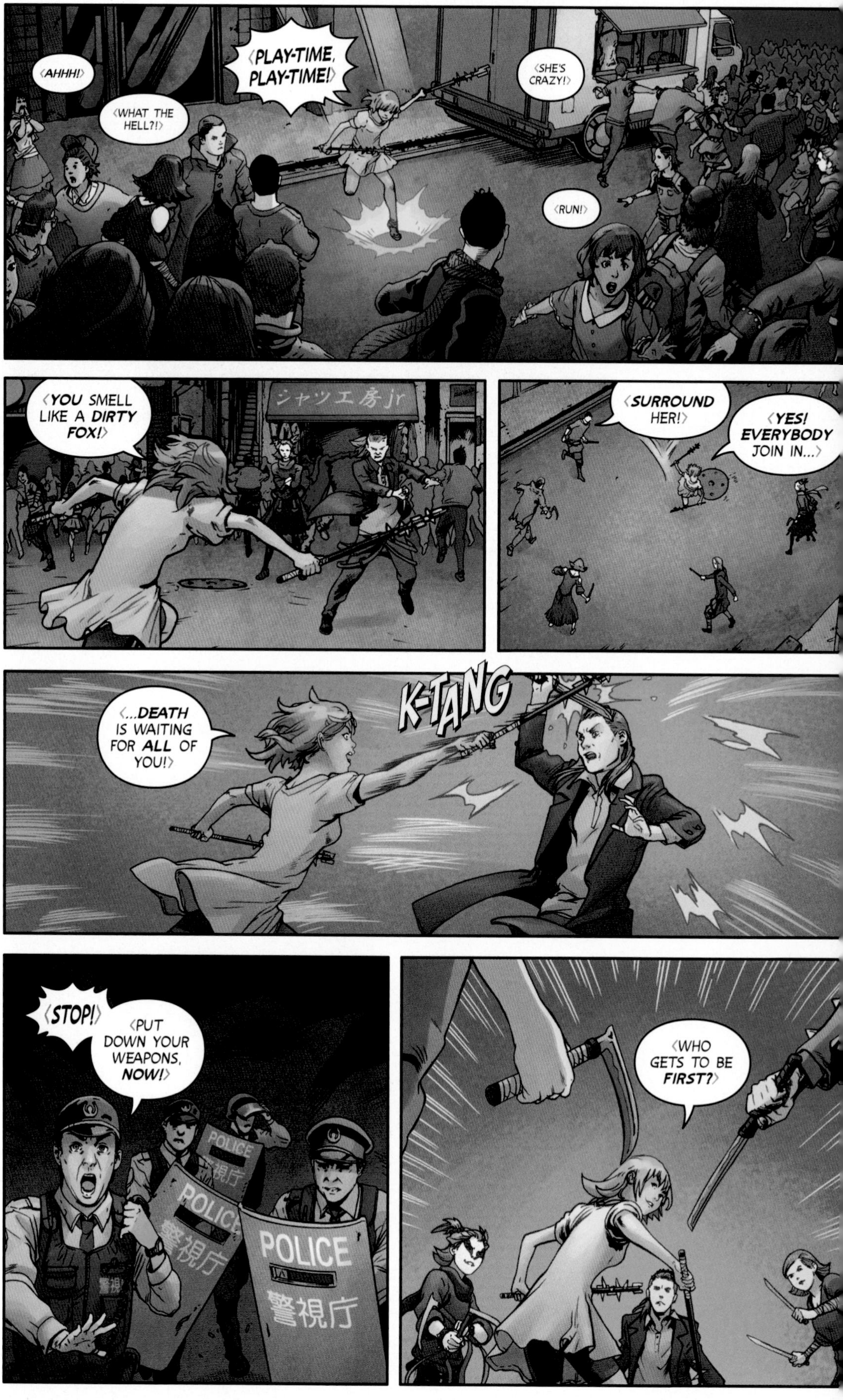

〈AHHH!〉
〈WHAT THE HELL?!〉
〈PLAY-TIME, PLAY-TIME!〉
〈SHE'S CRAZY!〉
〈RUN!〉
〈YOU SMELL LIKE A DIRTY FOX!〉
シャツ工房jr
〈SURROUND HER!〉
〈YES! EVERYBODY JOIN IN...〉
〈...DEATH IS WAITING FOR ALL OF YOU!〉
K-TANG
〈STOP!〉
〈PUT DOWN YOUR WEAPONS, NOW!〉
POLICE
警視庁
POLICE
警視庁
POLICE
警視庁
〈WHO GETS TO BE FIRST?〉

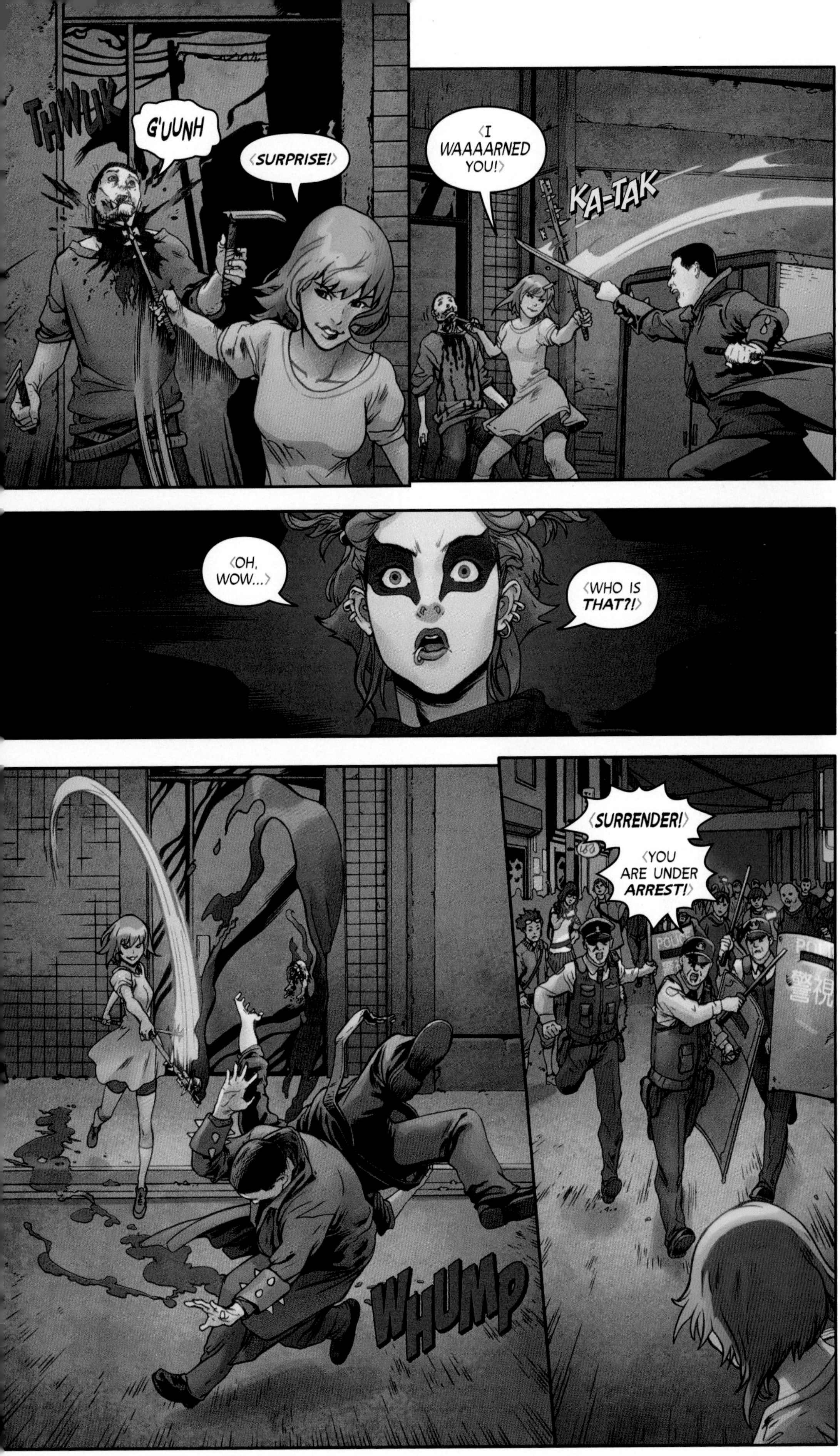
THWUK
G'UUNH
⟨SURPRISE!⟩
⟨I WAAAARNED YOU!⟩
KA-TAK
⟨OH, WOW...⟩
⟨WHO IS THAT?!⟩
WHUMP
⟨SURRENDER!⟩
⟨YOU ARE UNDER ARREST!⟩
POLICE

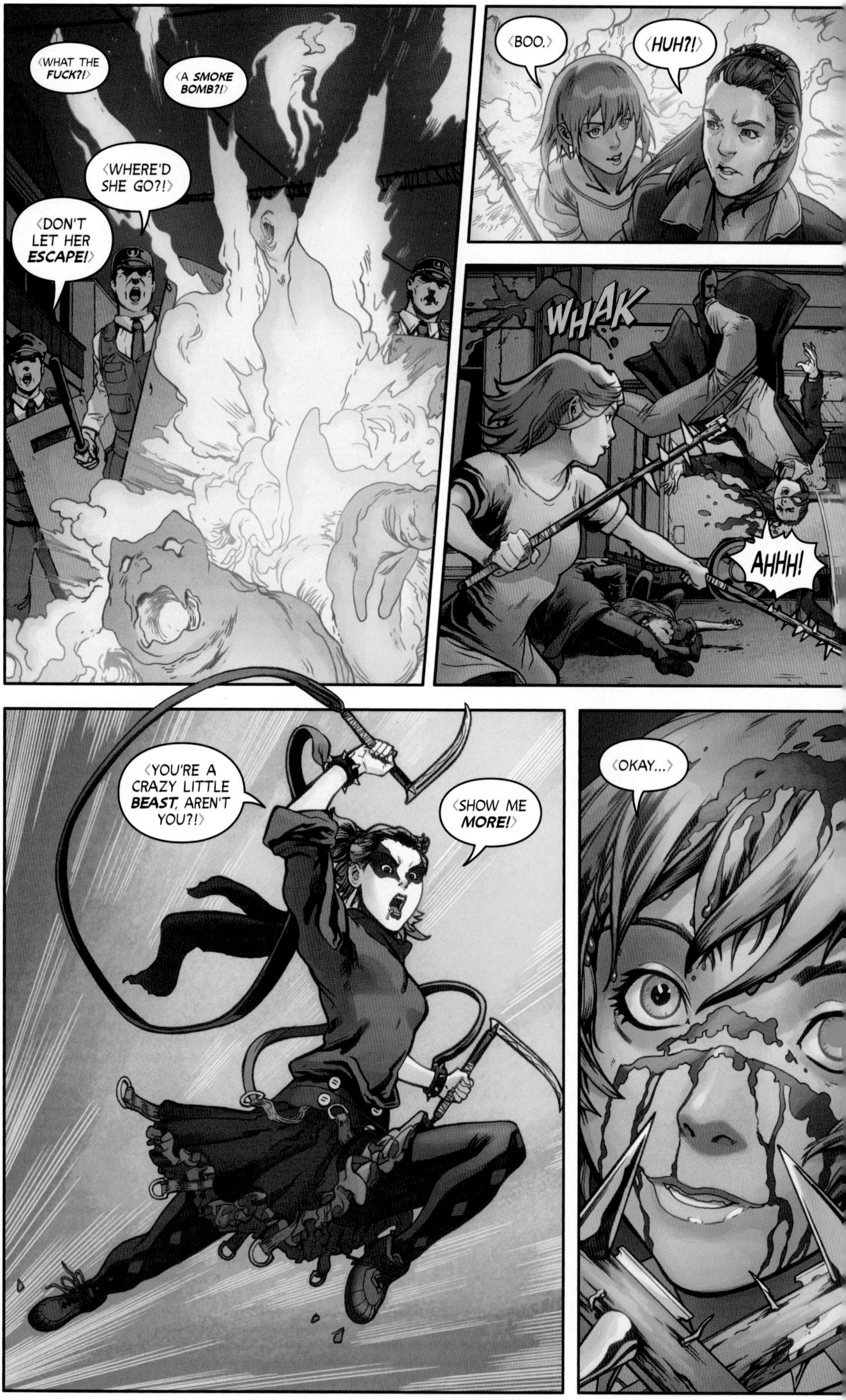
⟨WHAT THE *FUCK?!*⟩
⟨A *SMOKE BOMB?!*⟩
⟨WHERE'D SHE GO?!⟩
⟨DON'T LET HER *ESCAPE!*⟩
⟨BOO.⟩
⟨*HUH?!*⟩
WHAK
AHHH!
⟨YOU'RE A CRAZY LITTLE *BEAST*, AREN'T YOU?!⟩
⟨SHOW ME *MORE!*⟩
⟨OKAY...⟩

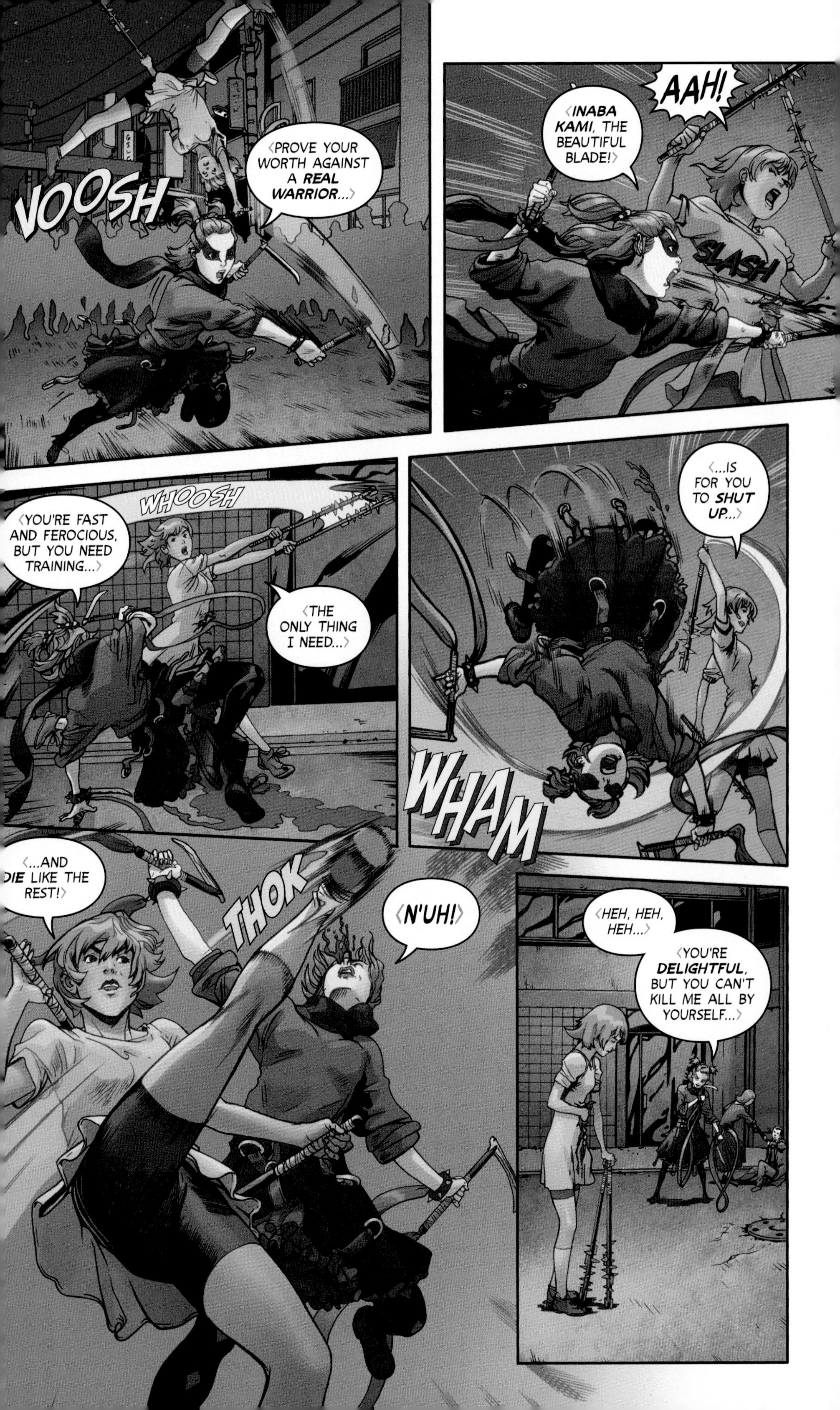
VOOSH
⟨PROVE YOUR WORTH AGAINST A **REAL WARRIOR**...⟩
⟨**INABA KAMI**, THE BEAUTIFUL BLADE!⟩
AAH!
SLASH
WHOOSH
⟨YOU'RE FAST AND FEROCIOUS, BUT YOU NEED TRAINING...⟩
⟨THE ONLY THING I NEED...⟩
⟨...IS FOR YOU TO **SHUT UP**...⟩
WHAM
⟨...AND **DIE** LIKE THE REST!⟩
THOK
⟨N'UH!⟩
⟨HEH, HEH, HEH...⟩
⟨YOU'RE **DELIGHTFUL**, BUT YOU CAN'T KILL ME ALL BY YOURSELF...⟩

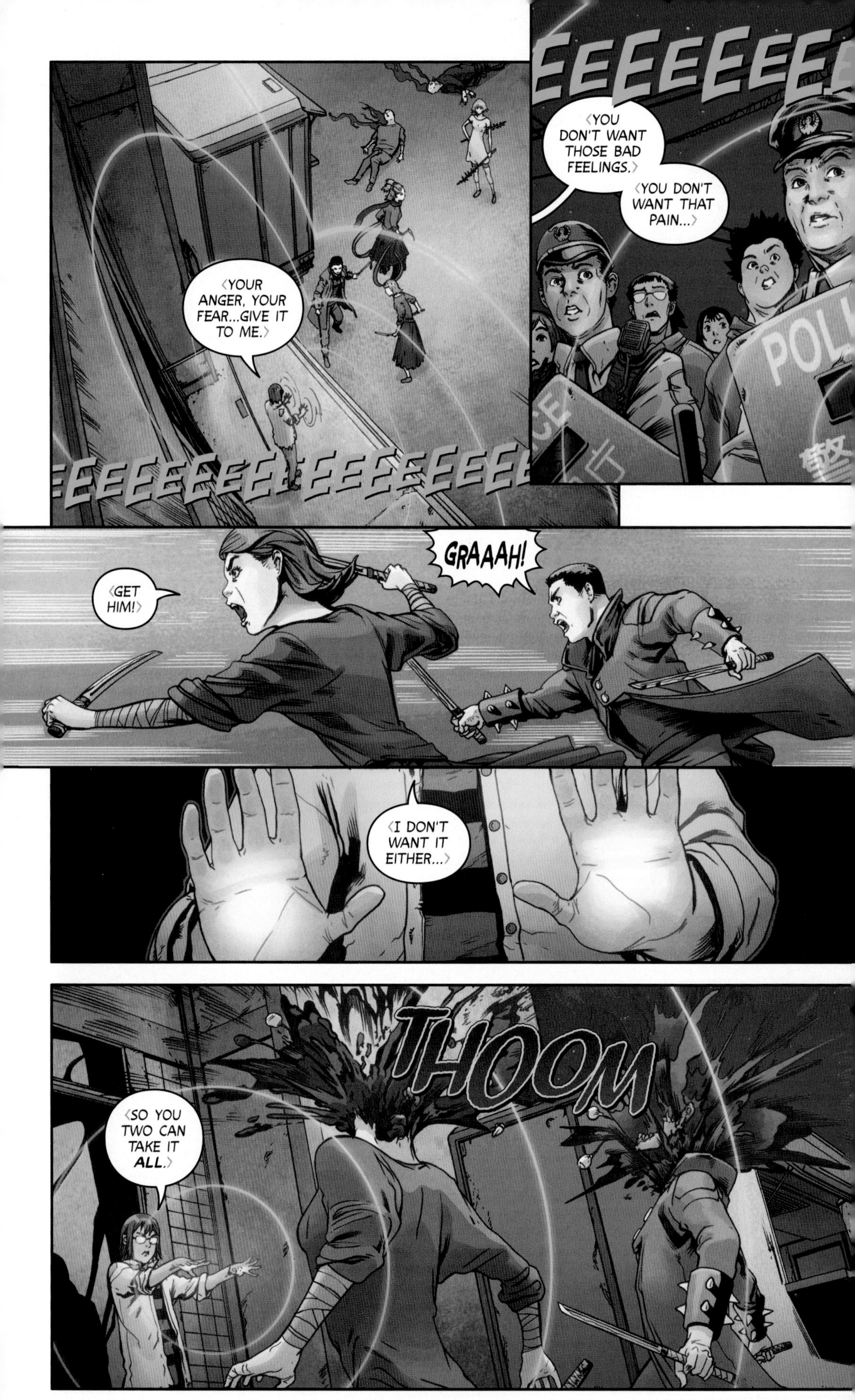

‹YOUR ANGER, YOUR FEAR...GIVE IT TO ME.›
EEEEEEEEEEEEEEEEEE
EEEEEEE
‹YOU DON'T WANT THOSE BAD FEELINGS.›
‹YOU DON'T WANT THAT PAIN...›
POLI
CE
‹GET HIM!›
GRAAAH!
‹I DON'T WANT IT EITHER...›
THOOM
‹SO YOU TWO CAN TAKE IT ALL.›

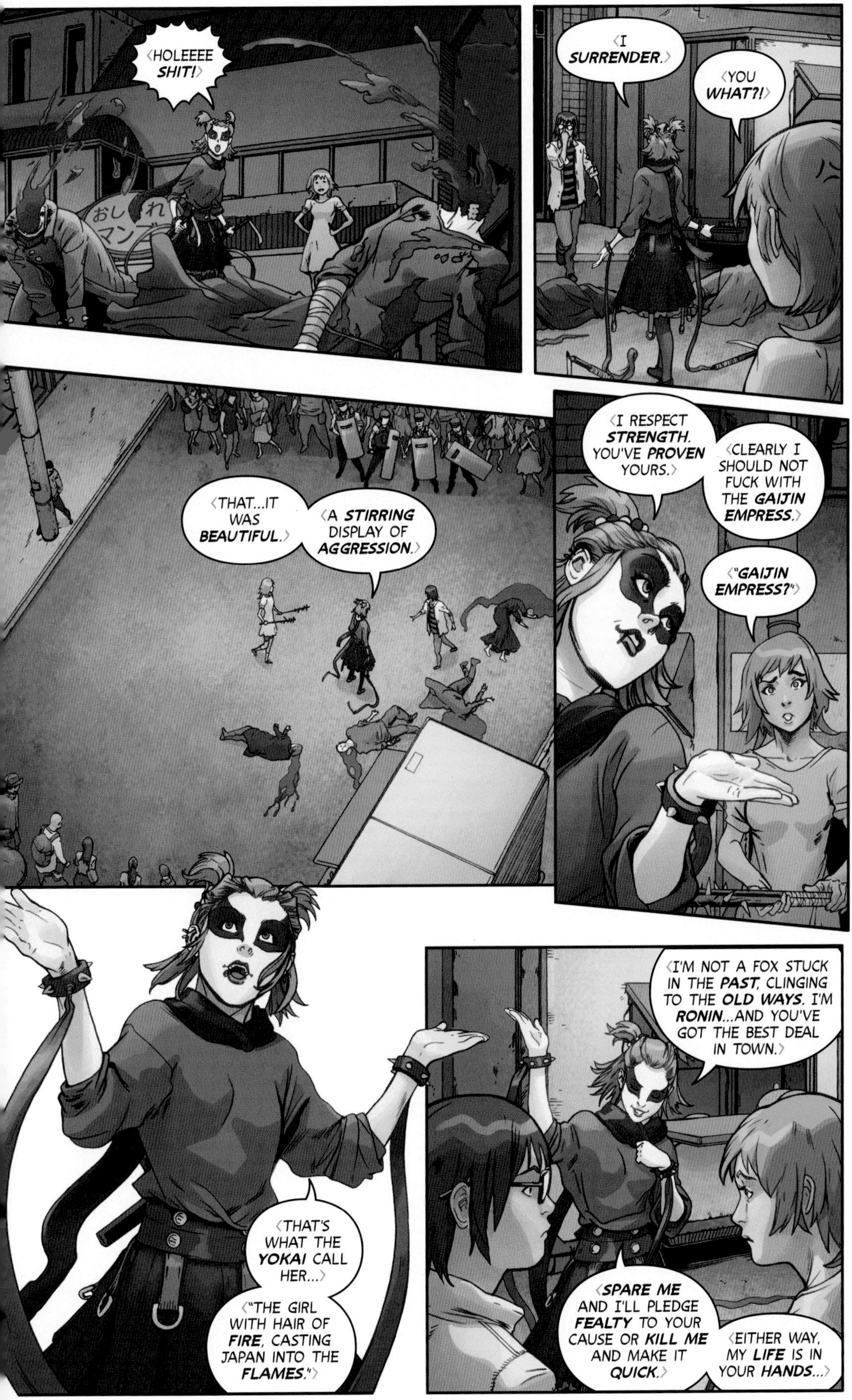

‹HOLEEEE SHIT!›
‹I SURRENDER.›
‹YOU WHAT?!›
‹THAT...IT WAS BEAUTIFUL.›
‹A STIRRING DISPLAY OF AGGRESSION.›
‹I RESPECT STRENGTH. YOU'VE PROVEN YOURS.›
‹CLEARLY I SHOULD NOT FUCK WITH THE GAIJIN EMPRESS.›
‹"GAIJIN EMPRESS?"›
‹THAT'S WHAT THE YOKAI CALL HER...›
‹"THE GIRL WITH HAIR OF FIRE, CASTING JAPAN INTO THE FLAMES."›
‹I'M NOT A FOX STUCK IN THE PAST, CLINGING TO THE OLD WAYS. I'M RONIN...AND YOU'VE GOT THE BEST DEAL IN TOWN.›
‹SPARE ME AND I'LL PLEDGE FEALTY TO YOUR CAUSE OR KILL ME AND MAKE IT QUICK.›
‹EITHER WAY, MY LIFE IS IN YOUR HANDS...›

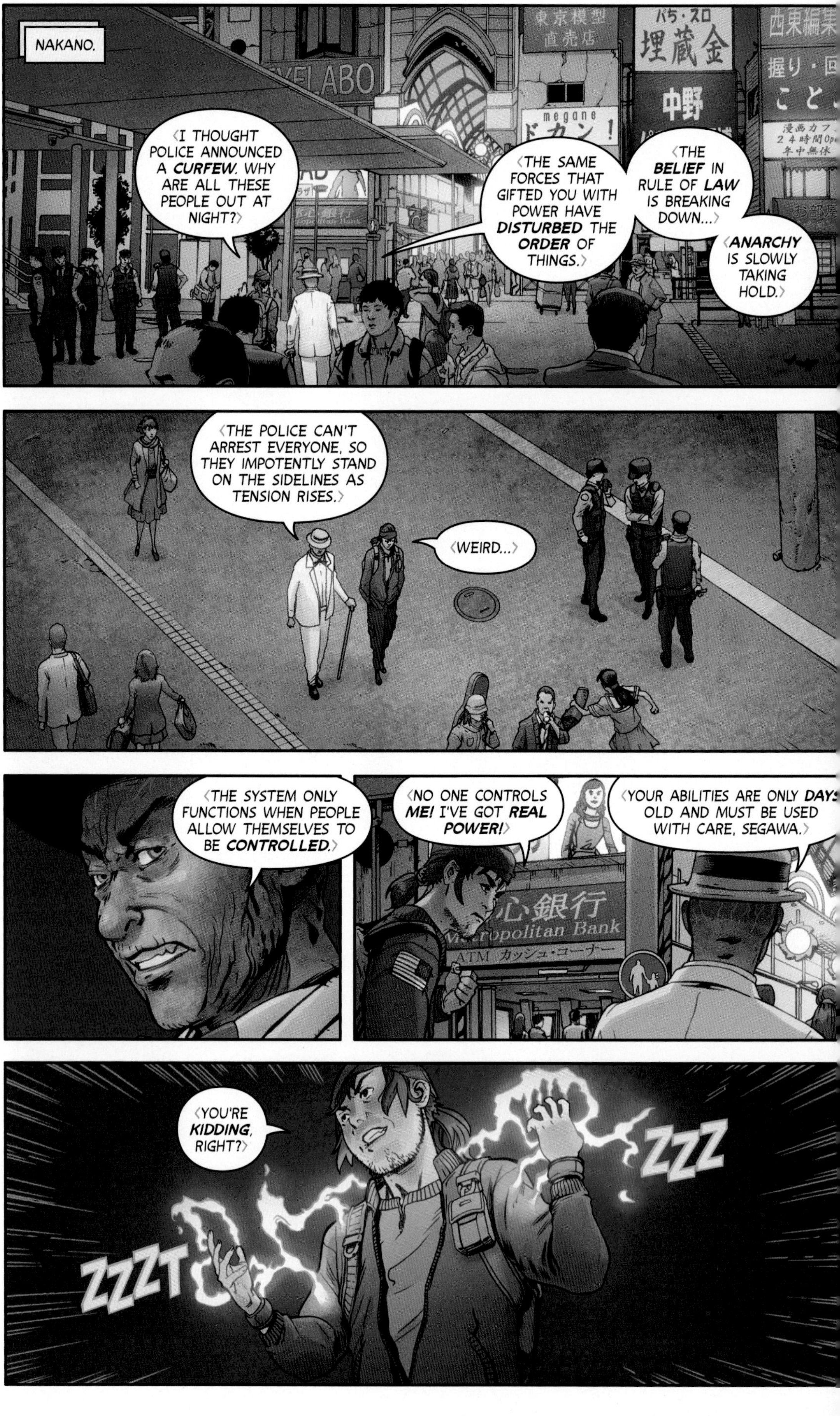
NAKANO.
〈I THOUGHT POLICE ANNOUNCED A CURFEW. WHY ARE ALL THESE PEOPLE OUT AT NIGHT?〉
〈THE SAME FORCES THAT GIFTED YOU WITH POWER HAVE DISTURBED THE ORDER OF THINGS.〉
〈THE BELIEF IN RULE OF LAW IS BREAKING DOWN...〉
〈ANARCHY IS SLOWLY TAKING HOLD.〉
〈THE POLICE CAN'T ARREST EVERYONE, SO THEY IMPOTENTLY STAND ON THE SIDELINES AS TENSION RISES.〉
〈WEIRD...〉
〈THE SYSTEM ONLY FUNCTIONS WHEN PEOPLE ALLOW THEMSELVES TO BE CONTROLLED.〉
〈NO ONE CONTROLS ME! I'VE GOT REAL POWER!〉
〈YOUR ABILITIES ARE ONLY DAYS OLD AND MUST BE USED WITH CARE, SEGAWA.〉
〈YOU'RE KIDDING, RIGHT?〉
ZZZ
ZZZT

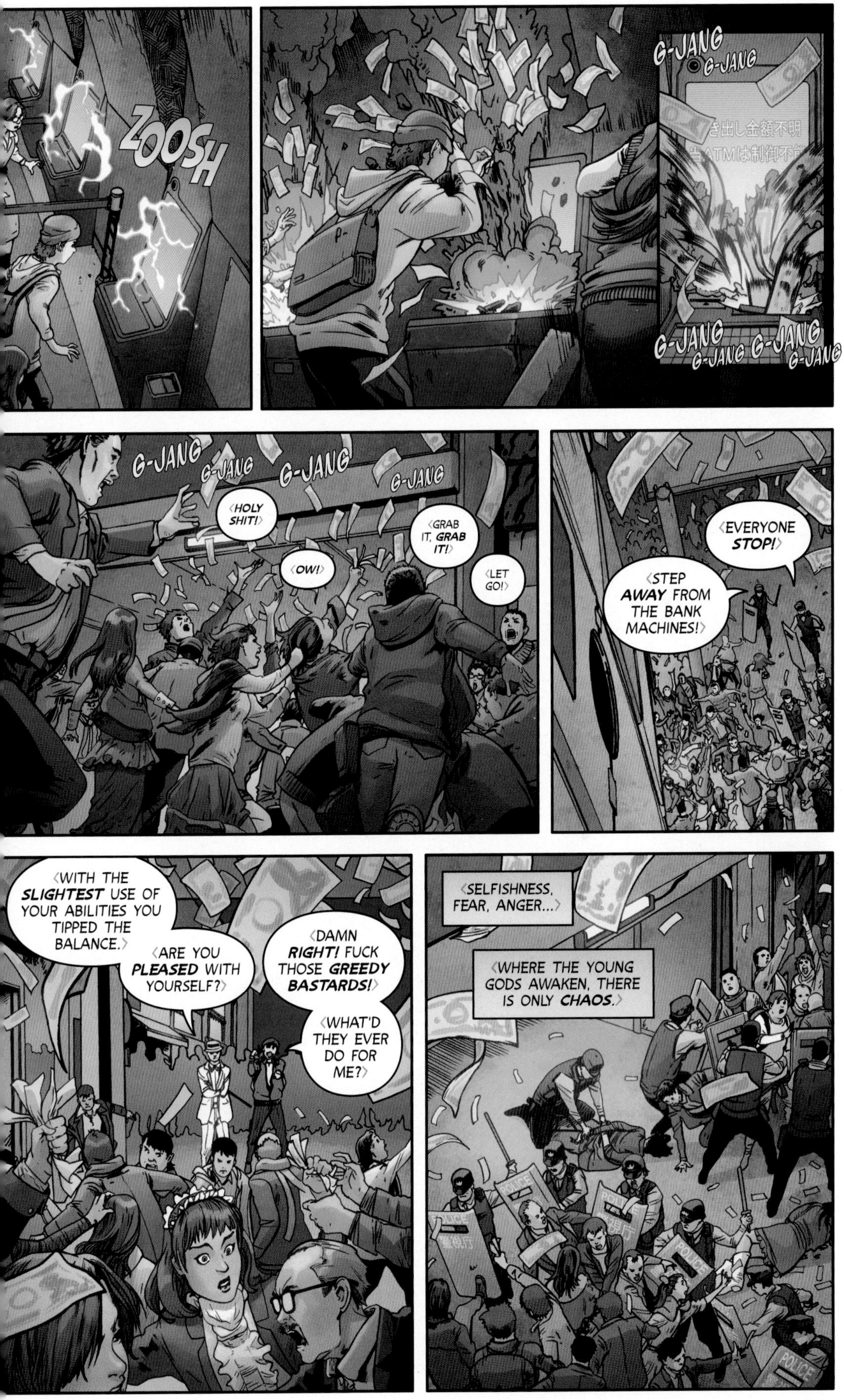
ZOOSH
G-JANG
G-JANG
き出し金額不明
当ATMは制御不
G-JANG
G-JANG
G-JANG
G-JANG
G-JANG
G-JANG
G-JANG
G-JANG
〈HOLY SHIT!〉
〈OW!〉
〈GRAB IT, GRAB IT!〉
〈LET GO!〉
〈EVERYONE STOP!〉
〈STEP AWAY FROM THE BANK MACHINES!〉
〈WITH THE SLIGHTEST USE OF YOUR ABILITIES YOU TIPPED THE BALANCE.〉
〈ARE YOU PLEASED WITH YOURSELF?〉
〈DAMN RIGHT! FUCK THOSE GREEDY BASTARDS!〉
〈WHAT'D THEY EVER DO FOR ME?〉
〈SELFISHNESS, FEAR, ANGER...〉
〈WHERE THE YOUNG GODS AWAKEN, THERE IS ONLY CHAOS.〉
POLICE
POLICE
POLICE
POLICE

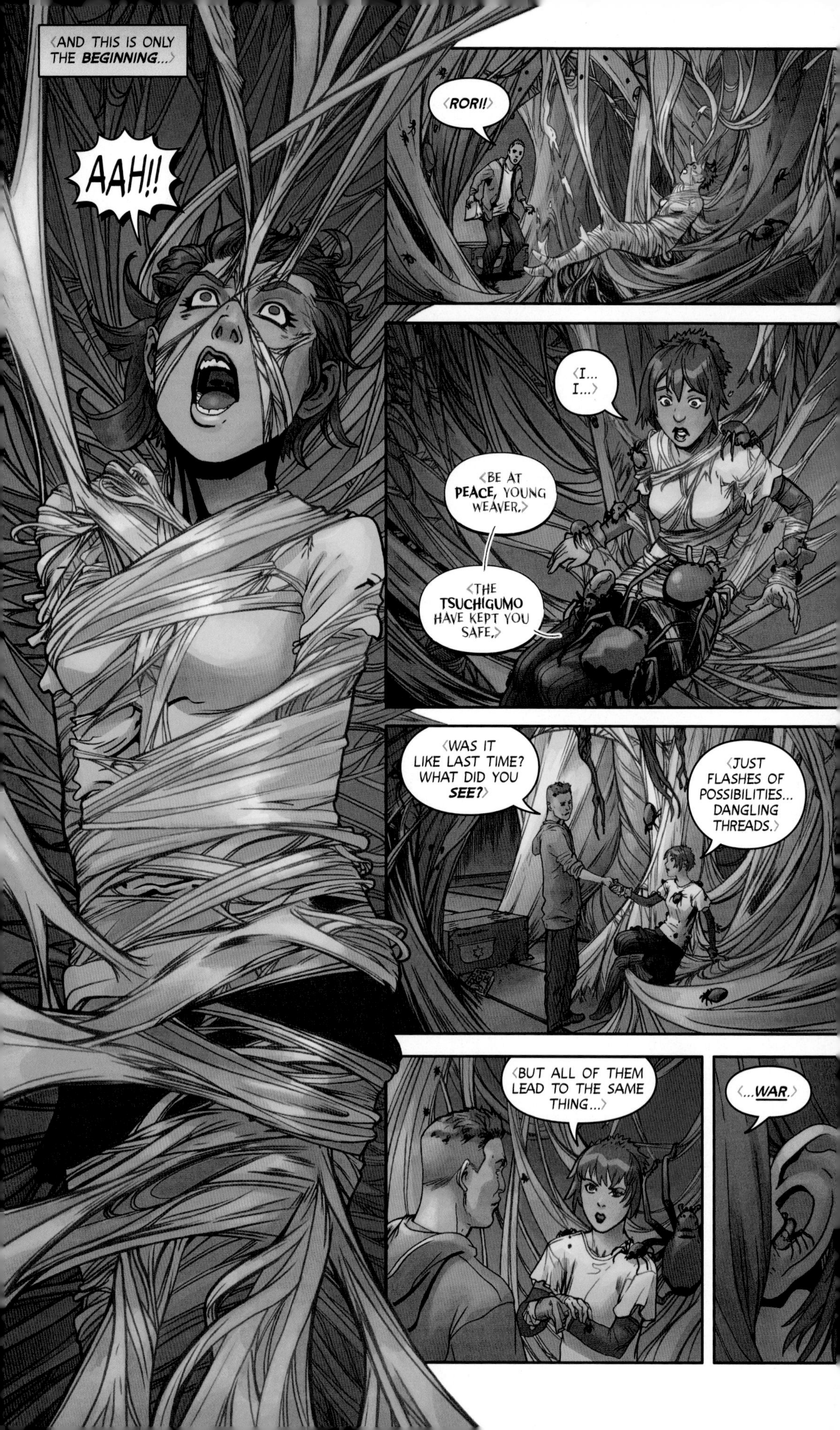

‹AND THIS IS ONLY THE BEGINNING...›
AAH!!
‹RORI!›
‹I... I...›
‹BE AT PEACE, YOUNG WEAVER.›
‹THE TSUCHIGUMO HAVE KEPT YOU SAFE.›
‹WAS IT LIKE LAST TIME? WHAT DID YOU SEE?›
‹JUST FLASHES OF POSSIBILITIES... DANGLING THREADS.›
‹BUT ALL OF THEM LEAD TO THE SAME THING...›
‹...WAR.›

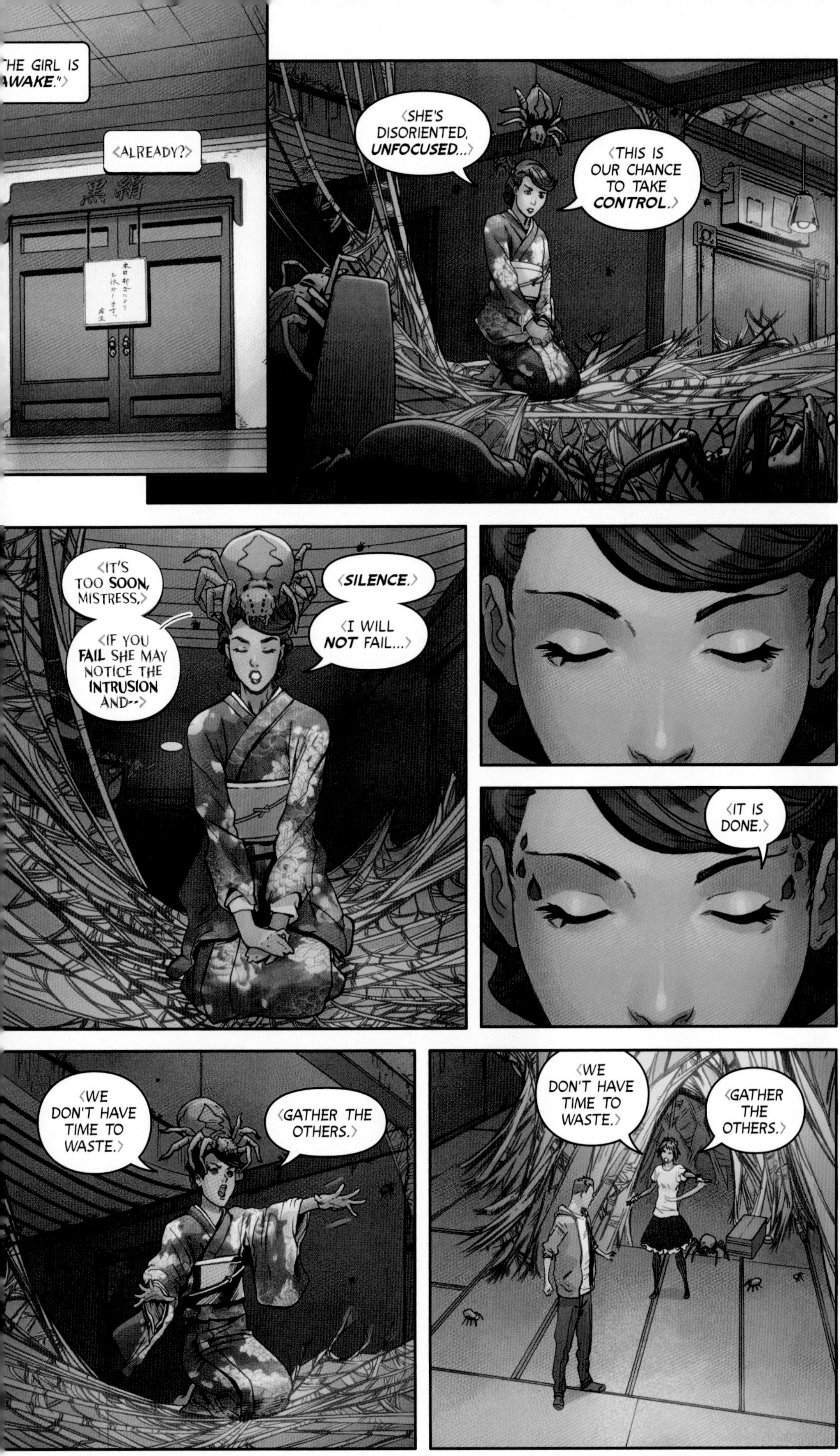

"THE GIRL IS AWAKE."›
‹ALREADY?›
‹SHE'S DISORIENTED, UNFOCUSED...›
‹THIS IS OUR CHANCE TO TAKE CONTROL.›
‹IT'S TOO SOON, MISTRESS.›
‹IF YOU FAIL SHE MAY NOTICE THE INTRUSION AND--›
‹SILENCE.›
‹I WILL NOT FAIL...›
‹IT IS DONE.›
‹WE DON'T HAVE TIME TO WASTE.›
‹GATHER THE OTHERS.›
‹WE DON'T HAVE TIME TO WASTE.›
‹GATHER THE OTHERS.›

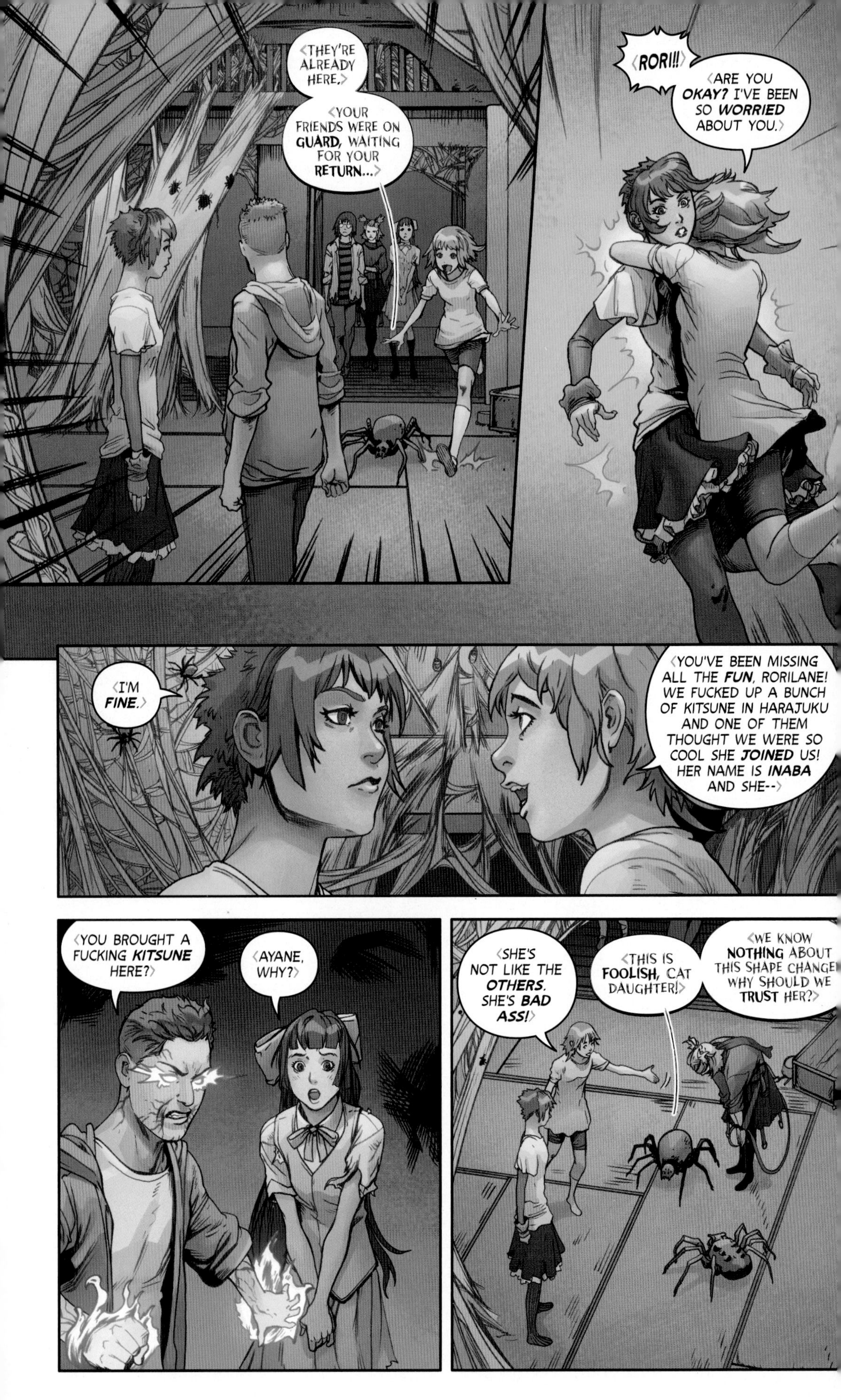

<THEY'RE ALREADY HERE.>
<YOUR FRIENDS WERE ON GUARD, WAITING FOR YOUR RETURN...>
<RORI!!>
<ARE YOU OKAY? I'VE BEEN SO WORRIED ABOUT YOU.>
<I'M FINE.>
<YOU'VE BEEN MISSING ALL THE FUN, RORILANE! WE FUCKED UP A BUNCH OF KITSUNE IN HARAJUKU AND ONE OF THEM THOUGHT WE WERE SO COOL SHE JOINED US! HER NAME IS INABA AND SHE-->
<YOU BROUGHT A FUCKING KITSUNE HERE?>
<AYANE, WHY?>
<SHE'S NOT LIKE THE OTHERS. SHE'S BAD ASS!>
<THIS IS FOOLISH, CAT DAUGHTER!>
<WE KNOW NOTHING ABOUT THIS SHAPE CHANGE WHY SHOULD WE TRUST HER?>

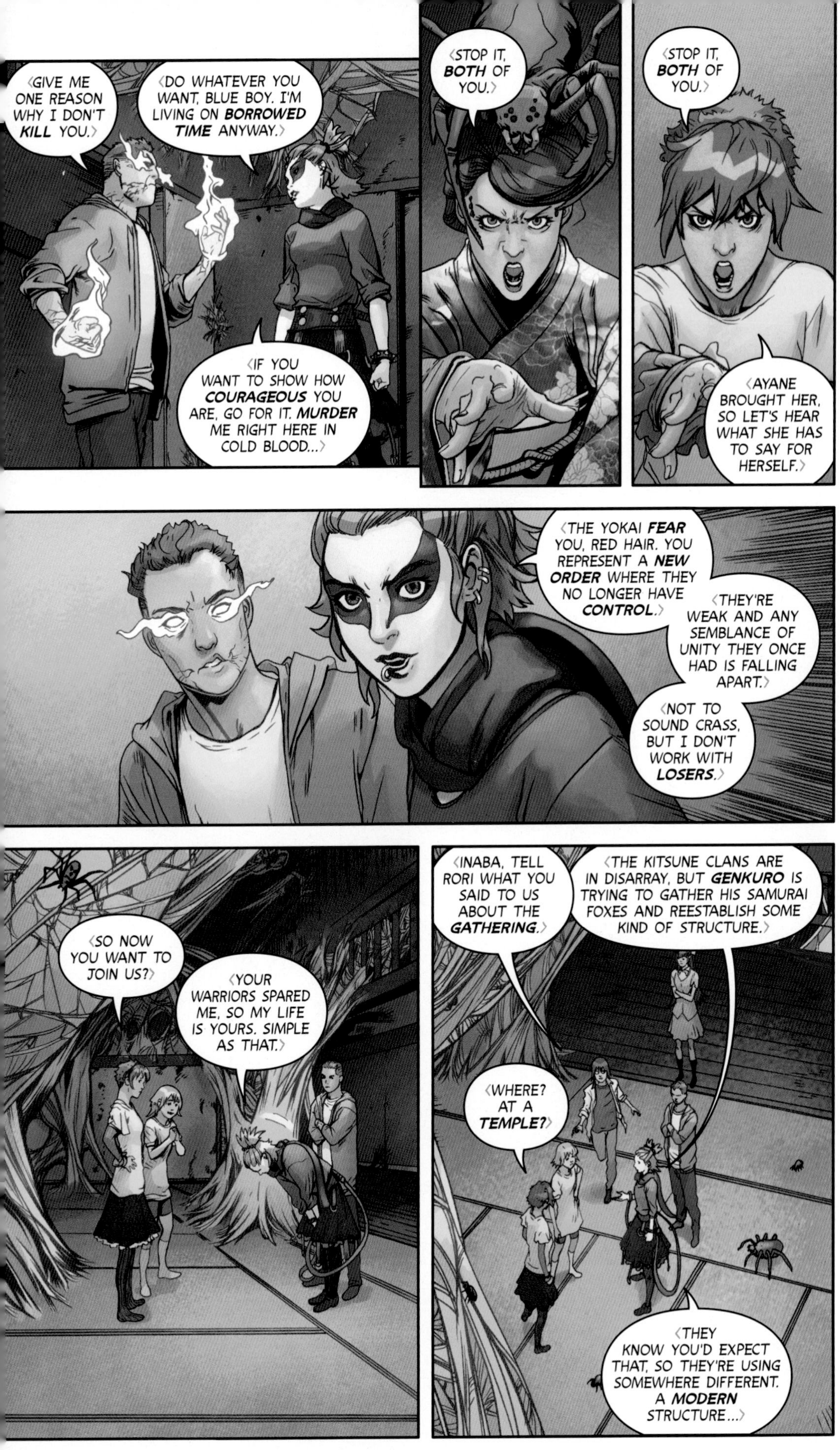

‹GIVE ME ONE REASON WHY I DON'T KILL YOU.›
‹DO WHATEVER YOU WANT, BLUE BOY. I'M LIVING ON BORROWED TIME ANYWAY.›
‹IF YOU WANT TO SHOW HOW COURAGEOUS YOU ARE, GO FOR IT. MURDER ME RIGHT HERE IN COLD BLOOD...›
‹STOP IT, BOTH OF YOU.›
‹STOP IT, BOTH OF YOU.›
‹AYANE BROUGHT HER, SO LET'S HEAR WHAT SHE HAS TO SAY FOR HERSELF.›
‹THE YOKAI FEAR YOU, RED HAIR. YOU REPRESENT A NEW ORDER WHERE THEY NO LONGER HAVE CONTROL.›
‹THEY'RE WEAK AND ANY SEMBLANCE OF UNITY THEY ONCE HAD IS FALLING APART.›
‹NOT TO SOUND CRASS, BUT I DON'T WORK WITH LOSERS.›
‹SO NOW YOU WANT TO JOIN US?›
‹YOUR WARRIORS SPARED ME, SO MY LIFE IS YOURS. SIMPLE AS THAT.›
‹INABA, TELL RORI WHAT YOU SAID TO US ABOUT THE GATHERING.›
‹THE KITSUNE CLANS ARE IN DISARRAY, BUT GENKURO IS TRYING TO GATHER HIS SAMURAI FOXES AND REESTABLISH SOME KIND OF STRUCTURE.›
‹WHERE? AT A TEMPLE?›
‹THEY KNOW YOU'D EXPECT THAT, SO THEY'RE USING SOMEWHERE DIFFERENT. A MODERN STRUCTURE...›

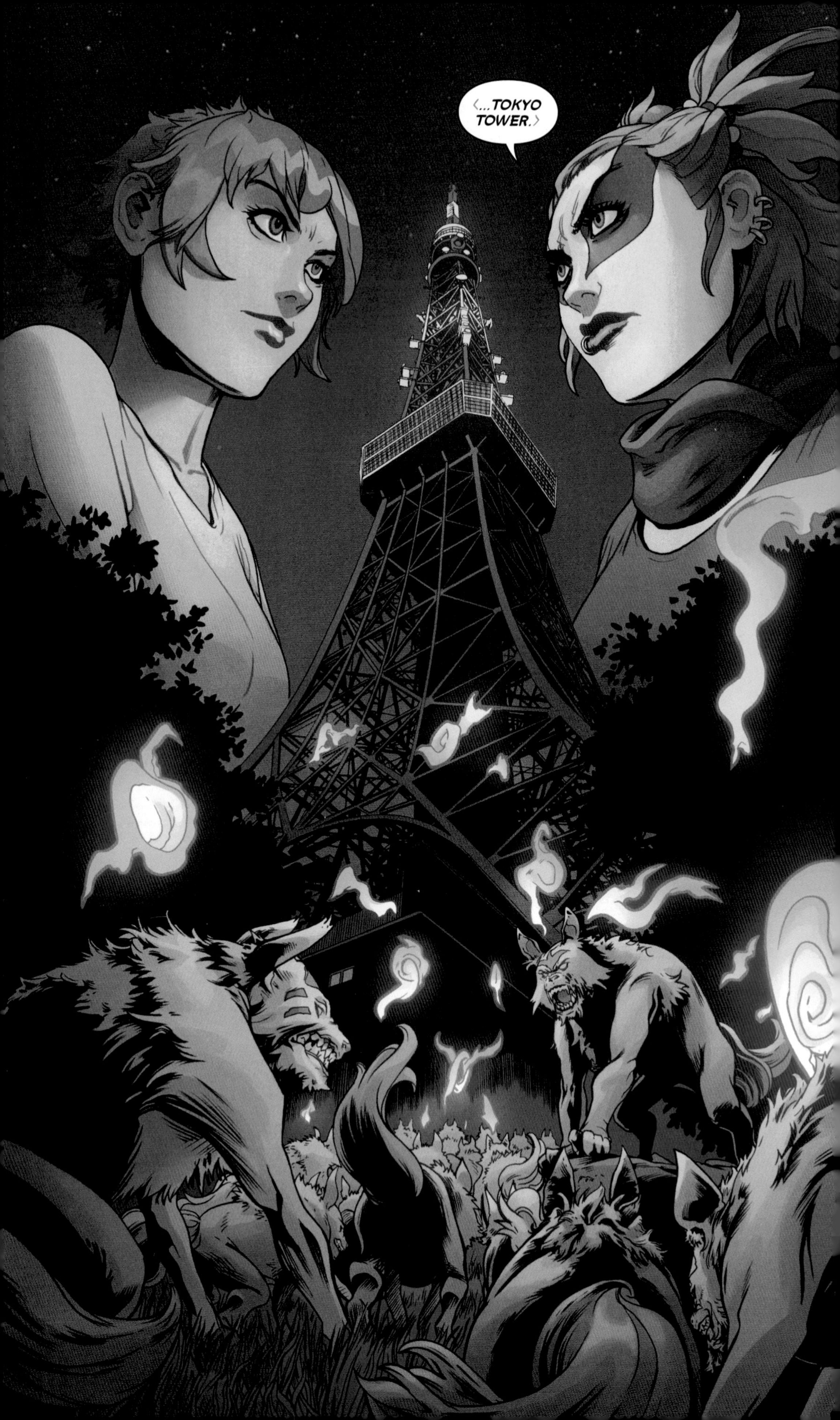
<...TOKYO TOWER.>

Chapter Thirteen

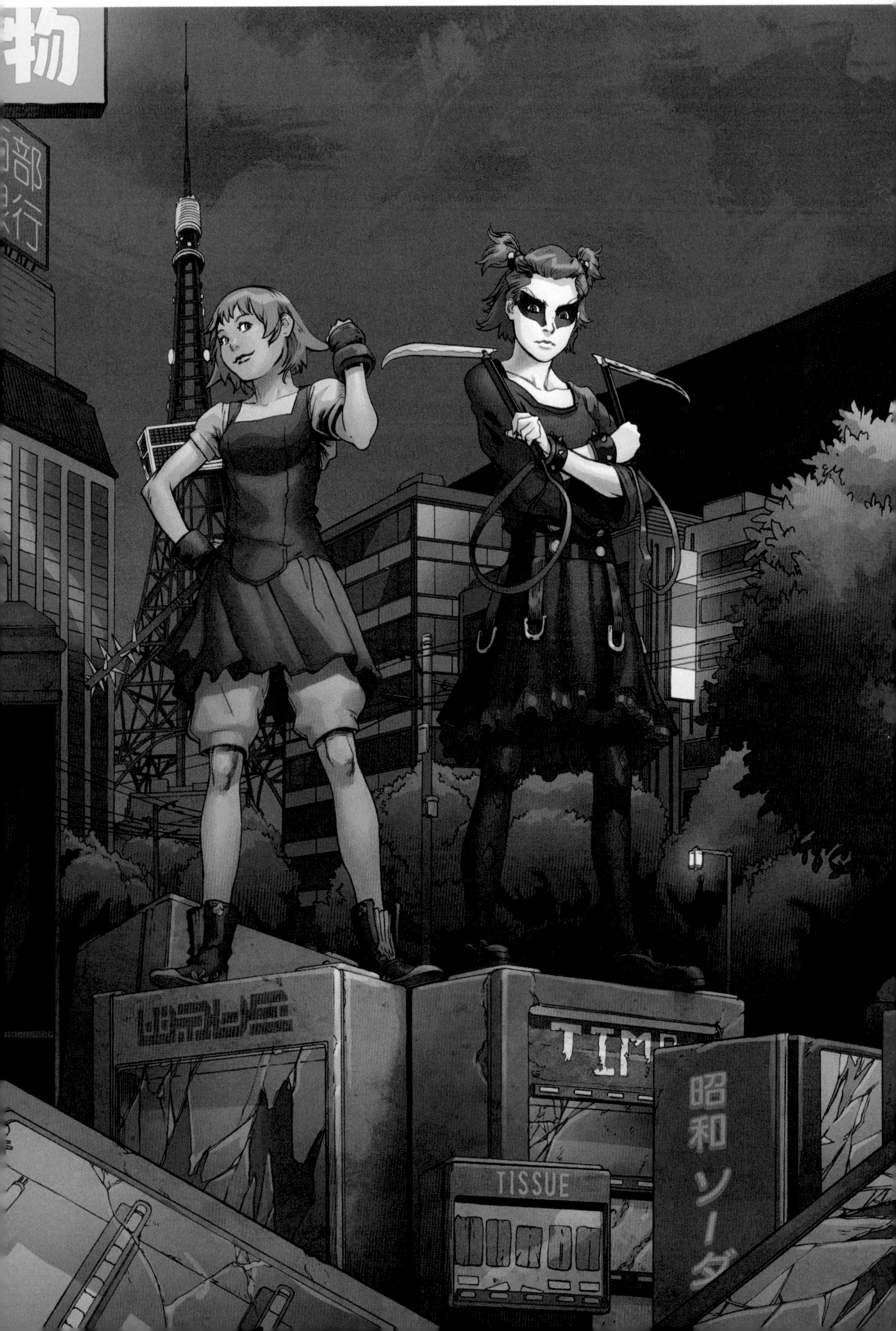
物
TISSUE
昭和ソーダ

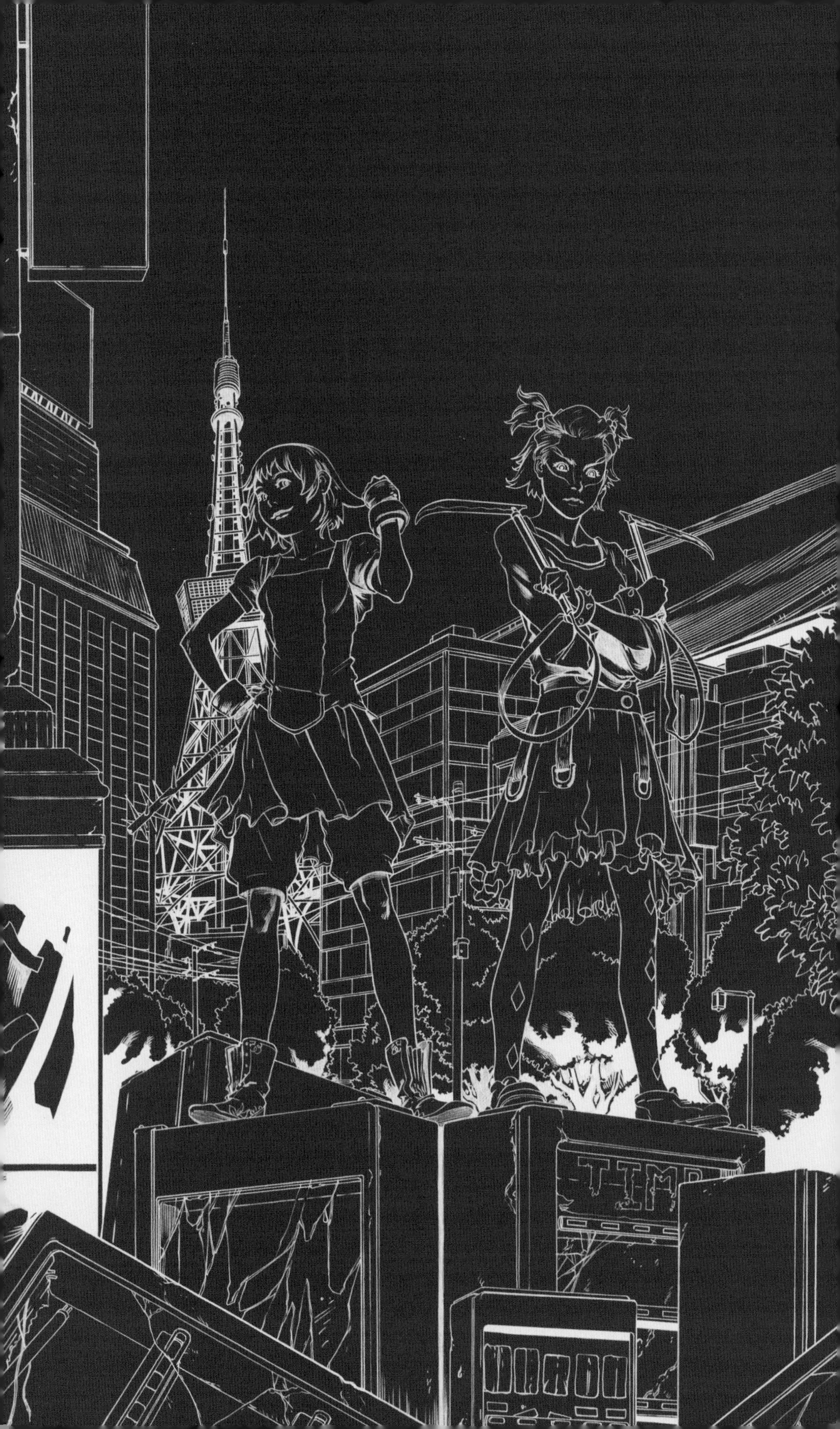

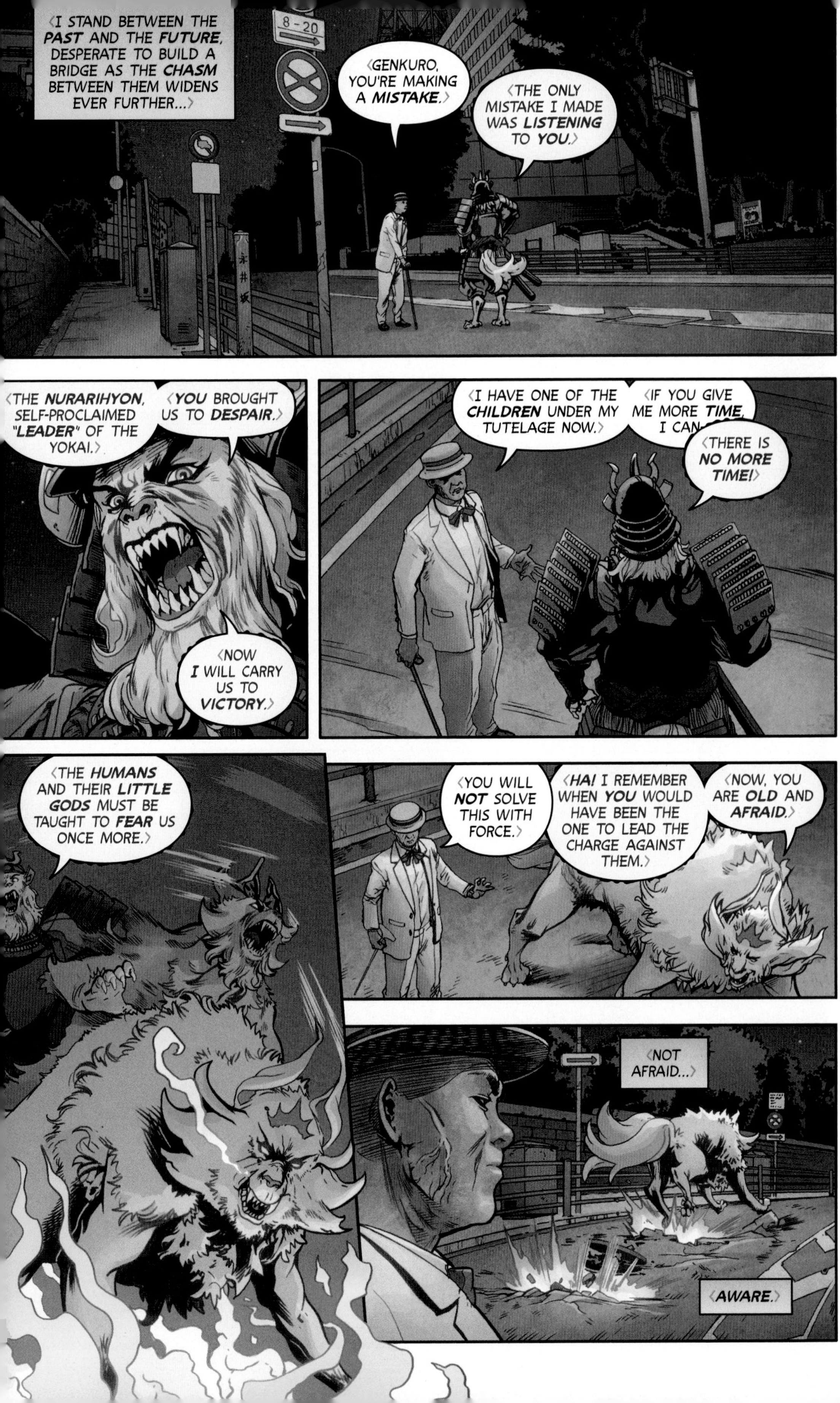
〈I STAND BETWEEN THE PAST AND THE FUTURE, DESPERATE TO BUILD A BRIDGE AS THE CHASM BETWEEN THEM WIDENS EVER FURTHER...〉
8-20
〈GENKURO, YOU'RE MAKING A MISTAKE.〉
〈THE ONLY MISTAKE I MADE WAS LISTENING TO YOU.〉
〈THE NURARIHYON, SELF-PROCLAIMED "LEADER" OF THE YOKAI.〉
〈YOU BROUGHT US TO DESPAIR.〉
〈NOW I WILL CARRY US TO VICTORY.〉
〈I HAVE ONE OF THE CHILDREN UNDER MY TUTELAGE NOW.〉
〈IF YOU GIVE ME MORE TIME, I CAN-
〈THERE IS NO MORE TIME!〉
〈THE HUMANS AND THEIR LITTLE GODS MUST BE TAUGHT TO FEAR US ONCE MORE.〉
〈YOU WILL NOT SOLVE THIS WITH FORCE.〉
〈HA! I REMEMBER WHEN YOU WOULD HAVE BEEN THE ONE TO LEAD THE CHARGE AGAINST THEM.〉
〈NOW, YOU ARE OLD AND AFRAID.〉
〈NOT AFRAID...〉
〈AWARE.〉

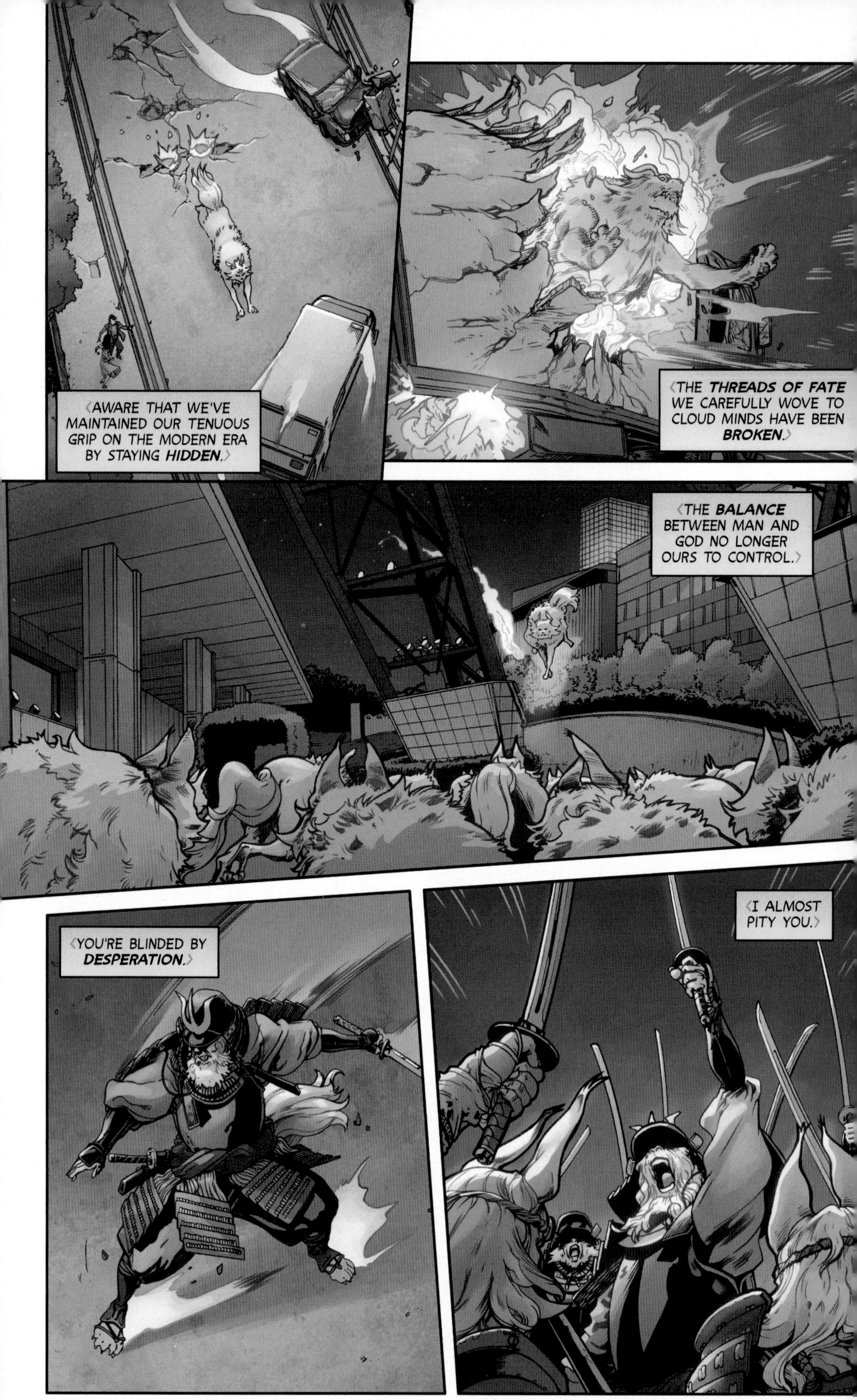

〈AWARE THAT WE'VE MAINTAINED OUR TENUOUS GRIP ON THE MODERN ERA BY STAYING *HIDDEN*.〉
〈THE *THREADS OF FATE* WE CAREFULLY WOVE TO CLOUD MINDS HAVE BEEN *BROKEN*.〉
〈THE *BALANCE* BETWEEN MAN AND GOD NO LONGER OURS TO CONTROL.〉
〈YOU'RE BLINDED BY *DESPERATION*.〉
〈I ALMOST PITY YOU.〉

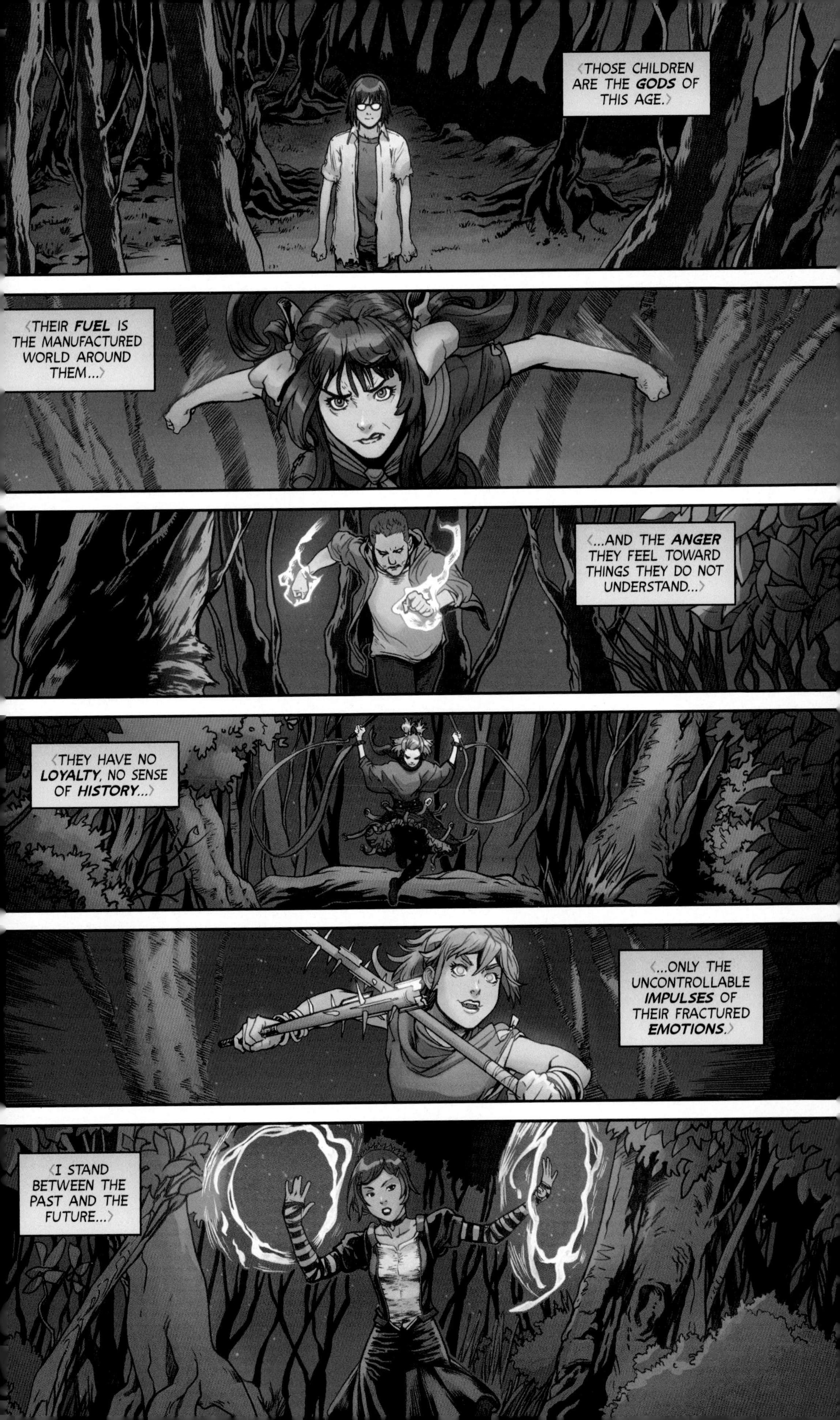
‹THOSE CHILDREN ARE THE ***GODS*** OF THIS AGE.›
‹THEIR ***FUEL*** IS THE MANUFACTURED WORLD AROUND THEM...›
‹...AND THE ***ANGER*** THEY FEEL TOWARD THINGS THEY DO NOT UNDERSTAND...›
‹THEY HAVE NO ***LOYALTY***, NO SENSE OF ***HISTORY***...›
‹...ONLY THE UNCONTROLLABLE ***IMPULSES*** OF THEIR FRACTURED ***EMOTIONS***.›
‹I STAND BETWEEN THE PAST AND THE FUTURE...›

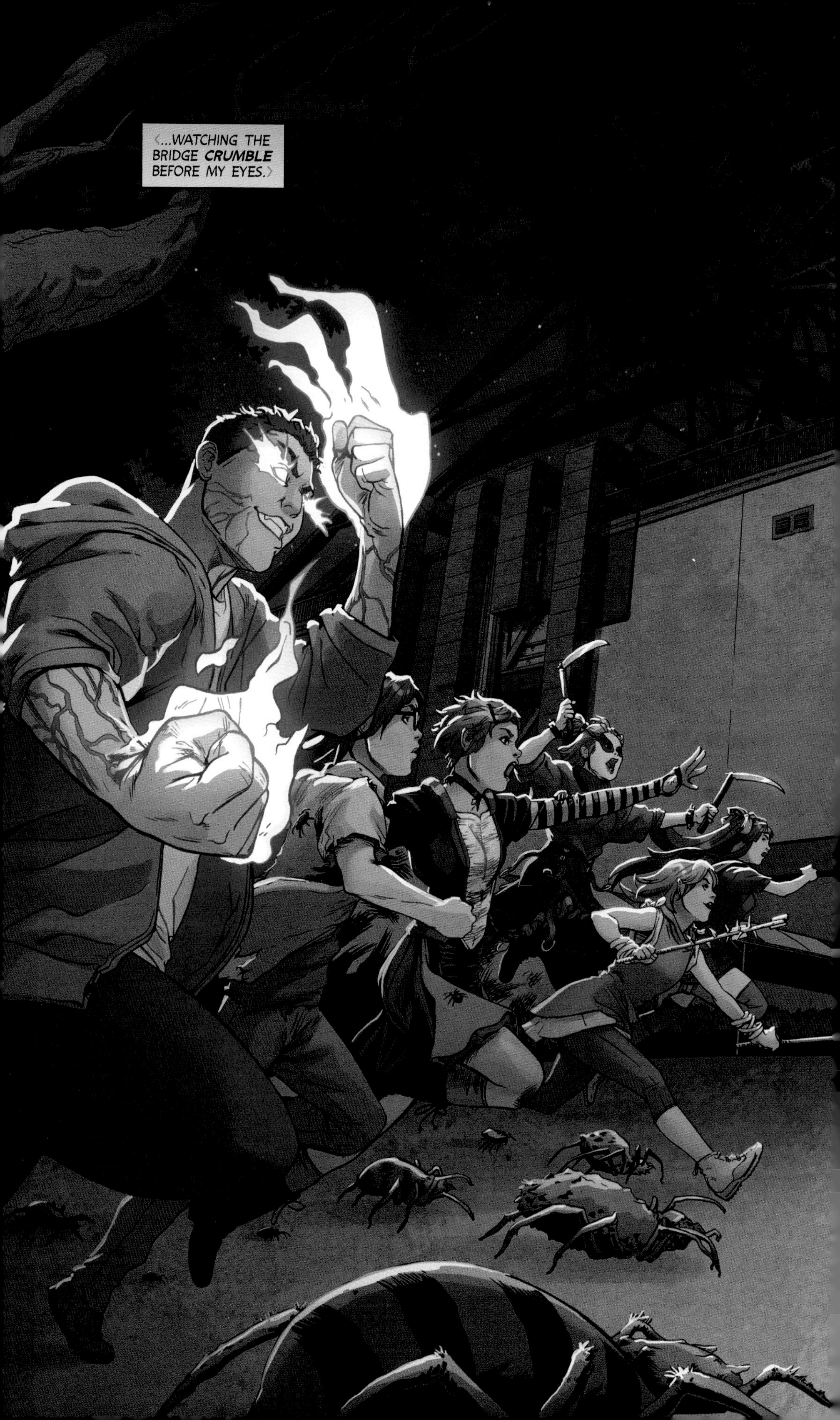
<...WATCHING THE BRIDGE *CRUMBLE* BEFORE MY EYES.>

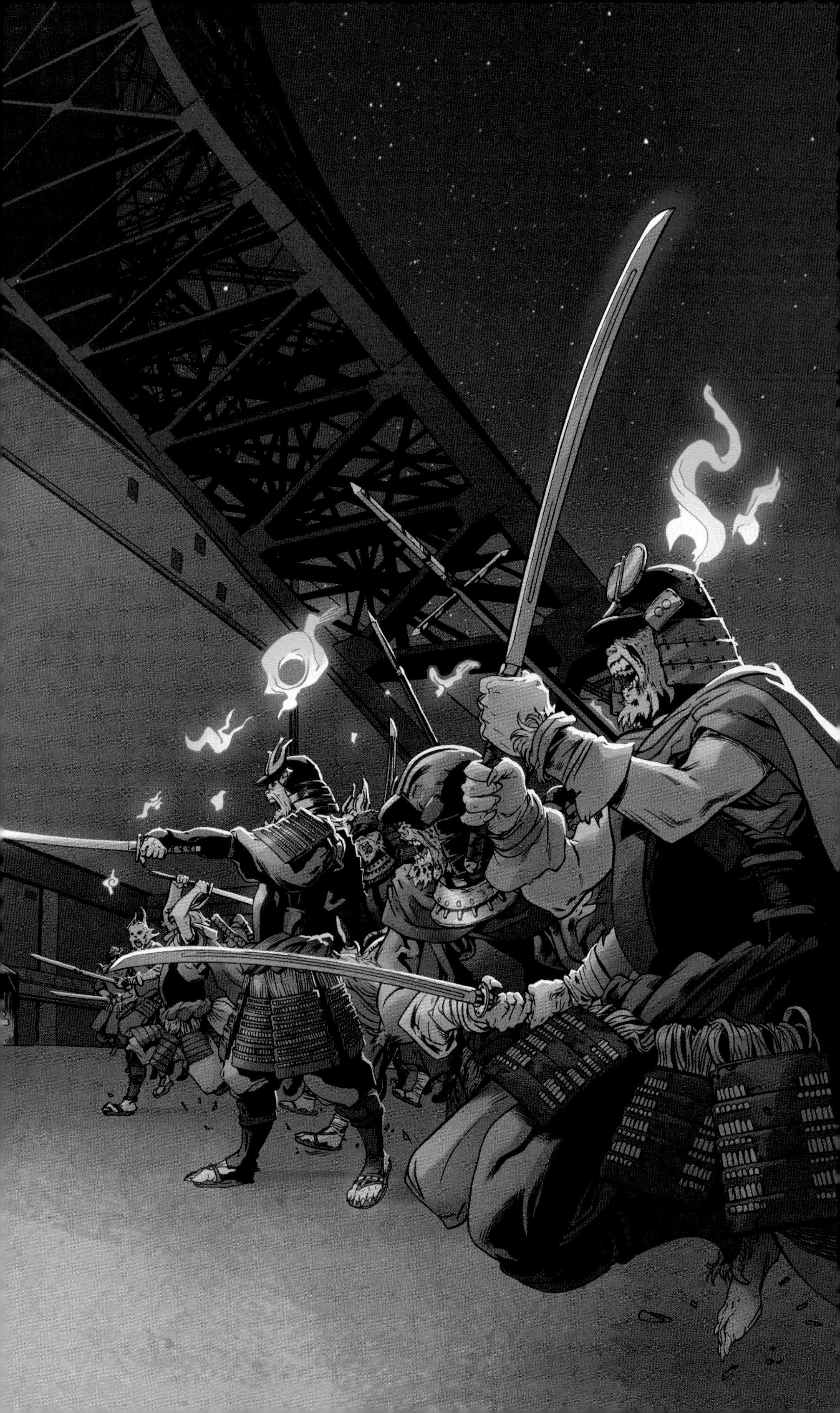

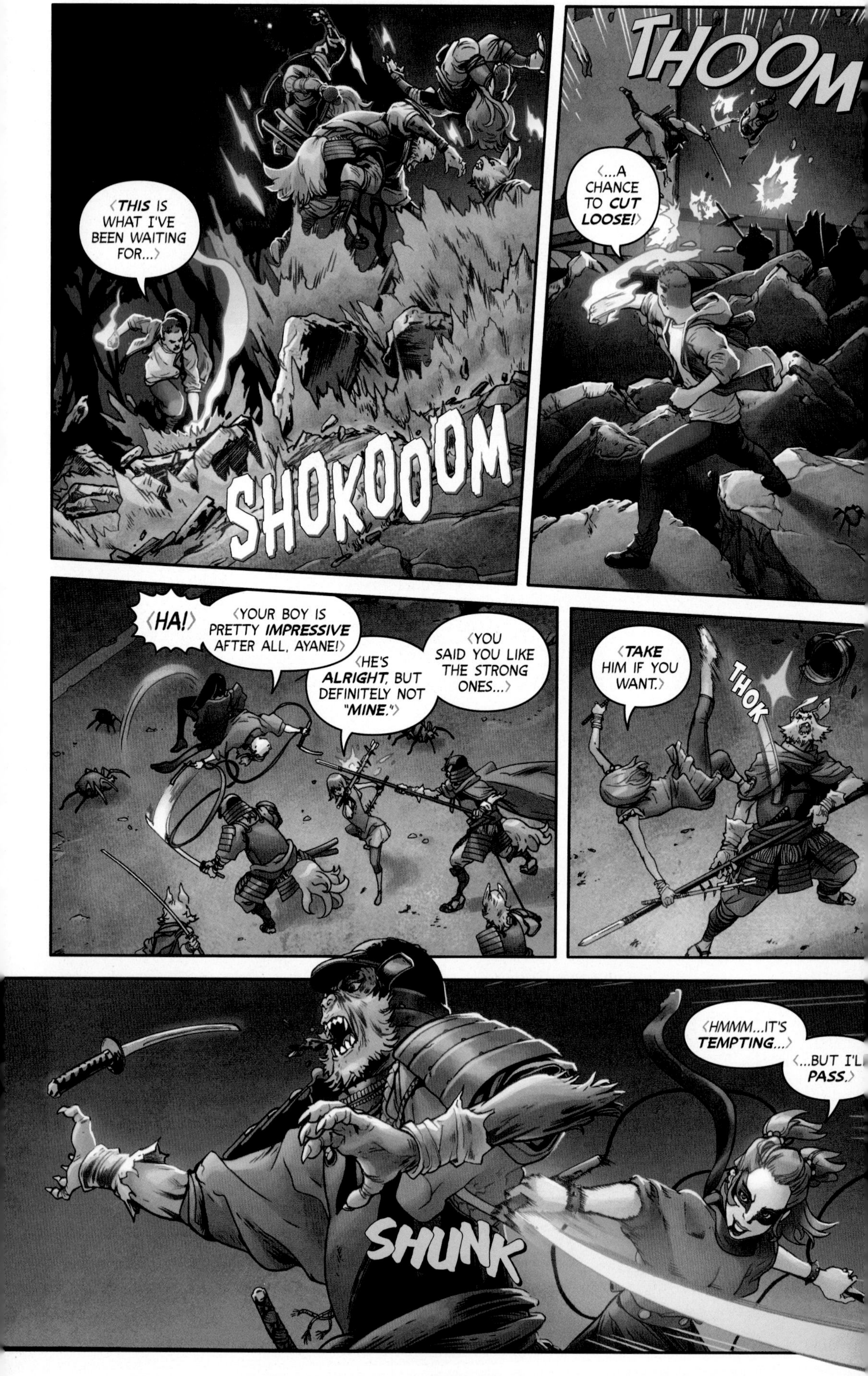

⟨THIS IS WHAT I'VE BEEN WAITING FOR...⟩
SHOKOOOM
THOOM
⟨...A CHANCE TO CUT LOOSE!⟩
⟨HA!⟩
⟨YOUR BOY IS PRETTY IMPRESSIVE AFTER ALL, AYANE!⟩
⟨HE'S ALRIGHT, BUT DEFINITELY NOT "MINE."⟩
⟨YOU SAID YOU LIKE THE STRONG ONES...⟩
⟨TAKE HIM IF YOU WANT.⟩
THOK
⟨HMMM...IT'S TEMPTING...⟩
⟨...BUT I'L PASS.⟩
SHUNK

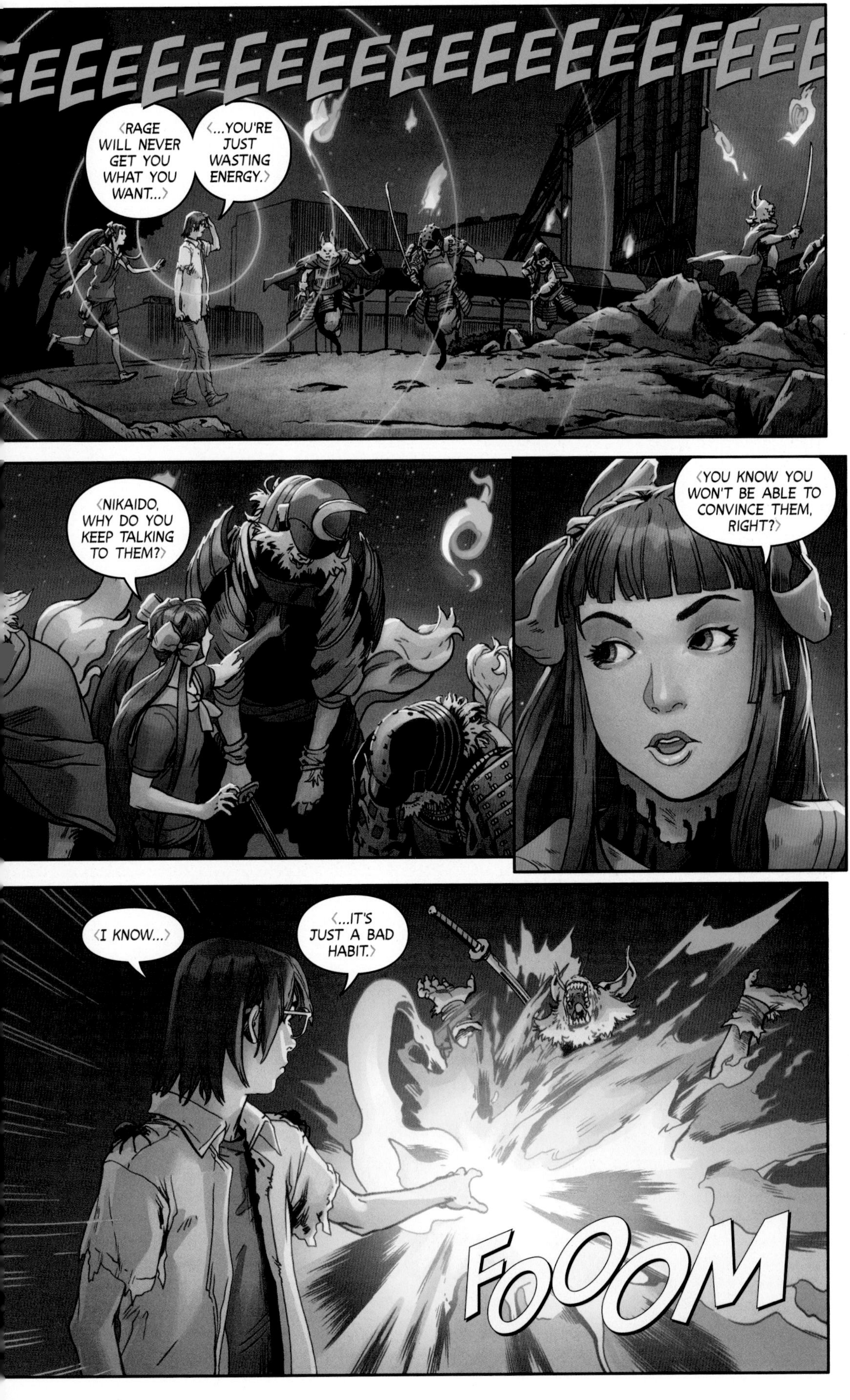
EEEEEEEEEEEEEEEEEEE
‹RAGE WILL NEVER GET YOU WHAT YOU WANT...›
‹...YOU'RE JUST WASTING ENERGY.›
‹NIKAIDO, WHY DO YOU KEEP TALKING TO THEM?›
‹YOU KNOW YOU WON'T BE ABLE TO CONVINCE THEM, RIGHT?›
‹I KNOW...›
‹...IT'S JUST A BAD HABIT.›
FOOOM

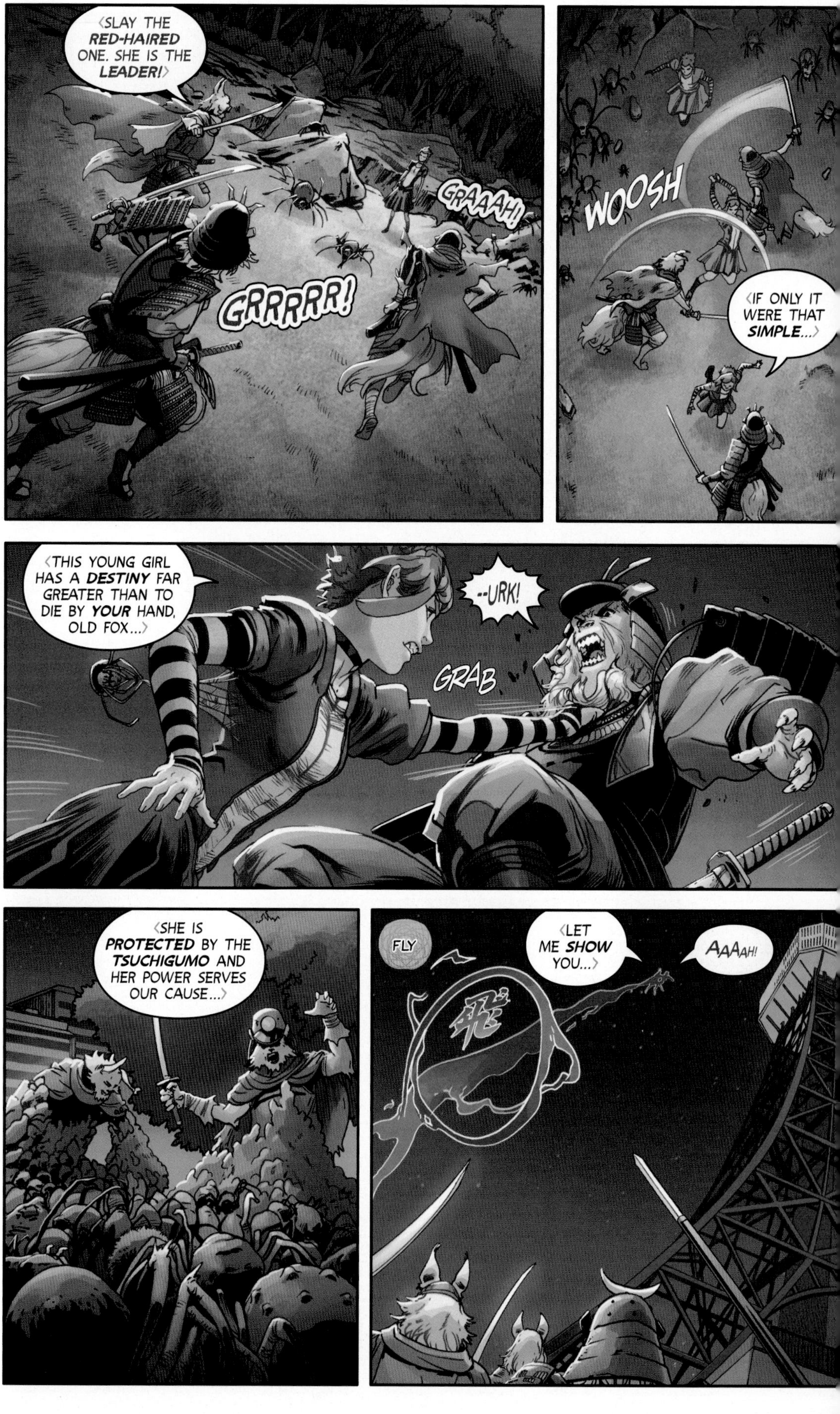

‹SLAY THE RED-HAIRED ONE. SHE IS THE LEADER!›
GRAAAH!
GRRRRR!
WOOSH
‹IF ONLY IT WERE THAT SIMPLE...›
‹THIS YOUNG GIRL HAS A DESTINY FAR GREATER THAN TO DIE BY YOUR HAND, OLD FOX...›
--URK!
GRAB
‹SHE IS PROTECTED BY THE TSUCHIGUMO AND HER POWER SERVES OUR CAUSE...›
FLY
‹LET ME SHOW YOU...›
AAAAH!

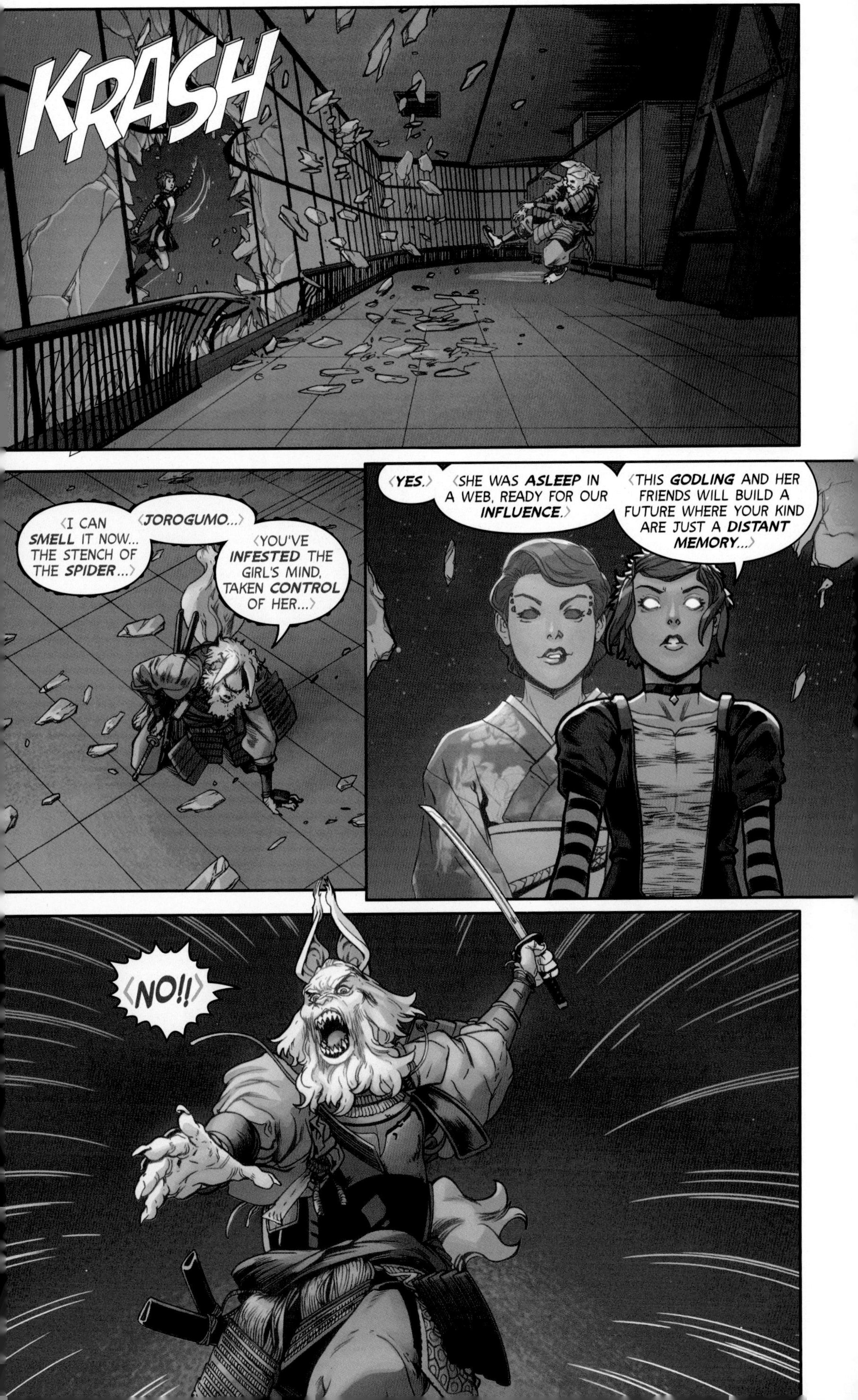
KRASH
⟨I CAN SMELL IT NOW... THE STENCH OF THE SPIDER...⟩
⟨JOROGUMO...⟩
⟨YOU'VE INFESTED THE GIRL'S MIND, TAKEN CONTROL OF HER...⟩
⟨YES.⟩
⟨SHE WAS ASLEEP IN A WEB, READY FOR OUR INFLUENCE.⟩
⟨THIS GODLING AND HER FRIENDS WILL BUILD A FUTURE WHERE YOUR KIND ARE JUST A DISTANT MEMORY...⟩
⟨NO!!⟩

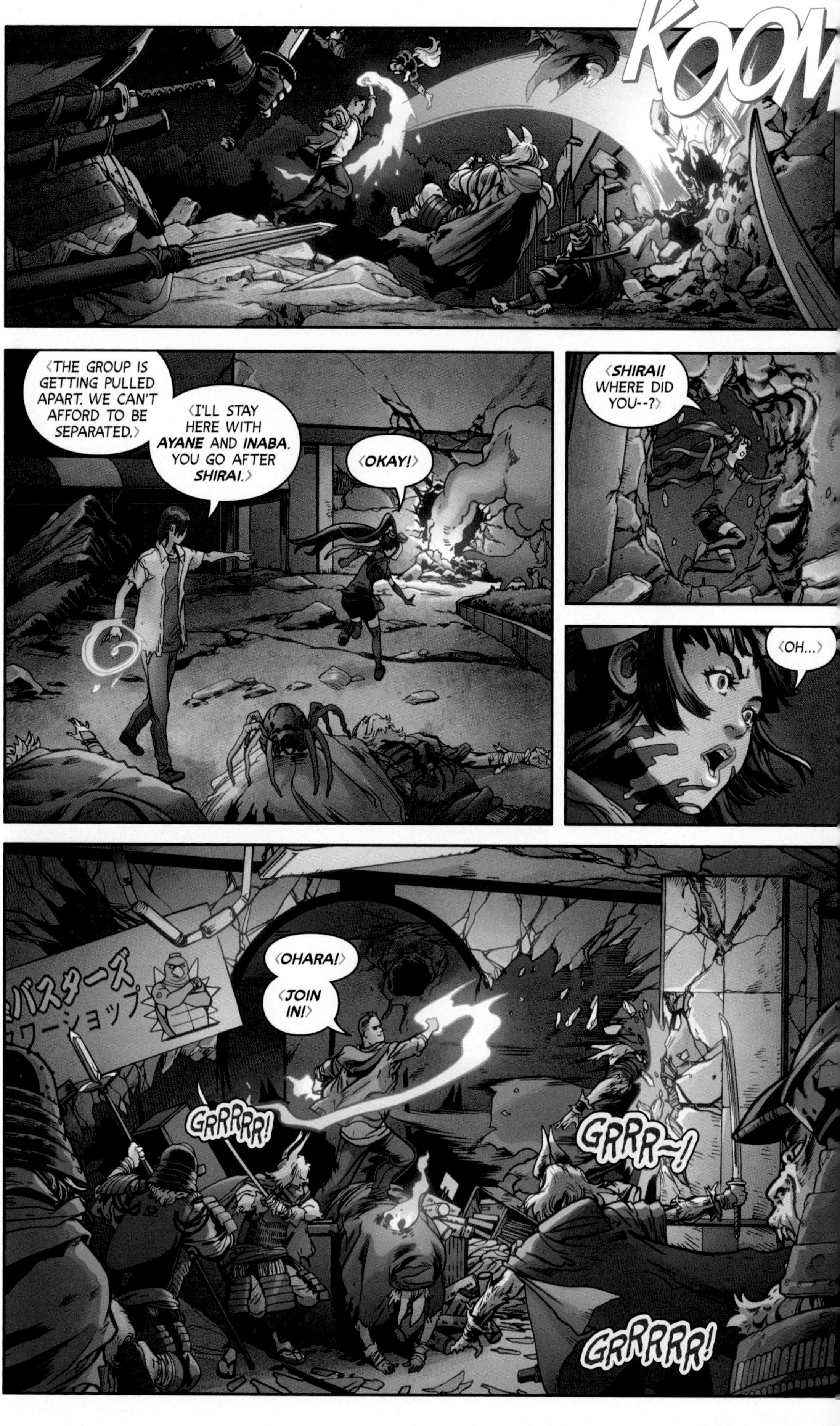
KOOM
‹THE GROUP IS GETTING PULLED APART. WE CAN'T AFFORD TO BE SEPARATED.›
‹I'LL STAY HERE WITH AYANE AND INABA. YOU GO AFTER SHIRAI.›
‹OKAY!›
‹SHIRAI! WHERE DID YOU--?›
‹OH...›
バスターズ
ワーショップ
‹OHARA!›
‹JOIN IN!›
GRRRRR!
GRRR~!
GRRRRR!

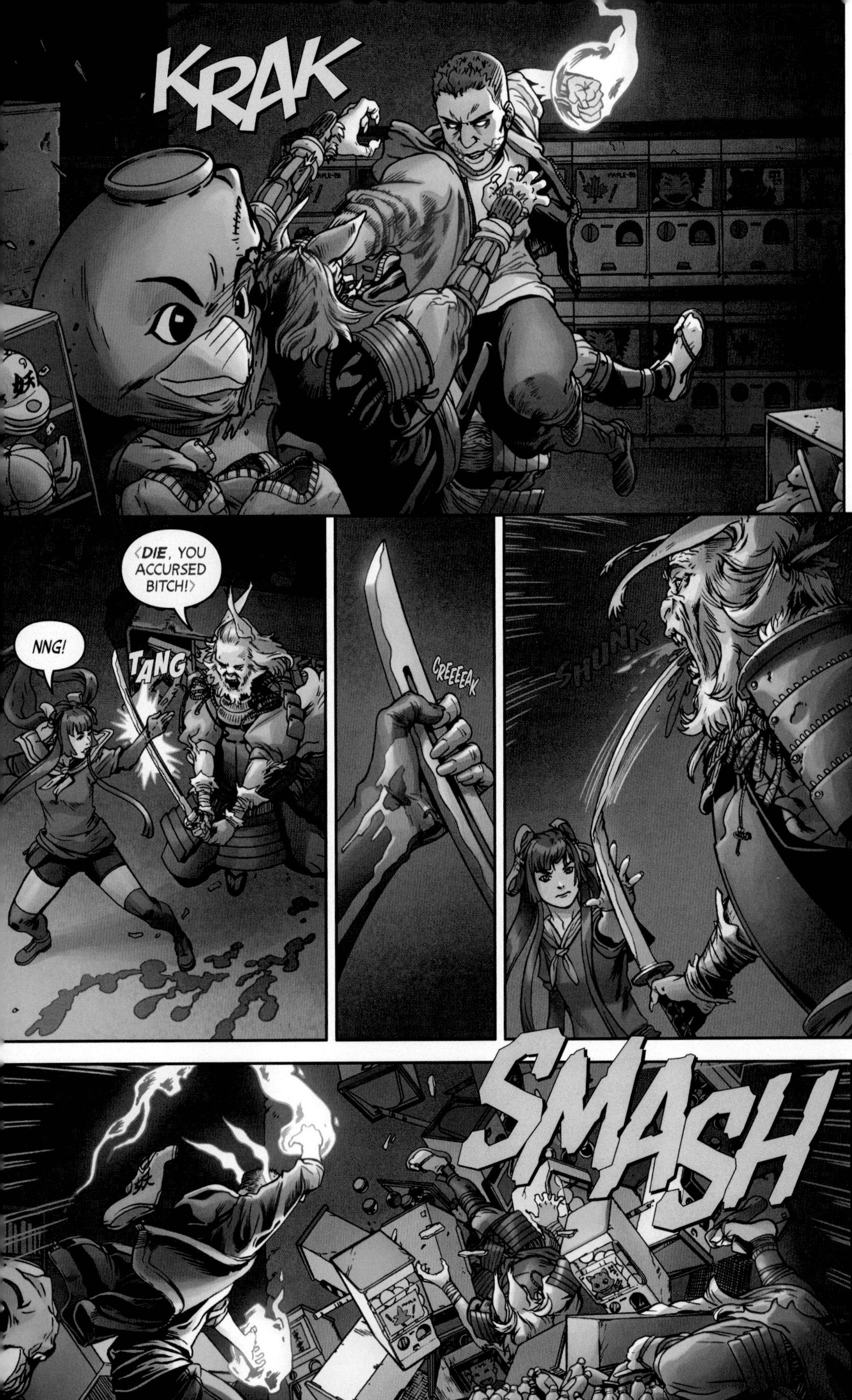
KRAK
<DIE, YOU ACCURSED BITCH!>
NNG!
TANG
CREEEEAK
SHUNK
SMASH

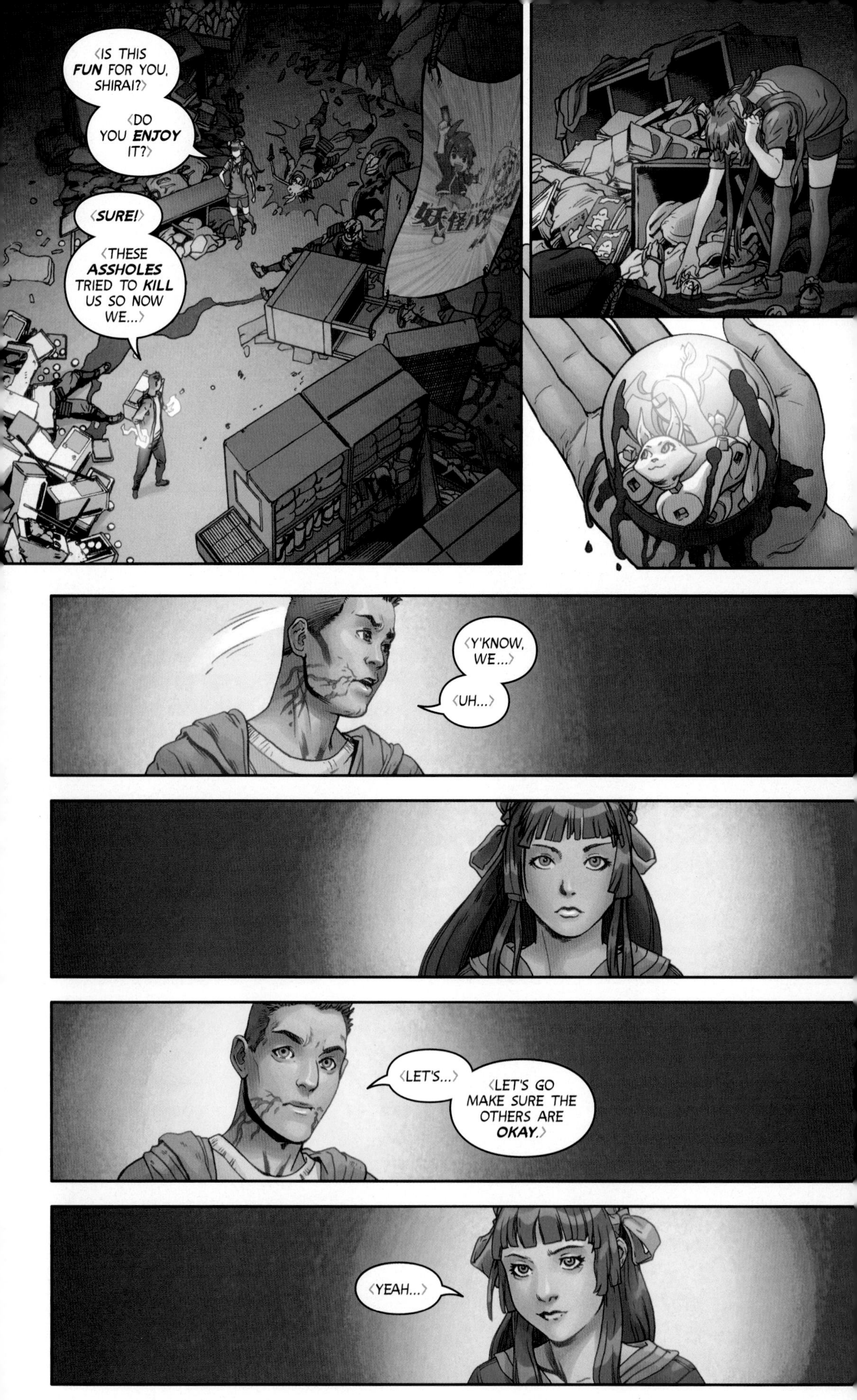
‹IS THIS FUN FOR YOU, SHIRAI?›
‹DO YOU ENJOY IT?›
‹SURE!›
‹THESE ASSHOLES TRIED TO KILL US SO NOW WE...›
‹Y'KNOW, WE...›
‹UH...›
‹LET'S...›
‹LET'S GO MAKE SURE THE OTHERS ARE OKAY.›
‹YEAH...›

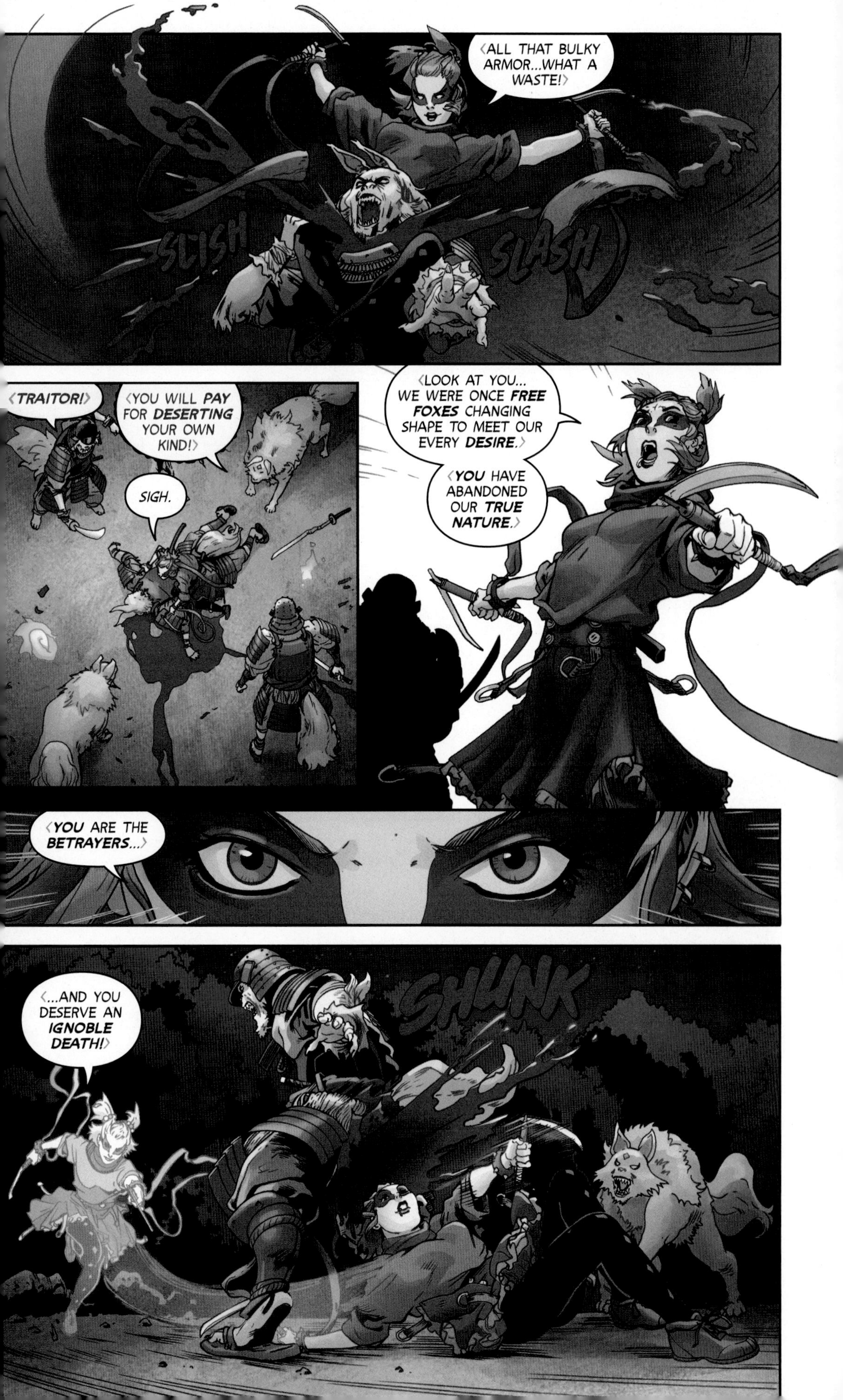

‹ALL THAT BULKY ARMOR...WHAT A WASTE!›
SLISH
SLASH
‹TRAITOR!›
‹YOU WILL PAY FOR DESERTING YOUR OWN KIND!›
SIGH.
‹LOOK AT YOU... WE WERE ONCE FREE FOXES CHANGING SHAPE TO MEET OUR EVERY DESIRE.›
‹YOU HAVE ABANDONED OUR TRUE NATURE.›
‹YOU ARE THE BETRAYERS...›
SHUNK
‹...AND YOU DESERVE AN IGNOBLE DEATH!›

GRAAAH!

SLASH

‹I'LL **PURGE** YOUR **SINS** ON THE EDGE OF MY **BLADE!**›

CHOMP

‹YOU THOUGHT SIDING WITH **CHILDREN** WOULD SAVE YOU?›

‹YOU LITTLE **FOOL**. WHERE ARE THEY **NOW?**›

‹ACTUALLY, THEY'RE RIGHT **BEHIND** YOU.›

FOOM

WHAM

‹I THINK THIS ONE'S A **KEEPER**, NIKI.›

‹HEH, THANKS.›

‹HAVE YOU **SEEN** RORI?›

‹SHE IS CONFRONTING **GENKURO**, LEADER OF THE ARMY OF OLD FOXES...›

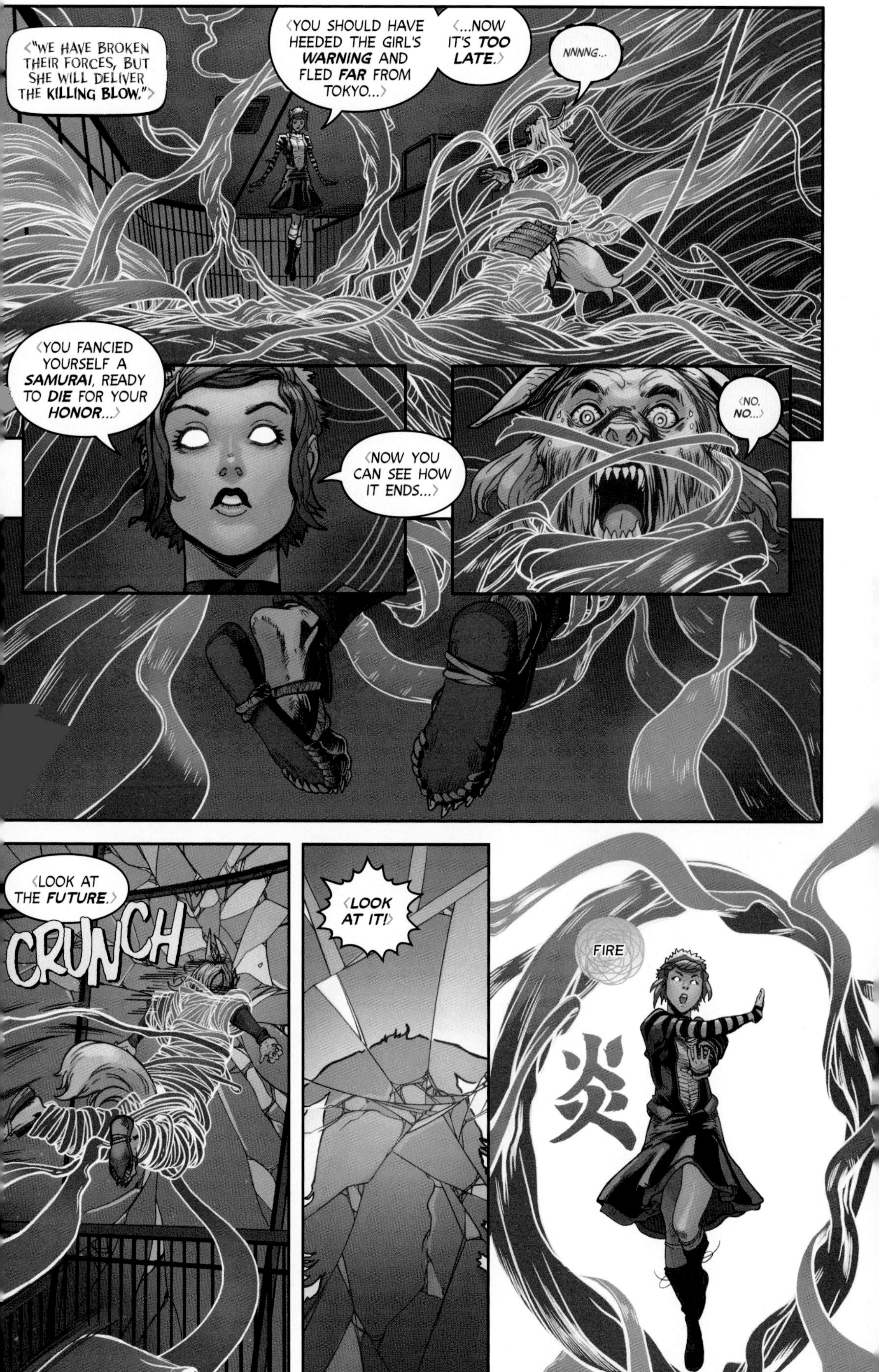

‹"WE HAVE BROKEN THEIR FORCES, BUT SHE WILL DELIVER THE KILLING BLOW."›
‹YOU SHOULD HAVE HEEDED THE GIRL'S WARNING AND FLED FAR FROM TOKYO...›
‹...NOW IT'S TOO LATE.›
NNNNG...
‹YOU FANCIED YOURSELF A SAMURAI, READY TO DIE FOR YOUR HONOR...›
‹NOW YOU CAN SEE HOW IT ENDS...›
‹NO. NO...›
‹LOOK AT THE FUTURE.›
CRUNCH
‹LOOK AT IT!›
FIRE
炎

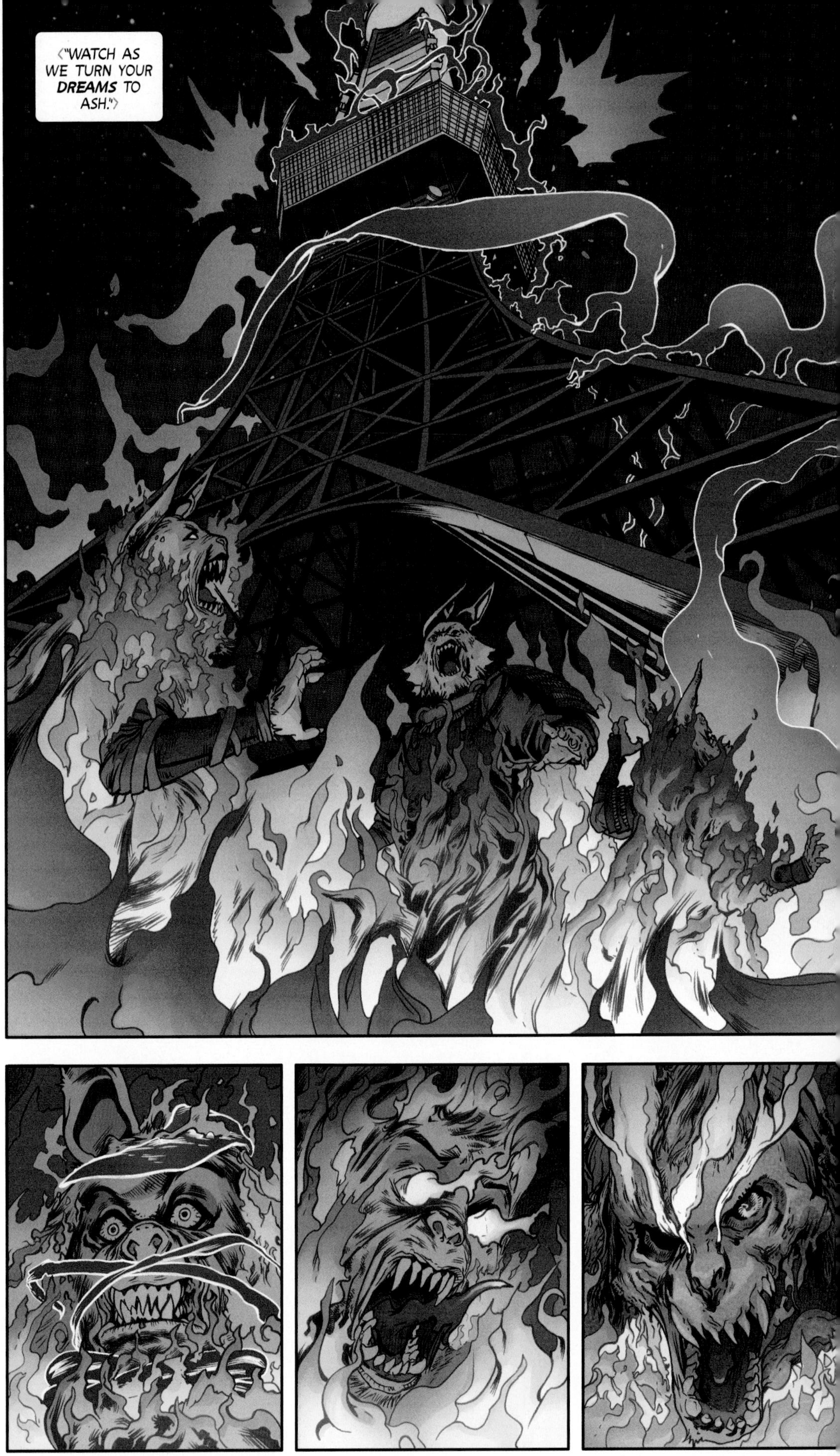
〈"WATCH AS WE TURN YOUR DREAMS TO ASH."〉

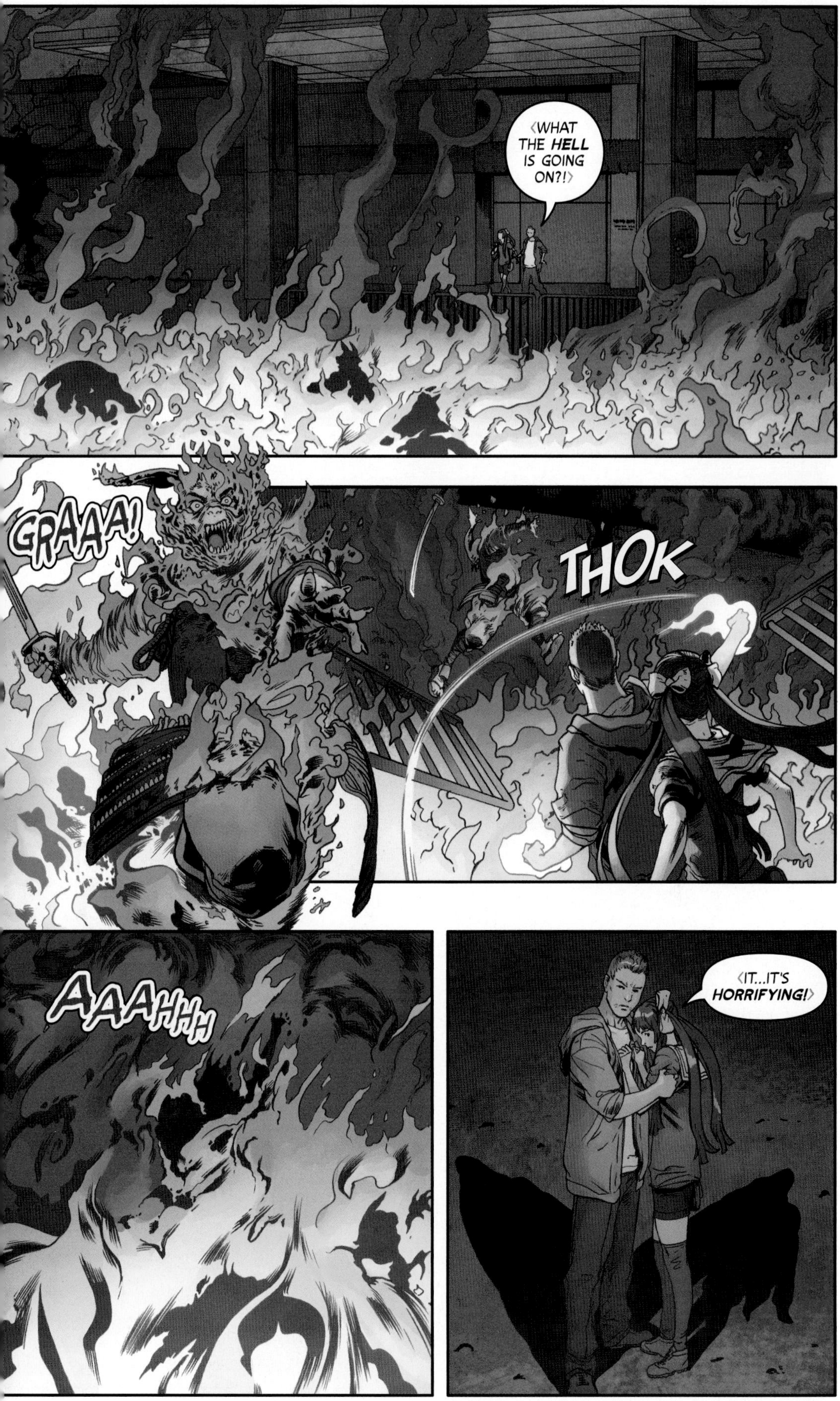

‹WHAT THE HELL IS GOING ON?!›
GRAAAA!
THOK
AAAHHH
‹IT...IT'S HORRIFYING!›

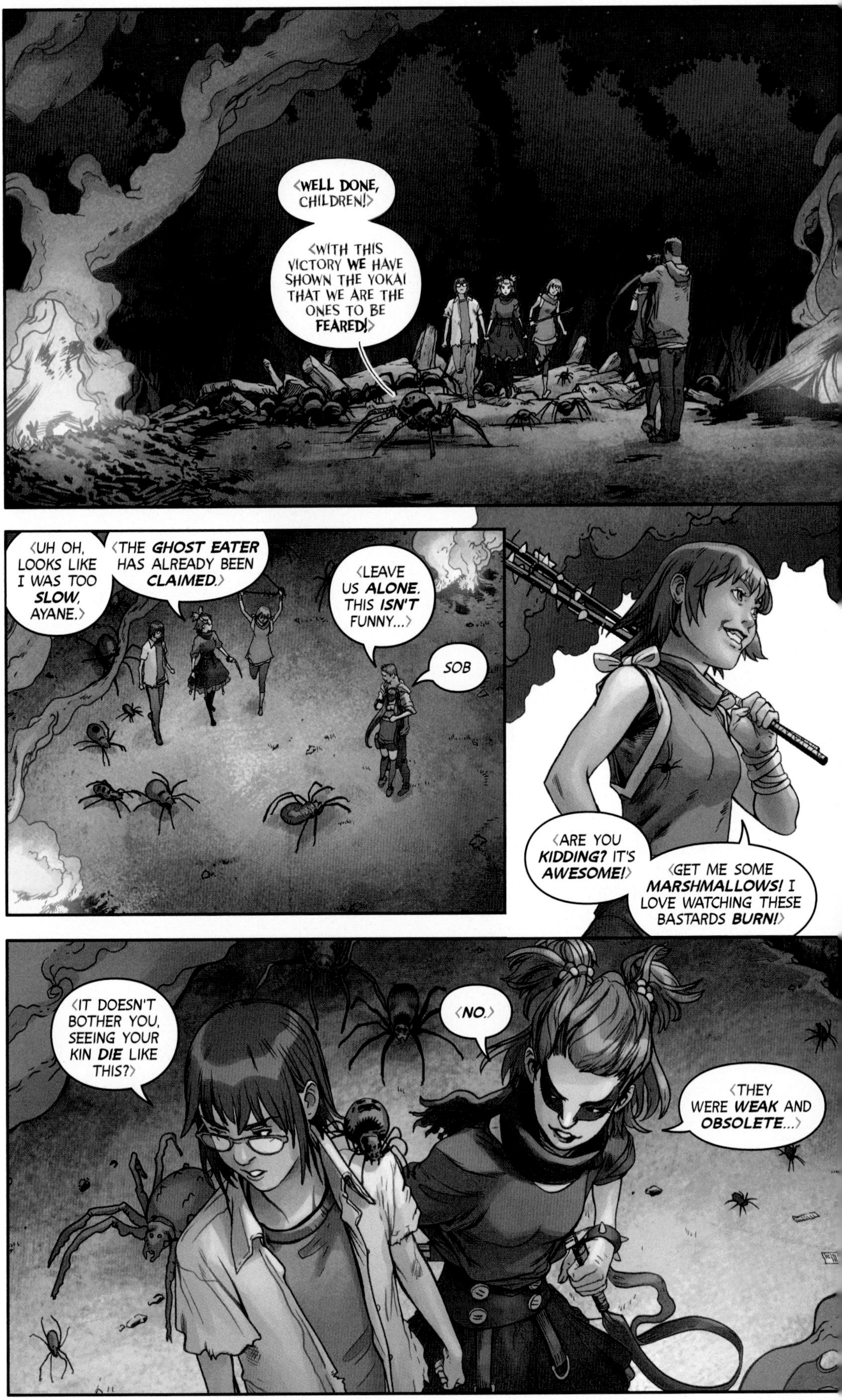
‹WELL DONE, CHILDREN!›
‹WITH THIS VICTORY WE HAVE SHOWN THE YOKAI THAT WE ARE THE ONES TO BE FEARED!›
‹UH OH, LOOKS LIKE I WAS TOO SLOW, AYANE.›
‹THE GHOST EATER HAS ALREADY BEEN CLAIMED.›
‹LEAVE US ALONE. THIS ISN'T FUNNY...›
SOB
‹ARE YOU KIDDING? IT'S AWESOME!›
‹GET ME SOME MARSHMALLOWS! I LOVE WATCHING THESE BASTARDS BURN!›
‹IT DOESN'T BOTHER YOU, SEEING YOUR KIN DIE LIKE THIS?›
‹NO.›
‹THEY WERE WEAK AND OBSOLETE...›

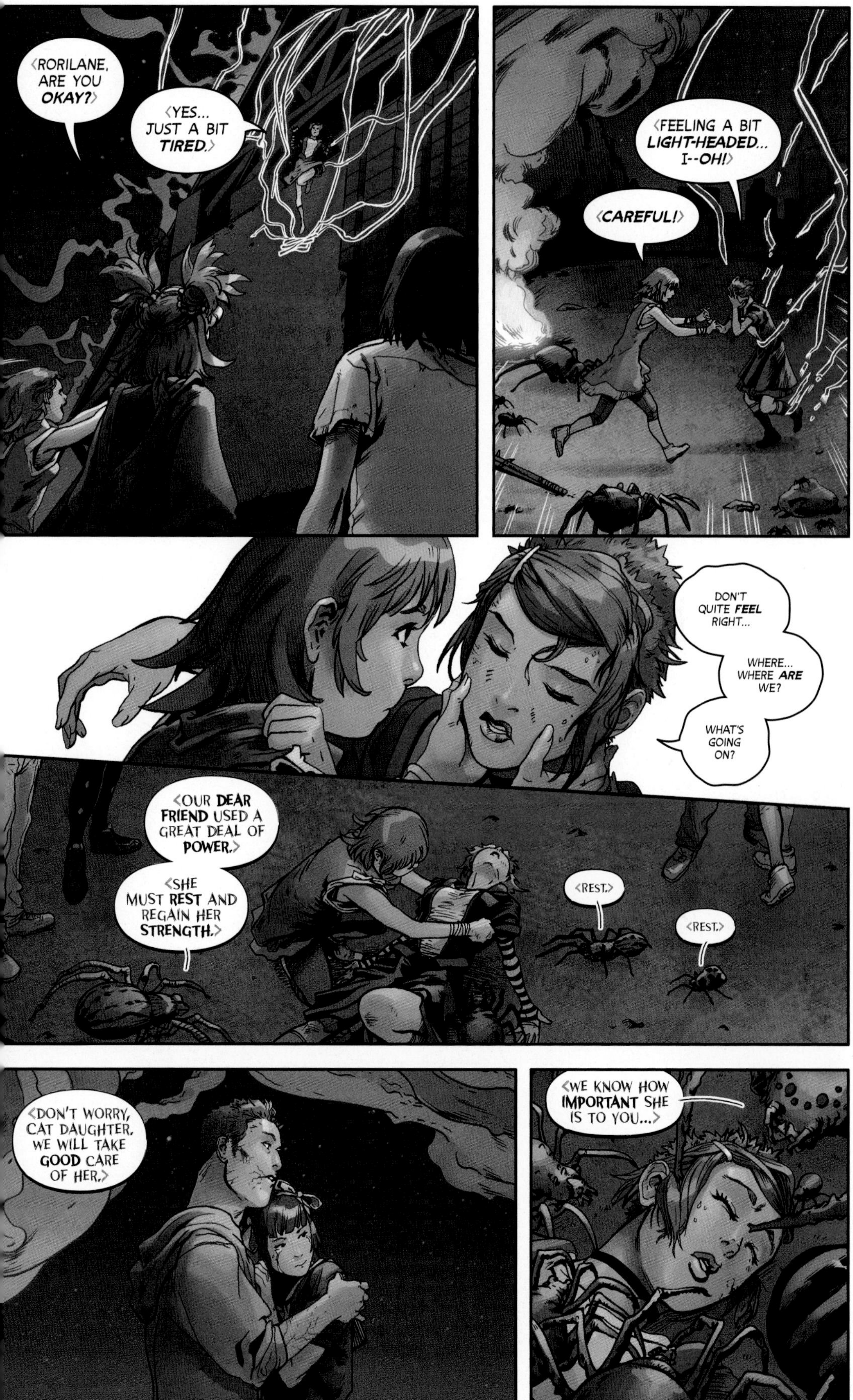

‹RORILANE, ARE YOU *OKAY?*›
‹YES... JUST A BIT *TIRED.*›
‹FEELING A BIT *LIGHT-HEADED...* I--*OH!*›
‹*CAREFUL!*›
DON'T QUITE **FEEL** RIGHT...
WHERE... WHERE ***ARE*** WE?
WHAT'S GOING ON?
‹OUR **DEAR FRIEND** USED A GREAT DEAL OF **POWER.**›
‹SHE MUST **REST** AND REGAIN HER **STRENGTH.**›
‹REST.›
‹REST.›
‹DON'T WORRY, CAT DAUGHTER. WE WILL TAKE **GOOD** CARE OF HER.›
‹WE KNOW HOW **IMPORTANT** SHE IS TO YOU...›

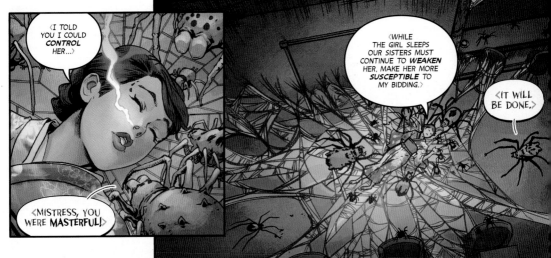

⟨I TOLD YOU I COULD *CONTROL* HER...⟩

⟨MISTRESS, YOU WERE *MASTERFUL!*⟩

⟨WHILE THE GIRL SLEEPS OUR SISTERS MUST CONTINUE TO *WEAKEN* HER, MAKE HER MORE *SUSCEPTIBLE* TO MY BIDDING.⟩

⟨IT WILL BE DONE.⟩

⟨PLEASE, STAY HERE, WE WILL BRING YOU *SUSTENANCE.*⟩

⟨*FINE*, BUT BE *QUICK* ABOUT IT.⟩

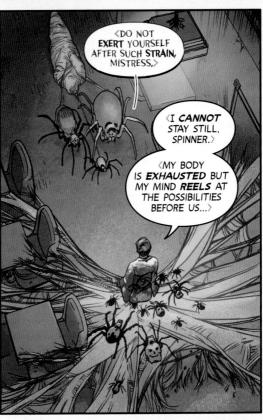

⟨DO NOT *EXERT* YOURSELF AFTER SUCH *STRAIN*, MISTRESS.⟩

⟨I *CANNOT* STAY STILL, SPINNER.⟩

⟨MY BODY IS *EXHAUSTED* BUT MY MIND *REELS* AT THE POSSIBILITIES BEFORE US...⟩

⟨WE *FINALLY* HAVE THE UPP[ER] HAND...⟩

⟨THE *STRINGS OF FATE* WILL AT LAST BE WOVEN INTO A *WEB* OF *OUR DESIGN...*⟩

⟨...WITH THE *TSUCHIGUMO* AT ITS *CENTER.*⟩

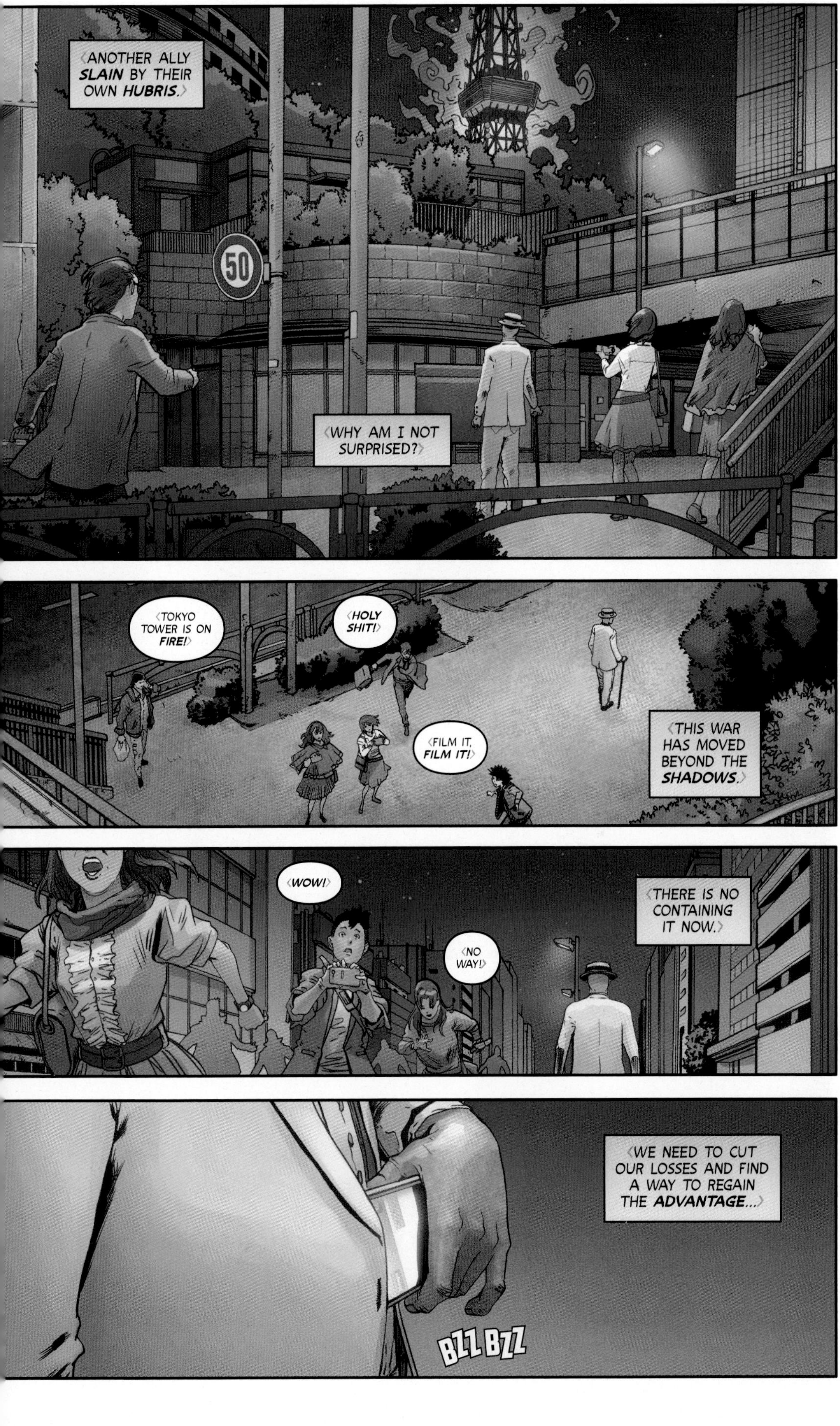

ANOTHER ALLY SLAIN BY THEIR OWN HUBRIS.
50
WHY AM I NOT SURPRISED?
TOKYO TOWER IS ON FIRE!
HOLY SHIT!
FILM IT, FILM IT!
THIS WAR HAS MOVED BEYOND THE SHADOWS.
WOW!
NO WAY!
THERE IS NO CONTAINING IT NOW.
WE NEED TO CUT OUR LOSSES AND FIND A WAY TO REGAIN THE ADVANTAGE...
BZZ BZZ

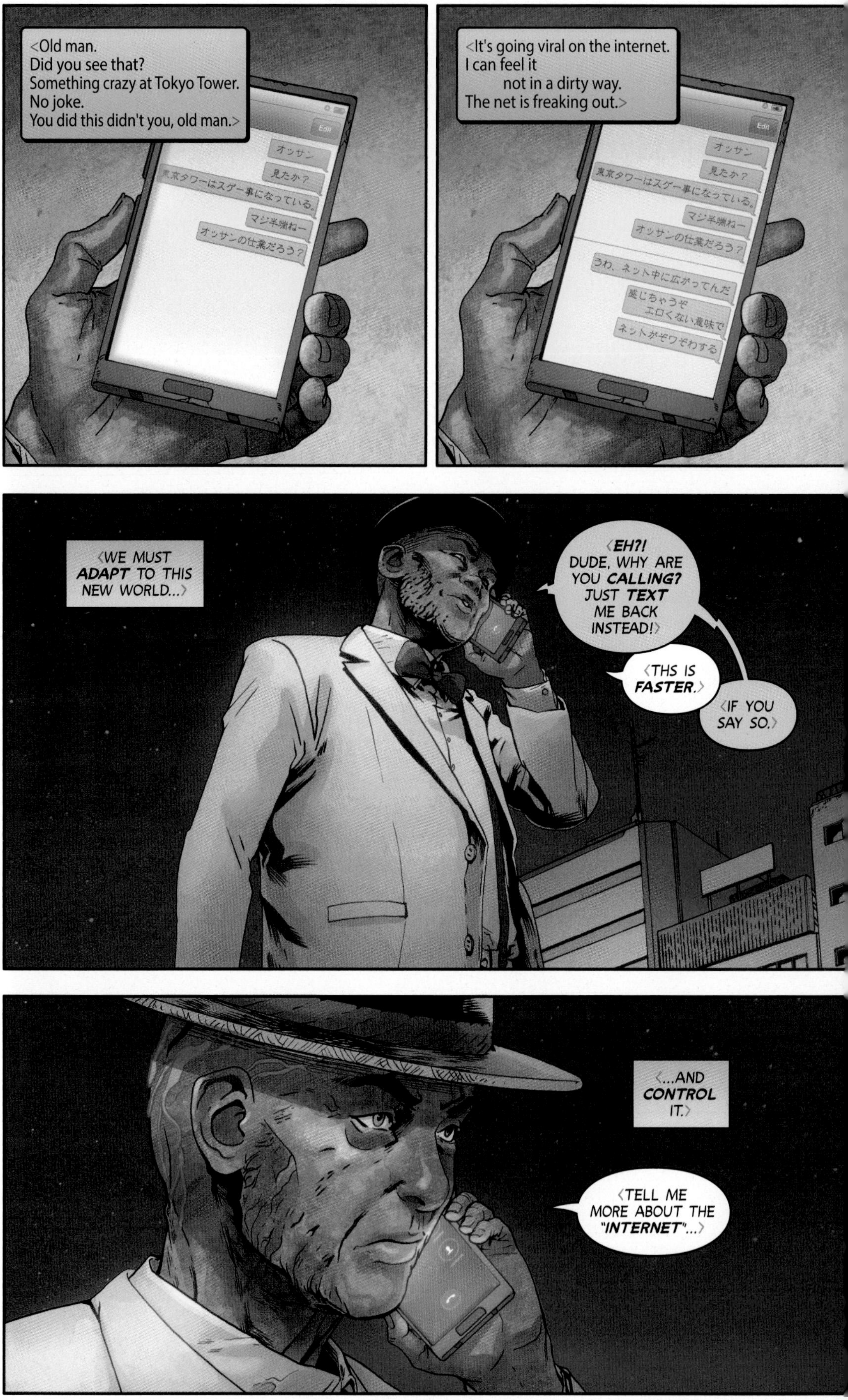
<Old man.
Did you see that?
Something crazy at Tokyo Tower.
No joke.
You did this didn't you, old man.>
Edit
オッサン
見たか？
東京タワーはスゲー事になっている。
マジ半端ねー
オッサンの仕業だろう？
<It's going viral on the internet.
I can feel it
not in a dirty way.
The net is freaking out.>
Edit
オッサン
見たか？
東京タワーはスゲー事になっている。
マジ半端ねー
オッサンの仕業だろう？
うわ、ネット中に広がってんだ
感じちゃうぞ エロくない意味で
ネットがぞワぞわする
<WE MUST ADAPT TO THIS NEW WORLD...>
<EH?! DUDE, WHY ARE YOU CALLING? JUST TEXT ME BACK INSTEAD!>
<THS IS FASTER.>
<IF YOU SAY SO.>
<...AND CONTROL IT.>
<TELL ME MORE ABOUT THE "INTERNET"...>

Chapter Fourteen

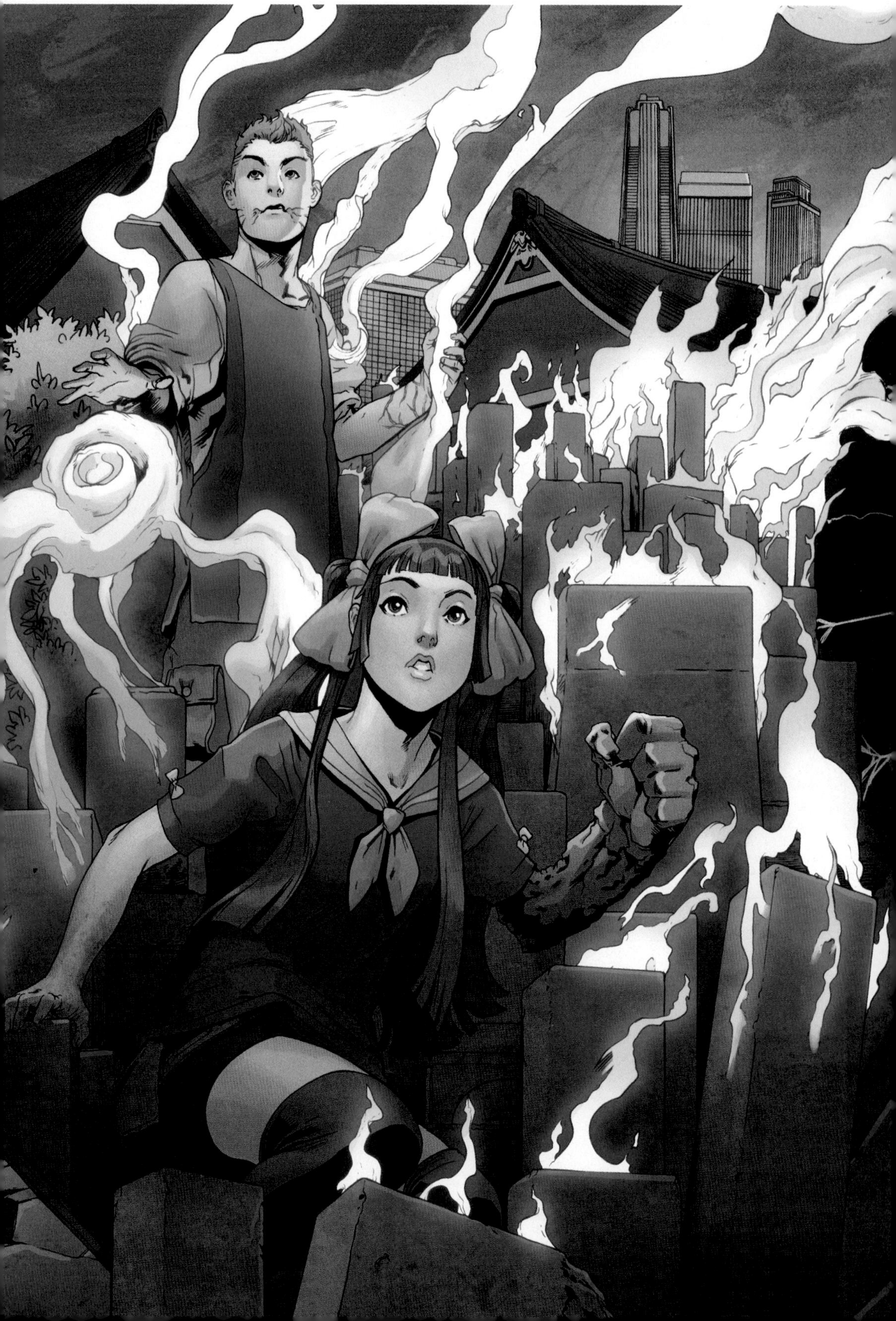

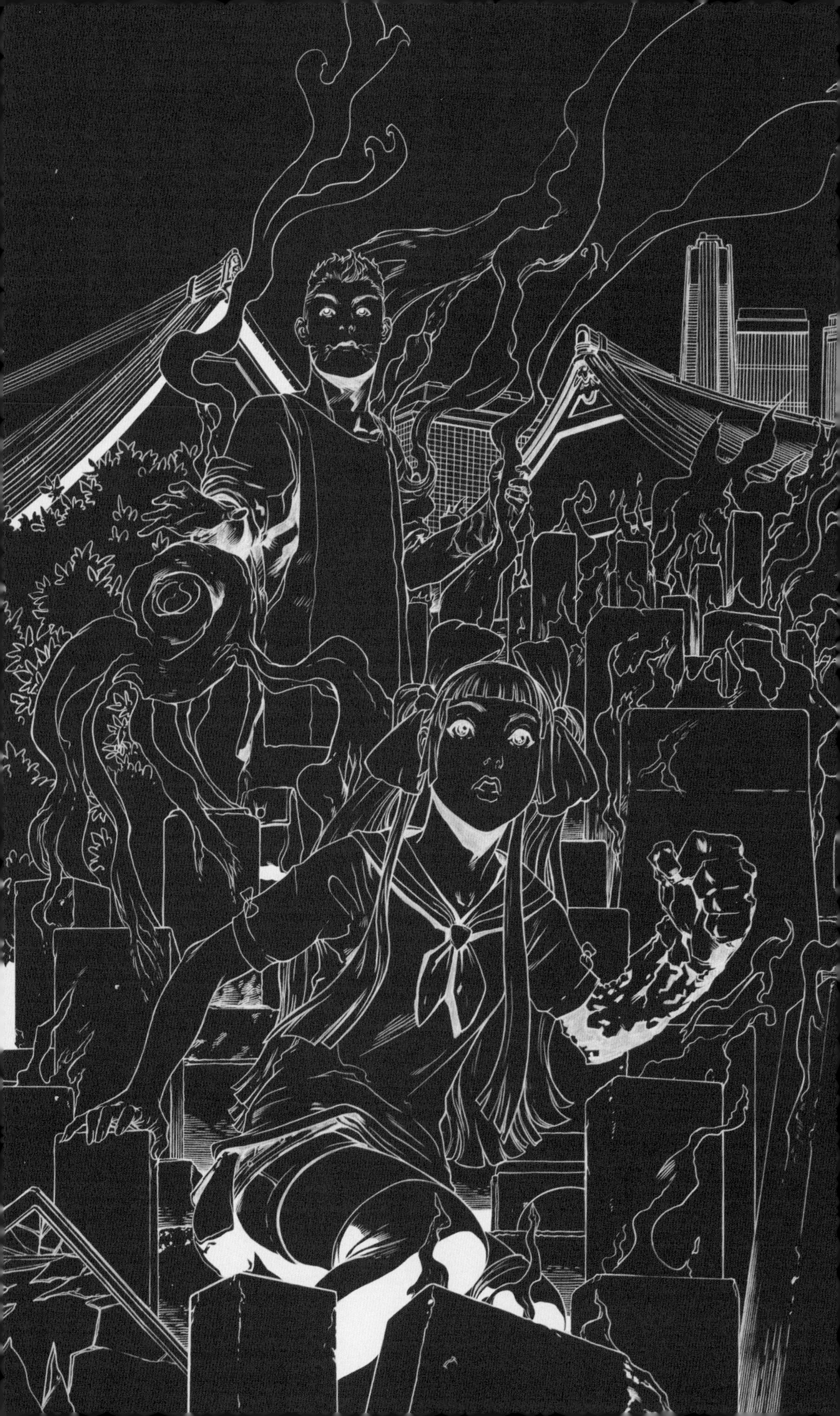

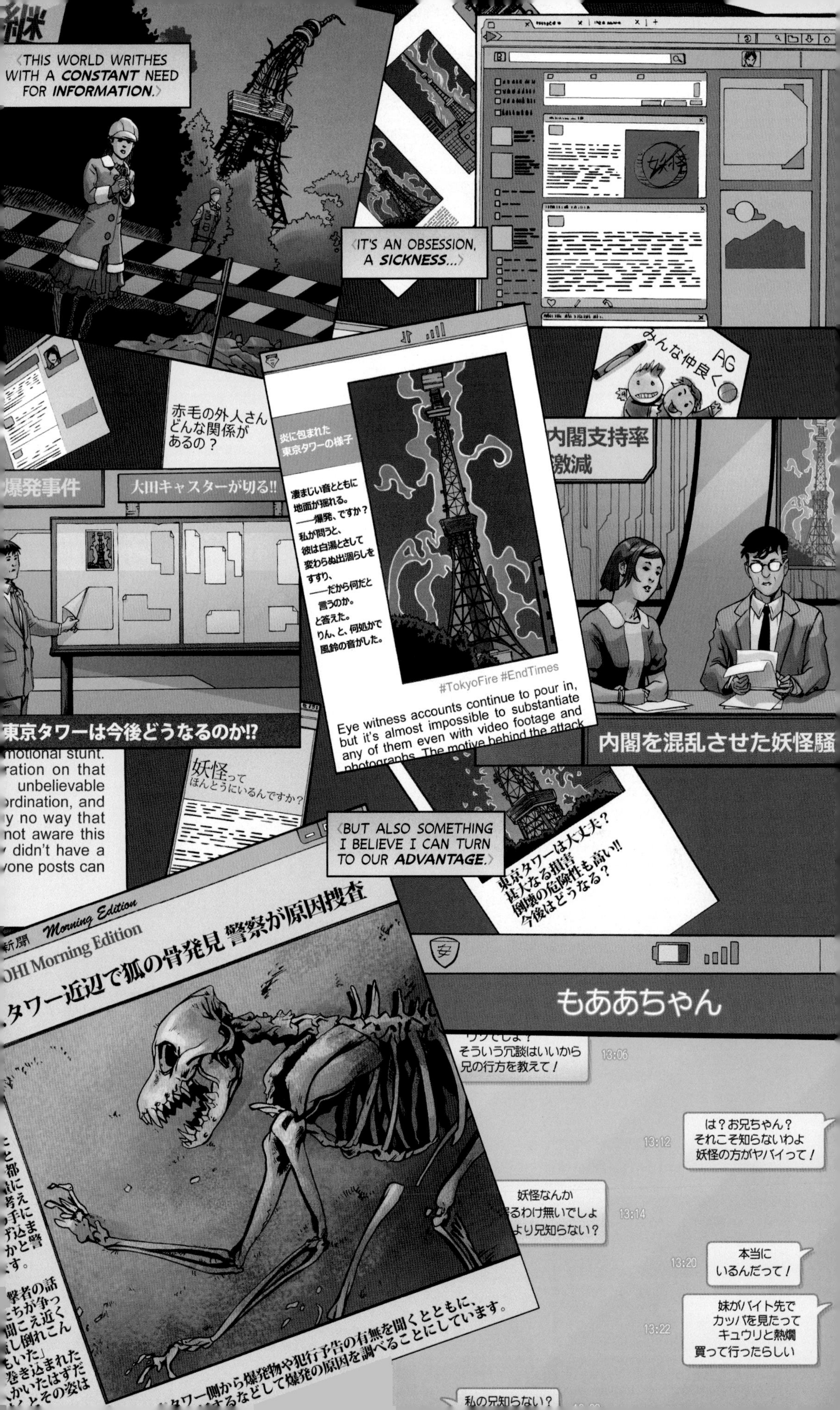

〈THIS WORLD WRITHES WITH A CONSTANT NEED FOR INFORMATION.〉
〈IT'S AN OBSESSION, A SICKNESS...〉
みんな仲良く
AG
赤毛の外人さん
どんな関係が
あるの？
炎に包まれた
東京タワーの様子
凄まじい音とともに
地面が揺れる。
――爆発、ですか？
私が問うと、
彼は白湯とさして
変わらぬ出涸らしを
すすり、
――だから何だと
言うのか。
と答えた。
りん、と、何処かで
風鈴の音がした。
#TokyoFire #EndTimes
Eye witness accounts continue to pour in, but it's almost impossible to substantiate any of them even with video footage and photographs. The motive behind the attack
内閣支持率
激減
爆発事件
大田キャスターが切る!!
東京タワーは今後どうなるのか!?
内閣を混乱させた妖怪騒
motional stunt.
ration on that
unbelievable
ordination, and
y no way that
not aware this
didn't have a
one posts can
妖怪って
ほんとうにいるんですか？
〈BUT ALSO SOMETHING I BELIEVE I CAN TURN TO OUR ADVANTAGE.〉
東京タワーは大丈夫？
甚大なる損害
倒壊の危険性も高い!!
今後はどうなる？
新聞 Morning Edition
OHI Morning Edition
タワー近辺で狐の骨発見 警察が原因捜査
と都
にえ
考えに
手込ま
かと警
す。
撃者の話
ちが争っ
聞こえ近く
し倒れこん
いた」
巻き込まれた
かいたはずだ
とその姿は
タワー側から爆発物や犯行予告の有無を聞くとともに、
するなどして爆発の原因を調べることにしています。
もあちゃん
そういう冗談はいいから
兄の行方を教えて！
13:06
は？お兄ちゃん？
それこそ知らないわよ
妖怪の方がヤバイって！
13:12
妖怪なんか
るわけ無いでしょ
より兄知らない？
13:14
本当に
いるんだって！
13:20
妹がバイト先で
カッパを見たって
キュウリと熱燗
買って行ったらしい
13:22
私の兄知らない？

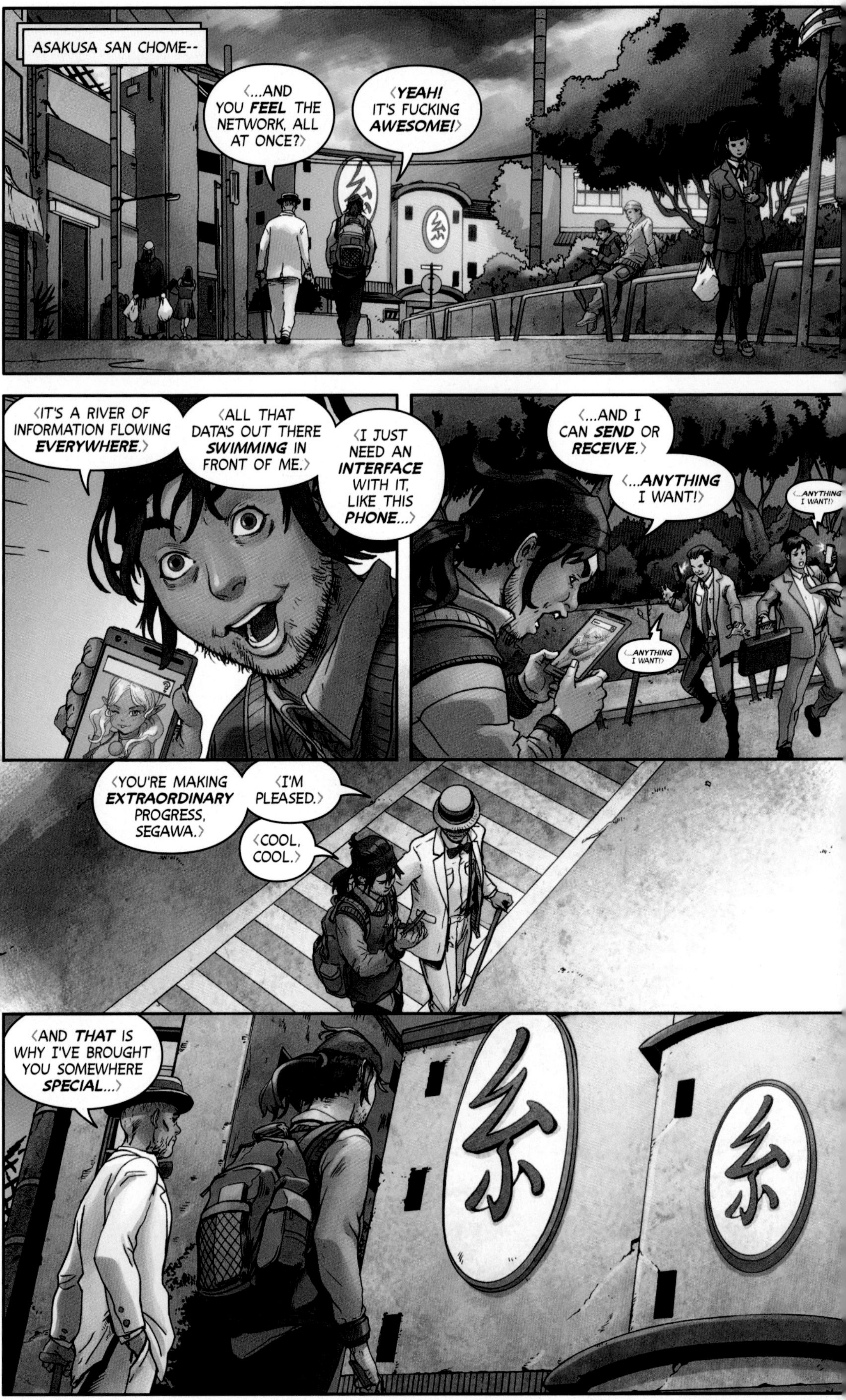
ASAKUSA SAN CHOME--
⟨...AND YOU FEEL THE NETWORK, ALL AT ONCE?⟩
⟨YEAH! IT'S FUCKING AWESOME!⟩
⟨IT'S A RIVER OF INFORMATION FLOWING EVERYWHERE.⟩
⟨ALL THAT DATA'S OUT THERE SWIMMING IN FRONT OF ME.⟩
⟨I JUST NEED AN INTERFACE WITH IT, LIKE THIS PHONE...⟩
⟨...AND I CAN SEND OR RECEIVE.⟩
⟨...ANYTHING I WANT!⟩
⟨...ANYTHING I WANT!⟩
⟨...ANYTHING I WANT!⟩
⟨YOU'RE MAKING EXTRAORDINARY PROGRESS, SEGAWA.⟩
⟨I'M PLEASED.⟩
⟨COOL, COOL.⟩
⟨AND THAT IS WHY I'VE BROUGHT YOU SOMEWHERE SPECIAL...⟩

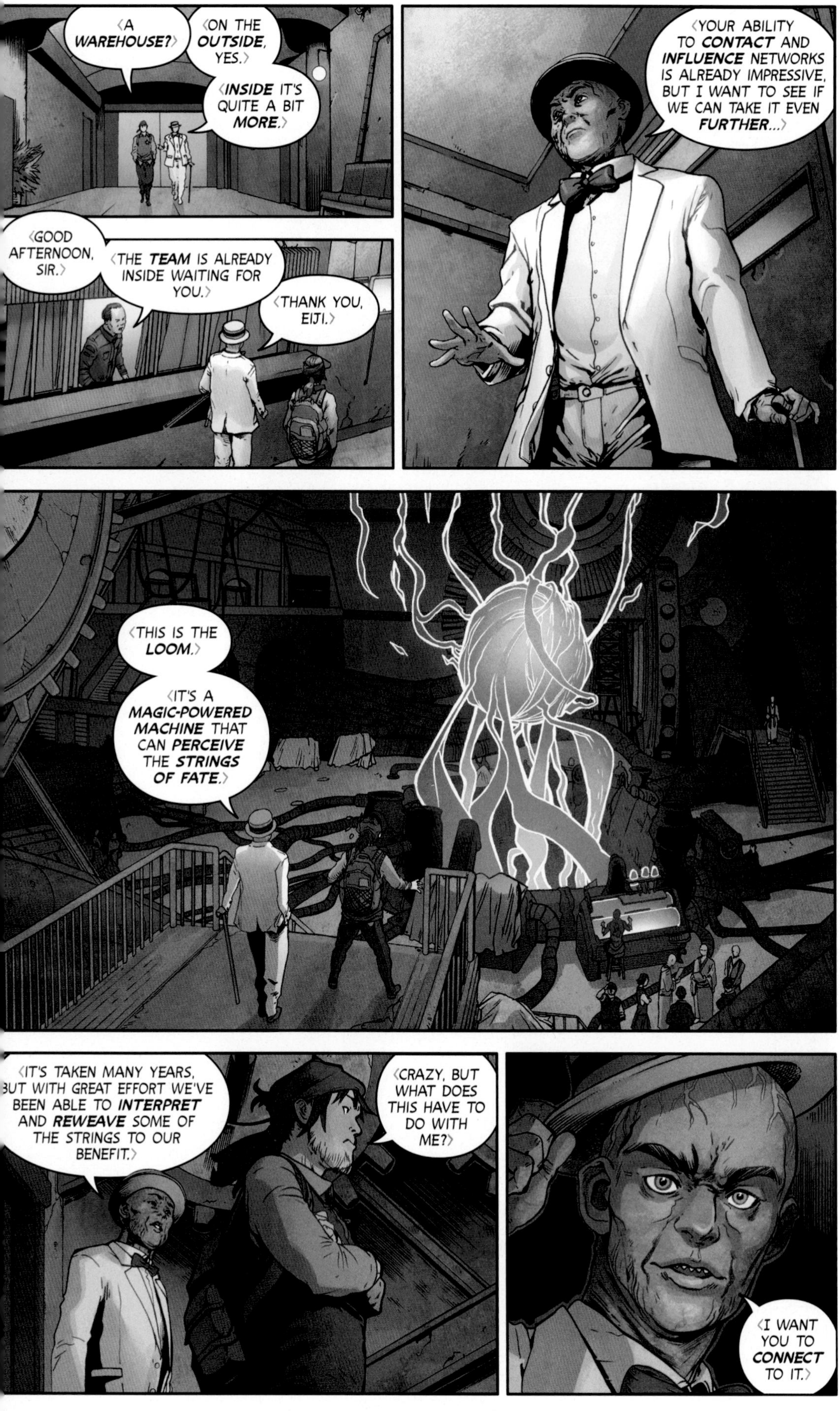

〈A WAREHOUSE?〉
〈ON THE OUTSIDE, YES.〉
〈INSIDE IT'S QUITE A BIT MORE.〉
〈YOUR ABILITY TO CONTACT AND INFLUENCE NETWORKS IS ALREADY IMPRESSIVE, BUT I WANT TO SEE IF WE CAN TAKE IT EVEN FURTHER...〉
〈GOOD AFTERNOON, SIR.〉
〈THE TEAM IS ALREADY INSIDE WAITING FOR YOU.〉
〈THANK YOU, EIJI.〉
〈THIS IS THE LOOM.〉
〈IT'S A MAGIC-POWERED MACHINE THAT CAN PERCEIVE THE STRINGS OF FATE.〉
〈IT'S TAKEN MANY YEARS, BUT WITH GREAT EFFORT WE'VE BEEN ABLE TO INTERPRET AND REWEAVE SOME OF THE STRINGS TO OUR BENEFIT.〉
〈CRAZY, BUT WHAT DOES THIS HAVE TO DO WITH ME?〉
〈I WANT YOU TO CONNECT TO IT.〉

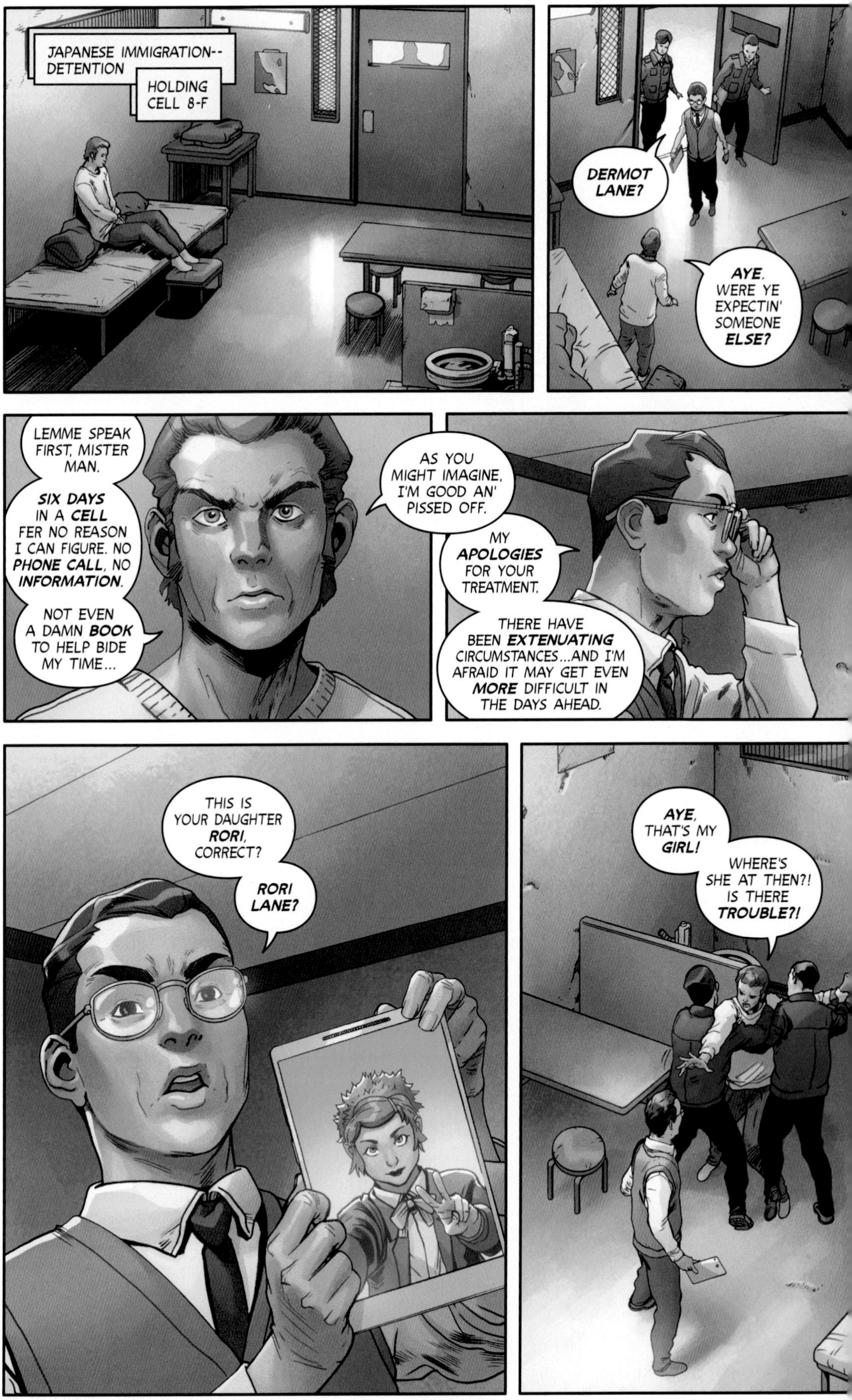
JAPANESE IMMIGRATION--DETENTION
HOLDING CELL 8-F
DERMOT LANE?
AYE. WERE YE EXPECTIN' SOMEONE ELSE?
LEMME SPEAK FIRST, MISTER MAN.
SIX DAYS IN A CELL FER NO REASON I CAN FIGURE. NO PHONE CALL, NO INFORMATION.
NOT EVEN A DAMN BOOK TO HELP BIDE MY TIME...
AS YOU MIGHT IMAGINE, I'M GOOD AN' PISSED OFF.
MY APOLOGIES FOR YOUR TREATMENT.
THERE HAVE BEEN EXTENUATING CIRCUMSTANCES...AND I'M AFRAID IT MAY GET EVEN MORE DIFFICULT IN THE DAYS AHEAD.
THIS IS YOUR DAUGHTER RORI, CORRECT?
RORI LANE?
AYE, THAT'S MY GIRL!
WHERE'S SHE AT THEN?! IS THERE TROUBLE?!

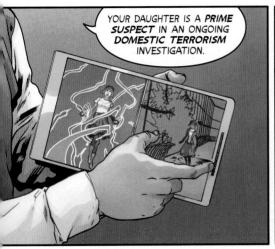

YOUR DAUGHTER IS A *PRIME SUSPECT* IN AN ONGOING *DOMESTIC TERRORISM* INVESTIGATION.

THERE HAVE BEEN MULTIPLE INCIDENTS OVER THE PAST FEW MONTHS INVOLVING *EXPLOSIVES* AND *INCENDIARY DEVICES* DEPLOYED AGAINST THE PEOPLE OF TOKYO.

MULTIPLE REPORTS PLACE *RORI* AND A GROUP OF OTHER *ANARCHISTS* AT EACH LOCATION.

YOU CAN'T BE *SERIOUS!* SHE-SHE'S JUST A *CHILD!*

EXACTLY. THAT'S WHY WE BELIEVE SHE MAY BE RECEIVING ORDERS FROM A *LARGER ORGANIZATION.* POSSIBLY ONE OF *FOREIGN* ORIGIN...

SO YOU THINK I'M SUM KINDA FUCKIN' *TERRORIST* THEN?

PERHAPS. PERHAPS NOT.

UNTIL WE CAN DETERMINE YOUR *INNOCENCE* OR VERIFY HER *LOCATION,* YOU WILL BE DETAINED HERE IN *IMMIGRATION DETENTION.*

DO YOU KNOW *WHERE* SHE IS?

DO YOU HAVE ANY WAY TO CONTACT HER?

IF I DID, DO YA THINK I'D JUMP ON A *FUCKIN' PLANE* AN' COME ROUND *HERE?*

VERY WELL.

I'LL RETURN WHEN I HAVE MORE *INFORMATION...*

FWUMP

[DADDY'S LITTLE GIRL...*]

*TRANSLATED FROM IRISH.

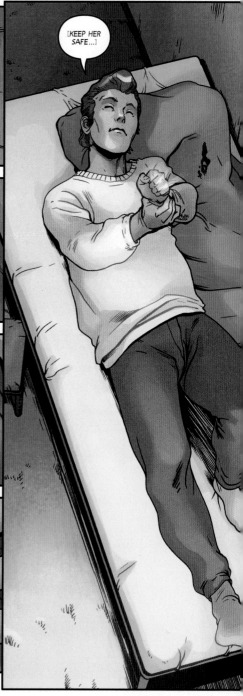

[KEEP HER SAFE...]

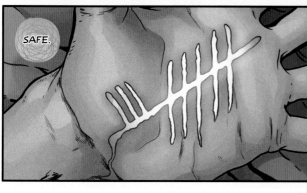

SAFE.

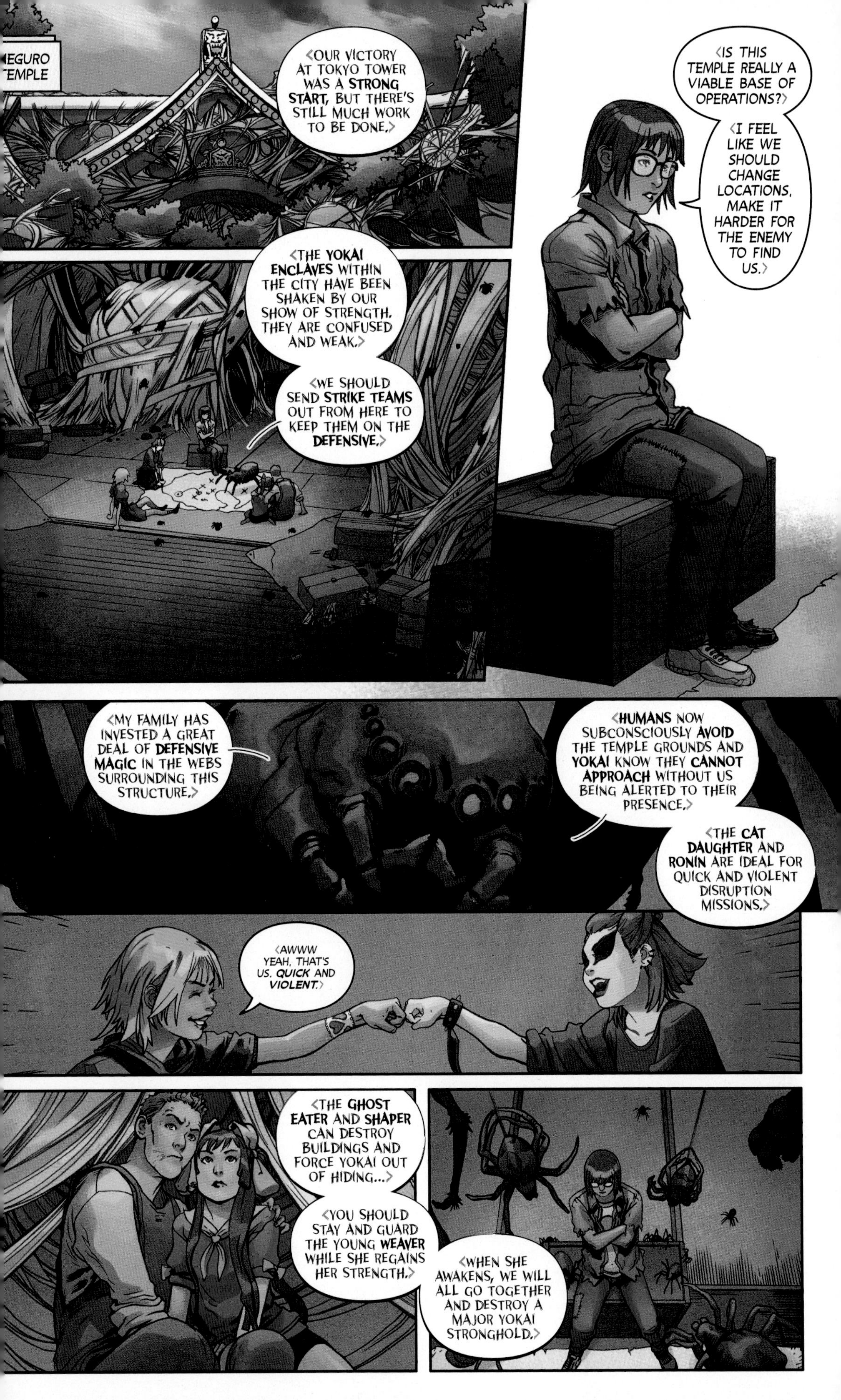
MEGURO TEMPLE
<OUR VICTORY AT TOKYO TOWER WAS A STRONG START, BUT THERE'S STILL MUCH WORK TO BE DONE.>
<IS THIS TEMPLE REALLY A VIABLE BASE OF OPERATIONS?>
<I FEEL LIKE WE SHOULD CHANGE LOCATIONS, MAKE IT HARDER FOR THE ENEMY TO FIND US.>
<THE YOKAI ENCLAVES WITHIN THE CITY HAVE BEEN SHAKEN BY OUR SHOW OF STRENGTH. THEY ARE CONFUSED AND WEAK.>
<WE SHOULD SEND STRIKE TEAMS OUT FROM HERE TO KEEP THEM ON THE DEFENSIVE.>
<MY FAMILY HAS INVESTED A GREAT DEAL OF DEFENSIVE MAGIC IN THE WEBS SURROUNDING THIS STRUCTURE.>
<HUMANS NOW SUBCONSCIOUSLY AVOID THE TEMPLE GROUNDS AND YOKAI KNOW THEY CANNOT APPROACH WITHOUT US BEING ALERTED TO THEIR PRESENCE.>
<THE CAT DAUGHTER AND RONIN ARE IDEAL FOR QUICK AND VIOLENT DISRUPTION MISSIONS.>
<AWWW YEAH, THAT'S US. QUICK AND VIOLENT.>
<THE GHOST EATER AND SHAPER CAN DESTROY BUILDINGS AND FORCE YOKAI OUT OF HIDING...>
<YOU SHOULD STAY AND GUARD THE YOUNG WEAVER WHILE SHE REGAINS HER STRENGTH.>
<WHEN SHE AWAKENS, WE WILL ALL GO TOGETHER AND DESTROY A MAJOR YOKAI STRONGHOLD.>

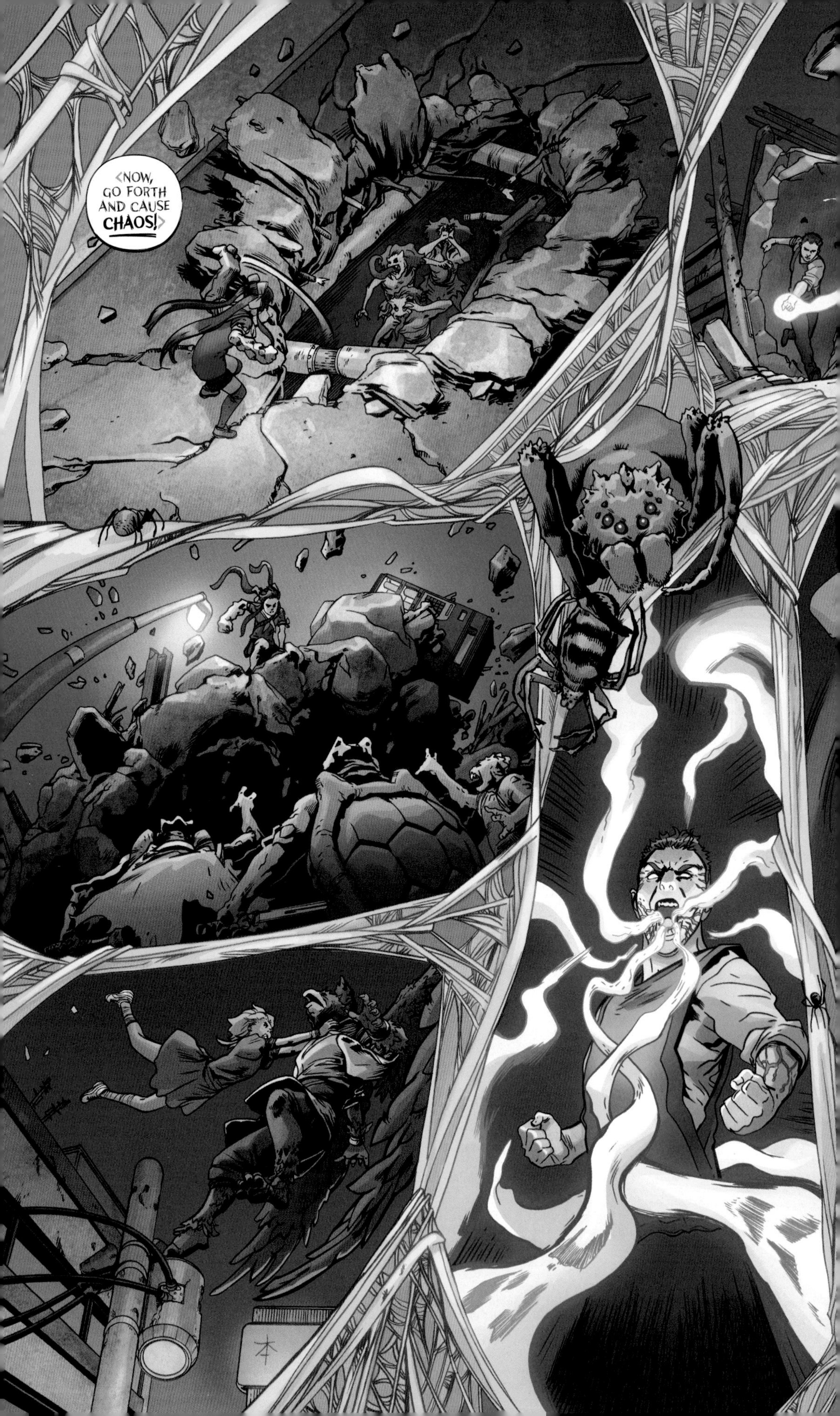
<NOW, GO FORTH AND CAUSE CHAOS!>
本

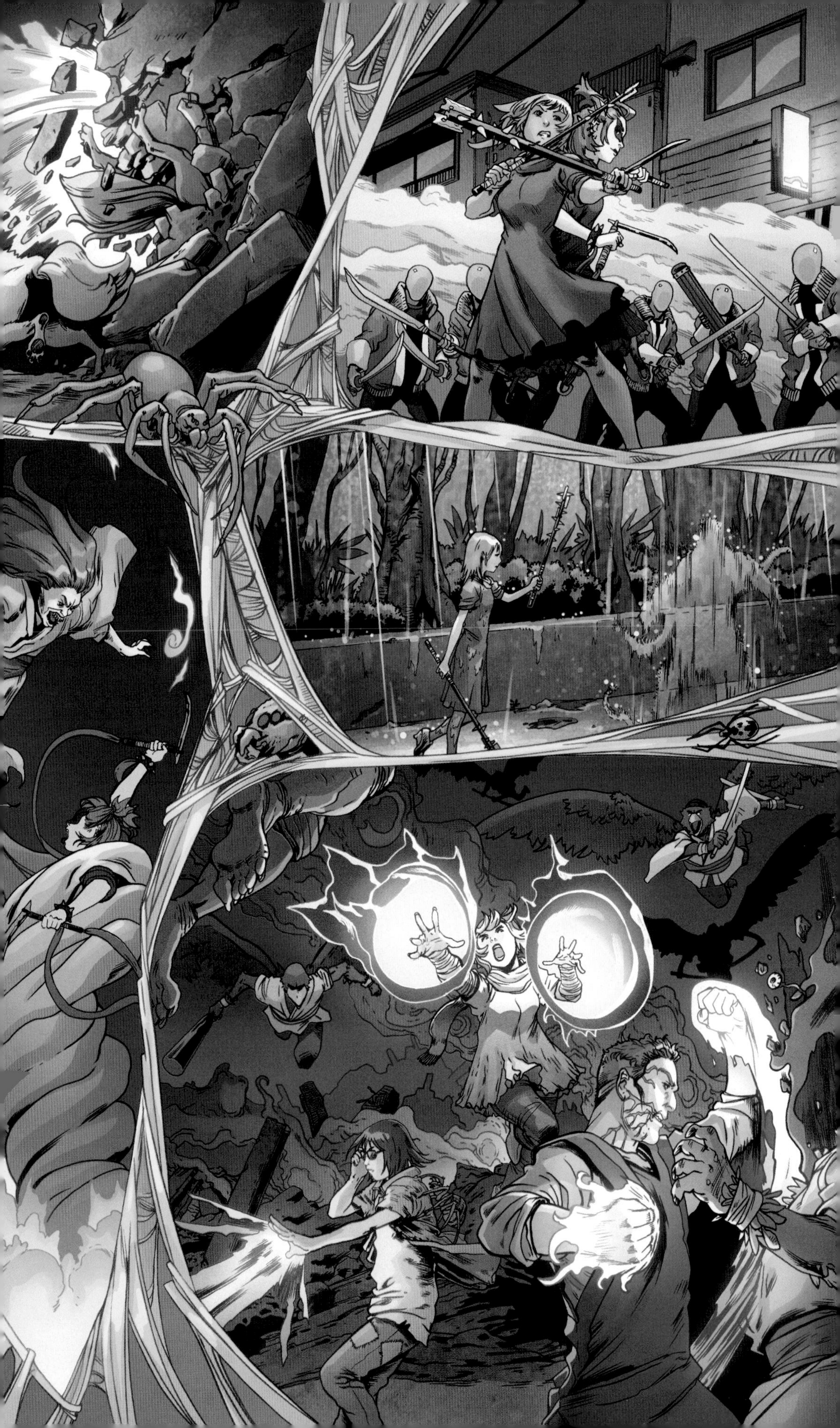

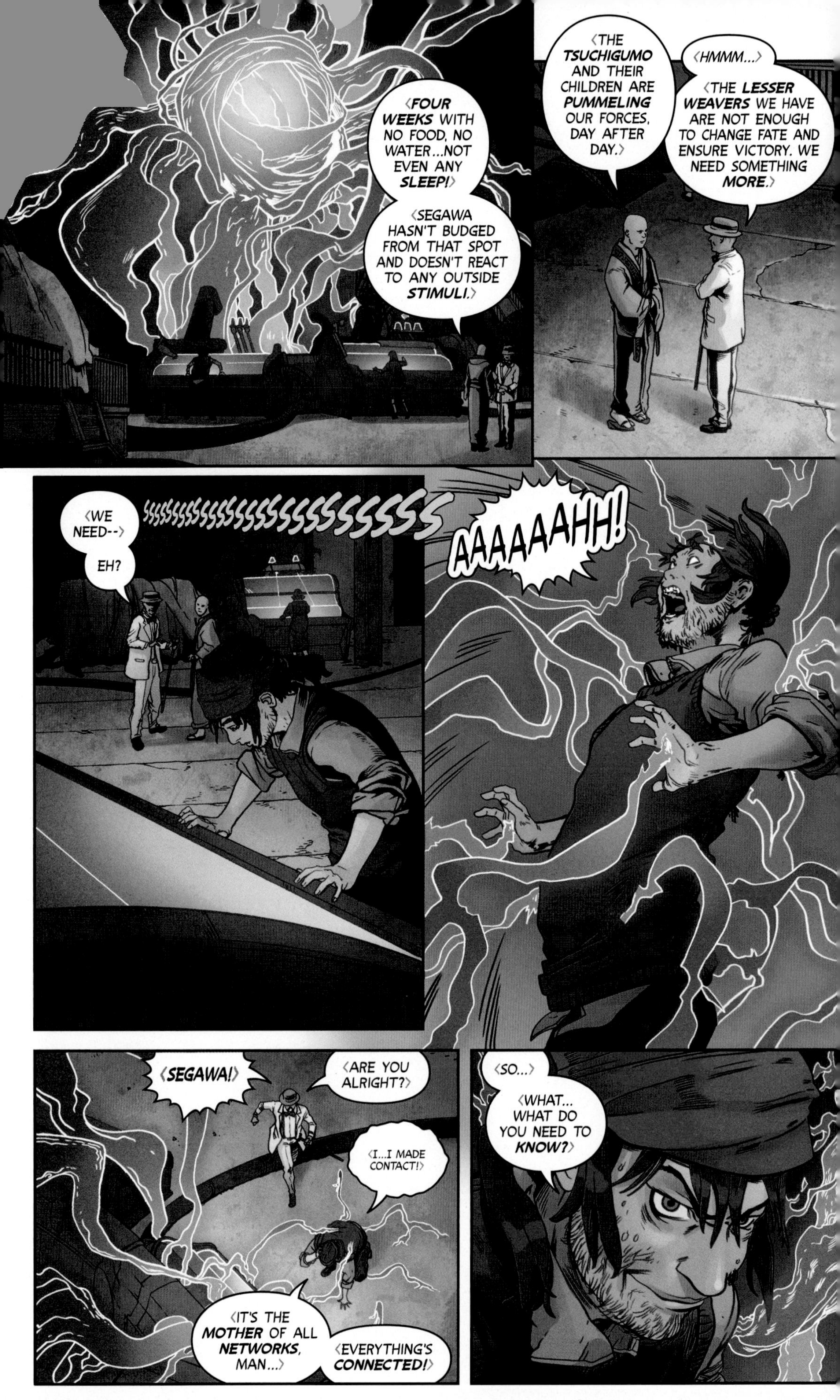
‹FOUR WEEKS WITH NO FOOD, NO WATER...NOT EVEN ANY SLEEP!›
‹SEGAWA HASN'T BUDGED FROM THAT SPOT AND DOESN'T REACT TO ANY OUTSIDE STIMULI.›
‹THE TSUCHIGUMO AND THEIR CHILDREN ARE PUMMELING OUR FORCES, DAY AFTER DAY.›
‹HMMM...›
‹THE LESSER WEAVERS WE HAVE ARE NOT ENOUGH TO CHANGE FATE AND ENSURE VICTORY. WE NEED SOMETHING MORE.›
‹WE NEED--›
EH?
SSSSSSSSSSSSSSSSSSSSSSSSSS
AAAAAAHH!
‹SEGAWA!›
‹ARE YOU ALRIGHT?›
‹I...I MADE CONTACT!›
‹IT'S THE MOTHER OF ALL NETWORKS, MAN...›
‹EVERYTHING'S CONNECTED!›
‹SO...›
‹WHAT... WHAT DO YOU NEED TO KNOW?›

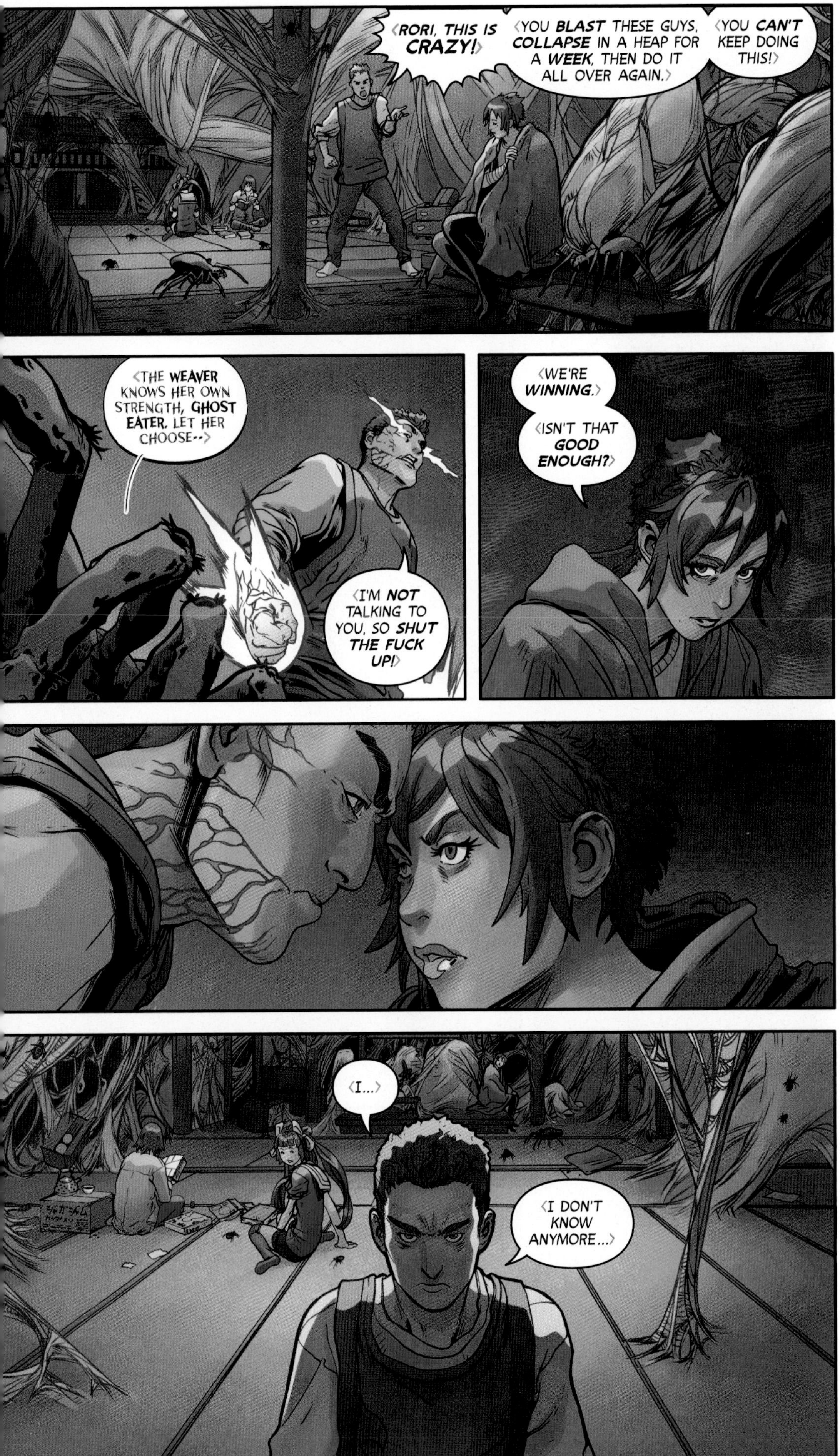
〈RORI, THIS IS CRAZY!〉
〈YOU BLAST THESE GUYS, COLLAPSE IN A HEAP FOR A WEEK, THEN DO IT ALL OVER AGAIN.〉
〈YOU CAN'T KEEP DOING THIS!〉
〈THE WEAVER KNOWS HER OWN STRENGTH, GHOST EATER. LET HER CHOOSE--〉
〈I'M NOT TALKING TO YOU, SO SHUT THE FUCK UP!〉
〈WE'RE WINNING.〉
〈ISN'T THAT GOOD ENOUGH?〉
〈I...〉
〈I DON'T KNOW ANYMORE...〉

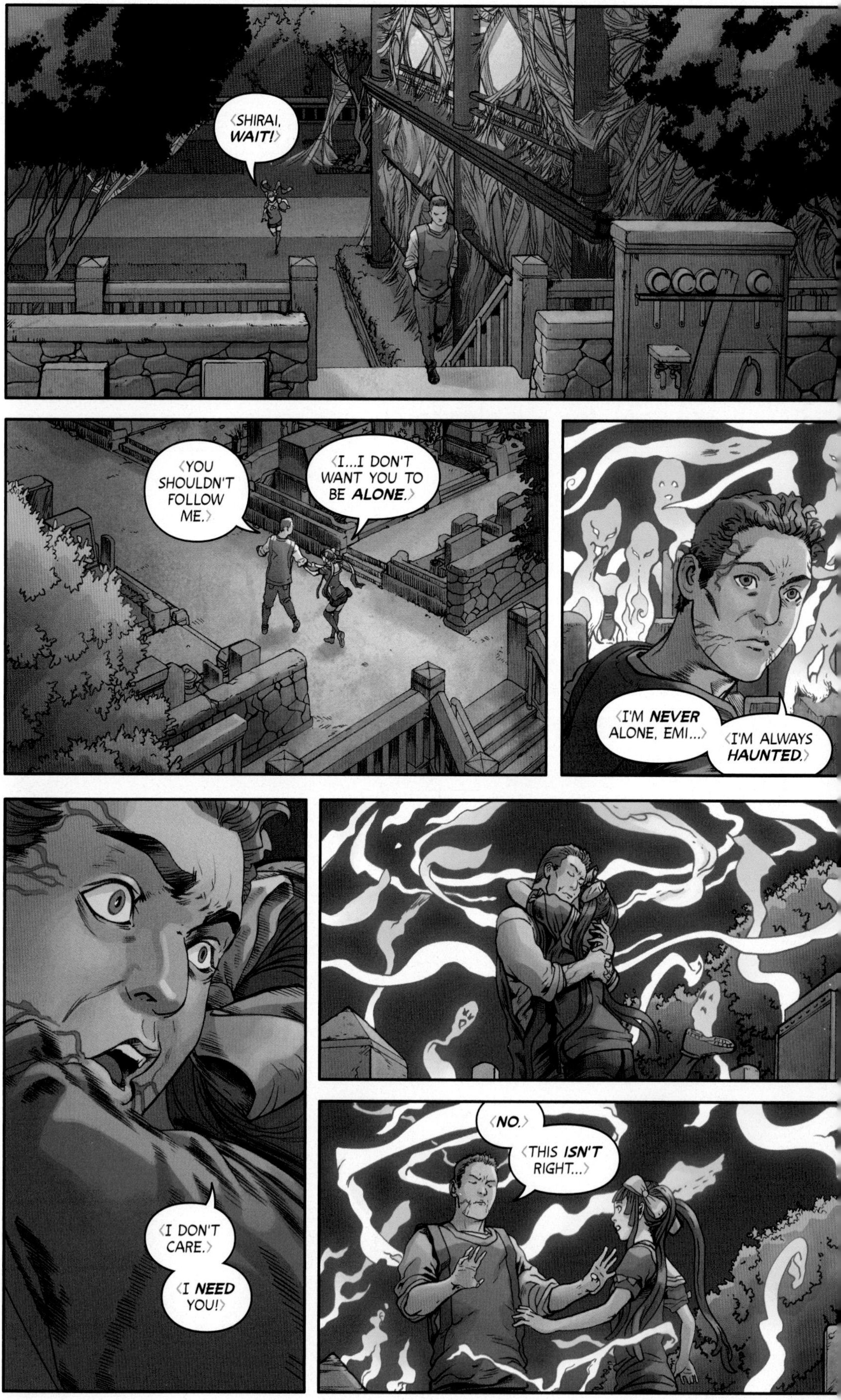

‹SHIRAI, **WAIT!**›
‹YOU SHOULDN'T FOLLOW ME.›
‹I...I DON'T WANT YOU TO BE **ALONE**.›
‹I'M **NEVER** ALONE, EMI...›
‹I'M ALWAYS **HAUNTED**.›
‹I DON'T CARE.›
‹I **NEED** YOU!›
‹**NO**.›
‹THIS **ISN'T** RIGHT...›

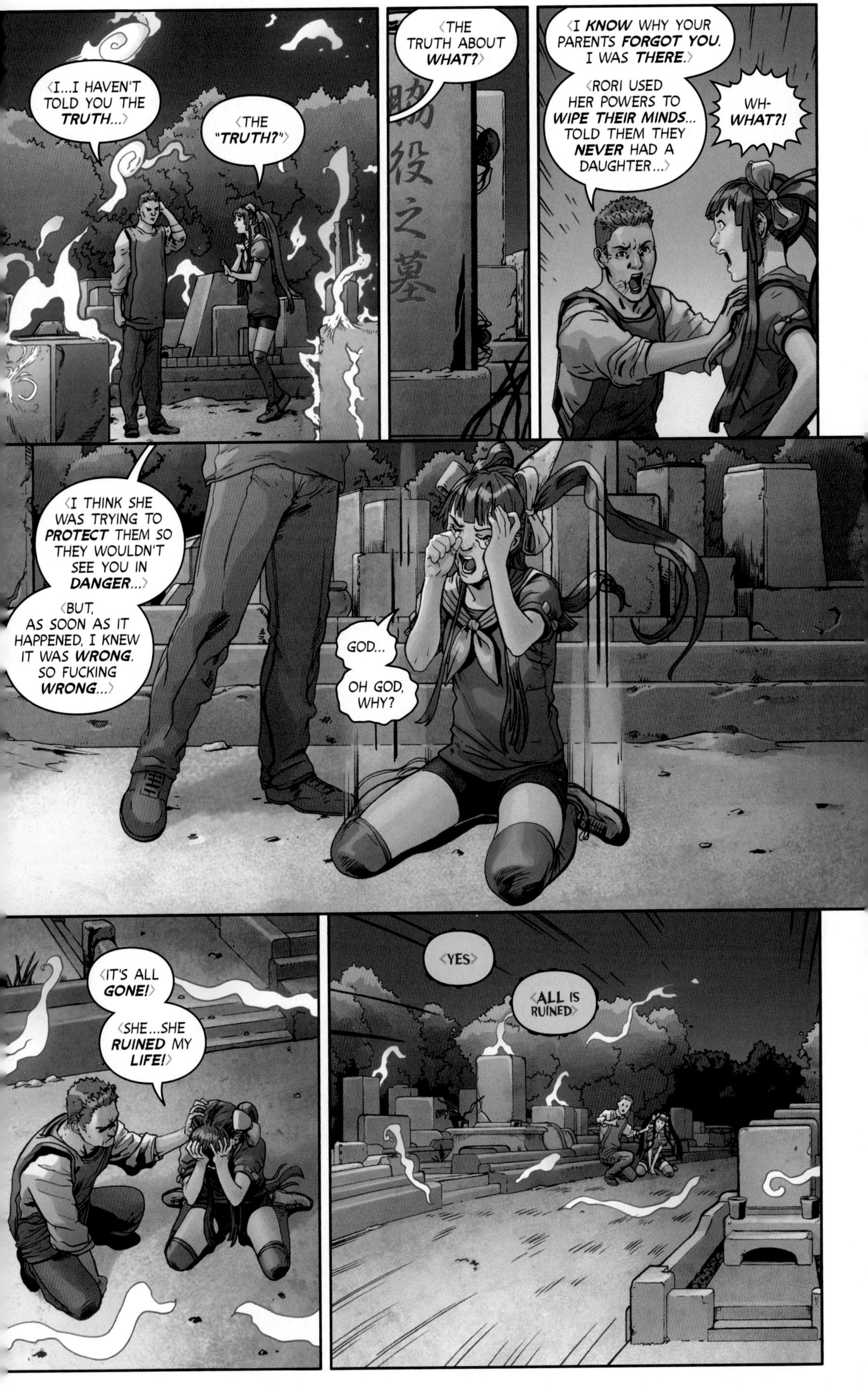
‹I...I HAVEN'T TOLD YOU THE TRUTH...›
‹THE "TRUTH?"›
‹THE TRUTH ABOUT WHAT?›
‹I KNOW WHY YOUR PARENTS FORGOT YOU. I WAS THERE.›
‹RORI USED HER POWERS TO WIPE THEIR MINDS... TOLD THEM THEY NEVER HAD A DAUGHTER...›
WH- WHAT?!
‹I THINK SHE WAS TRYING TO PROTECT THEM SO THEY WOULDN'T SEE YOU IN DANGER...›
‹BUT, AS SOON AS IT HAPPENED, I KNEW IT WAS WRONG, SO FUCKING WRONG...›
GOD...
OH GOD, WHY?
‹IT'S ALL GONE!›
‹SHE...SHE RUINED MY LIFE!›
‹YES›
‹ALL IS RUINED›

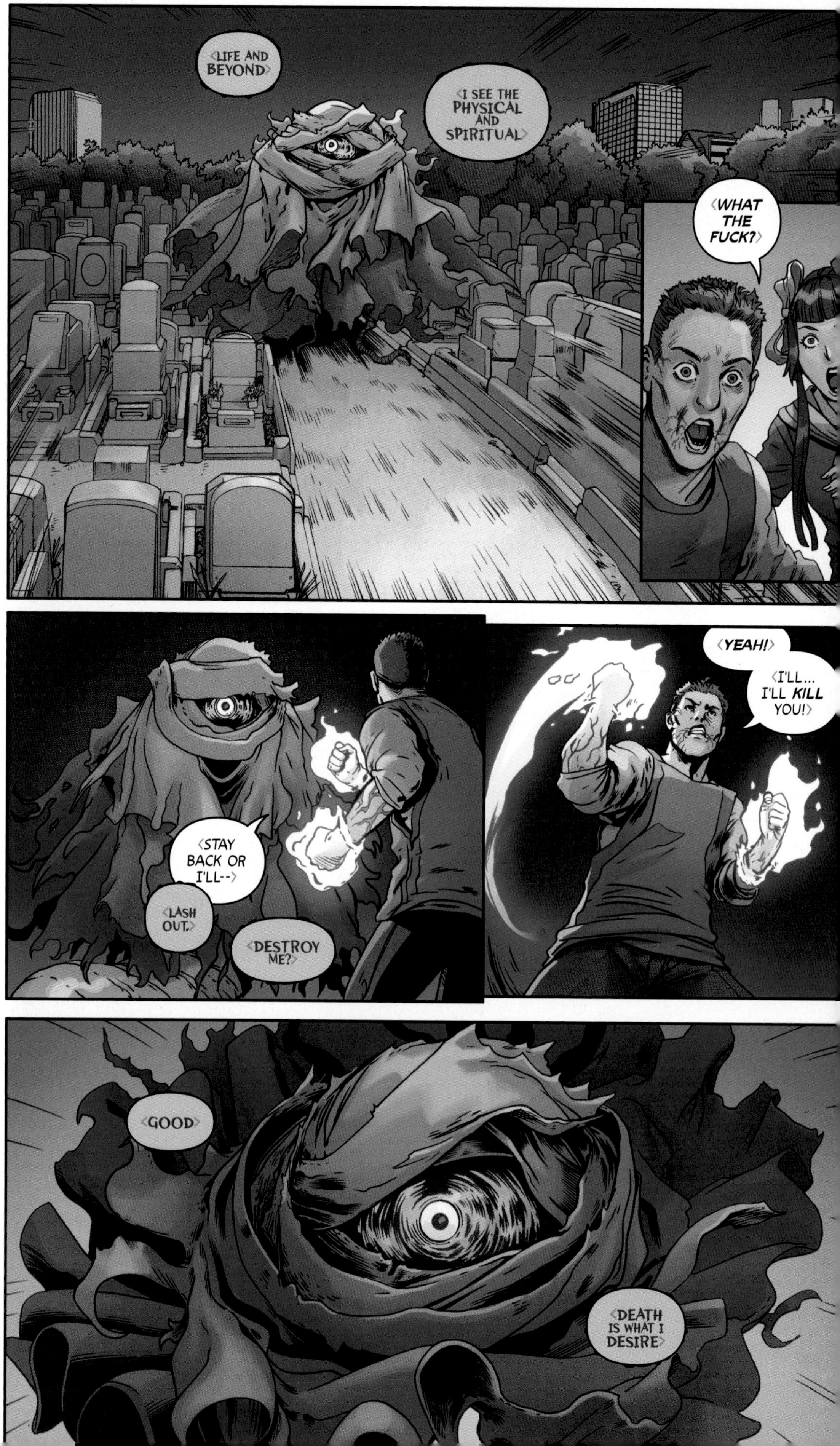
<LIFE AND BEYOND>
<I SEE THE PHYSICAL AND SPIRITUAL>
<WHAT THE FUCK?>
<STAY BACK OR I'LL-->
<LASH OUT.>
<DESTROY ME?>
<YEAH!>
<I'LL... I'LL KILL YOU!>
<GOOD>
<DEATH IS WHAT I DESIRE>

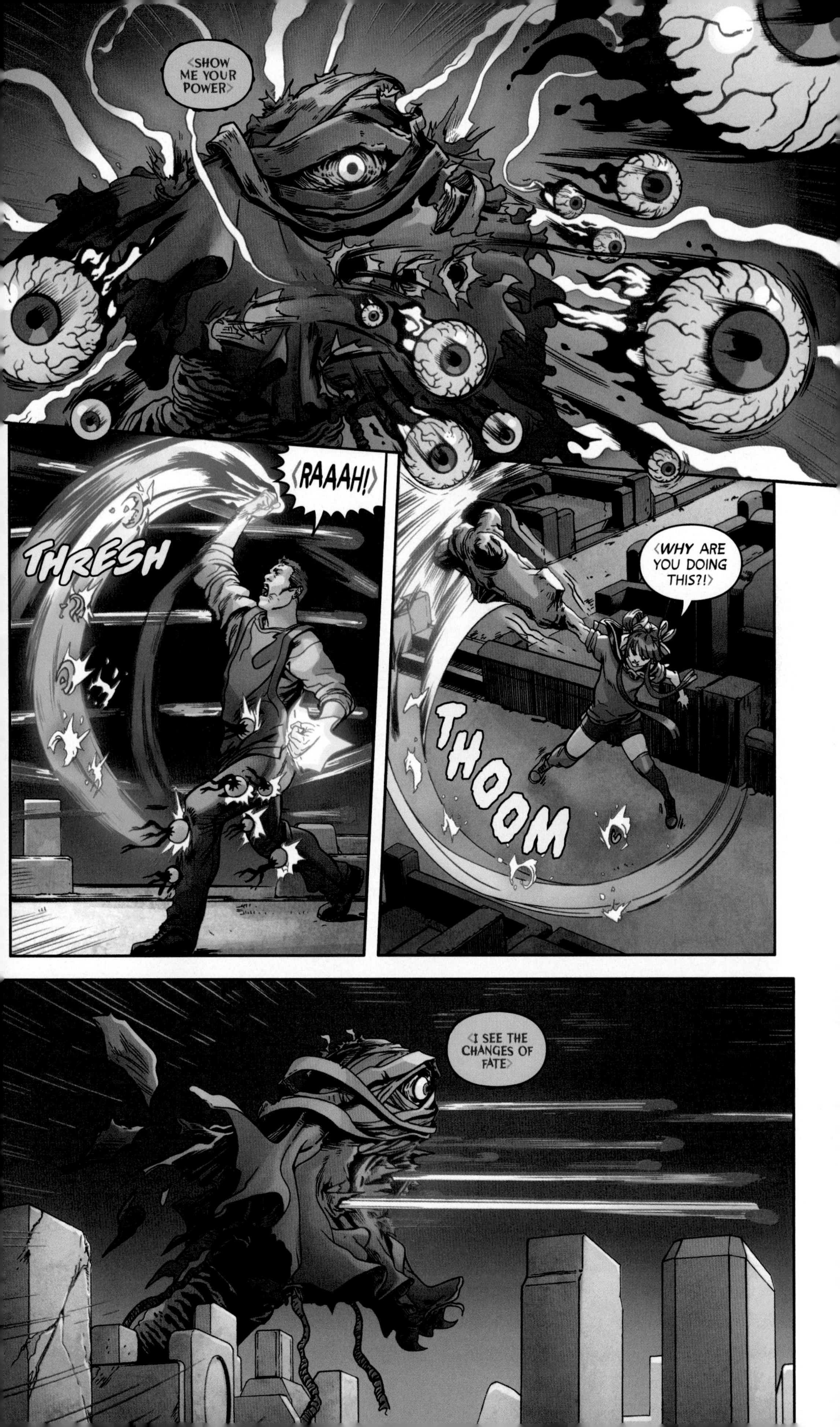
<SHOW ME YOUR POWER>
<RAAAH!>
THRESH
<WHY ARE YOU DOING THIS?!>
THOOM
<I SEE THE CHANGES OF FATE>

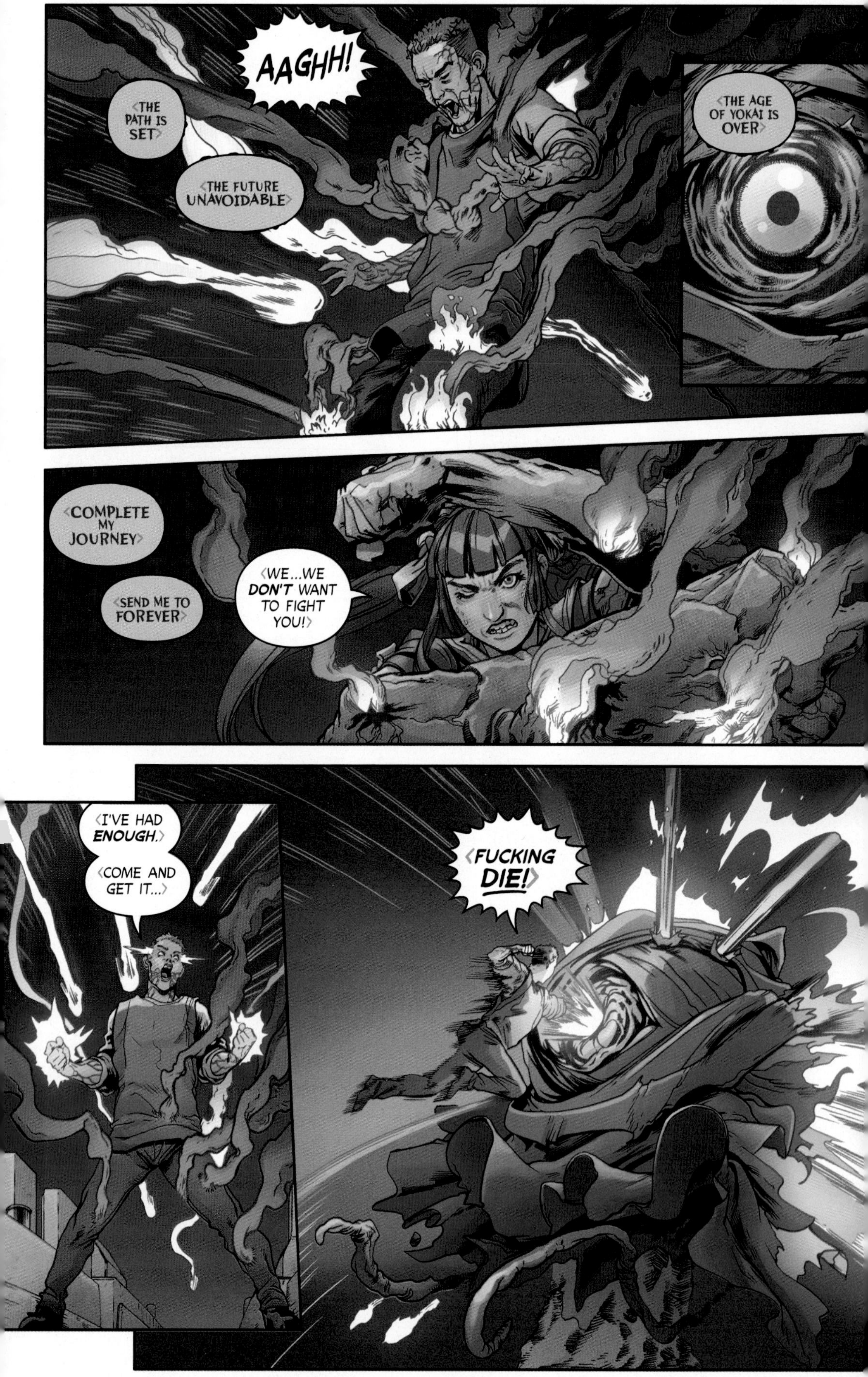
AAGHH!
‹THE PATH IS SET›
‹THE FUTURE UNAVOIDABLE›
‹THE AGE OF YOKAI IS OVER›
‹COMPLETE MY JOURNEY›
‹SEND ME TO FOREVER›
‹WE...WE DON'T WANT TO FIGHT YOU!›
‹I'VE HAD ENOUGH.›
‹COME AND GET IT...›
‹FUCKING DIE!›

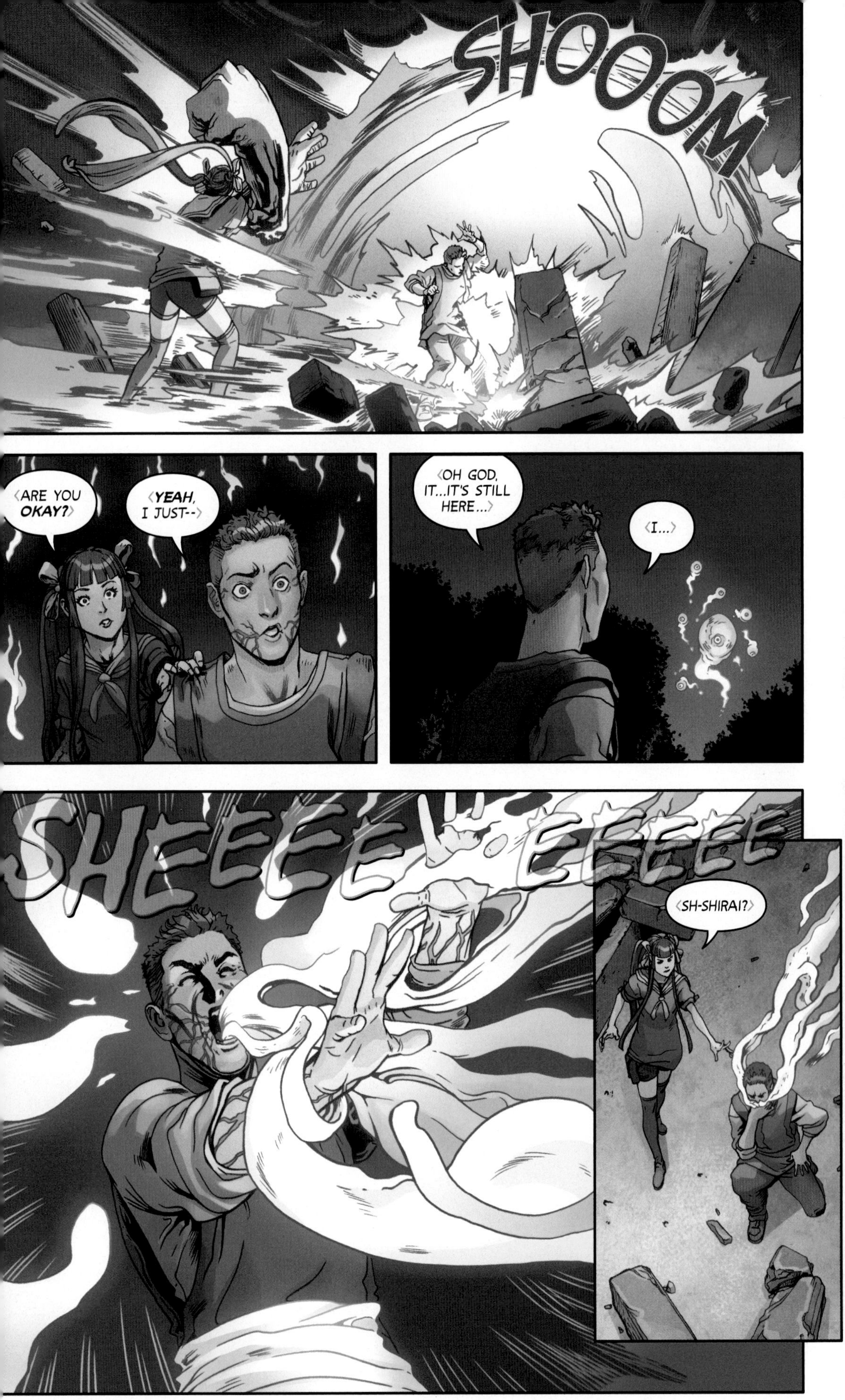
SHOOOM
ARE YOU OKAY?
YEAH, I JUST--
OH GOD, IT...IT'S STILL HERE...
I...
SHEEEE EEEEE
SH-SHIRAI?

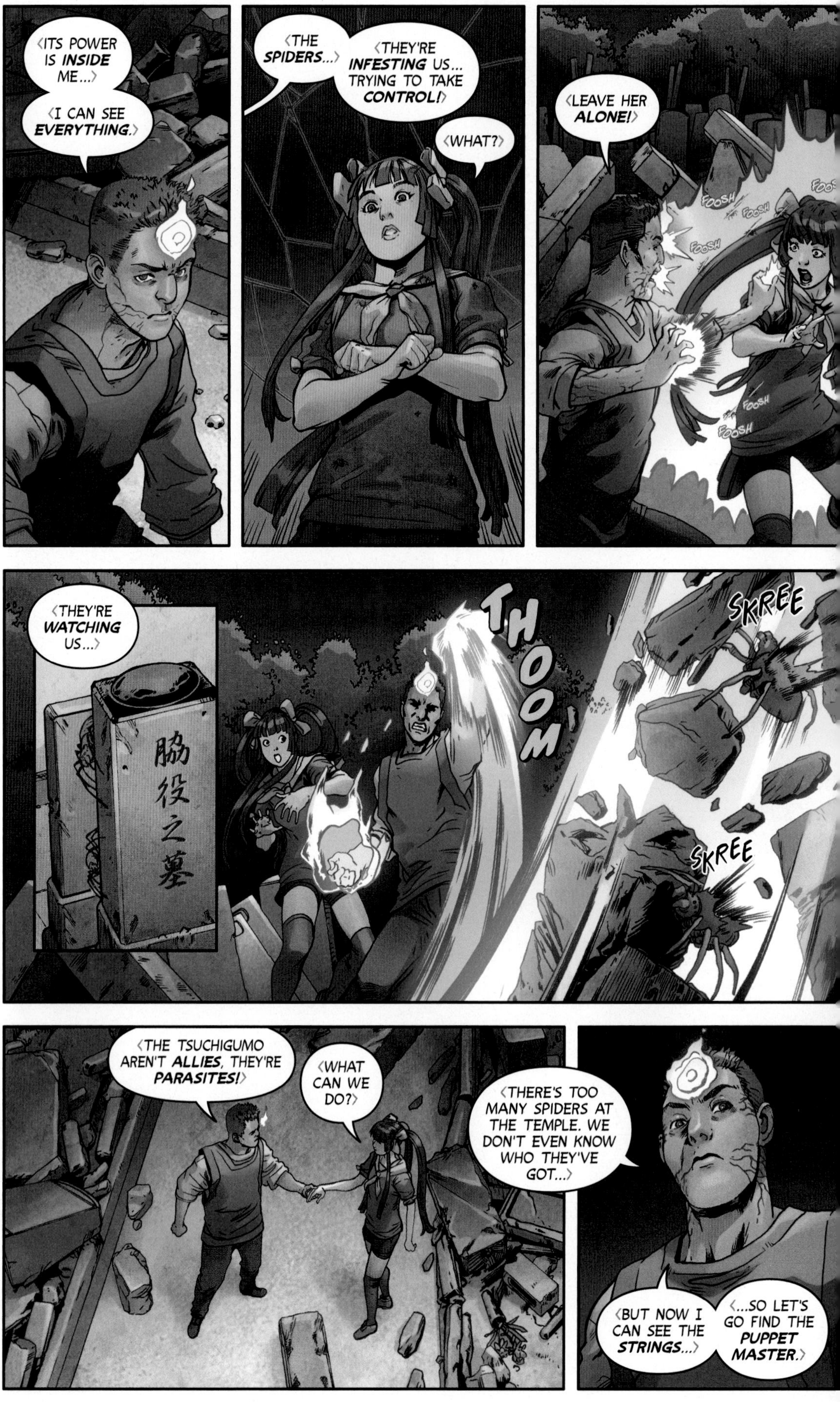

‹ITS POWER IS INSIDE ME...›
‹I CAN SEE EVERYTHING.›
‹THE SPIDERS...›
‹THEY'RE INFESTING US... TRYING TO TAKE CONTROL!›
‹WHAT?›
‹LEAVE HER ALONE!›
FOOSH
FOOSH
FOOSH
FOOSH
FOOSH
FOOSH
‹THEY'RE WATCHING US...›
脇役之墓
THOOM
SKREE
SKREE
‹THE TSUCHIGUMO AREN'T ALLIES, THEY'RE PARASITES!›
‹WHAT CAN WE DO?›
‹THERE'S TOO MANY SPIDERS AT THE TEMPLE. WE DON'T EVEN KNOW WHO THEY'VE GOT...›
‹BUT NOW I CAN SEE THE STRINGS...›
‹...SO LET'S GO FIND THE PUPPET MASTER.›

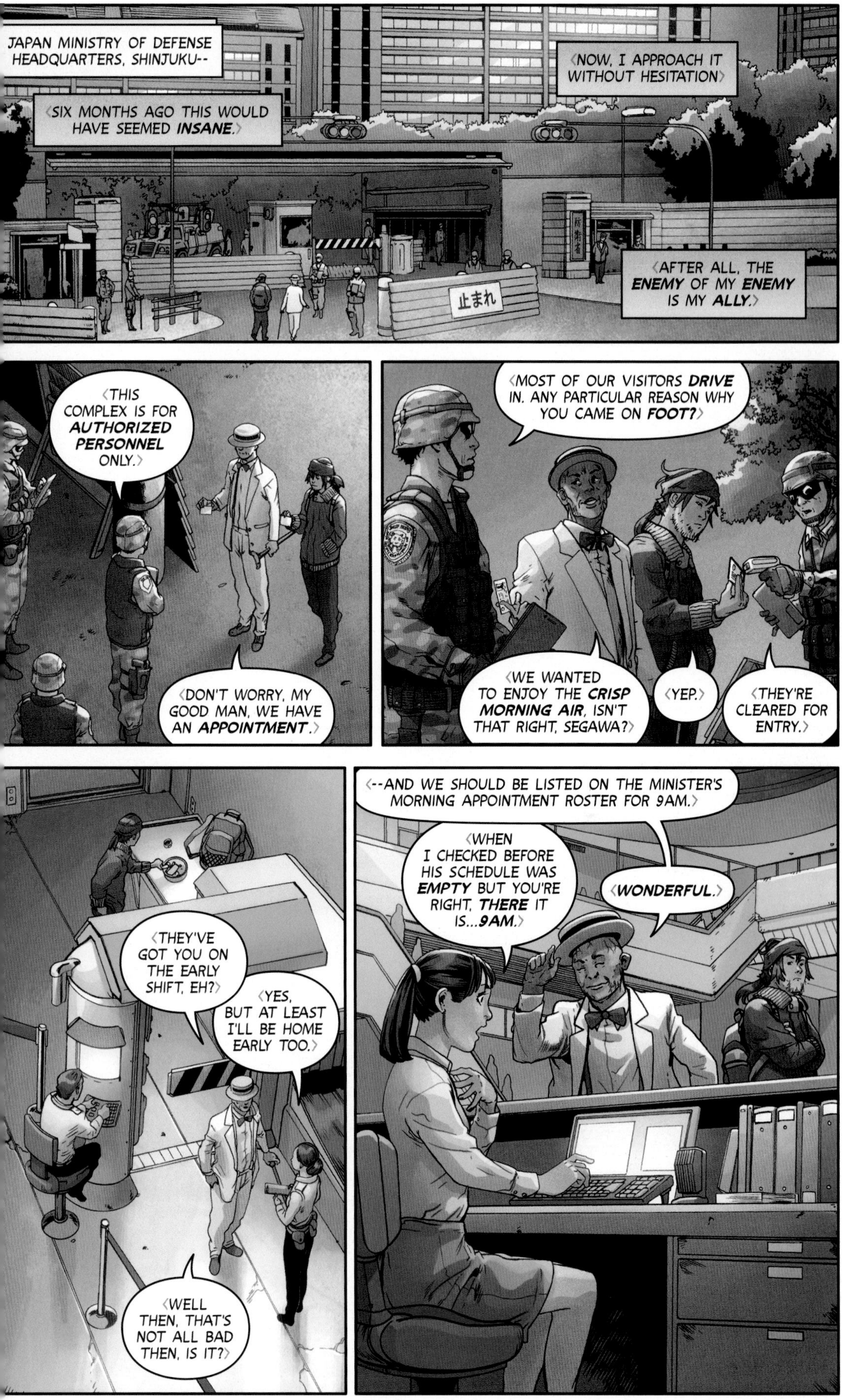
JAPAN MINISTRY OF DEFENSE HEADQUARTERS, SHINJUKU--
‹SIX MONTHS AGO THIS WOULD HAVE SEEMED INSANE.›
‹NOW, I APPROACH IT WITHOUT HESITATION›
止まれ
‹AFTER ALL, THE ENEMY OF MY ENEMY IS MY ALLY.›
‹THIS COMPLEX IS FOR AUTHORIZED PERSONNEL ONLY.›
‹DON'T WORRY, MY GOOD MAN, WE HAVE AN APPOINTMENT.›
‹MOST OF OUR VISITORS DRIVE IN. ANY PARTICULAR REASON WHY YOU CAME ON FOOT?›
‹WE WANTED TO ENJOY THE CRISP MORNING AIR, ISN'T THAT RIGHT, SEGAWA?›
‹YEP.›
‹THEY'RE CLEARED FOR ENTRY.›
‹THEY'VE GOT YOU ON THE EARLY SHIFT, EH?›
‹YES, BUT AT LEAST I'LL BE HOME EARLY TOO.›
‹WELL THEN, THAT'S NOT ALL BAD THEN, IS IT?›
‹--AND WE SHOULD BE LISTED ON THE MINISTER'S MORNING APPOINTMENT ROSTER FOR 9AM.›
‹WHEN I CHECKED BEFORE HIS SCHEDULE WAS EMPTY BUT YOU'RE RIGHT, THERE IT IS...9AM.›
‹WONDERFUL.›

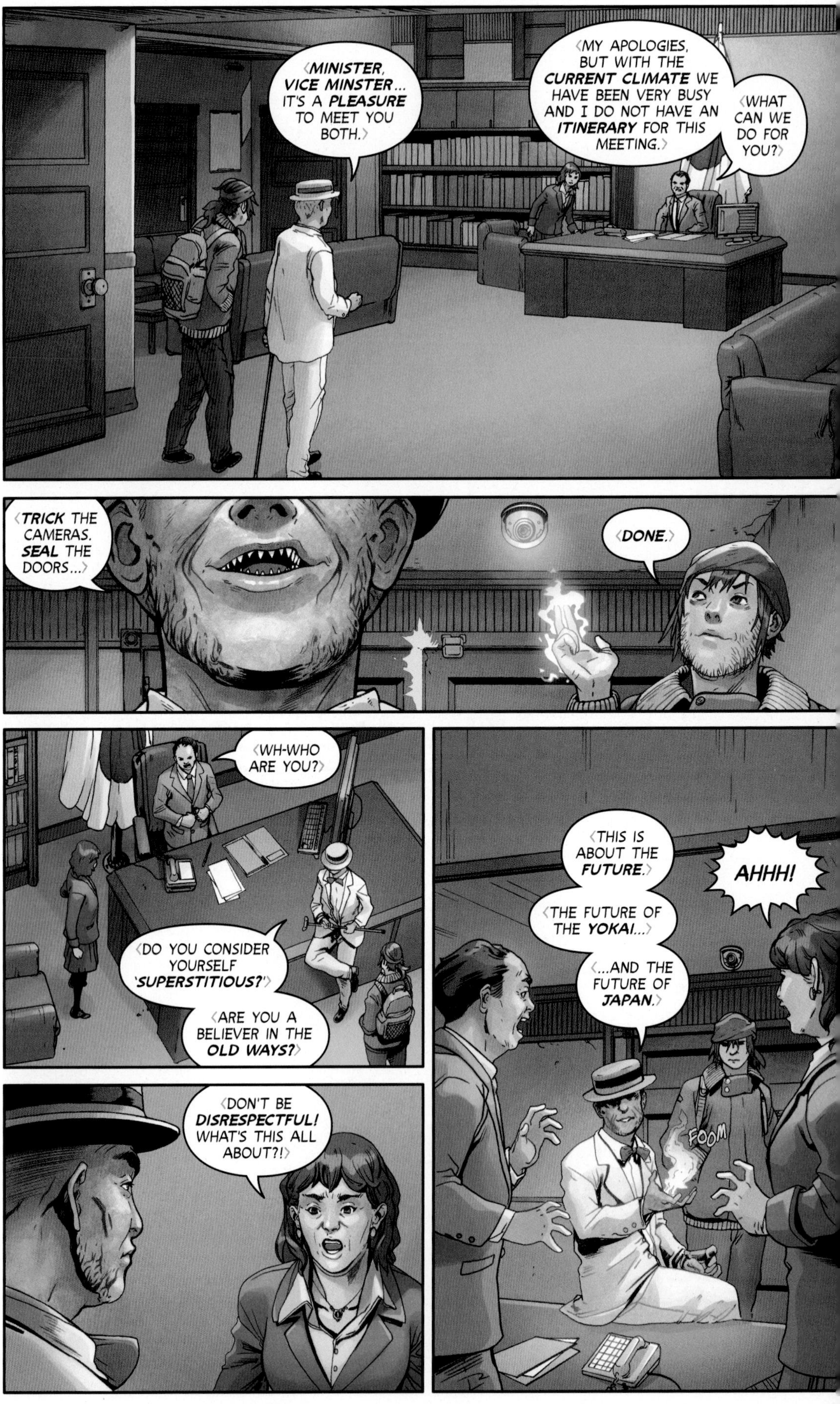

‹MINISTER, VICE MINSTER... IT'S A PLEASURE TO MEET YOU BOTH.›
‹MY APOLOGIES, BUT WITH THE CURRENT CLIMATE WE HAVE BEEN VERY BUSY AND I DO NOT HAVE AN ITINERARY FOR THIS MEETING.›
‹WHAT CAN WE DO FOR YOU?›
‹TRICK THE CAMERAS. SEAL THE DOORS...›
‹DONE.›
‹WH-WHO ARE YOU?›
‹DO YOU CONSIDER YOURSELF 'SUPERSTITIOUS?'›
‹ARE YOU A BELIEVER IN THE OLD WAYS?›
‹DON'T BE DISRESPECTFUL! WHAT'S THIS ALL ABOUT?!›
‹THIS IS ABOUT THE FUTURE.›
‹THE FUTURE OF THE YOKAI...›
‹...AND THE FUTURE OF JAPAN.›
AHHH!
FOOM

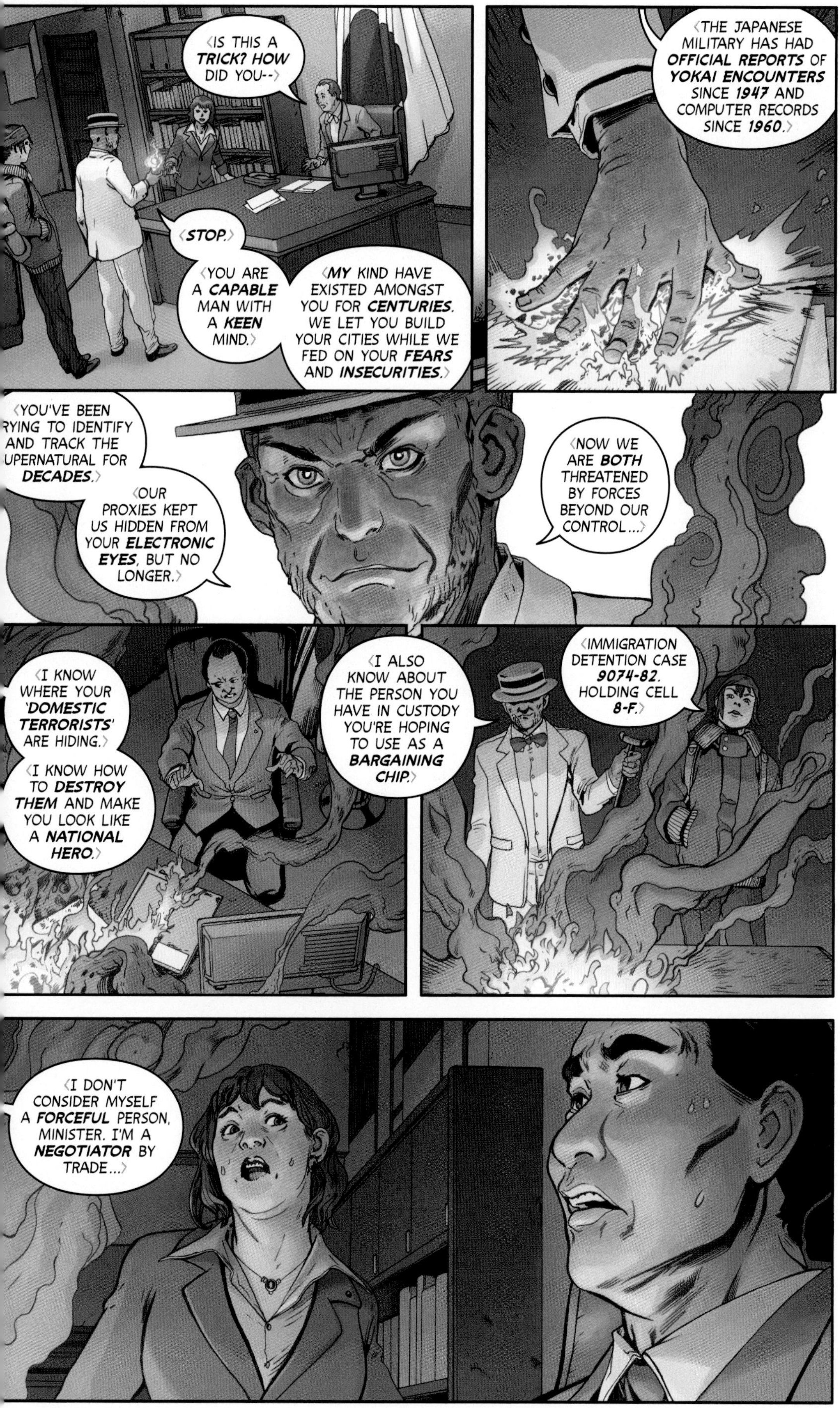

‹IS THIS A TRICK? HOW DID YOU--›
‹STOP.›
‹YOU ARE A CAPABLE MAN WITH A KEEN MIND.›
‹MY KIND HAVE EXISTED AMONGST YOU FOR CENTURIES. WE LET YOU BUILD YOUR CITIES WHILE WE FED ON YOUR FEARS AND INSECURITIES.›
‹THE JAPANESE MILITARY HAS HAD OFFICIAL REPORTS OF YOKAI ENCOUNTERS SINCE 1947 AND COMPUTER RECORDS SINCE 1960.›
‹YOU'VE BEEN RYING TO IDENTIFY AND TRACK THE UPERNATURAL FOR DECADES.›
‹OUR PROXIES KEPT US HIDDEN FROM YOUR ELECTRONIC EYES, BUT NO LONGER.›
‹NOW WE ARE BOTH THREATENED BY FORCES BEYOND OUR CONTROL...›
‹I KNOW WHERE YOUR 'DOMESTIC TERRORISTS' ARE HIDING.›
‹I KNOW HOW TO DESTROY THEM AND MAKE YOU LOOK LIKE A NATIONAL HERO.›
‹I ALSO KNOW ABOUT THE PERSON YOU HAVE IN CUSTODY YOU'RE HOPING TO USE AS A BARGAINING CHIP.›
‹IMMIGRATION DETENTION CASE 9074-82. HOLDING CELL 8-F.›
‹I DON'T CONSIDER MYSELF A FORCEFUL PERSON, MINISTER. I'M A NEGOTIATOR BY TRADE...›

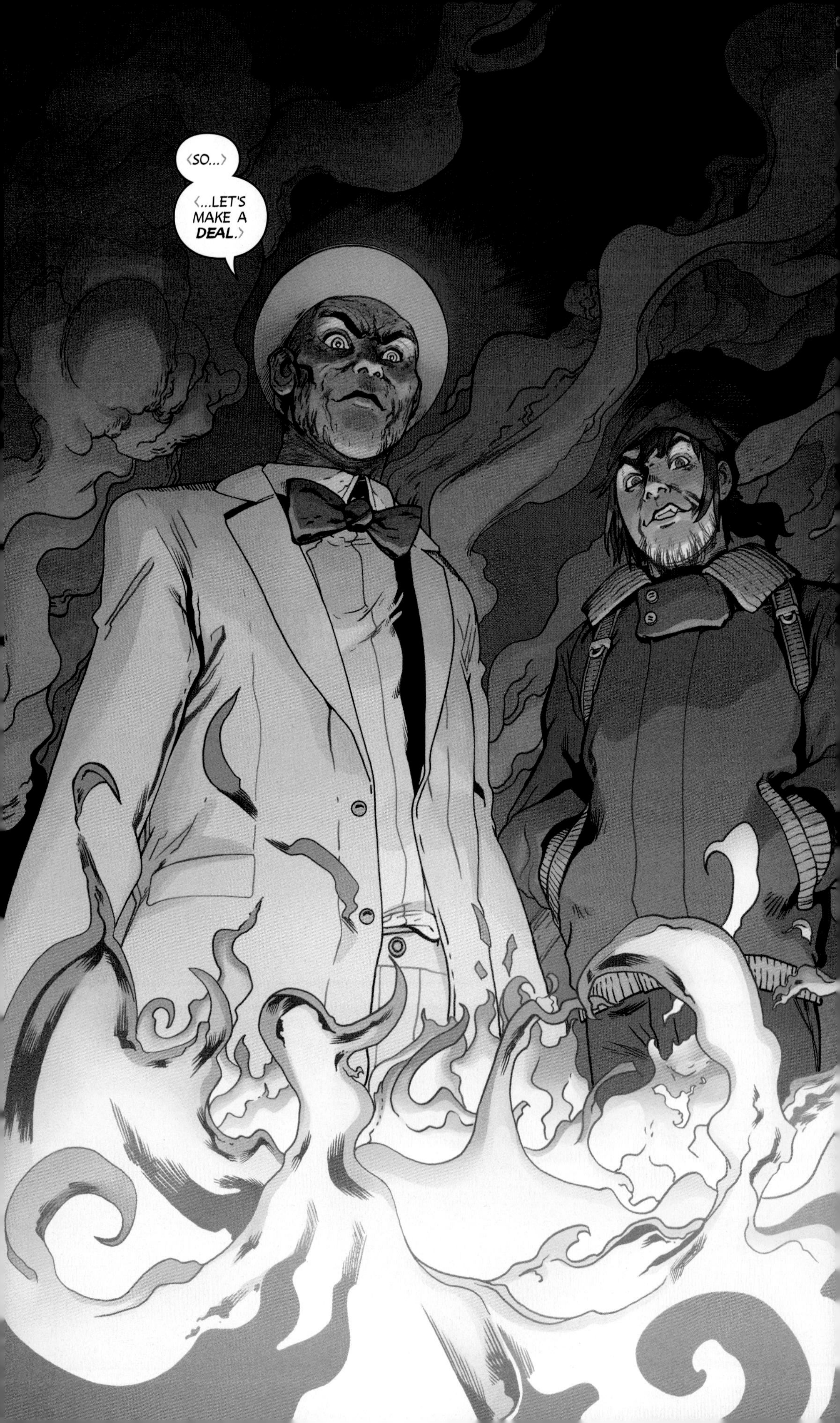
‹SO...›
‹...LET'S MAKE A DEAL.›

Chapter Fifteen

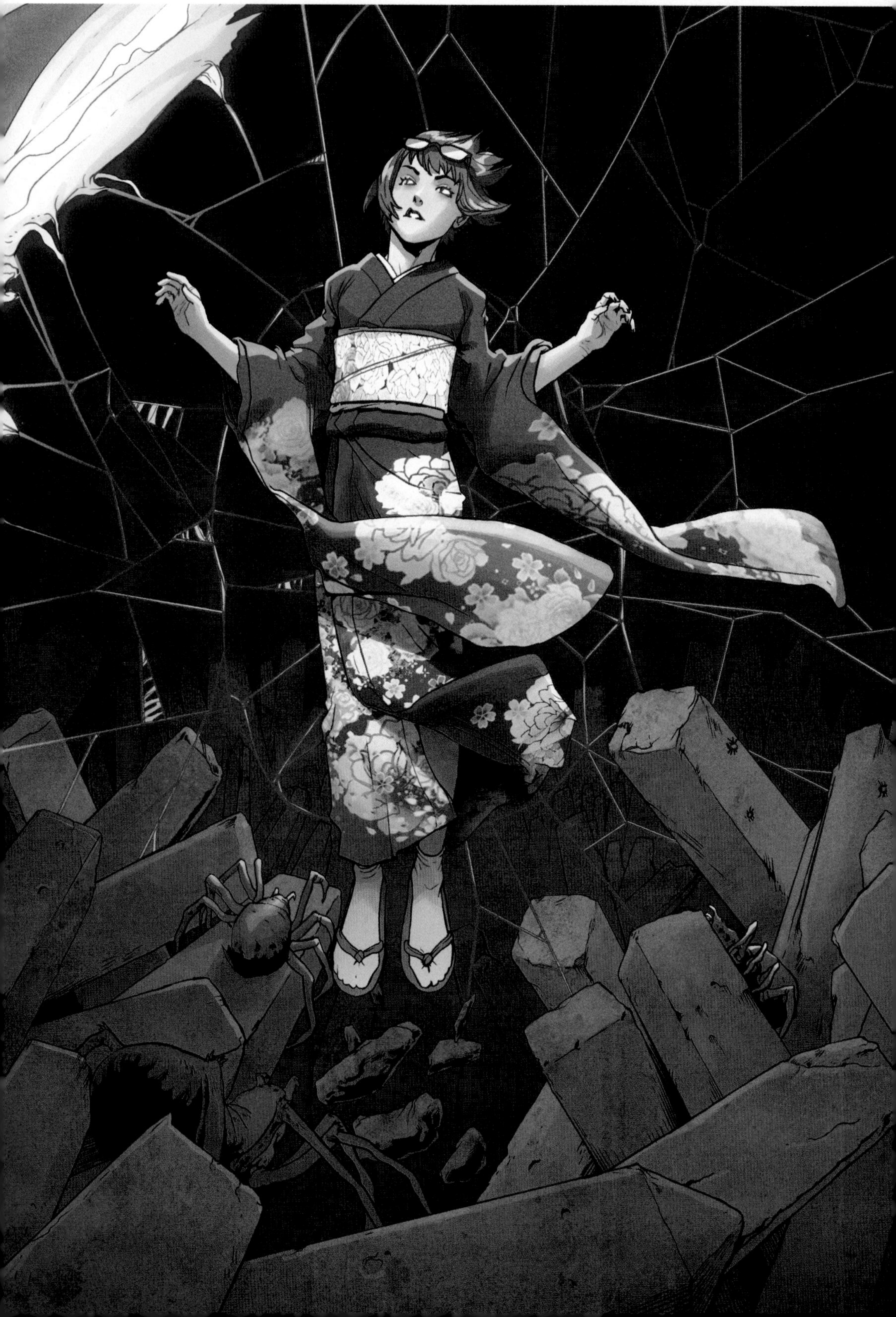

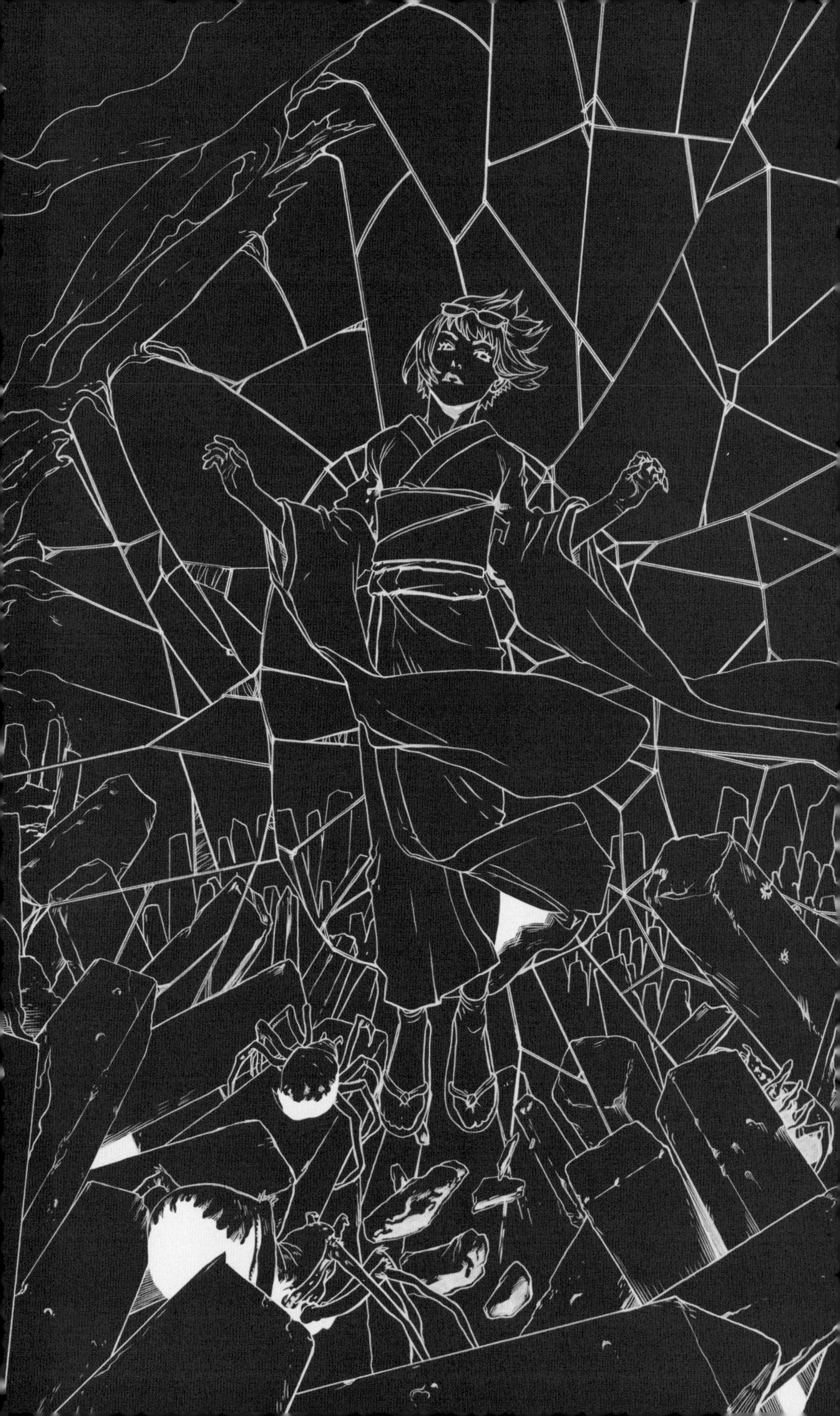

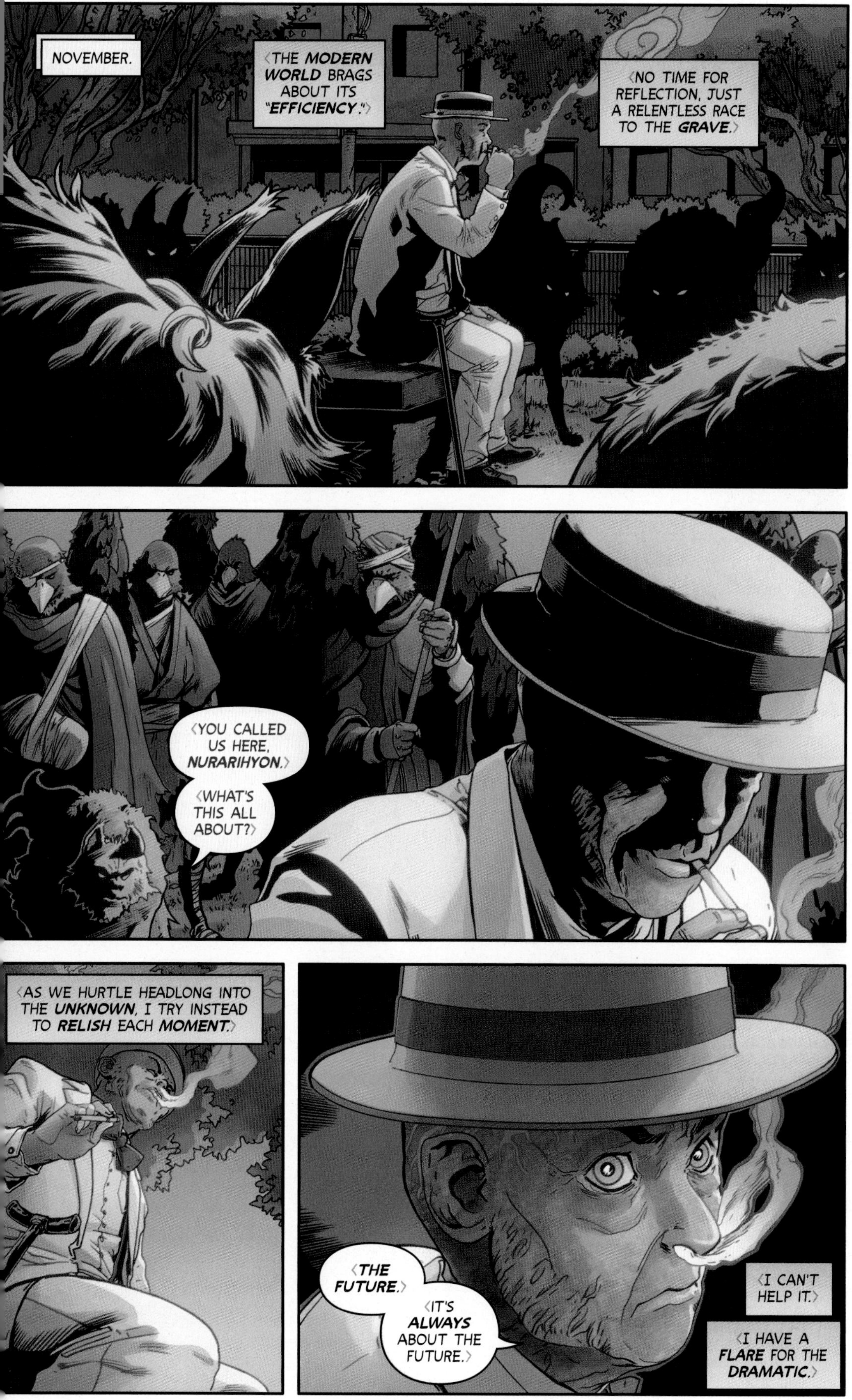
NOVEMBER.
‹THE ***MODERN WORLD*** BRAGS ABOUT ITS "***EFFICIENCY***."›
‹NO TIME FOR REFLECTION, JUST A RELENTLESS RACE TO THE ***GRAVE***.›
‹YOU CALLED US HERE, ***NURARIHYON***.›
‹WHAT'S THIS ALL ABOUT?›
‹AS WE HURTLE HEADLONG INTO THE ***UNKNOWN***, I TRY INSTEAD TO ***RELISH*** EACH ***MOMENT***.›
‹***THE FUTURE***.›
‹IT'S ***ALWAYS*** ABOUT THE FUTURE.›
‹I CAN'T HELP IT.›
‹I HAVE A ***FLARE*** FOR THE ***DRAMATIC***.›

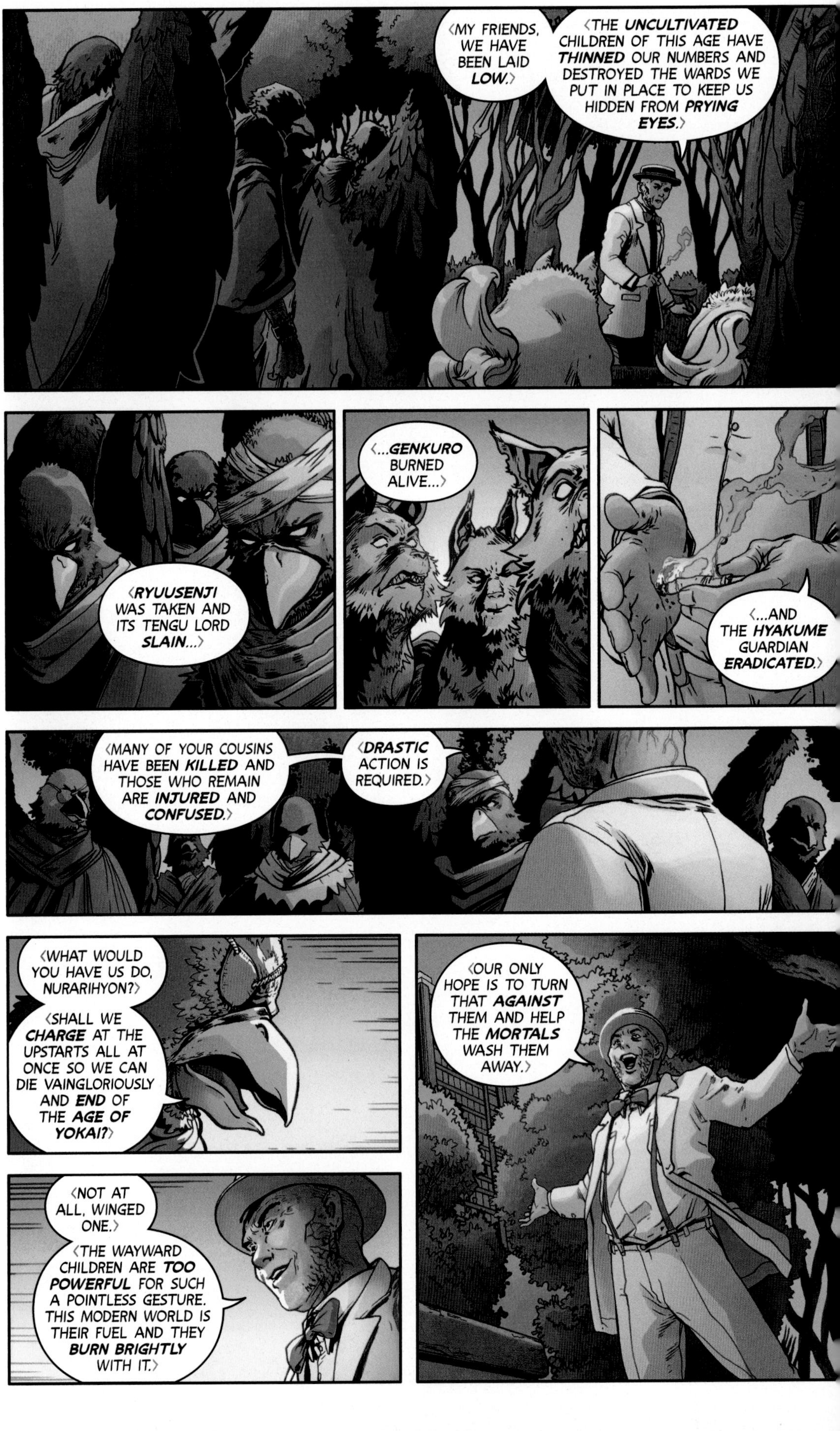
‹MY FRIENDS, WE HAVE BEEN LAID LOW.›
‹THE UNCULTIVATED CHILDREN OF THIS AGE HAVE THINNED OUR NUMBERS AND DESTROYED THE WARDS WE PUT IN PLACE TO KEEP US HIDDEN FROM PRYING EYES.›
‹RYUUSENJI WAS TAKEN AND ITS TENGU LORD SLAIN...›
‹...GENKURO BURNED ALIVE...›
‹...AND THE HYAKUME GUARDIAN ERADICATED.›
‹MANY OF YOUR COUSINS HAVE BEEN KILLED AND THOSE WHO REMAIN ARE INJURED AND CONFUSED.›
‹DRASTIC ACTION IS REQUIRED.›
‹WHAT WOULD YOU HAVE US DO, NURARIHYON?›
‹SHALL WE CHARGE AT THE UPSTARTS ALL AT ONCE SO WE CAN DIE VAINGLORIOUSLY AND END OF THE AGE OF YOKAI?›
‹NOT AT ALL, WINGED ONE.›
‹THE WAYWARD CHILDREN ARE TOO POWERFUL FOR SUCH A POINTLESS GESTURE. THIS MODERN WORLD IS THEIR FUEL AND THEY BURN BRIGHTLY WITH IT.›
‹OUR ONLY HOPE IS TO TURN THAT AGAINST THEM AND HELP THE MORTALS WASH THEM AWAY.›

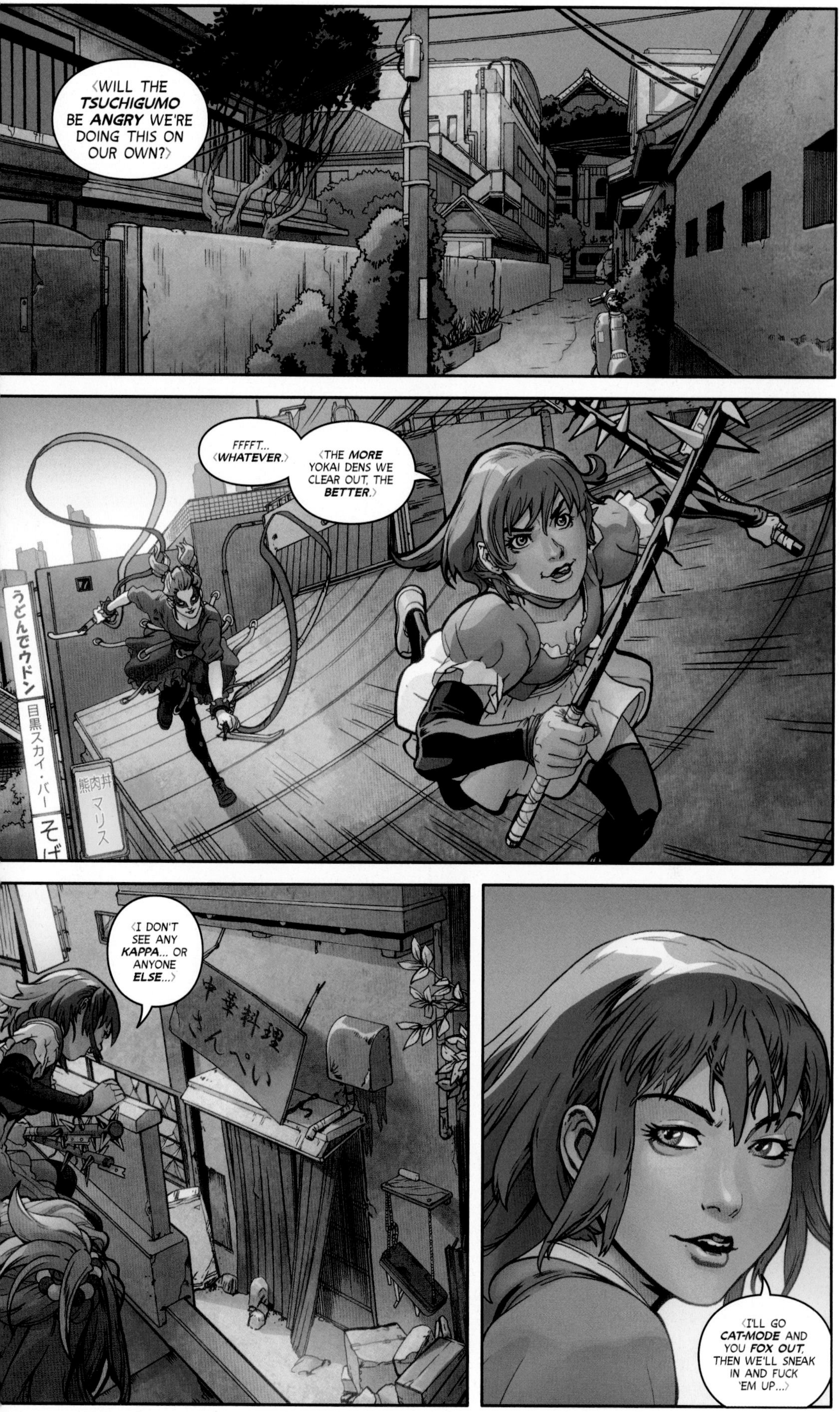
〈WILL THE **TSUCHIGUMO** BE **ANGRY** WE'RE DOING THIS ON OUR OWN?〉
FFFFT... 〈***WHATEVER.***〉
〈THE **MORE** YOKAI DENS WE CLEAR OUT, THE **BETTER.**〉
うどんでウドン
目黒スカイ・バー
熊肉丼 マリス
〈I DON'T SEE ANY **KAPPA**... OR ANYONE **ELSE**...〉
中華料理 さんぺい
〈I'LL GO **CAT-MODE** AND YOU **FOX OUT,** THEN WE'LL SNEAK IN AND FUCK 'EM UP...〉

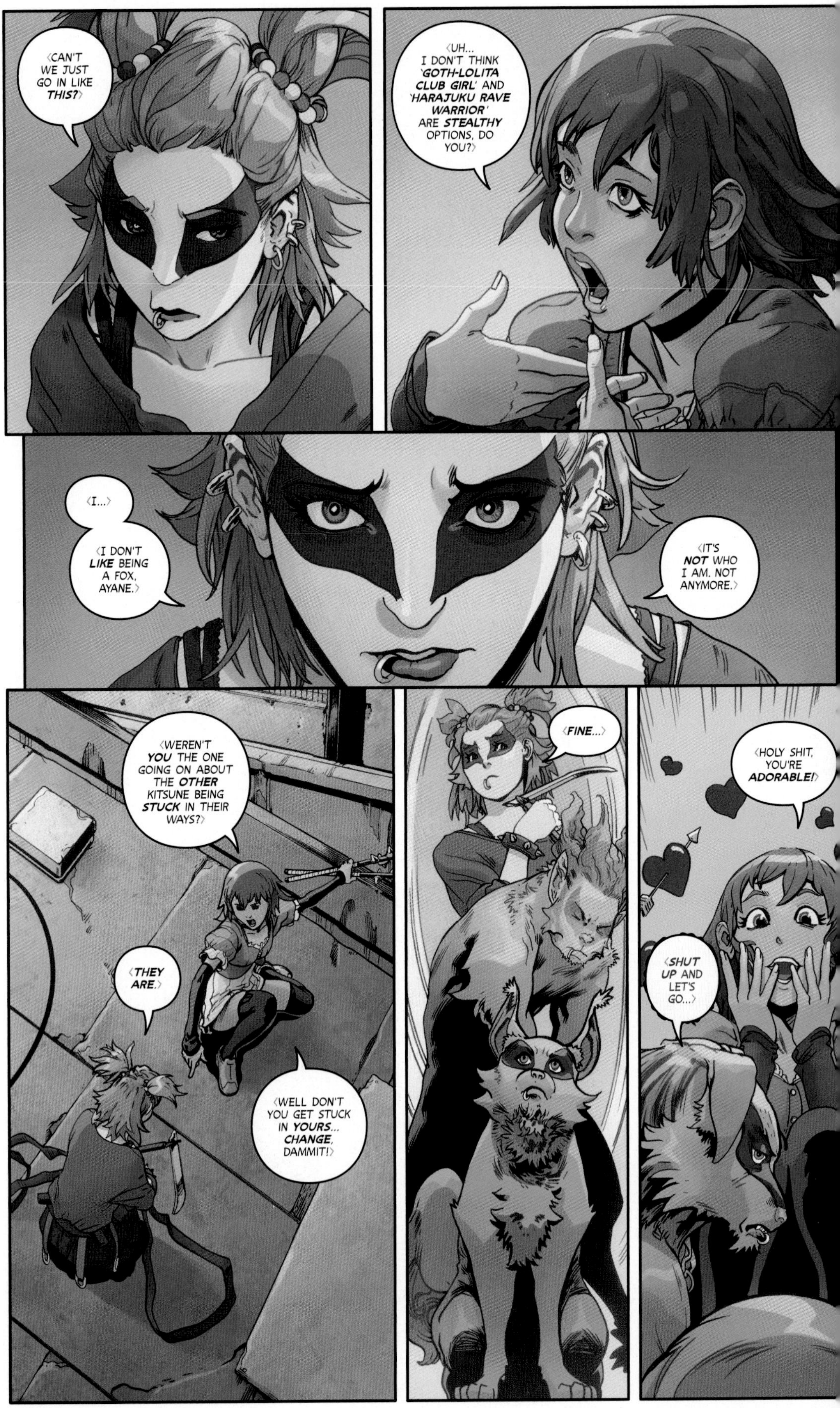
⟨CAN'T WE JUST GO IN LIKE *THIS?*⟩
⟨UH... I DON'T THINK *'GOTH-LOLITA CLUB GIRL'* AND *'HARAJUKU RAVE WARRIOR'* ARE *STEALTHY* OPTIONS, DO YOU?⟩
⟨I...⟩
⟨I DON'T *LIKE* BEING A FOX, AYANE.⟩
⟨IT'S *NOT* WHO I AM. NOT ANYMORE.⟩
⟨WEREN'T *YOU* THE ONE GOING ON ABOUT THE *OTHER* KITSUNE BEING *STUCK* IN THEIR WAYS?⟩
⟨*THEY ARE*.⟩
⟨WELL DON'T YOU GET STUCK IN *YOURS*... *CHANGE*, DAMMIT!⟩
⟨*FINE*...⟩
⟨HOLY SHIT, YOU'RE *ADORABLE!*⟩
⟨*SHUT UP* AND LET'S GO...⟩

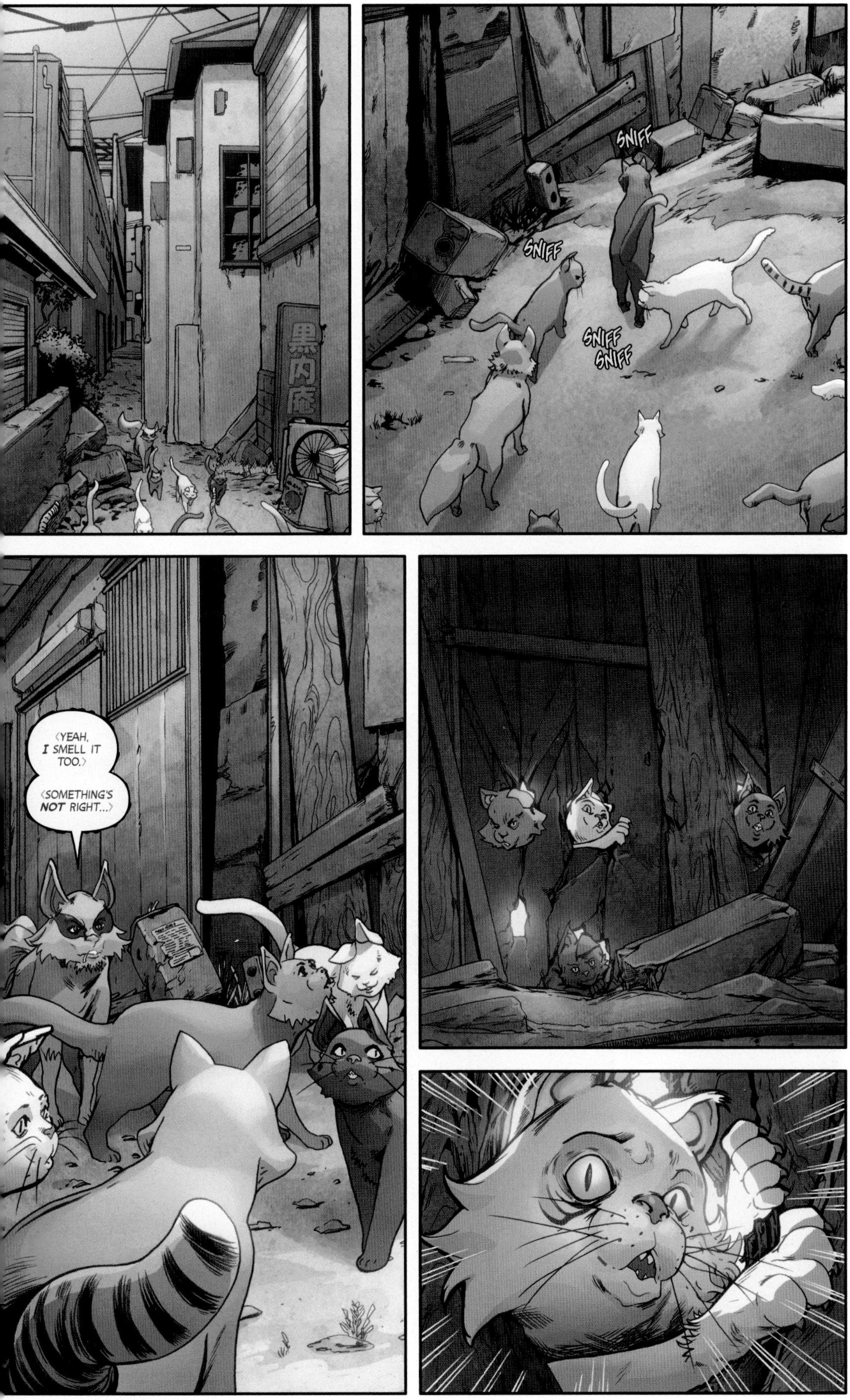
黒内庵
SNIFF
SNIFF
SNIFF SNIFF
‹YEAH, I SMELL IT TOO.›
‹SOMETHING'S NOT RIGHT...›

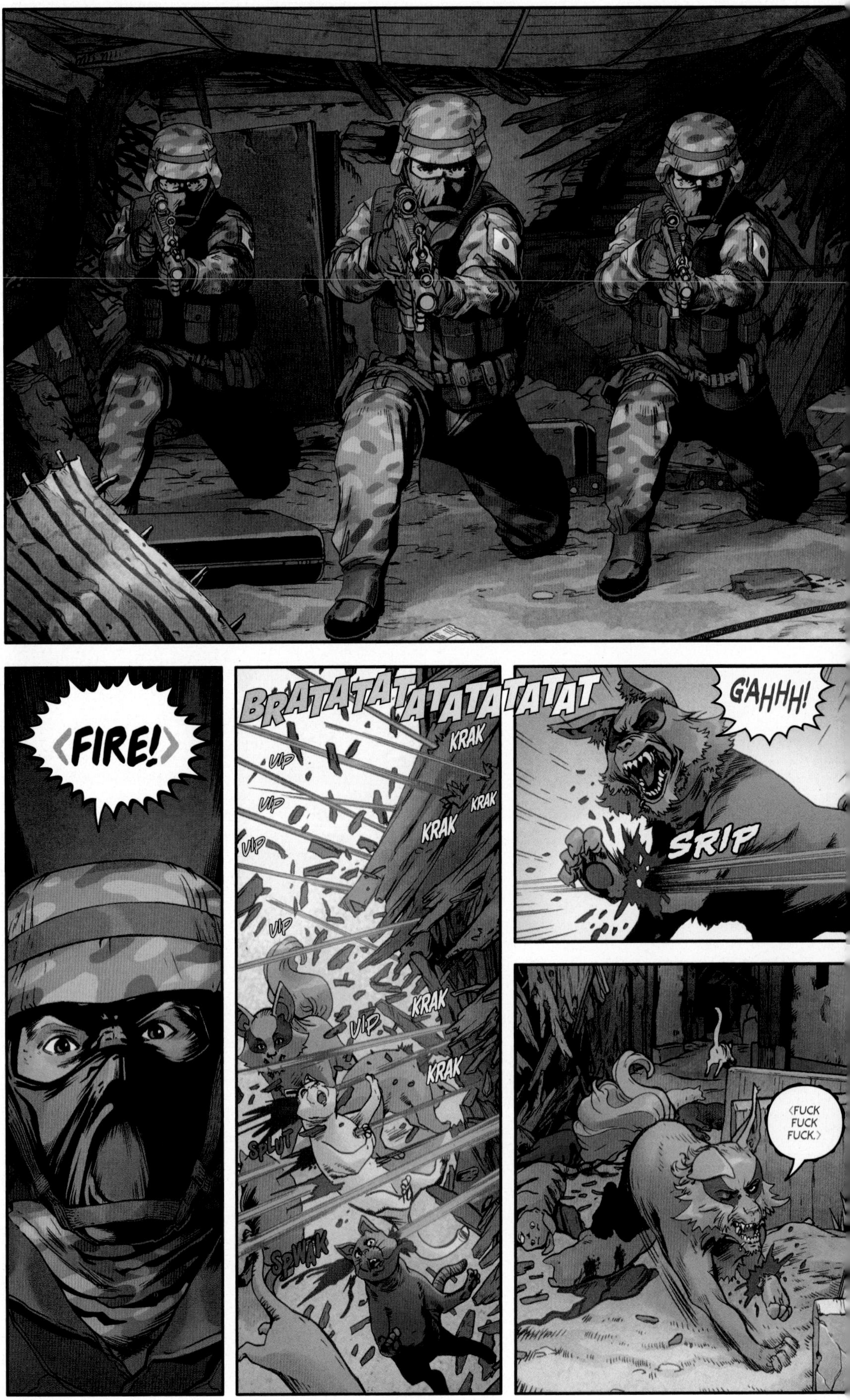

‹FIRE!›
BRATATATATATATATATAT
KRAK
VIP
VIP
KRAK
KRAK
VIP
VIP
KRAK
VIP
KRAK
SPLUT
SPWAK
G'AHHH!
SRIP
‹FUCK FUCK FUCK.›

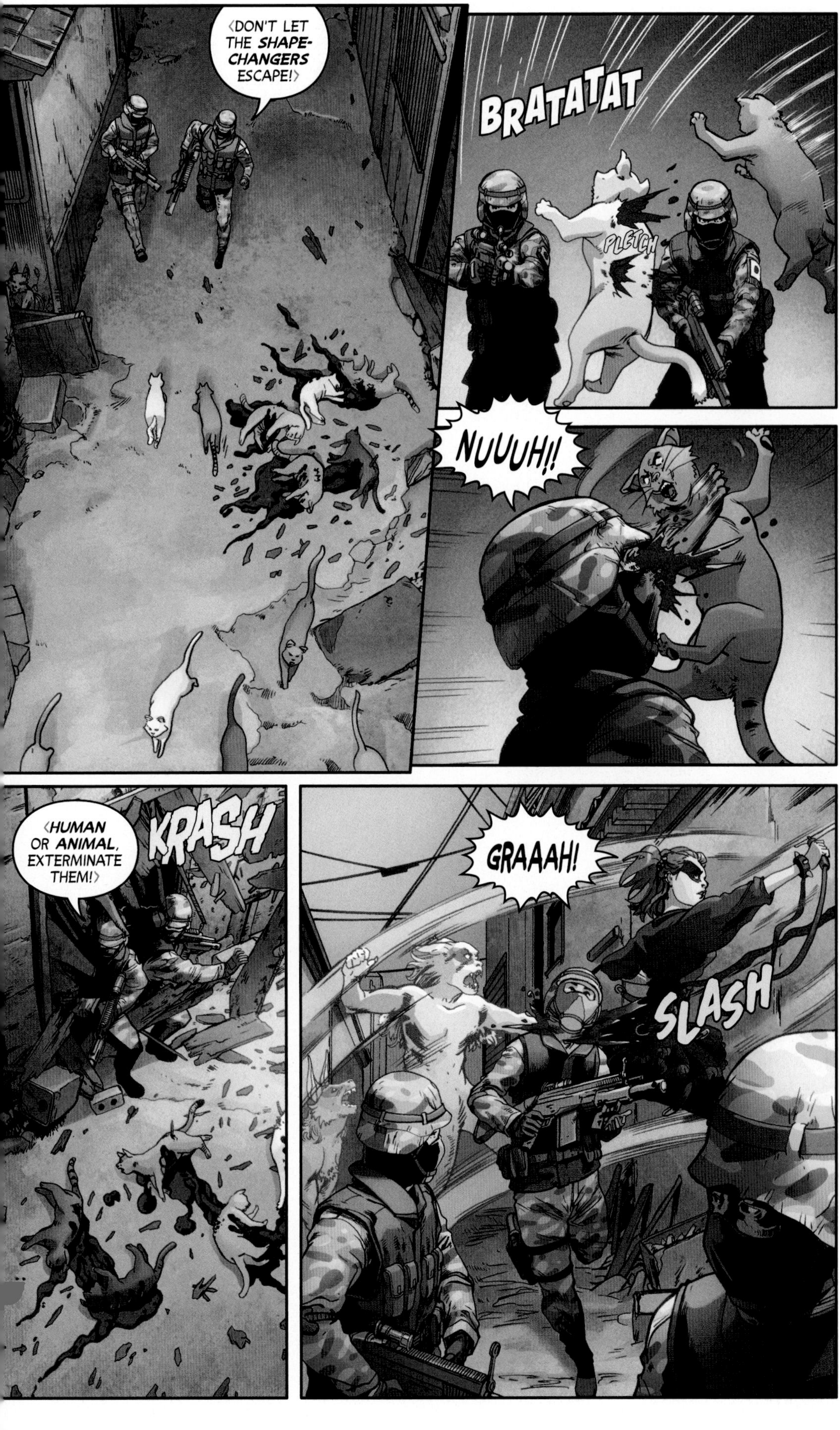
⟨DON'T LET THE *SHAPE-CHANGERS* ESCAPE!⟩
BRATATAT
PLETCH
NUUUH!!
⟨*HUMAN* OR *ANIMAL*, EXTERMINATE THEM!⟩
KRASH
GRAAAH!
SLASH

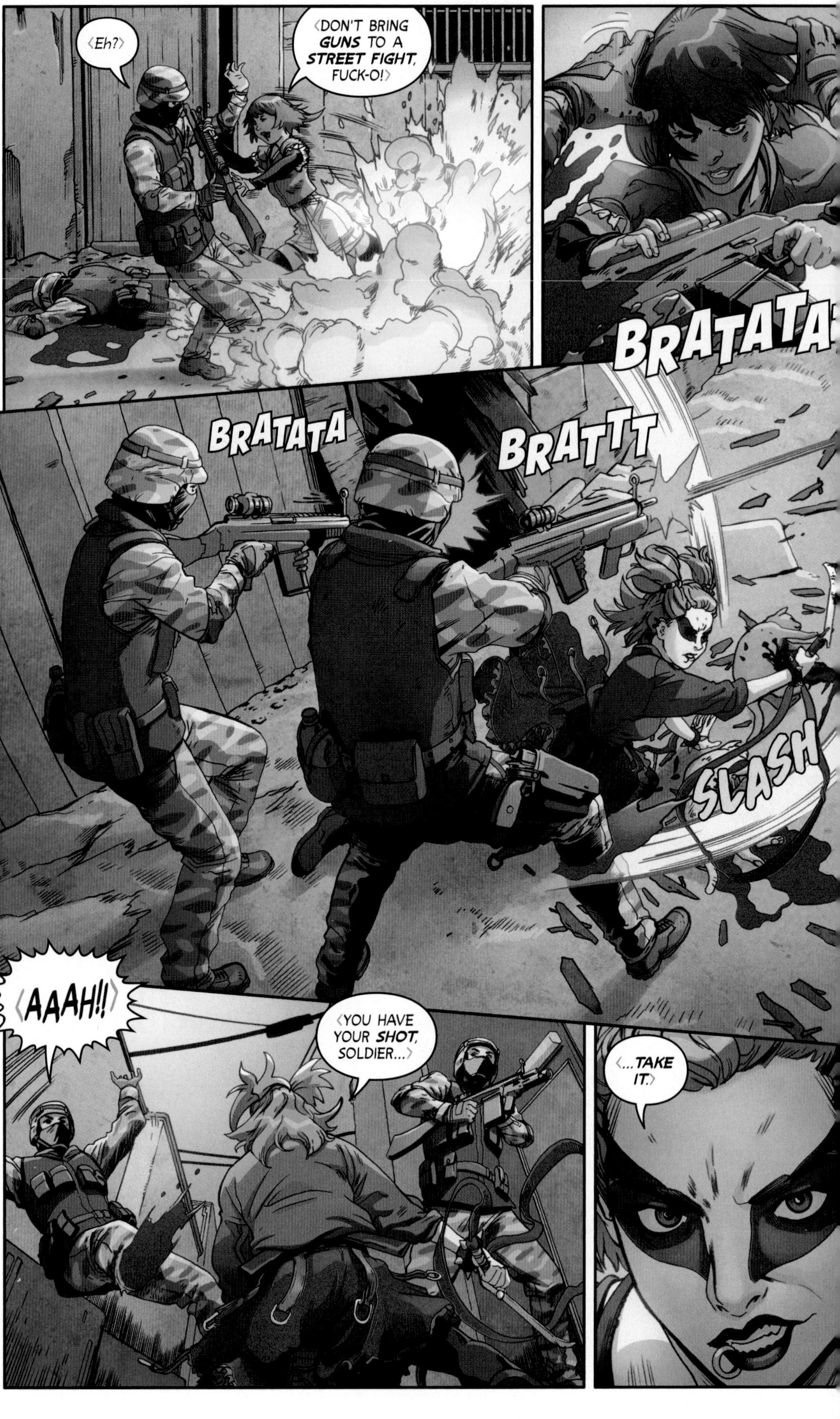

‹Eh?›
‹DON'T BRING GUNS TO A STREET FIGHT, FUCK-O!›
BRATATA
BRATATA
BRATTT
SLASH
‹AAAH!!›
‹YOU HAVE YOUR SHOT, SOLDIER...›
‹...TAKE IT.›

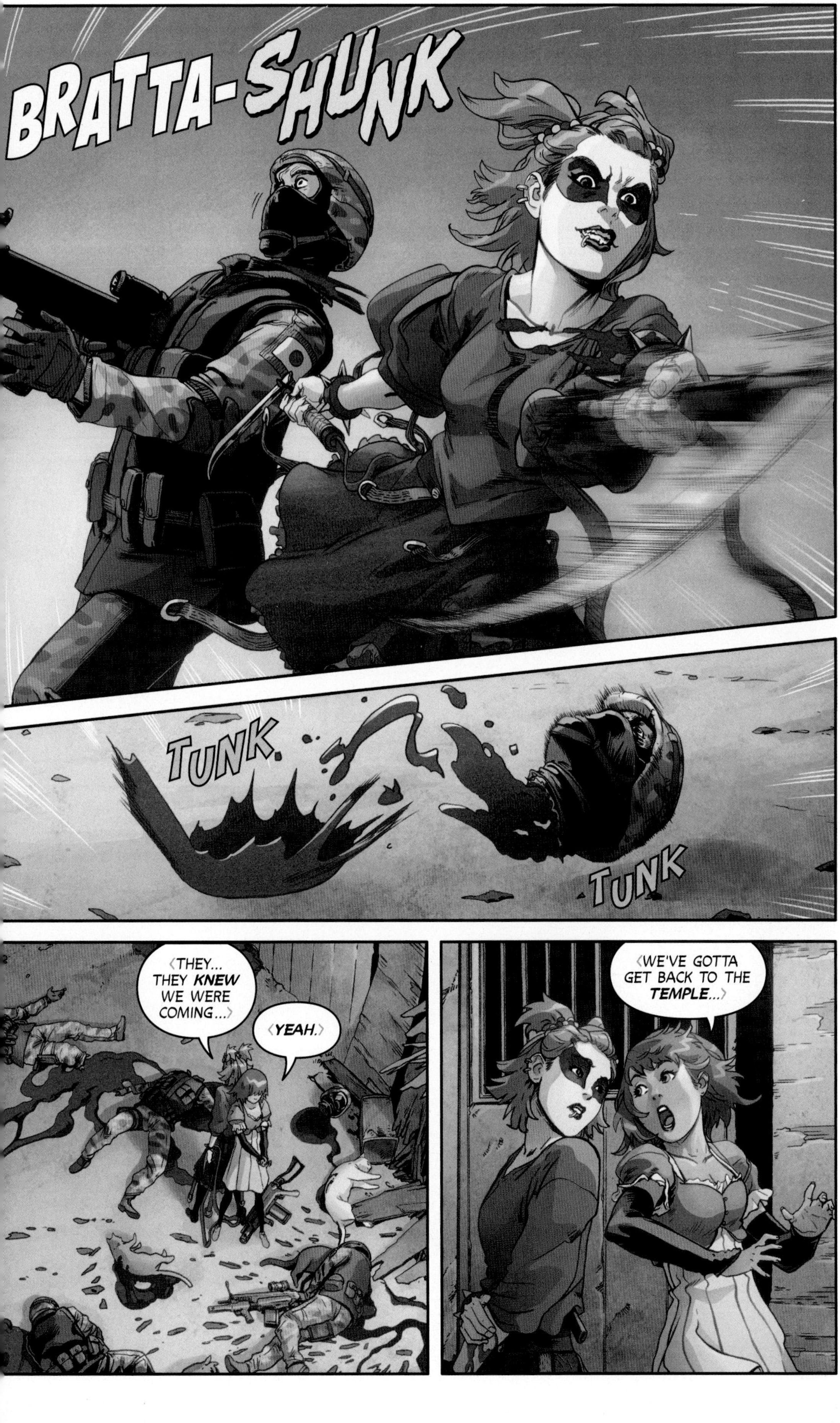
BRATTA-SHUNK
TUNK
TUNK
⟨THEY... THEY KNEW WE WERE COMING...⟩
⟨YEAH.⟩
⟨WE'VE GOTTA GET BACK TO THE TEMPLE...⟩

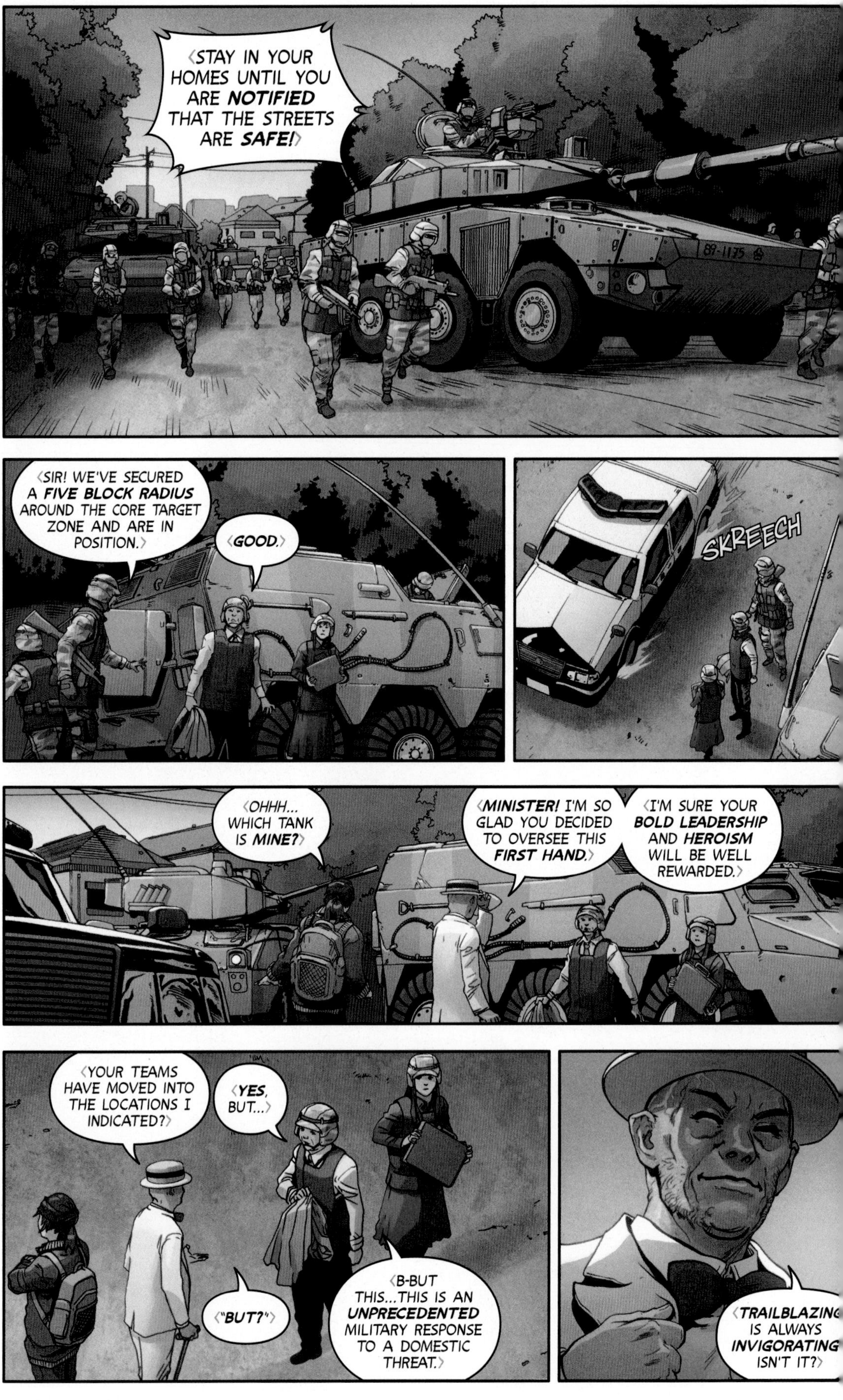
‹STAY IN YOUR HOMES UNTIL YOU ARE NOTIFIED THAT THE STREETS ARE SAFE!›
‹SIR! WE'VE SECURED A FIVE BLOCK RADIUS AROUND THE CORE TARGET ZONE AND ARE IN POSITION.›
‹GOOD.›
SKREECH
‹OHHH... WHICH TANK IS MINE?›
‹MINISTER! I'M SO GLAD YOU DECIDED TO OVERSEE THIS FIRST HAND.›
‹I'M SURE YOUR BOLD LEADERSHIP AND HEROISM WILL BE WELL REWARDED.›
‹YOUR TEAMS HAVE MOVED INTO THE LOCATIONS I INDICATED?›
‹YES, BUT...›
‹"BUT?"›
‹B-BUT THIS...THIS IS AN UNPRECEDENTED MILITARY RESPONSE TO A DOMESTIC THREAT.›
‹TRAILBLAZING IS ALWAYS INVIGORATING, ISN'T IT?›

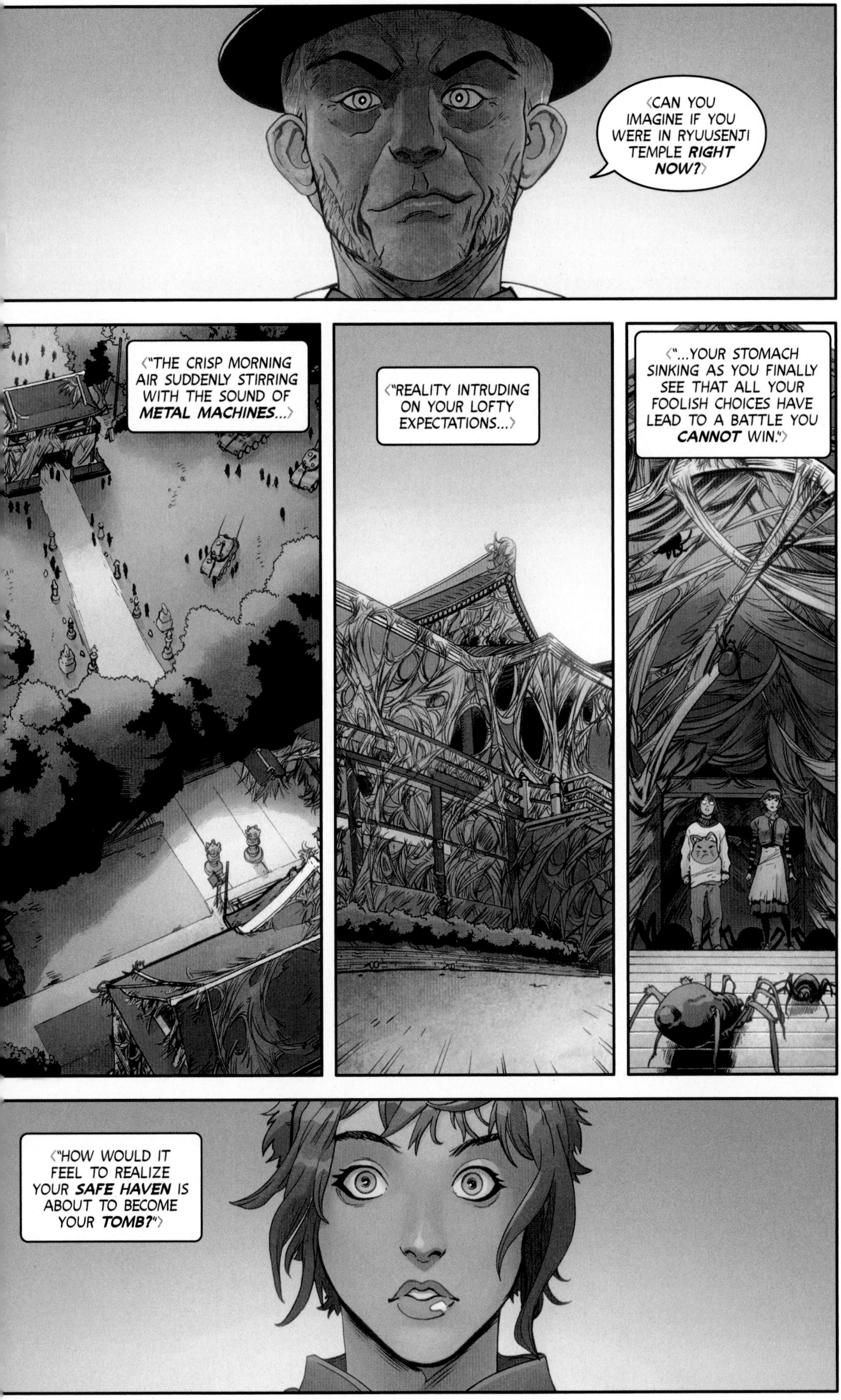

‹CAN YOU IMAGINE IF YOU WERE IN RYUUSENJI TEMPLE **RIGHT NOW?**›
‹"THE CRISP MORNING AIR SUDDENLY STIRRING WITH THE SOUND OF **METAL MACHINES**...›
‹"REALITY INTRUDING ON YOUR LOFTY EXPECTATIONS...›
‹"...YOUR STOMACH SINKING AS YOU FINALLY SEE THAT ALL YOUR FOOLISH CHOICES HAVE LEAD TO A BATTLE YOU **CANNOT** WIN."›
‹"HOW WOULD IT FEEL TO REALIZE YOUR **SAFE HAVEN** IS ABOUT TO BECOME YOUR **TOMB?**"›

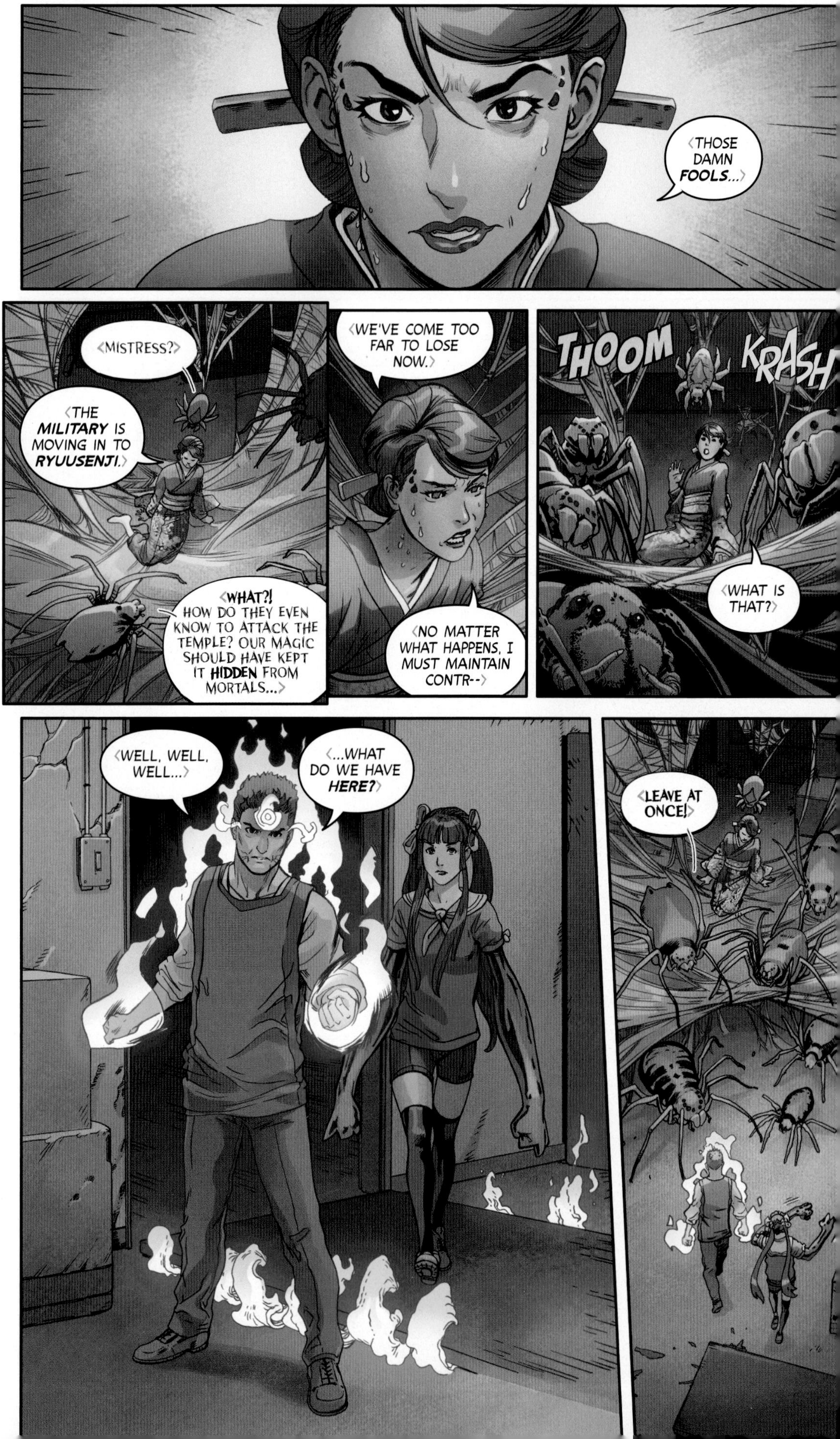

‹THOSE DAMN FOOLS...›
‹MISTRESS?›
‹THE MILITARY IS MOVING IN TO RYUUSENJI.›
‹WHAT?! HOW DO THEY EVEN KNOW TO ATTACK THE TEMPLE? OUR MAGIC SHOULD HAVE KEPT IT HIDDEN FROM MORTALS...›
‹WE'VE COME TOO FAR TO LOSE NOW.›
‹NO MATTER WHAT HAPPENS, I MUST MAINTAIN CONTR--›
THOOM
KRASH
‹WHAT IS THAT?›
‹WELL, WELL, WELL...›
‹...WHAT DO WE HAVE HERE?›
‹LEAVE AT ONCE!›

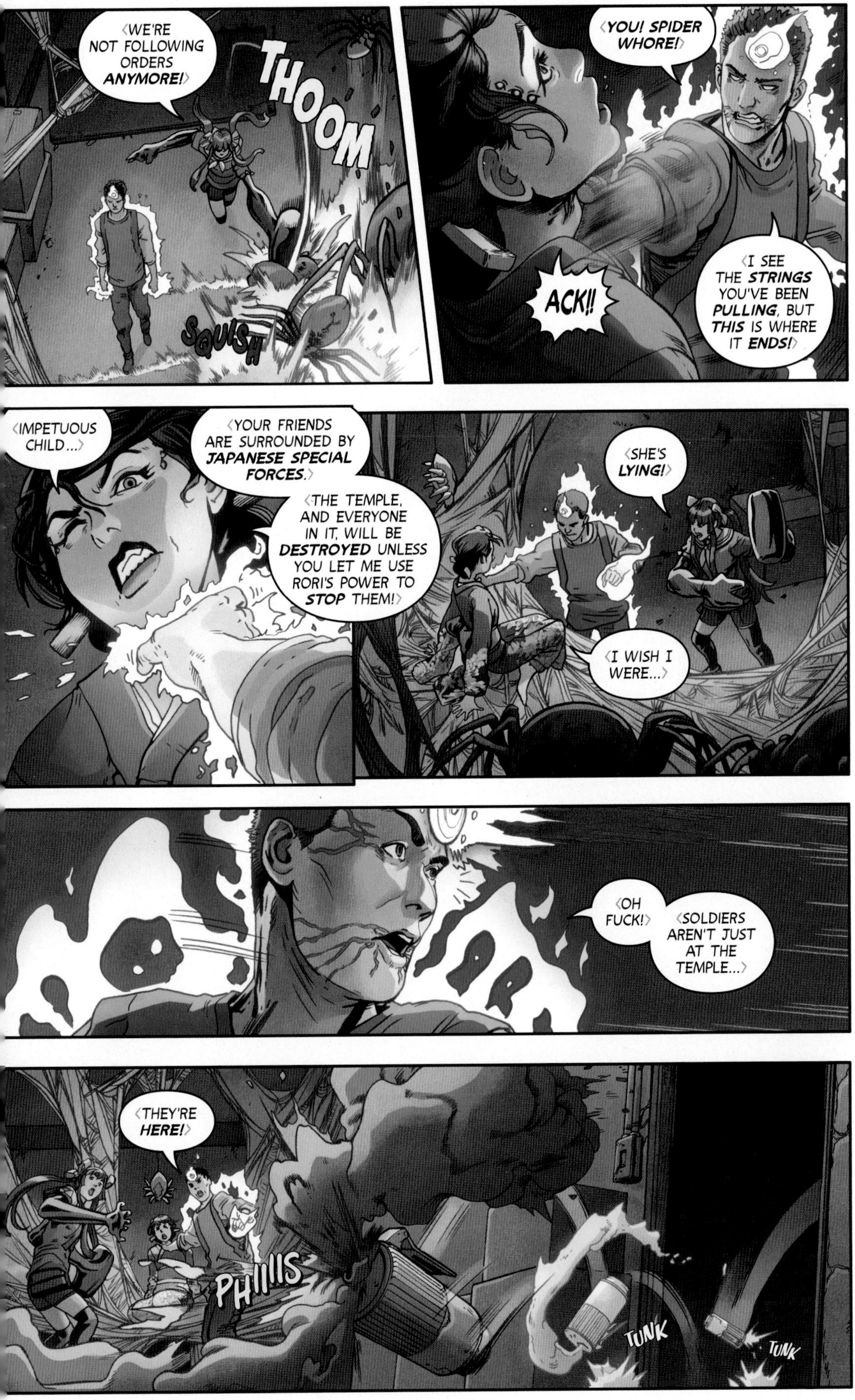

⟨WE'RE NOT FOLLOWING ORDERS ANYMORE!⟩
THOOM
SQUISH
⟨YOU! SPIDER WHORE!⟩
ACK!!
⟨I SEE THE STRINGS YOU'VE BEEN PULLING, BUT THIS IS WHERE IT ENDS!⟩
⟨IMPETUOUS CHILD...⟩
⟨YOUR FRIENDS ARE SURROUNDED BY JAPANESE SPECIAL FORCES.⟩
⟨THE TEMPLE, AND EVERYONE IN IT, WILL BE DESTROYED UNLESS YOU LET ME USE RORI'S POWER TO STOP THEM!⟩
⟨SHE'S LYING!⟩
⟨I WISH I WERE...⟩
⟨OH FUCK!⟩
⟨SOLDIERS AREN'T JUST AT THE TEMPLE...⟩
⟨THEY'RE HERE!⟩
PHIIIIS
TUNK
TUNK

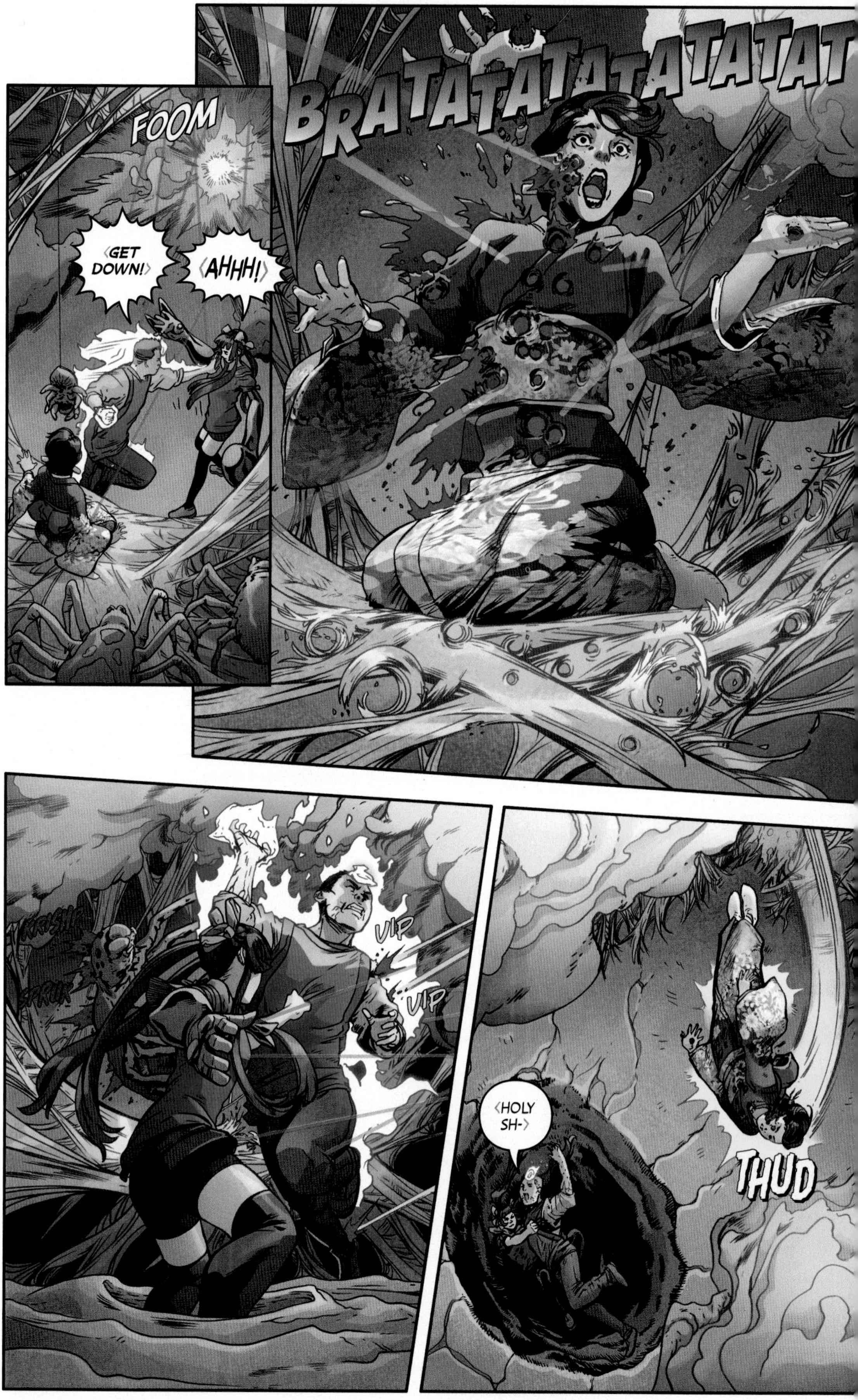
FOOM
‹GET DOWN!›
‹AHHH!›
BRATATATATATATAT
KRISH
SPRUK
VIP
VIP
‹HOLY SH-›
THUD

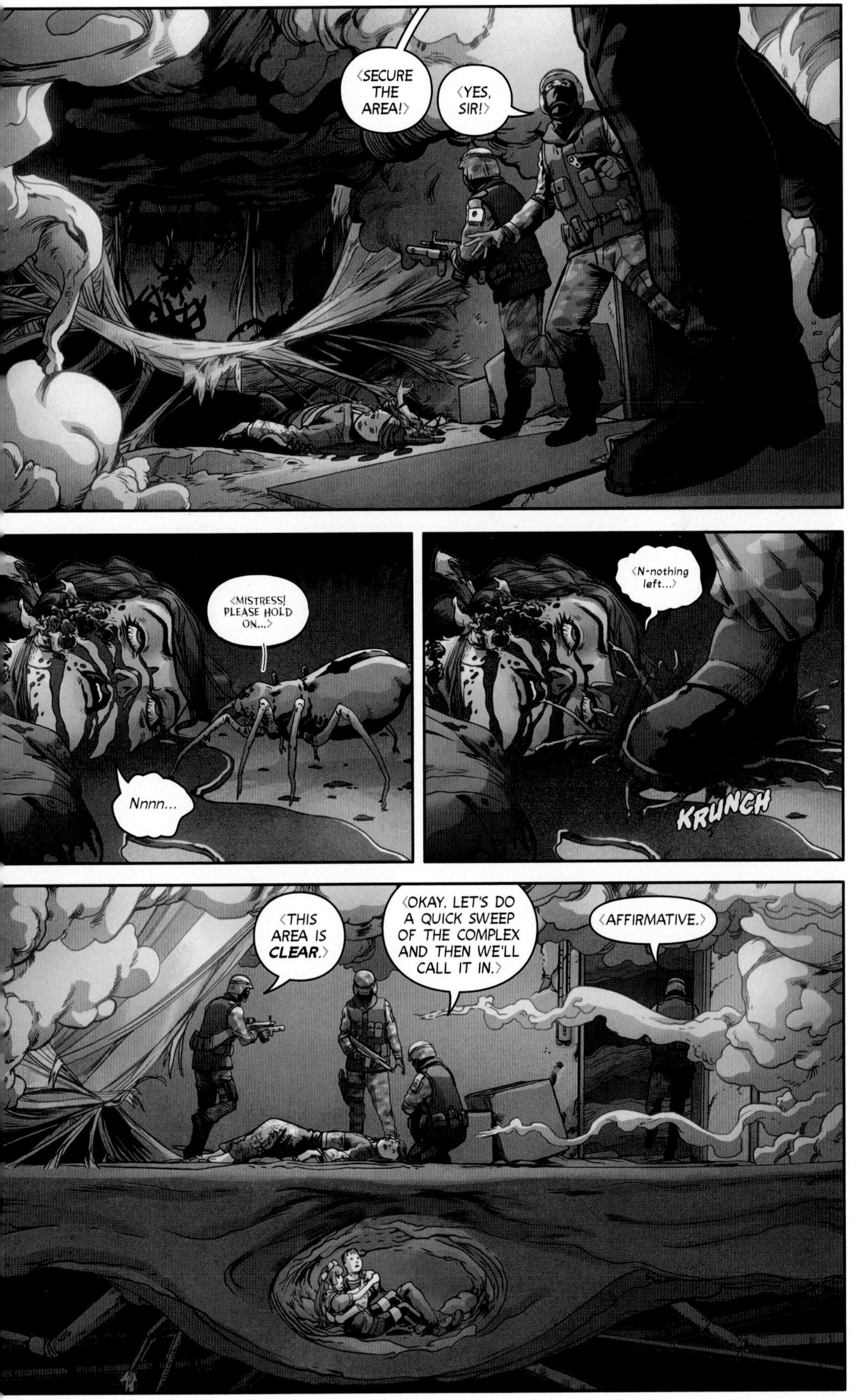
〈SECURE THE AREA!〉
〈YES, SIR!〉
〈MISTRESS! PLEASE HOLD ON...〉
Nnnn...
〈N-nothing left...〉
KRUNCH
〈THIS AREA IS **CLEAR**.〉
〈OKAY. LET'S DO A QUICK SWEEP OF THE COMPLEX AND THEN WE'LL CALL IT IN.〉
〈AFFIRMATIVE.〉

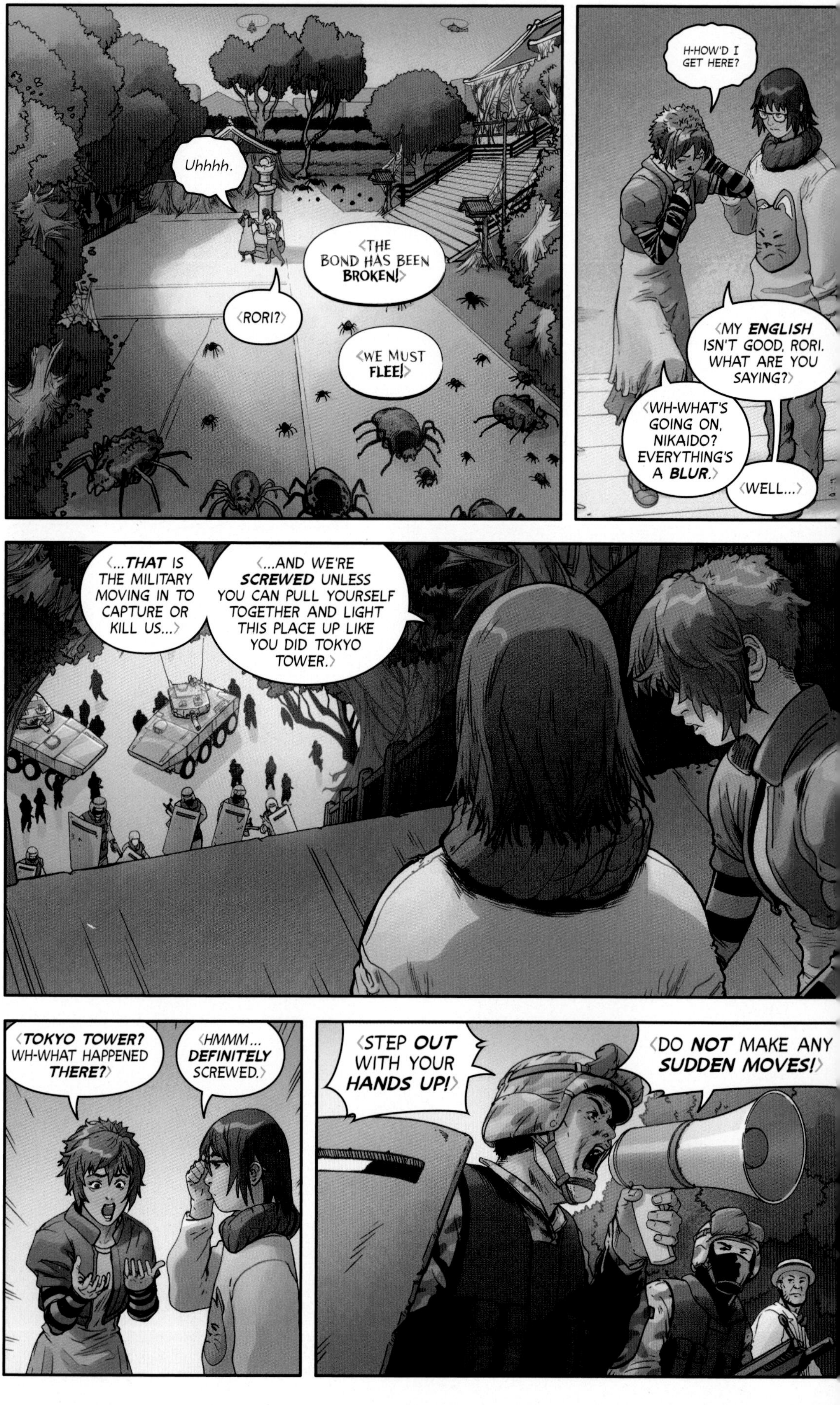
Uhhhh.
⟨THE BOND HAS BEEN BROKEN!⟩
⟨RORI?⟩
⟨WE MUST FLEE!⟩
H-HOW'D I GET HERE?
⟨MY ENGLISH ISN'T GOOD, RORI. WHAT ARE YOU SAYING?⟩
⟨WH-WHAT'S GOING ON, NIKAIDO? EVERYTHING'S A BLUR.⟩
⟨WELL...⟩
⟨...THAT IS THE MILITARY MOVING IN TO CAPTURE OR KILL US...⟩
⟨...AND WE'RE SCREWED UNLESS YOU CAN PULL YOURSELF TOGETHER AND LIGHT THIS PLACE UP LIKE YOU DID TOKYO TOWER.⟩
⟨TOKYO TOWER? WH-WHAT HAPPENED THERE?⟩
⟨HMMM... DEFINITELY SCREWED.⟩
⟨STEP OUT WITH YOUR HANDS UP!⟩
⟨DO NOT MAKE ANY SUDDEN MOVES!⟩

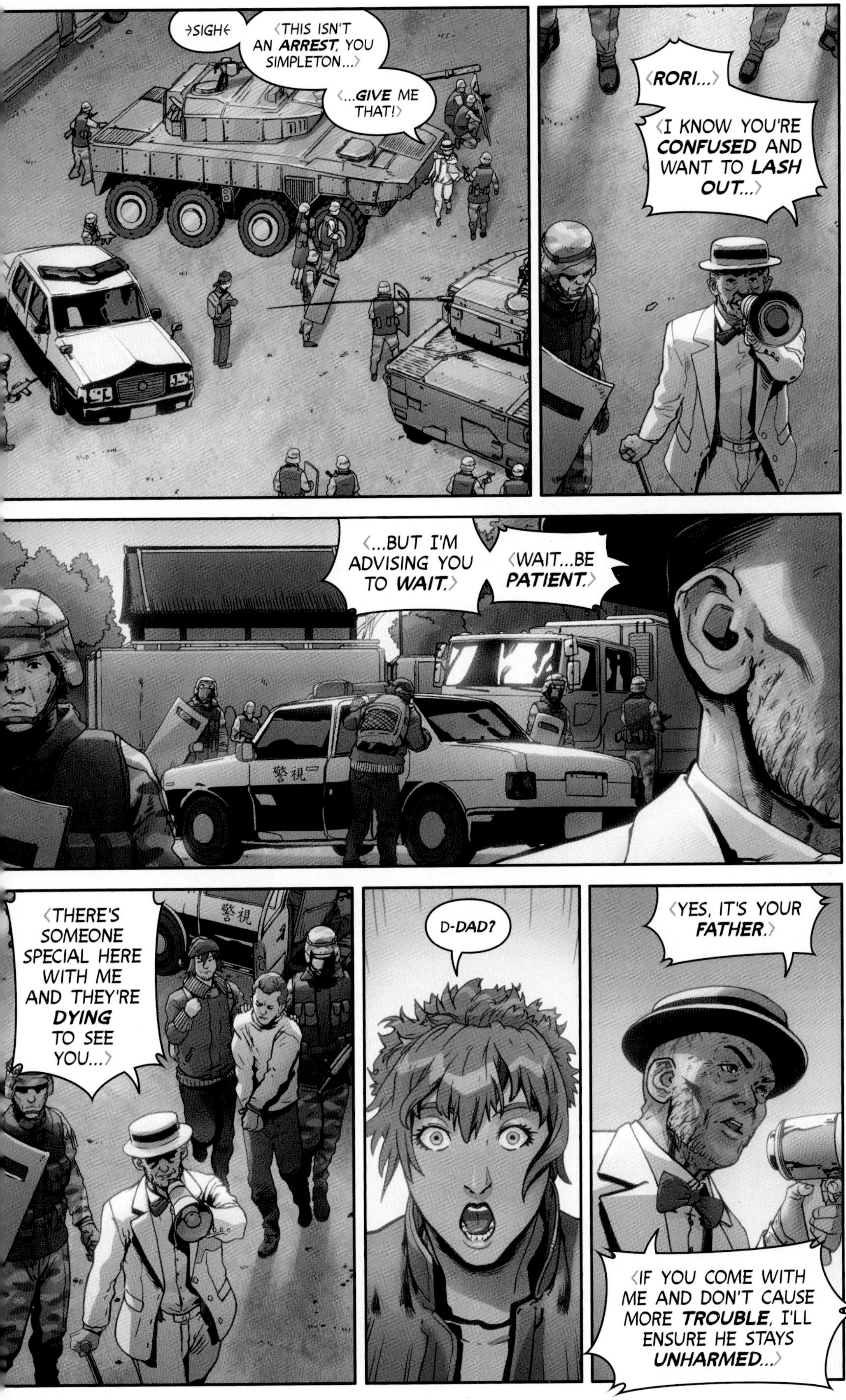

→SIGH←
‹THIS ISN'T AN ARREST, YOU SIMPLETON...›
‹...GIVE ME THAT!›
‹RORI...›
‹I KNOW YOU'RE CONFUSED AND WANT TO LASH OUT...›
‹...BUT I'M ADVISING YOU TO WAIT.›
‹WAIT...BE PATIENT.›
警視
‹THERE'S SOMEONE SPECIAL HERE WITH ME AND THEY'RE DYING TO SEE YOU...›
D-DAD?
‹YES, IT'S YOUR FATHER.›
‹IF YOU COME WITH ME AND DON'T CAUSE MORE TROUBLE, I'LL ENSURE HE STAYS UNHARMED...›

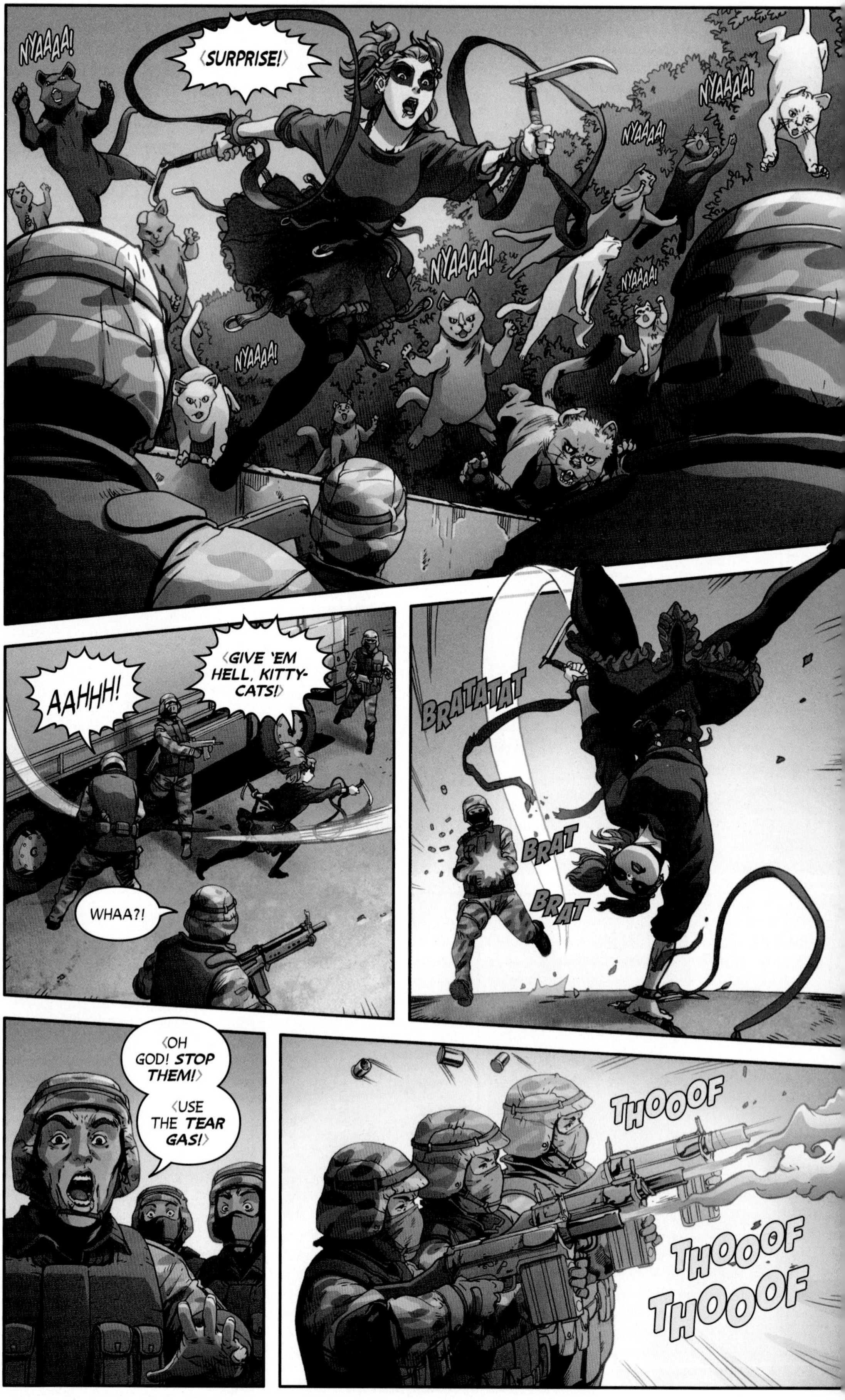
NYAAAA!
⟨SURPRISE!⟩
NYAAAA!
NYAAAA!
NYAAAA!
NYAAAA!
NYAAAA!
AAHHH!
⟨GIVE 'EM HELL, KITTY-CATS!⟩
WHAA?!
BRATATAT
BRAT
BRAT
⟨OH GOD! STOP THEM!⟩
⟨USE THE TEAR GAS!⟩
THOOOF
THOOOF
THOOOF

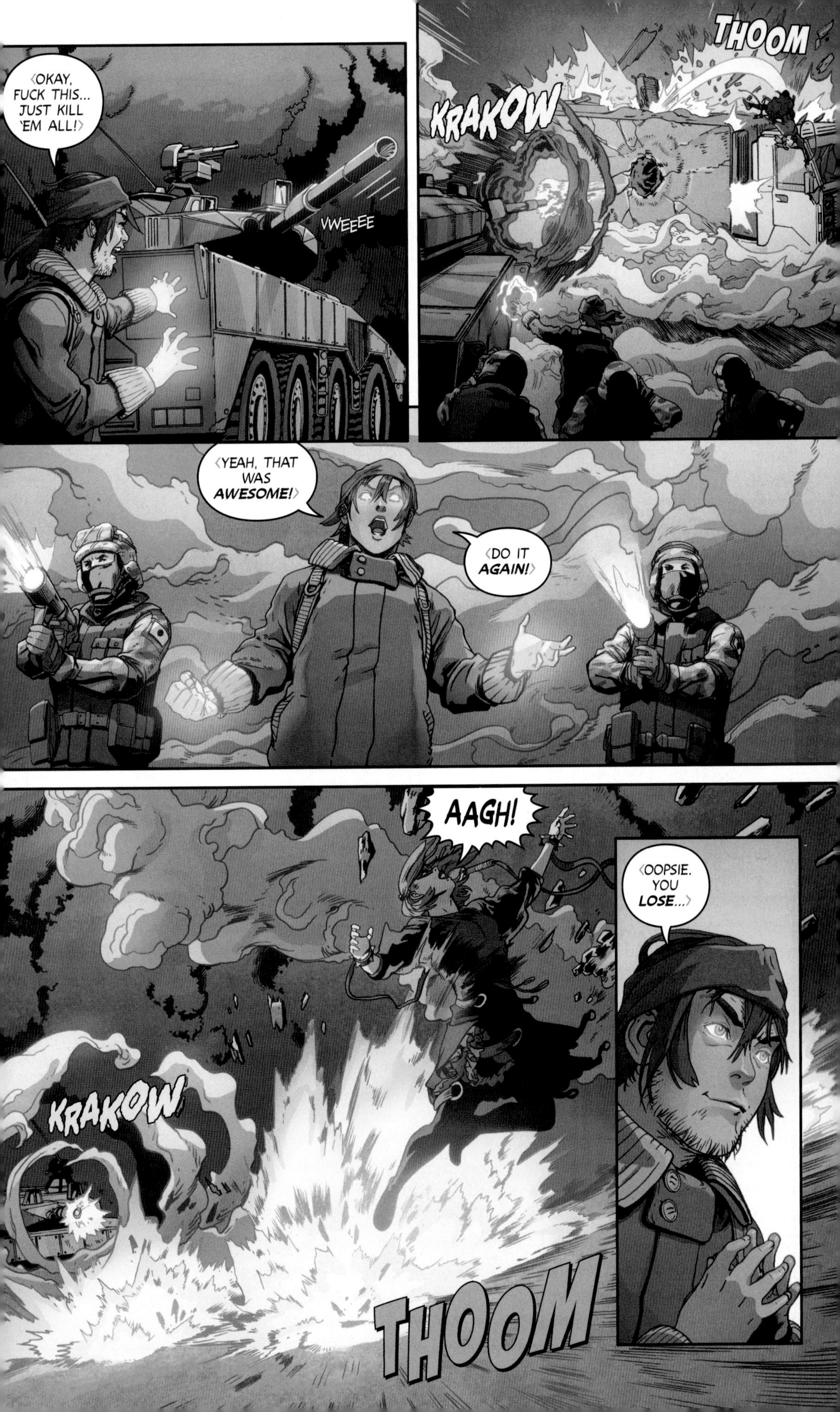

‹OKAY, FUCK THIS... JUST KILL 'EM ALL!›
VWEEEE
THOOM
KRAKOW
‹YEAH, THAT WAS AWESOME!›
‹DO IT AGAIN!›
AAGH!
KRAKOW
THOOM
‹OOPSIE. YOU LOSE...›

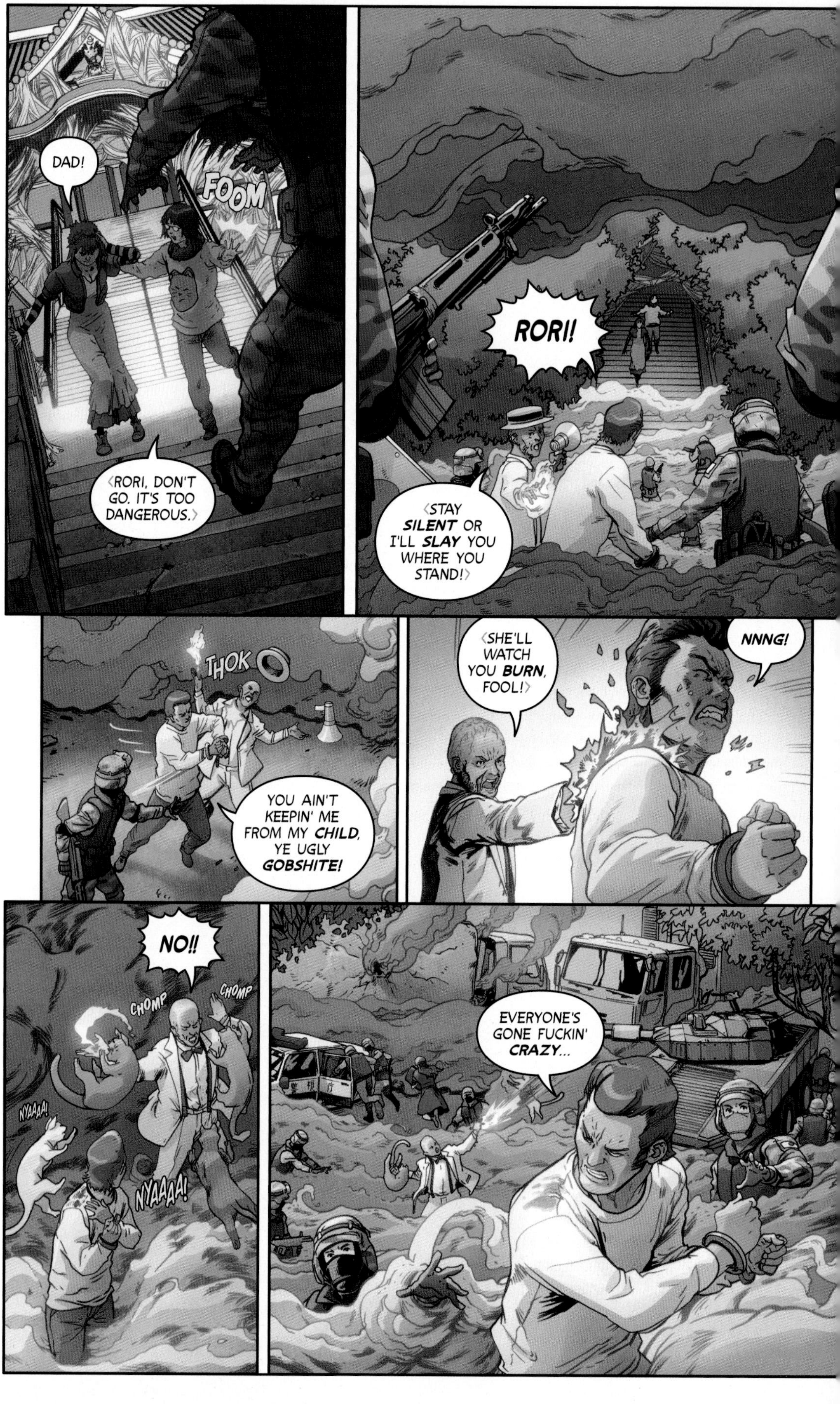
DAD!
FOOM
<RORI, DON'T GO. IT'S TOO DANGEROUS.>
RORI!
<STAY SILENT OR I'LL SLAY YOU WHERE YOU STAND!>
THOK
YOU AIN'T KEEPIN' ME FROM MY CHILD, YE UGLY GOBSHITE!
<SHE'LL WATCH YOU BURN, FOOL!>
NNNG!
NO!!
CHOMP
CHOMP
NYAAAA!
NYAAAA!
EVERYONE'S GONE FUCKIN' CRAZY...

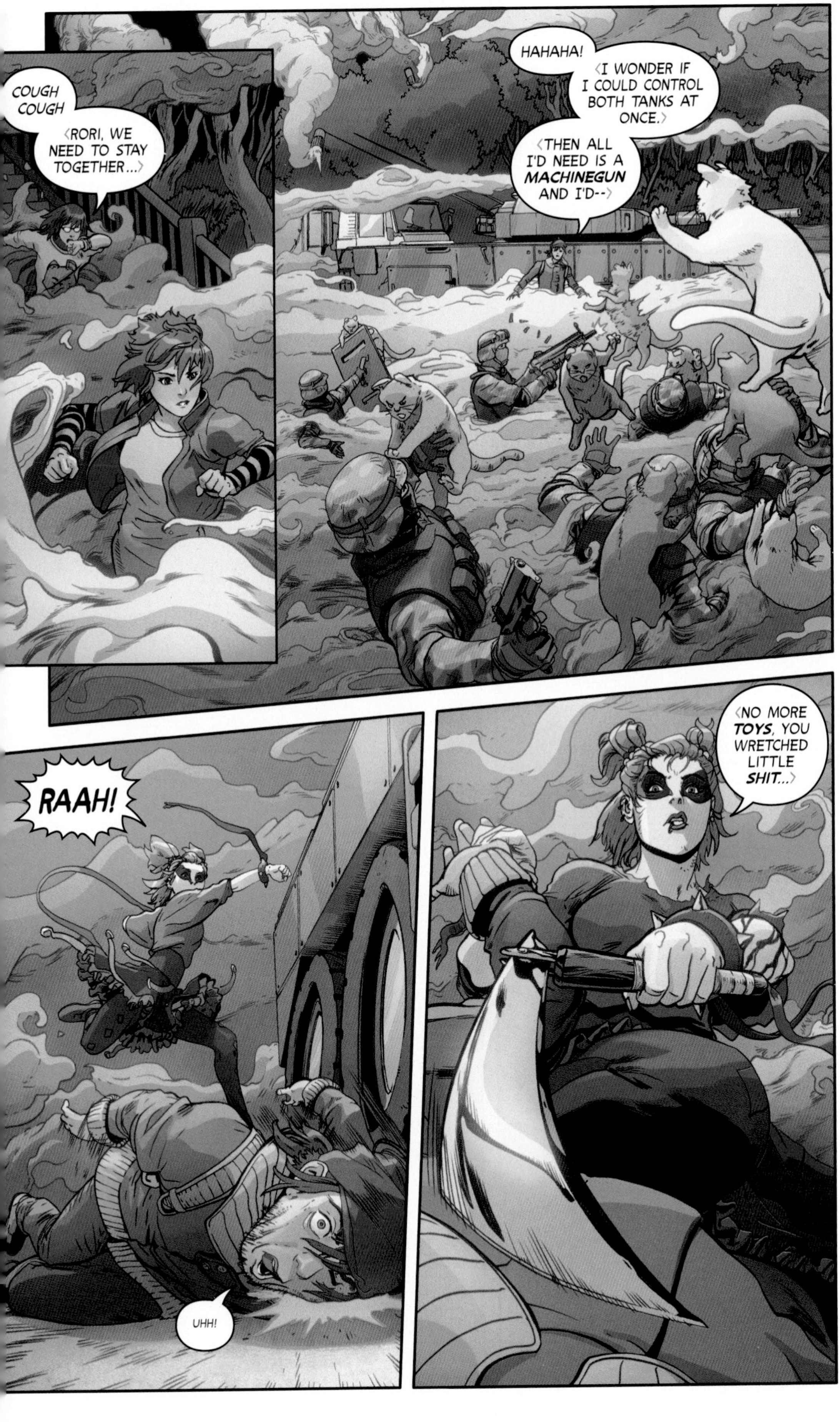
COUGH COUGH
‹RORI, WE NEED TO STAY TOGETHER...›
HAHAHA!
‹I WONDER IF I COULD CONTROL BOTH TANKS AT ONCE.›
‹THEN ALL I'D NEED IS A MACHINEGUN AND I'D--›
RAAH!
UHH!
‹NO MORE TOYS, YOU WRETCHED LITTLE SHIT...›

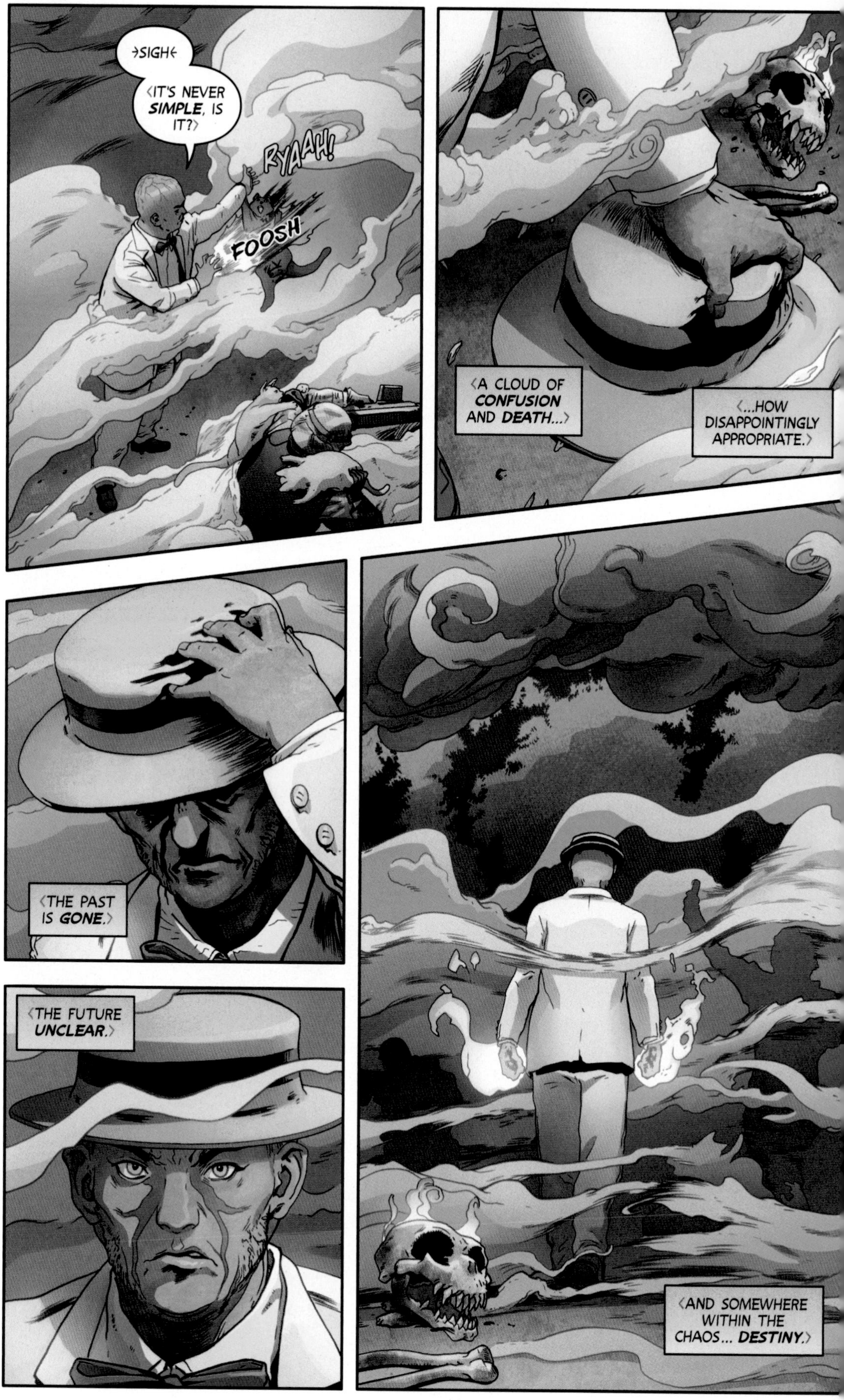

>SIGH<
<IT'S NEVER SIMPLE, IS IT?>
RYAAH!
FOOSH
<A CLOUD OF CONFUSION AND DEATH...>
<...HOW DISAPPOINTINGLY APPROPRIATE.>
<THE PAST IS GONE.>
<THE FUTURE UNCLEAR.>
<AND SOMEWHERE WITHIN THE CHAOS... DESTINY.>

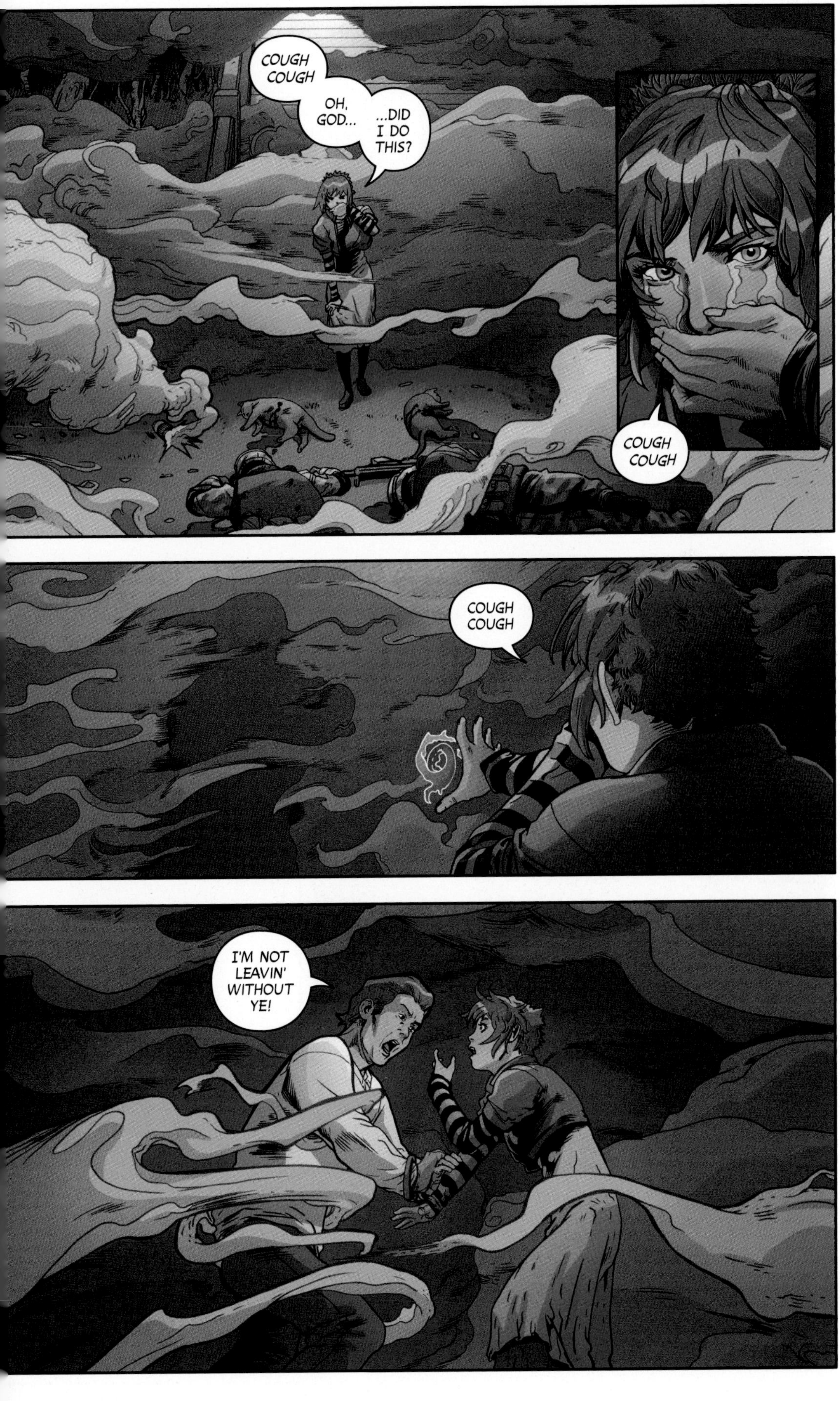
COUGH COUGH
OH, GOD...
...DID I DO THIS?
COUGH COUGH
COUGH COUGH
I'M NOT LEAVIN' WITHOUT YE!

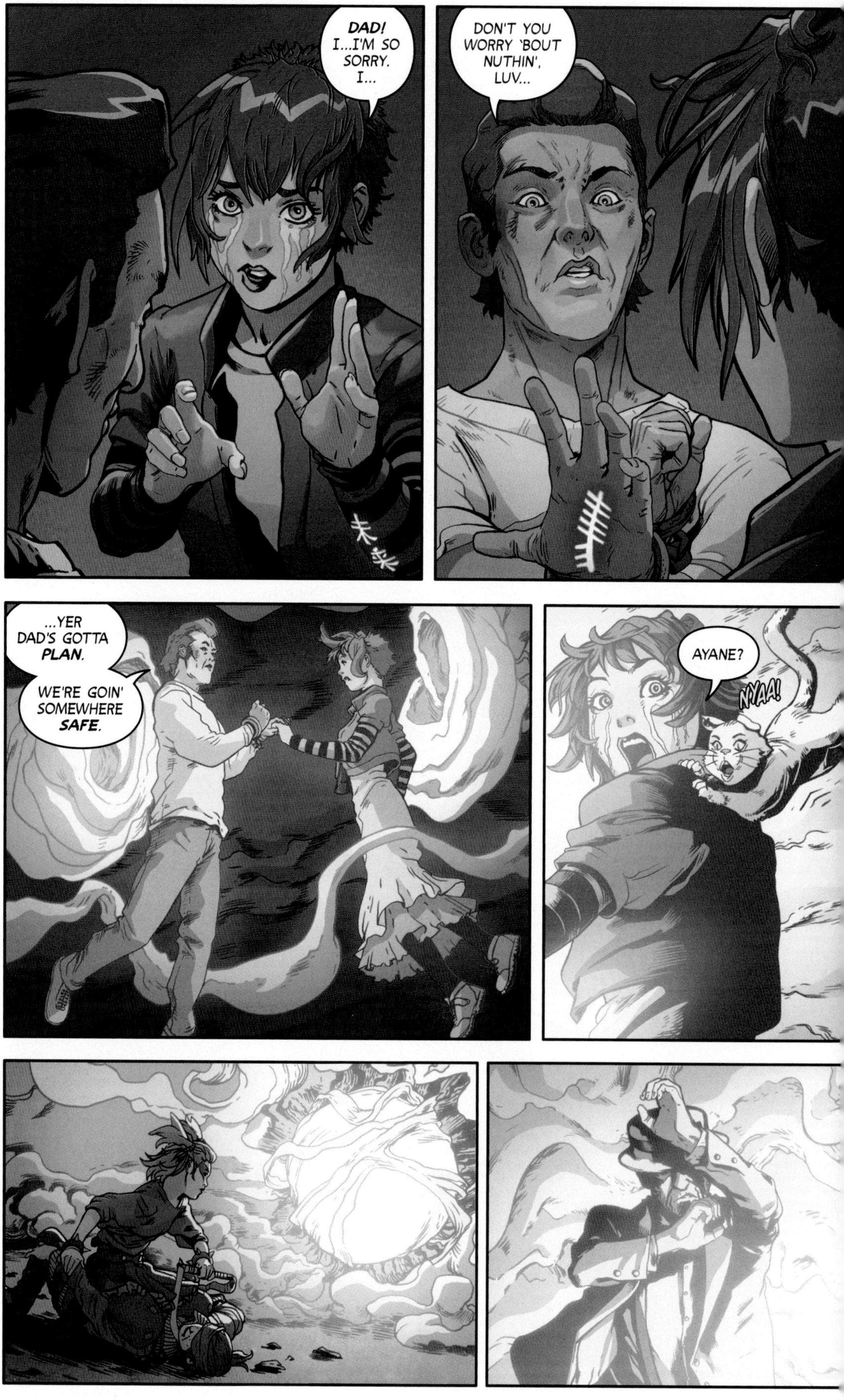
DAD! I...I'M SO SORRY. I...
DON'T YOU WORRY 'BOUT NUTHIN', LUV...
...YER DAD'S GOTTA PLAN.
WE'RE GOIN' SOMEWHERE SAFE.
AYANE?
NYAA!

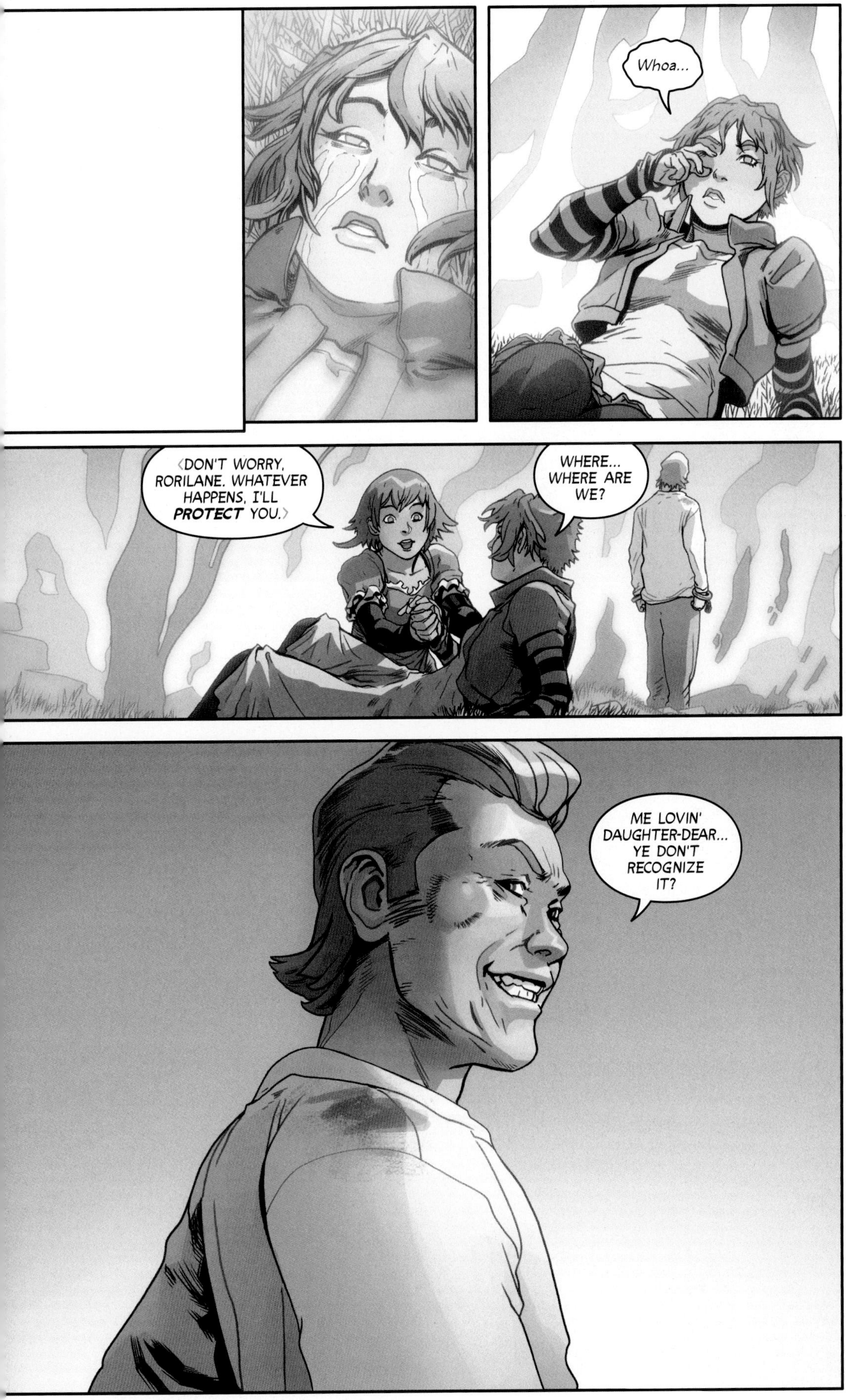
Whoa...
‹DON'T WORRY, RORILANE. WHATEVER HAPPENS, I'LL **PROTECT** YOU.›
WHERE... WHERE ARE WE?
ME LOVIN' DAUGHTER-DEAR... YE DON'T RECOGNIZE IT?

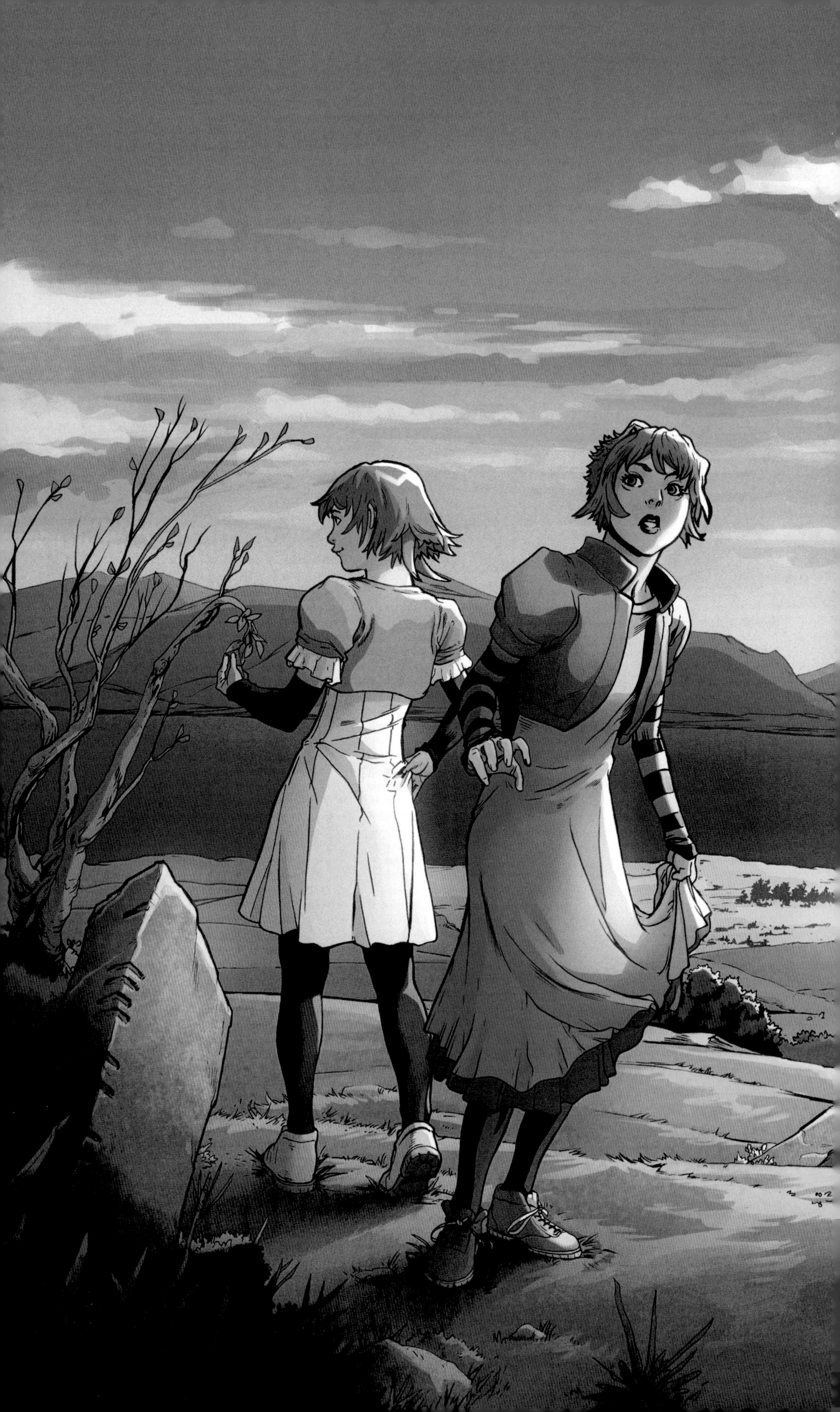

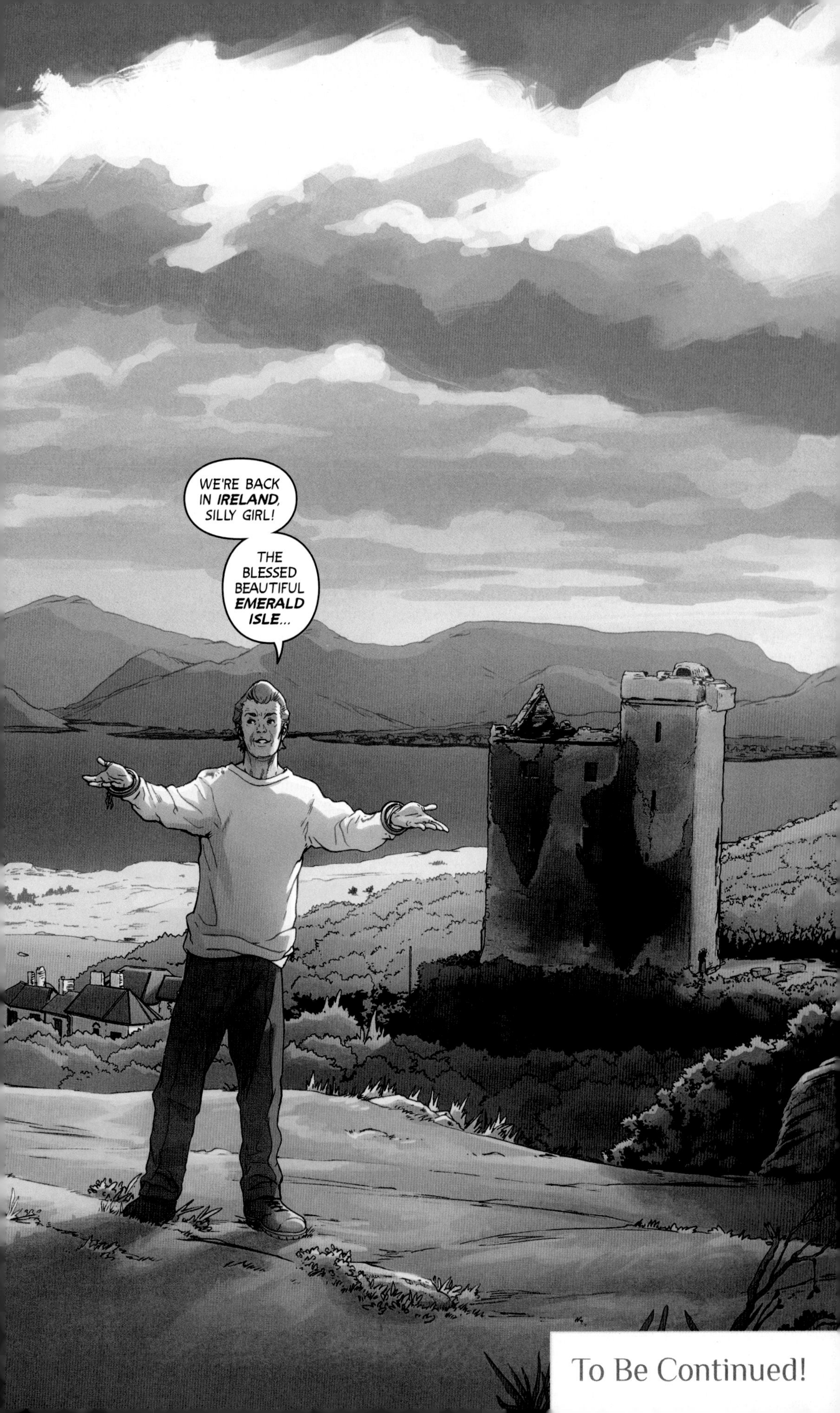
WE'RE BACK IN IRELAND, SILLY GIRL!
THE BLESSED BEAUTIFUL EMERALD ISLE...

To Be Continued!

During the Meiji period, the Japanese government declared war on yokai. Not a traditional war; they didn't attack with bullets and bombs. Instead they used more effective weapons. Politics. And ideas. As Francisco Goya said, "The sleep of reason produces monsters." In the 1860s, reason awoke and banished the monsters.

First a little context:

Japan is sometimes described as a "unique country." It's a controversial statement, wrapped in Japanese nationalism and the study of "Japaneseness" called *nihonjinron*. But political points aside, there is one defining aspect of Japanese history that is highly unusual, to say the least.

When Tokugawa Iemitsu—third shogun of the Tokugawa shogunate—takes power in 1623, he has a problem. His grandfather's compatriot Oda Nobunaga allowed Jesuit missionaries and traders to gain a foothold in Japan. They occupy the southern island of Kyushu and the port of Nagasaki, where they actively attempt to subvert Japanese culture. Missionaries encourage Japanese people to take "Christian names" and abandon kimono and geta sandals in favor of "proper" clothes. On top of this, local lords are too powerful, growing rich on Western trade and technology. Iemitsu's solution is swift

and absolute. He expels all foreigners from t country, and slams shut the gates of Japan. Fr 1633, he institutes *sakoku*—the country in chair

Foreigners are banned on pain of death. A Japanese person outside the country is forbidd reentry. Trade is limited to the Dutch, a contained on the artificial island of Dejima. T rest of Japan is hermetically sealed and preserv For 220 years, they incubate in insolation. Jap turns inward—a self-contained microco focused on the endless refining of the arts. A called the Edo period, most of the *things Japane* —like artisanal geishas and woodblock prints— developed during this period. And yokai. As te before, the country is consumed with belief in t supernatural.

Fast forward to 1853. The American Commode Matthew Perry knocks on the locked doors Japan with cannon fire. Using his four black warsh in an act of Gunboat Diplomacy, Perry gives Jap the choice to open its gates to trade—or conquered. They relent.

Japan is a time capsule. The country has n advanced technologically for two centuries. Pe and his shipmates might as well be spacesh landing, complete with laser guns and robot butl for all the wide divide between Japan's spears a rowboats and Perry's canons and steamships. T leaders of Japan are deeply ashamed when th see the scientific accomplishments and ideas the Western nations, compared to their ow backwards, superstitious people. It's a ru awakening.

Change happens rapidly. Civil war. Strife. By 18 the shogunate is overthrown. 16-year old Mutsuh returns imperial power to Japan when he enthroned as Emperor Meiji in the Meiji Restorati The last charge of the samurai in the 1877 Satsu Rebellion proves the folly of bringing swords t rifle fight. The Edo period is finished. An age enlightenment dawns; and the attack on yo begins.

Leading the charge is "yokai professor" Ino Enryo. A crusader against superstition, declares that the "unknowable" nature of yo can be elucidated using the twin tools of scier and psychology. In his 2,000 page magnum op *Lecture on Yokai Studies*, he rigorously disse and defines the various types of yokai, categoriz m as celestial phenomena, terrestrial calamities, ural species of plants and animals, or delusions the mind. In further books, such as *Tenguron* *ıdy of Tengu*) and *The Dissolution of Superstition*, labels belief in yokai as a psychological disorder. ue is no atheist; he believes deeply in the nkai--the True Mystery that lies beyond the ders of human perception, smaller than atoms l larger than the universe. Inoue espouses that ty folktales and ghosts distract from this more portant mystery. They must be swept away.

ue's influence is pervasive. Eager to shift the pulace towards the modern miracles of science l industry, the new Japanese government also nts to eliminate regional cultures in favor of a ntrollable, national identity. Key to this is nolishing belief in local guardian deities and ines and refocusing the population on a single gion of worshiping the Emperor as the God of an. Using Inoue's writings, they institute several *perial Rescripts on Education*. Included is the olute statement that yokai do not exist.

government campaigns to remove all references yokai. The supernatural is stripped from art, rature, and the theater. Famed storyteller nyutei Encho is forbidden to use the word *dan* and forced to write a prologue to his new rk Mystery of Kasane Swamp saying "... there is such thing as ghosts, they are all merely rosis..." The dread haunter Oiwa is reinterpreted ner husband's guilty conscious. The yokai side-ws of Asakusa are banned. The government is ost as effective at expelling yokai as Iemitsu l been two centuries before in removing eigners from Japan. What was once invisible, became visible, is made invisible again.

attack on yokai is not an absolute success. re are safe havens. Yanagita Kunio gathers l shelters yokai in the protected towers of demia. The opposite side of the coin to Inoue yo, Yanagita focuses on commoners. Known as "*Japanese Brothers Grimm*," he hikes the ntryside with fellow researcher Sasaki Kizen. y collect and preserve vanishing beliefs and ratives like kappa and the child spirts *zashiki rashi*. Recorded as *Tales of Tono* (*Tono nogatari*), they wait to be rediscovered by er, less skeptical generations.

other man, a foreigner living in Japan named cadio Hearn, is equally fascinated by ancient legends. He writes the stories his Japanese wife tells him in his 1889 book *In Ghostly Japan*. In 1903 he publishes his masterpiece *Kwaidan: Stories and Studies of Strange Things*. With Hearn's books, yokai travel abroad.

And in the isolated fishing village of Sakaiminato, a withered old nurse named Nononba tells stories remembered from her childhood to a young boy named Shigeru Mizuki—who will grow up to reintroduce yokai to Japan through the modern entertainment called *manga*. And the country will fall in love with its monsters all over again.

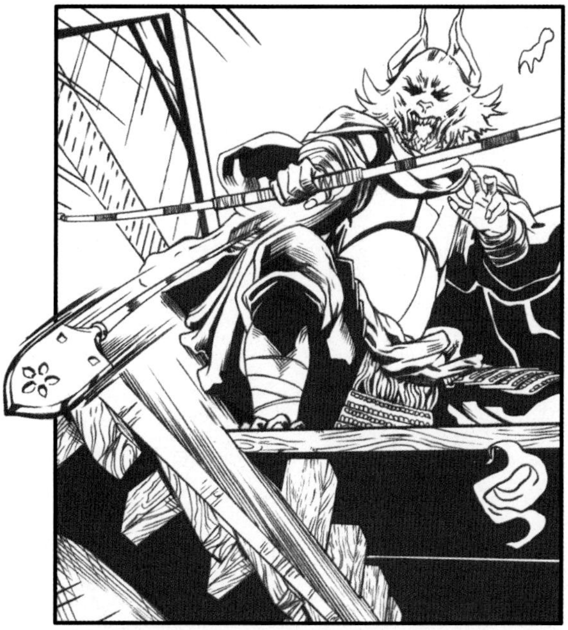

If you find yourself on the losing side—if your lord to whom you have sworn fealty lies bleeding in the dirt—what do you do? Do you hold true to your ideals, your training; do you choose honorable death, even if it is by your own hand? Or do you turn tail on everything you have ever lived for, throw down your flag and run fleeing into the night, to live on as an honorless deserter—a ronin.

The word ronin has meant many things over the centuries, from farm workers to laid-off business-men. But it has never meant anything good. The translation is a weird one; the kanji that make up the word (浪人) read as "wave person" and are meant to invoke unreliability. Loyalty is one of the core factors of Japanese society, especially loyalty to a superior. Switching teams is frowned upon. Social harmony demands that everyone knows their place, and does what is expected. By contrast, ronin are flotsam and jetsam, adrift on the tides of an inconstant ocean. Wanders, vagrants, vagabonds, drifters—they are people without foundation, without loyalty or respect.

The term originated during the Nara period, where it labeled peasants who fled their master's lands. Unable to return home, these wave people drifted the countryside as migrant laborers, rarely staying in one place and scratching out a meager existence. As Japanese culture evolved, masters assembled

armies, built castles, and declared themselv lords. They took personal bodyguards whom th called *samurai* —a word which literally transla as "servant." With the rise of clans, ronin appli more and more to freelance fighters and sellswor those without loyalty who fought for the highe bidder.

The golden age of ronin was the Sengoku peri the time of Warring States when Japan w engaged in seemingly endless civil war. With al these lords vying for power, they needed bod and weren't too particular about where they them. Any disgruntled farmer's son could thr down his spade, pilfer a spear and armor from o of the multitude of dead bodies, and present hims at some castle walls ready to fight.

Some of these ronin did well for themselves. T lord Tōdō Takatora famously served ten differe masters before allying himself with the futu shogun Tokugawa Ieyasu. Saitō Dōsan was wealthy shop keeper who put down his balar book and picked up a sword, seizing power Mino province and becoming known as the Vip of Mino. This was a rare time in Japanese histc when social mobility was possible.

One of the most famous ronin of all was Toyotc Hideyoshi. A peasant's son, he fought his way samurai rank and status—and then immediate made it so that no one could follow in his footste Toyotomi enacted laws establishing samurai as separate noble class. Things got even tougl when Tokugawa Ieyasu seized power as the s ruler of Japan. As you will recall from a previc essay, Tokugawa instituted societal controls usi neo-Confucianism. To ensure stability, he establisl the shi-nō-kō-shō system where everyo was sorted as either a farmer, mercha artisan, or samurai.

During the Edo period the role of samurai chang drastically. No longer necessary as warriors, th became bureaucrats—middle managers, accountar tax agents, scribes, and occasionally ceremor body guards. Great lords realized that they did need massive armies anymore. They went throu a period of downsizing. Pretexts were made consolidate castles and fiefdoms, and hundreds thousands of samurai were effectively laid off.

Due to the strict rules of shi-nō-kō-shō, the samurai could not seek an occupation or ever w master. They had only two options available; e expected path of suicide to cleanse their ame, or throw away honor completely and turn nin. Generally this meant finding employment a robber, thug, or swellsword. It is estimated at under the third shogun Tokugawa Iemitsu, ose to half a million displaced samurai wandered e country as ronin. This lead to the Keian Uprising 1651, and an eventual relaxing of the strict laws at forbade seeking employment. It turned out at putting ronin back to work was a more equitable lution than demanding mass suicide.

e final bow of the ronin took place in 1703, in at is called the event of the *47 Loyal Ronin*. A nor country lord Asano attacked the court official ra Yoshinaka in the shogun's palace. Asano as clearly in the wrong, and sentenced to icide. His lands and clan were disbanded. ano's three hundred samurai were turned ronin. wever, forty seven of them remained faithful their lord, and in an incredible display of loyalty otted over two years to take revenge on Kira. eir actions moved the country deeply, and eir story has been called Japan's "national gend."

e of the keys of the 47 Ronin tale is precisely at Lord Asano *did not deserve their loyalty*. He as a hot-headed jerk who sacrificed the lives of who depended on him just because he couldn't ep his temper. What so impressed Japan, and ny these forty seven are venerated to this y, is that even in the most harrowing circumstances they stayed loyal— oyalty that was given, not earned. On a darker te, these forty seven were held as ideals for ldiers during WWII, when absolute loyalty was mmanded at the cost of their own lives.

modern Japan, ronin has changed again with e times. It still refers to vagrants, but now it is ose lost in a society that no longer needs them. pan's modern ronin are students who failed eir college entrance exams, or downsized business ople. Like the wave people of old, they drift rough the world trying to find their place. As nin have always been, they are looked down on and disgraced—even if it through no fault their own. They discovered that loyalty given esn't always result in loyalty returned. lesson that is by no means unique to Japan.

Left: Inaba Kami design sketch by Steven Cummings. Colors by Jim Zub.

A lingering shadow cast against a wall when no one is there. The silhouette of a woman in a window coming from an empty room. These are all signs of one of the shyest, most ellusive yokai of all—kage onna, the shadow woman.

Very little is known about the kage onna. It is said she appears on moonlit nights, and that the shimmer of moonbeams reveal her true form. She is never seen in detail, only the outline of a woman cast against an illuminated surface. What she wants, who she is—nobody knows.

Like many yokai, she can be traced back to Toriyama Sekien's Konjaku Hyakki Shūi (今昔百鬼拾遺; *Supplement to The Hundred Demons from the Present and the Past*). The third volume in his yokai encyclopedia collection, by this time Toriyama had run out of traditional folklore yokai and begun inventing his own. Toriyama often started with a frightening or evocotive name, then imagined a yokai to match. That is almost certainly the case with the kage onna.

However, in her book Tohoku Kaidan no Tabi (*Travels through the Yokai of Tohoku*) novelist Yamada Norio said that the kage onna is a traditional yokai from Yamagata prefecture. She tells the story of a man visiting his friend's house, and seeing the shadow of a women in the garden. When asking his friend who this mystery woman is, the friend laughs it off, saying he must have seen the kage onna who haunts the place. So is the kage onna a haunting spirit or just a convenient excuse for a man attempting to cover up an illicit love affair? In the world of the yokai, the answer is most likely both.

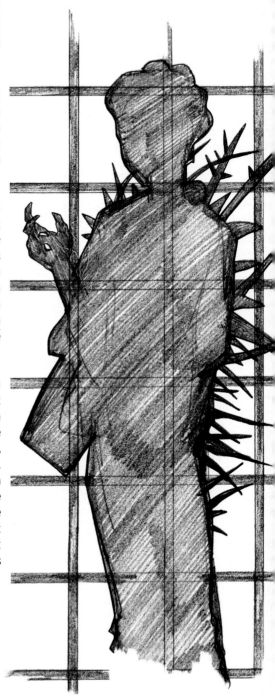

a story that could be repeated by every Japanese ild, a man coming home late at night encounters stranger whose face is as smooth as an egg. eeing in terror, he meets a police officer (or a nen seller, in some versions) and screams out story. The police officer then smiles, raises a nd to his face and wipes down, asking the man if ooked "something like this" –revealing himself as other of those self-same monsters, a faceless parition called nopperabo.

pperabo are one of the most well-known of an's yokai. Almost all encounters are variations the above story, with slight variations. Tales st started to appearing in the early Edo period, pearing in kaidan collections like the 1663 *Sorori nogatari*. Nopperabo were one of the first ve of new urban yokai that accompanied an's shift from villages to cities. There stories vays contain some element of city life, from lice officers to ramen shops.

counts vary as to whether nopperabo are a ique species of yokai, or just one of Japan's ny prankster spirits playing games with hapless mans. When Lafcadio Hearn told their story in 1903 book *Kwaidan: Stories and Studies of ange Things*, he titled it *Mujina*, which are one apan's shapeshifting animal yokai along h tanuki, kitsune, cats, and weasels. atever the case, nopperabo are atively harmless—they seek only startle, not to harm.

No face
Flat Skull/Face. No bridge of nose or anything that can be Seen in profile.
Slightly muscular
Armed with a Minimum of a Medium blade.

pperabo are one of the few Japanese yokai to vel outside their native country. Sightings have en reported in Hawaii as recently as the 1950s, ving many to believe that when Japanese immigrants nt to Hawaii to work, not all of them were ctly human. It looks like a few yokai went along the trip as well.

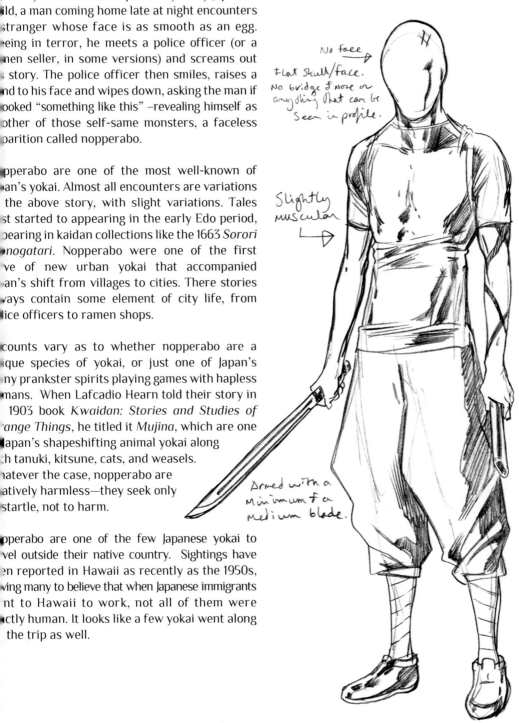

If you think you are safe from prying eyes on the second story of the house of pleasure, you haven't reckoned with this yokai's abilities. The taka onna can stretch her body as far as required to peek in on the illicit goings-on. Her own horrible face keeps her from joining in on the fun inside, but the taka onna has a different fetish—she likes to watch.

Toriyama Seiken was either not feeling particularly creative when he drew the taka onna for Gazu Hyakki Yagyō (*The Illustrated Night Parade of a Hundred Demons*), or he felt her story was so well known that she needed no explanation. In either case, all we know of her origins are Toriyama's picture and her name. Unlike other yokai in the collection, Toriyama supplied no backstory or further information about the tall woman.

That hasn't stopped people from filling in the blanks. In his book Yokai Gadan Zenshu (*Complete Discussions of Yokai*), folklorist Fujisawa Morihiko first recorded the story of the taka onna as a woman peeking into brothel windows. Fujisawa speculates that these stories were most likely inspired by Toriyama's picture, and not the other way around. In Tohoku Kaidan no Tabi (*Travels through the Yokai of Tohoku*), novelist Yamada Norio added the detail of the taka onna being a woman consumed by jealousy and lust but too ugly to get a man. She then transforms into the taka onna and menaces anyone enjoying the pleasures of the flesh she was denied.

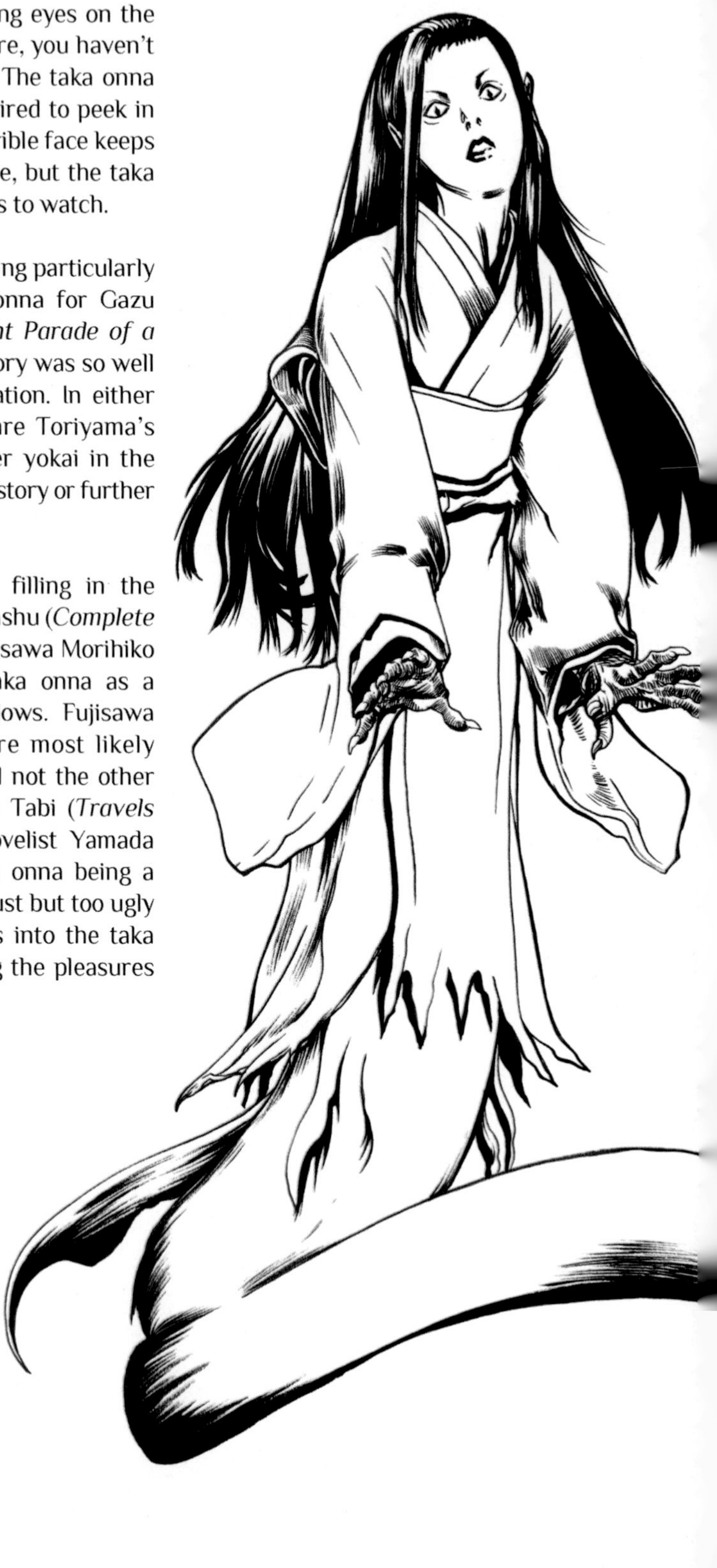

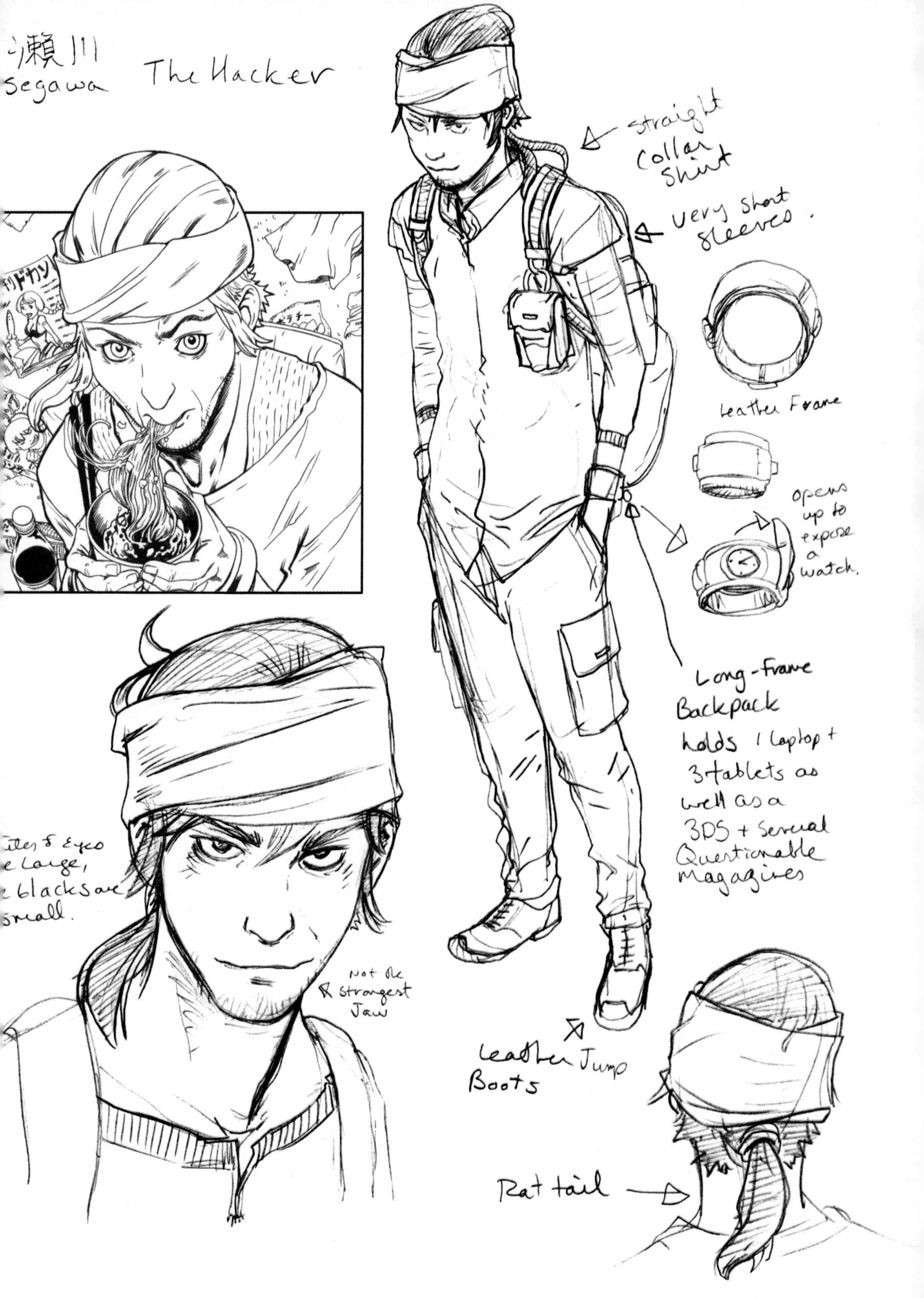
瀬川
Segawa
The Hacker
straight Collar Shirt
Very Short Sleeves.
Leather Frame
opens up to expose a watch.
Long-Frame Backpack
holds 1 laptop + 3 tablets as well as a 3DS + Several Questionable Magazines
ites of Eyes
e Large,
e blacks are
small.
Not the strongest Jaw
Leather Jump Boots
Rat tail

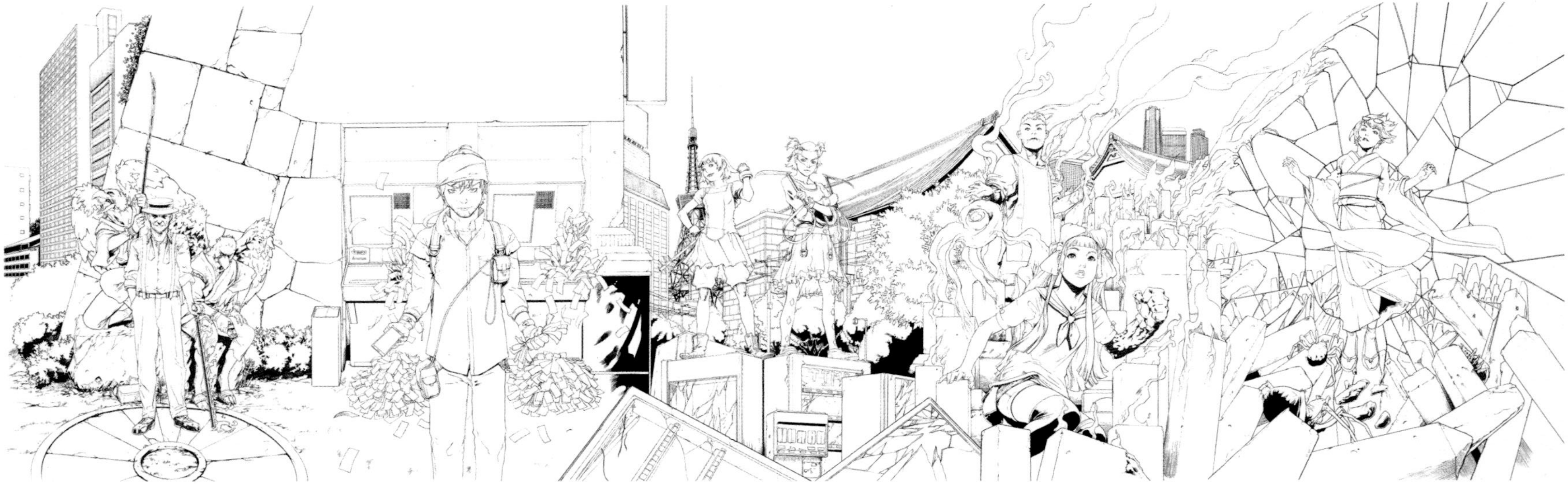

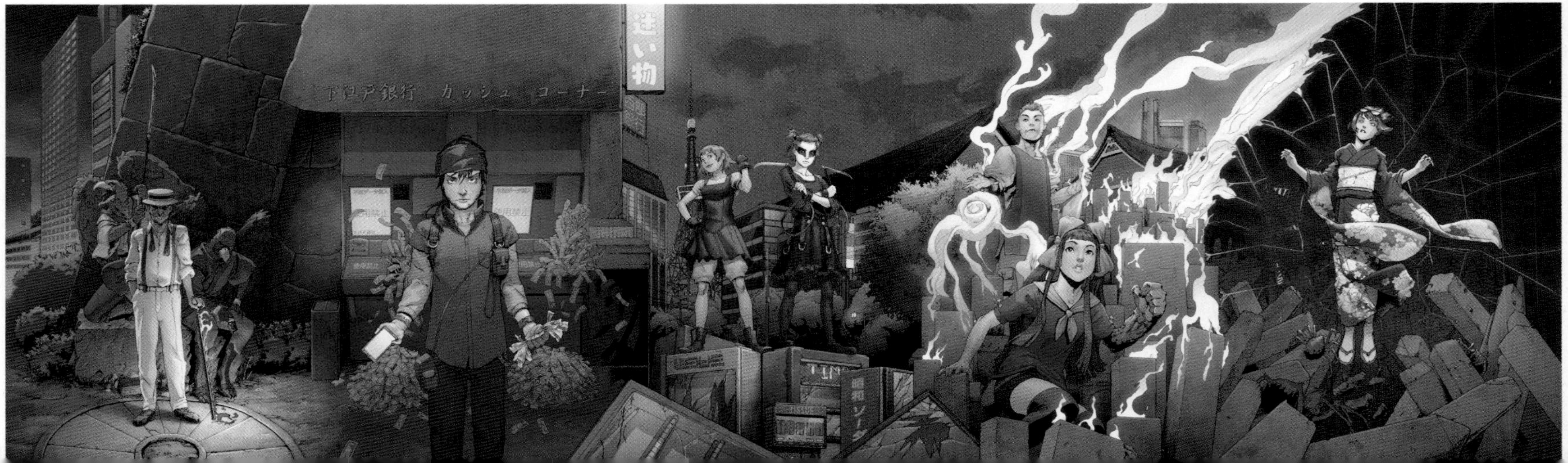
下江戸銀行　カッシュ　コーナー
迷い物